PERFECT KILLER

FORGE BOOKS BY LEWIS PERDUE

Daughter of God
Slatewiper
The Da Vinci Legacy
Perfect Killer

PeRfecT KiLLeR

LEWIS PERDUE

FORGE®

A
TOM DOHERTY
ASSOCIATES
BOOK

NEW YORK

This is a work of fiction. Much of it is inspired by historically and scientifically accurate information. References to real people and real events are included to provide authenticity to the story, which, while a product of my imagination, is inspired by serious concern regarding the real military medical research and the cultural and ethnic struggles of my home state of Mississippi.

PERFECT KILLER

This book is printed on acid-free paper.

Map design by Jeffrey Ward

Book design by Heather Saunders

A Forge Book
Published by Tom Doherty Associates, LLC
175 Fifth Avenue
New York, NY 10010

www.tor.com

Forge® is a registered trademark of Tom Doherty Associates, LLC.

ISBN 0-765-30110-5
EAN 978-0-765-30110-9

First Edition: September 2005

Printed in the United States of America

0 9 8 7 6 5 4 3 2 1

CONTENTS

ACKNOWLEDGMENTS

This book would not have been possible without the help and guidance of many people who selflessly gave their time and effort.

I am forever indebted to the numerous hours so freely given by Dr. Bradford Stone and Jasmine Thompson and the unfettered access to their notes, archives, and other research they were able to hide when Homeland Security seized the bulk of their files during that memorable and unconstitutional predawn raid.

I would also like to thank:

- Sergeant Vince Sloane, Sonoma County Sheriff's Department (Ret.), for technical assistance.
- Reserve Deputy David Simon, Los Angeles County Sheriff's Department, for inspiration.
- Colonel Richard Gabriel, U.S. Army (Ret.), for his scholarly works, especially *No More Heroes*, which first raised the issue of the "brave pill."
- Al Thompson and Lena Grayson, who kept me from hanging myself and taught me grace and self-reliance.
- Jay Shanker, who could single-handedly change society's images of attorneys if they would all behave like him.
- Rex and Dr. Anita McNabb, for being such valued friends and for helping my mother during her final years.
- Steve La Vere, who has helped preserve Robert Johnson's legacy and advanced the cause of the Delta's original bluesmen.
- Tyrone Freed for advice and ideas.
- Dr. Arthur C. Guyton, who supported my love for and education in science and medicine.
- Dr. Jeff Flowers, for helping explain and interpret the various types of brain scans.
- My deepest gratitude to General Clark Braxton (U.S. Army, Ret.), for the generous time he gave me along with the tours of Castello

Da Vinci and tastings of his wine, and to his assistant Laura La-Haye for coordinating my access.

- Retired sheriff's deputy sergeant John Myers and Tyrone Freedman, for allowing me access to some awesome, disturbing, and historically important photos.
- Bill Waller, former Mississippi governor and my onetime boss, who had the courage to go after the assassin of Medgar Evers back when it was dangerous to do so.
- Stephen Huntington at sirrushosting.net, the world's best Web-hosting service, and tech Gary Anagnostis, who has made everything look so easy.
- For the opposite reasons, I am still grateful to the judge who offered a look into the power structure that ran Mississippi for so long. I am also grateful to have spent so much time on Mossy Plantation and fishing on the lake and having the hell scared out of me by the cotton gin in Itta Bena.

FOREWORD

I am donating 15 percent of my royalties from the sale of this book to three remarkable organizations: the Sunflower County Freedom Project, the Mississippi Center for Justice, and the National Military Family Association (all of which will receive 5 percent each from my royalties).

The Sunflower County Freedom Project (www.sunflowerfreedom.org) is a remarkably effective education/mentoring program in the Mississippi Delta. Founded in 1998, the SCFP is an independent, nonprofit organization that aims to create a corps of academically capable, socially conscious, and mentally disciplined young leaders.

The SCFP's mission is to provide intensive academic enrichment and leadership development to give young people in rural Mississippi the academic ability, social awareness, and life experience they need to make free, informed decisions about their lives. In addition to being named as a finalist for the Ford Foundation Leadership for a Changing World Award in 2003—one of only two organizations from the rural South so honored—the Freedom Project has been cited by the American Youth Policy Forum for their "wonderful" work in "encouraging youth to strive for excellence and be truly prepared for college."

The Mississippi Center for Justice (www.mscenterforjustice.org) is a Mississippi nonprofit corporation designed to resurrect a capacity for statewide, systemic legal advocacy on behalf of racially disadvantaged and low-income people and communities. The Center's legal advocacy intends to advance racial and economic justice in Mississippi. In the 1960s and 1970s, nonprofit public-interest law firms provided critical legal support to Mississippi's civil rights movement. In the 1980s and 1990s, federal funding from the Legal Services Corporation supported statewide advocacy for low-income people in such areas as voting rights, housing, public benefits, and consumer rights. With the advent of the 21st century, however, Mississippi no longer had a concerted, statewide capacity for legal advocacy to combat continuing problems of discrimination and poverty. The board of directors of the Mississippi Center for Justice is committed to build an organization that meets this challenge.

The National Military Family Association (www.nmfa.org) is an independent, nonprofit 501(c)(3) organization staffed principally by volunteers and financed by tax-deductible dues and donations. It is the only private national organization dedicated to identifying and resolving issues of concern to military families. NMFA's mission is to serve the families of the seven uniformed services through education, information and advocacy including programs to educate the military community, the Congress, and the public on the rights of military families and their benefits, and to advocate an equitable quality of life for those families.

—Lewis Perdue

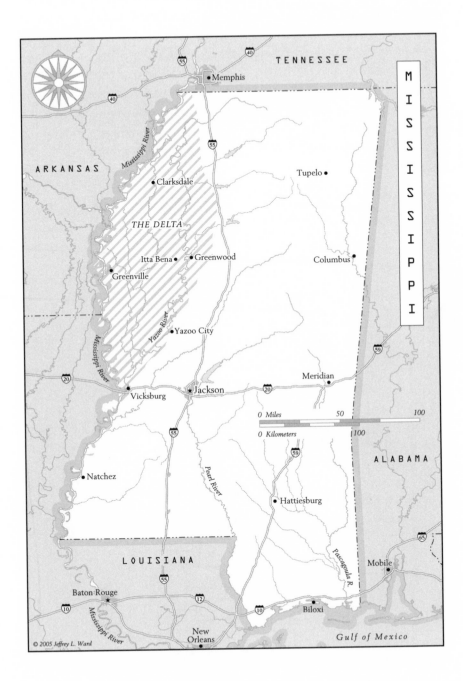

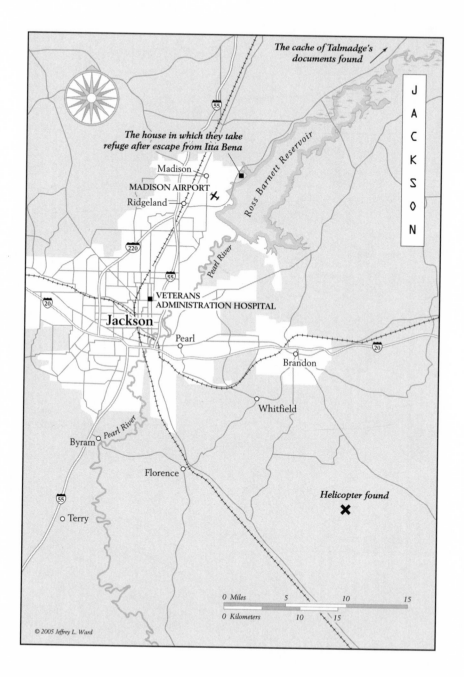

The cache of Talmadge's documents found

JACKSON

The house in which they take refuge after escape from Itta Bena

Madison
MADISON AIRPORT
Ridgeland

Ross Barnett Reservoir

Pearl River

VETERANS
ADMINISTRATION HOSPITAL

Jackson
Pearl

Brandon

20

Whitfield

Pearl River
Byram

Florence

Helicopter found
✕

55
Terry

0 Miles   5   10   15

0 Kilometers   10   15

© 2005 Jeffrey L. Ward

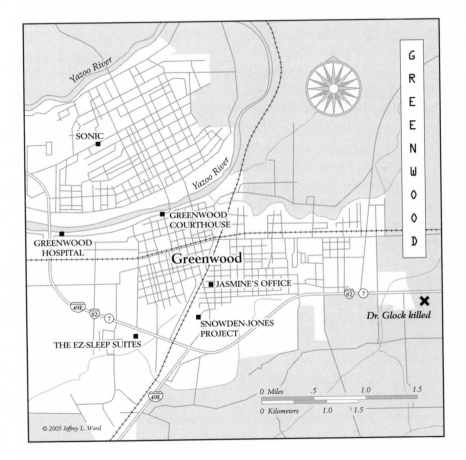

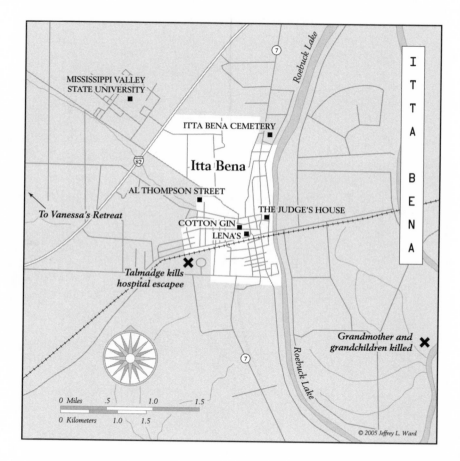

ITTA BENA

MISSISSIPPI VALLEY
STATE UNIVERSITY

7 Roebuck Lake

ITTA BENA CEMETERY

Itta Bena

82

AL THOMPSON STREET

To Vanessa's Retreat

THE JUDGE'S HOUSE

COTTON GIN
LENA'S

✕
Talmadge kills
hospital escapee

Grandmother and
grandchildren killed ✕

7 Roebuck Lake

0 Miles   .5   1.0   1.5
0 Kilometers   1.0   1.5

© 2005 Jeffrey L. Ward

I got to keep moving, I got to keep moving . . .
There's a hellhound on my trail.

—Mississippi Delta blues icon
ROBERT JOHNSON,
who, legend holds, gained
his musical gift by selling
his soul to the devil

Anyone who claims to understand quantum theory
is either lying or crazy.

—RICHARD P. FEYNMAN,
winner of the 1965
Nobel Prize in Physics

PERFECT KILLER

A moonless black-on-black night shrouded the Mississippi Delta in shades of dark and darker that flattened the feverishly humid world into a two-dimensional caricature.

Heard, felt but unseen, mosquitoes boiled out of the killing fields' stagnant pools like a biblical plague. In the distance, a scattering of lights glowed beyond a low embankment that kept the Columbus and Greenville Railroad tracks above water even in flood season. From beyond the embankment came strains of a church hymn drifting from the general direction of Balance Due, the notoriously impoverished black quarter of Itta Bena, where raw sewage fermented in open ditches along rutted dirt roads lined with battered wooden shacks.

At one with this deepest of nights, Darryl Talmadge squatted in the tall, soggy grass and held his suppressed Colt .45 Model 1911 well out of the swamp water seeping into his boots. He breathed silently through his mouth and listened with his whole body, trying to feel his quarry as much as hear him. A freight train rumbled distantly from the east, and from the darkness near the C&G berm came the sounds of a desperate man making his way through mud and tall grass. Talmadge knew all he had to do was be patient. Like hunting deer, he thought. Bag a big buck. The thought made him smile.

Talmadge had been a hunting guide in the Delta before the Korean War, before the head wound they'd fixed up so well. They'd saved his life, and for that he did what they asked. That and because he needed the medicine they gave him to keep the visions and memories away.

A sucking sound riveted Talmadge's attention. Over to his left, maybe twenty-five yards away. Then another and another. Feet liberating themselves from muck, slowly, cautiously at first, then with a labored acceleration making an angle toward the railroad tracks.

Perfect.

Talmadge stood up and in a single fluid motion aimed the Colt. It took only a split second to spot the faintest of shadows, night modeled on night. He sighted, squeezed the trigger, registered the mild cough of the shot and the shriek of pain as the shadow dropped with a wallowing splash.

"Give it up, nigger!" Talmadge yelled as he crashed through the mud and high grass. Then he picked up the panicked thrashes of a wounded man stumbling away.

"Shit a brick," Talmadge mumbled. This was number four in the past ten days, and he was simply tired of tracking down these boys.

Ahead of him, his prey's shadow moved right, reversed course, then sprinted toward the tracks. As the freight rumbled closer, Talmadge knew the boy would rush across the tracks in front of the engine and let the rest of the train shelter his escape, or hop a boxcar.

Either way worked for him, Talmadge thought as he swiftly made his way to the edge of the clinker stone at the base of the berm and hunkered down behind a clump of dead grass. He leaned against the slope and aimed the Colt down the berm, steadying it with his left arm.

Behind him the light from the train engine played shadows atop the berm. In moments, Talmadge spotted a shadow maybe thirty yards away detach itself from the brush and start up the slope. In another instant the locomotive's headlight lit up a wounded man, red across his shoulder where the last shot had winged him.

Talmadge fired, then cursed when the slug scattered gravel immediately behind the man's feet. The man scrambled faster. Talmadge felt no anger, no emotion, no disappointment. He kept the aim of his last shot and its trajectory precisely in mind as he corrected his sights for the spot he figured the man would reach at the top of the tracks.

Talmadge fired as the locomotive blew its horn. The man with the wounded shoulder froze as his face turned toward the train. The slug punched through the man's torso, bent him forward over the nearby track, and fed him to the locomotive's wheels.

Monday lay on the land as gray and stone cold as a corpse. Slate clouds, winter-frosted grass, pale headstones, sucked the color and life from the Itta Bena I had loved as a child.

Down the gently sloping field beyond the rusting iron pickets of the cemetery fence, and across the pitted, often-patched asphalt of the access road, the trunks of naked trees waded in the chill, muddy shadows of Roebuck Lake. The day promised little for the handful of mourners due to gather on this raw January morning to say good-bye to my mother.

I stood alone next to a half dozen folding chairs beside the freshly dug grave. Timeworn Astroturf carpeted the ground but did little to mask the pile of dirt next to the headstone carrying the name of Mama's second husband. She'd married him only after previously marrying and divorcing my father three times.

The morning silence gave way infrequently to the occasional car or pickup passing by on Highway 7. A wan breeze brought me faint, episodic snatches of conversation from two distant men whose yellow coveralls lent the day an Impressionistic splash of color. I watched them lean against a muddy yellow backhoe a hundred yards away, smoking one cigarette after another.

When the wind strengthened, it struck my bare forehead like an ice-cream headache and slashed through my brand-new dark wool suit bought for this occasion. The gusts snatched at me with sharp fingers, which sent my testicles climbing tight and desperate against my groin. I turned my back to the wind and shoved my hands deeper into the pants pockets and felt the icy handprints on my thighs. It reminded me of cold evenings in high school when football practice would run until it was too dark to see the ball, and we'd jam our hands right down into our jockstraps to keep our fingers limber enough to function and yell loudly for coach to put us in because no matter how dead tired you were, it was even worse to stand on the sidelines and have the wind refrigerate the sweat soaking your practice jersey.

Where the hell was everyone? I turned in a half circle, taking in the deserted little cemetery. As I did, a sudden movement caught my eye over toward the stately magnolia tree's waxy evergreen leaves. I saw nothing now, but convinced someone lurked near the magnolia, I closed my eyes and tried to recall the brief image flashing across the vague edge of my peripheral vision. Nothing.

I shook my head. Stress again, I reasoned as I opened my eyes. Regardless, I walked among the dead, heading toward the tree and thinking that even if no one was there, a little walk would get my blood moving, generate some heat.

The headstones reminded me how dead people continue to hold us long after their deaths, binding us with memories as strong as love. I studied these things in my work. I tried to tease through the fabric of neurons and skeins of synapses to determine what makes us conscious, what makes us, us. But none of my scientific conclusions mattered now, only sorrow's dark gravity holding my heart in its irresistible orbit.

I navigated among the graves of children who died too young and the rusting iron Southern Crosses of Confederate soldiers who died for no good reason. So much sorrow here, each grave its own epicenter of pain and loss, each marker a final punctuation mark for a life story increasingly forgotten as its memories faded as those who could remember dwindled.

The death hurts not only because we face the inevitability of our own death, but also because it opens a hole in our memories and robs us of the warm breathing evidence of who we have been. The loss forces us to redefine ourselves.

When I reached the magnolia, I found an old Ford hubcap, cigarette butts, two used condoms, and enough malt liquor cans to verify this as a major after-hours entertainment spot, life continuing, surrounded by death. I walked on and quickly found myself at the southern end of the cemetery, next to the Stone family plot holding the remains of my grandparents, my uncle William, and my uncle Wester, whom I had never known because, like so many in the rural South of the 1920s, he died as an infant from some now-treatable disease. The small angel on his headstone, meant to imply his innocence and express ticket to heaven, looked vaguely sinister to me this morning.

The low, powerful growl of a truck's exhaust drew my attention to the cemetery entrance. I watched as a limousine-sized, four-door, deep metallic gray pickup truck with a matching shell over the full-size bed pulled in and parked behind my rental. Behind the wheel sat Rex, his shaved head gleaming as if he had waxed and power-buffed it. He was a young contractor who had occasionally worked at my mother's apartment complex and had taken a liking to her sweetness and anachronistic Southern charm. For the past three years, he'd looked in on her almost every day, taken special care of her, installed all the special bathroom railings and fixtures needed for a woman whose mobility had been compromised by age.

Rex and his wife, Anita, a physician at the nearby University Medical School, had taken care of Mama and always made sure "Miss Anabel" did well. He refused to take my money for any of this and yet kept me posted on Mama's needs and condition and helped me secretly funnel funds and provide some level of extra care Mama would never take directly because she was determined she would never "be a burden to my children."

Rex was a tough man of few words and an uncertain past, which may or may not have included warrants connected with murder and mayhem. By the time I met him and learned enough about his past to confuse and concern me, he had already adopted Mama.

Rex waved at me when he got out of his truck and started toward me. He stood a head shorter than me, with a physique like a muscular tank. In his pin-striped, double-breasted suit, he looked like a dapper Mafia hit man and I wondered if he was packing.

2

Rex climbed down from his truck and waved as he started toward me.

I returned Rex's greeting and took a last look at the family plot. My mother had often told me she wanted to be buried here, but her younger brother William had beat her to the last available real estate in the plot. She had really wanted to be buried next to her father, whom she called Daddy and others called the Judge even though he had never been elected or appointed to the judiciary and felt those sorts of public office were not for gentlemen like him. It was, he felt, the duty of true Southern gentlemen like him to anoint those who would stand for election and appointment and who would do his bidding once in office.

The success of his theory was attested to by a file cabinet full of personal correspondence from governors and senators and congressmen and lesser elected officials and lower mortals all assuring the Judge they would do his bidding. Mama had inherited the papers half a century ago, and when she'd moved out of her big house into the little apartment across Lakeland Drive from St. Dominic's Hospital in Jackson, she'd passed the papers along to me. Out of respect for her, I had not thrown the papers away, but after one slapdash glance through a couple of the hundred or so file storage boxes (the accreted paper residue of the Judge's forty years of law practice and power brokering), I had stashed them all in mini-storage and forgotten about them until now.

The Judge's elitism and especially his attitude toward public officials formed the basis for his everlasting contempt for my father, whose family tree hung heavy with elected officials including a congressman and a famous U.S. senator, my great-great-grandfather J. Z. George, who, according to history books, was the first to formalize Jim Crow segregation when he wrote the Mississippi state constitution in 1890 and embodied in it the literacy test and the poll tax that disenfranchised half the state's population for the next three-quarters of a century.

For this, they put my great-great-grandfather in the U.S. Capitol's Statuary Hall next to Confederate president Jefferson Davis. I never quite understood the Judge's contempt for my family's dark legacy, since it had produced a masterpiece of constitutional handiwork allowing the Judge to keep the black sharecroppers on both his plantations in virtual slavery.

For all these familial reasons and because my father worked for the governor at the time, I scandalized the family with my expulsion from Ole Miss in the fall of 1967 for leading a civil rights march. The Judge disinherited me from his substantial estate faster than you could say *scalawag*. They were all thankful when I enlisted in the Army and shipped out.

I turned away from this past—yet again—and headed toward Rex.

He had called me at my office on Thursday, something he had never done before. Mama, he said, had gone to the hospital that morning. Like any relatively affluent and extensively insured eighty-seven-year-old, Mama had a battalion of medical experts she visited on a regular basis. And on a regular basis they sent her to the hospital for in-patient tests.

And likewise regularly, she had her doctors forward copies of her test results to me. She and I would discuss these results extensively. We would have had nothing to talk about had I never gone to medical school. She disapproved of where I lived, how I lived, most of what I believed in, and never failed to complain about my accent and how I sounded "like a blank Yankee." My mother was far too genteel to say *damn*. Southern ladies, in her mind, never used coarse language.

And make no mistake about it, Mama was a Southern lady of the very old school, an unreconstructed Delta belle born on a plantation who never understood why happy darkies no longer wanted to stay in their place as God had ordained like bluebirds not mixing with the sparrows. For this reason, our conversations tended to focus on her medical history. She loved me as only a mother could, but she never understood me or why I had turned out the way I had. Neither had I.

Rex and I met now, one hundred hours later, by a headstone bearing the Stallings name.

"Hey, Doc."

I held out my hand, but instead of shaking it, he stepped closer and gave me a bear hug. I returned it genuinely but briefly. Hugs from men—other than from my father, who was dead, and my son, who died far too short of being a man—made me uncomfortable.

"Thanks for coming." I knew it sounded lame even before Rex frowned at me. "Nice suit," I tried. He shrugged and turned to face the gravesite. "I owe you big time, man,"

Rex gave me a curious look.

"If you hadn't called me, I'd never have seen her alive again."

"How's that?"

"After you called me, I phoned Mama at the hospital. She gave me all her usual chatter about how I shouldn't come because my patients surely needed my attention more than she did, and wouldn't it be wonderful if I would take that endowed chair the University of Mississippi Medical School had offered me right there in Jackson."

Rex smiled. "She never stopped talking about that; that's for sure."

I shrugged. "Well, I just had a feeling this time. I'm glad you called me."

The religious would say it was a divine message, but I think maybe it was more the tone in her voice, or simply that she was getting old and my own professional medical judgment told me that the accretion of illnesses would soon overwhelm her stubborn grip on life. Regardless, I canceled my patient appointments and hospital rounds and took a red-eye from LAX Thursday night. When I got to her room at St. Dominic's Hospital early afternoon Friday, I sat down with a pale, dry husk of the woman I had seen only months before. It took a moment for her to open her eyes. They were lethargic, flat, and filled with tears when she recognized me. Colon cancer, she said. Terminal, the doctors said. She wanted no special measures, no interim surgeries or chemo.

"I spent the afternoon with her," I said as we walked toward the gravesite. "She was drifting in and out, and the few times she spoke, her voice was so faint I had to lean over the bed and hold my breath to hear her."

"What did you talk about?" Rex's voice had an odd tone, not fear but not simple curiosity.

"Mostly I read to her from the Bible, especially Psalm 121, over and over."

"That's it?"

I nodded and his usual poker face showed me something like relief. Something like a secret that had not been divulged. That confounded me and I put that down to yet another artifact of stress, like the person who wasn't by the magnolia.

"Yeah." I felt the regret. "That was it. When the light from the window got too dim to read by any longer, I told her I needed some sleep, because I didn't have any on the red-eye from L.A. I kissed her, gave her a hug, and told her I would be back in the morning."

He gave me a knowing look, as if he already knew what I had said and what I was about to say.

Movement interrupted my thoughts. In the distance, a hearse turned into the cemetery off Highway 7. It glided to a dignified stop behind Rex's truck.

"Nothing more until the phone call from the hospital at maybe four thirty in the dark to tell me she was dead." I stopped and looked at Rex closely. "They told me she had apparently gotten up to get a cigarette, lost her balance, hit her head as she fell in the darkness."

Rex stopped and looked back at me.

"She died all alone on the cold, hard linoleum floor." I shook my head as the image tore through my heart again. "You cannot possibly imagine how many times I have prayed that she had been knocked out by the blow on the way down. I can't stand to think that she ended up on the floor, conscious for a long time, dying all alone in the dark. I wonder if she called for help or simply gave up, closed her eyes, and let go?"

The detail in Rex's eyes gave my stress-worn nerves the impression that he somehow knew the answer to that.

In the distance, an older, four-door Chevrolet sedan with clergy license plates pulled into the cemetery behind the hearse. A bent, old gentleman in a dark suit climbed painfully from the sedan, his ragged white hair stirring in the wicked wind.

Rex and I turned toward him.

"Mama stage-managed everything, you know," I said. "Right down to the last detail."

Rex raised his eyebrows.

"Right there in the safe-deposit box with her will," I said. "She'd paper-clipped a note to the prepaid funeral papers and specified everything she was to be dressed in right down to hosiery and undergarments, which pastor to call, and what Scripture he would read."

I couldn't help but smile as I thought of her lifelong theological rebellion against one of the foundations of Christianity.

"What's so funny?" Rex asked me.

"The note was very clear that when we recited the Apostles' Creed during the service, we would absolutely, positively *not* say the part about Jesus descending into hell." I shook my head. "No matter how much she ragged on me about my heretical religious beliefs, she never managed to accept her personal savior spending time in hell."

"You mean *Hades*," Rex corrected me.

I smiled again at the memory. To Mama, *hell* was profanity and she was always too much of a lady to say those sorts of words.

As we drew closer to the hearse, two large men in dark suits got out of it and met the bent, old man at the rear of the vehicle. I pegged him as the minister rustled up by the local funeral home.

The funeral attendants were well dressed and professionally bland. The minister's face was chapped and red, patched all over with scars I recognized as from a workmanlike removal of skin lesions. I counted at least a dozen more precancerous patches in need of treatment. His left hand clutched a cracked and worn leather-covered Bible. His free hand was cupped gently and trembled faintly like a farmer sowing seed.

I shook the trembling hand and thanked him for coming and introduced Rex.

"I remember your mother," the minister said. "And especially the

Judge—but then, who doesn't?—particularly during the spring floods of 1929 when the levees threatened to burst, all of them except the ones the Judge built when he was president of the Levee Board. Yessiree, he was a man all right."

The well-practiced funeral home functionaries interceded then and pulled the old preacher back to the present. Rex and I slid Mama's pewter-finish casket—the one she had picked out herself God-only-knew how many years ago—out of the back of the hearse and carried it to the gravesite and placed it on the aluminum structure over the hole. Rex and I stood silently during the brief ceremony. Psalm 121 again, and the usual dust to dust. During the final prayer, as I closed my eyes and tried without success to visualize Mama in any other setting than the hospital or in her casket, I heard a car pull to a halt on the gravel access road behind us.

When the minister said the last amen, the men from the funeral home tripped some hidden lever and Mama descended into the hole.

Rex and I stood at the side of the hole as the sound of the backhoe grew louder. I picked up a handful of dirt and tossed it on the top of the coffin. The impact of the dirt, the hollow, dull sound the frozen dirt clods made as they rolled off the metal, tore a membrane in my heart, and suddenly I saw nothing for the tears. I swiped at my eyes with the cuff of my new suit and cursed at the sky for not showing even a little sunshine for Mama. I thought about cursing God as well, but I've never been much for existentially futile gestures.

Finally, I turned and saw that Rex had walked away and stood with his back to me and head bowed. On the other side of the dirt mound the backhoe idled restlessly. The two men in overalls looked expectantly at me. I nodded, then turned and made my way to the minister, who stood discreetly at a small distance. I thanked him for coming, mentioned that he should have his face looked at closely by a competent dermatologist, then slipped him an envelope containing two hundred-dollar bills.

As he walked away, I saw a tall woman with mocha skin climb out of a bright red Mercedes sedan parked behind Rex's truck.

"Well, I guess the bodies are spinning in their graves now," Rex said as he stopped by my side. He nodded at the woman walking toward us. She looked awfully familiar to me.

"Meaning?"

"Dude. This is a cemetery for white folks only," Rex said. "Even the labor with shovels're white."

I resented Rex's comments, wanted nothing to do with skin-color ir-relevancies right now. But I turned toward the backhoe anyway and realized he was right. What's more, the men stood stock-still, their heads tracking the woman as she made her way toward us. Likewise, the two funeral home attendants and the minister were shocked into immobility by the sight of a dark-skinned woman in a white cemetery.

I suppose I shouldn't have been surprised, but the disappointment tasted like dirt. I hadn't been here to Itta Bena in twenty years, and that absence from Delta reality had allowed me to construct a convenient lit-tle fiction of self-congratulation that my modest efforts in the civil rights movement and the phenomenal dedication of many others had changed things here into a culture of meritorious equal opportunity. But, clearly, life here in the Delta, more than in the rest of Mississippi, more than in the rest of the Deep South, and more than most any other where in America, still revolved about a deeply rutted axis of race, class, and misunderstanding.

I started to verbalize this to Rex when my heart stopped: the woman walking toward us was Vanessa Thompson. *The* Vanessa Thompson, moneyed securities attorney, former head of the Securities and Ex-change Commission, whose striking face had made the cover of *Time* magazine when she'd shuttered her lucrative New York law practice to move back to Mississippi almost ten years ago to use her money to pro-vide legal services for the state's poor, because "it was time to give back." But I also remembered quotes in the article from some of the more cyn-ical observers who thought her move was "more like payback than give back." I still had that copy of *Time* in a drawer in my living room in Playa Del Rey.

But it wasn't the powerful, wealthy crusader Vanessa Thompson who arrested my pulse. No, it was the teenage Vanessa Thompson, my high school heartthrob and the ultimate forbidden fruit, who momen-tarily flatlined my EKG precisely as she had done more than thirty years before.

Her appearance didn't entirely surprise me because she and I had swapped e-mails over the past month about a strange, cold hate-crime case. While I kept e-mailing her that I didn't do forensics, Vanessa per-sisted, attaching her e-mails with file after file crammed with informa-tion about Darryl Talmadge, a local white man who had recently been convicted of murdering a black man in the 1960s. I could not fathom why Vanessa wanted me to help save Talmadge from the gas chamber.

Vanessa Thompson had single-handedly deflected the trajectory of my life from that of privileged, multigenerational son of the Confederacy to a traitorous scalawag, who betrayed his race and turned his back on a heritage filled with statues and oil portraits in public buildings. I met Vanessa in 1965 when court-ordered integration placed her in my Jackson high school as part of a handful of token black students. I'd like to believe I changed way back then because Vanessa showed me how wrong the old system was. But it wasn't that way at all, not that clean and simple.

"You sure as hell know how to piss folks off, my friend," Rex mumbled to me as we made our way toward Vanessa.

I looked around and saw the white-hot hate stares shift from Vanessa to me and back.

"Comes naturally, I guess."

"Damn straight," Rex said. "So how is it you know the famed Vanessa Thompson?"

"High school," I said, remembering the wild sweetness of adolescence and the intoxicating hormone rushes. "She was in my history class. She always spoke up—"

"That sure hasn't changed."

"—spoke up and always had something interesting to say. Things I had never considered. Dangerous ideas."

"Y'Mama thought you had way too many dangerous ideas. I imagine one of those started with her?" Rex nodded toward Vanessa.

"Not exactly."

"How exactly?"

"I fell in love with her a long time before her words really mattered."

Rex grimaced and made a sucking sound with his front teeth. "Lordy!"

I nodded.

The meaning of her words would grow paramount as time passed, but at first it was her voice, the tones and timbre of the words, the steel of commitment reinforcing her voice, the energy of her emotions, and mostly the inexorable gravity of her wisteria-colored eyes that pulled me into orbit and made me hers.

And the testosterone.

"Vanessa and the other black students took the same classes, ate lunch by themselves at the same table every day, and pretty much kept to themselves," I said. "White students ignored them, like they were invisible. I started out the same way until American history."

"Let me guess," Rex said. "You committed the unpardonable sin of talking to them."

"To Vanessa," I said, nodding. "Sometimes just a few seconds between classes. But that was enough."

"Nigger lover."

The word still hit me like a physical slap. No matter how much hip-hop practitioners gratuitously tossed the word around, it felt like a profanity of the soul.

"Scratched into my locker, painted on my car, spelled out on the front lawn with used motor oil. I think they tried to set the oil on fire, but Papa chased them off with his twelve-gauge.

"The principal called me into his office and told me to stop fraternizing with the enemy, something about 'godless Communists' being behind it all. He called my parents. My mother cried; my father said he'd lose his job."

"So she turned your head around?"

"In a manner of speaking," I said. The old irresistible rush fluttered in my gut as Vanessa drew closer. How could this be? How could this feeling endure over the distance of so many decades?

"I was in love. Civil rights started out as a way to her heart. It took a while for it to become an end of its own." I nodded at the memories that played out in my head. "I asked her what to read, who to listen to, how to find the subversive literature behind the movement.

"Not surprisingly, Vanessa's dad was one of the leaders. He was a professor at Tougaloo. The whole thing came to a head right before Christmas when Vanessa invited me to a discussion-group party at her house. I told Mama I had to do some research at the library, then drove north on old Highway Fifty-one toward Tougaloo. When I got to Vanessa's house, it was the most amazing thing I had ever seen. That plain little tract house was packed—I mean literally jammed—with people of every color." I shook my head. "Black, white, Asian, Latino—" I turned to Rex. "I remember that day like it was this morning. I'd never, ever, been anywhere before in my entire life where blacks and whites and everybody else just . . . just hung around together as equals.

"I wasn't all that surprised to find all three of the Jewish students at my high school or the owner of the only real deli in town. But I was floored to find my physics teacher there, and that was my first indication that there were white people who didn't hate.

"When Vanessa took my arm, I was on cloud nine as she led me around and introduced me to people there. It was almost like the initiation into a secret society."

I felt the euphoria again as Rex and I covered the remaining few steps toward Vanessa. Now, as then, I felt the euphoria turn dark and ugly, remembering how all hell had broken loose when she'd introduced me to her parents. Her father was furious, and his deep, booming anger silenced the assembled crowd.

"How dare you step foot in my house!" he yelled at me. "You of all people! Your entire family and your ancestors have done more damage to my people than anybody else in this state's sorry history!"

He was convinced that at worst, I was there as a spy, and at the very best, a fulminating embarrassment.

He and Vanessa's brother Quincy escorted me to my car and told me never to speak to her again. Vanessa transferred out of my high school the next week, and I had not seen her face-to-face again until this moment.

Now on this bitter day, next to one of the many graves bearing a rusty iron Southern Cross, Vanessa and I met again. She reached out and touched my forearm with her fingers.

"Brad."

Seismic plates moved again in my heart.

"I'm so sorry about your mother."

I opened my arms and she stepped into them as if the past thirty-five years had never rolled by. She returned my embrace, then slipped a hand inside my suit coat to make the hug even more intimate. She took a step back then. Reluctantly, I let her go.

"I'm very, very sorry to barge in at a time like this, but this Talmadge thing has gotten out of control in the past few days. We really need your help and I hoped to convince you in person."

As Vanessa spoke, movement from behind her caught my eye. Again, I found myself staring toward the big magnolia tree; this time, I registered movement far beyond, in the trees down by Roebuck Lake.

Before I could react, a rifle shot thundered through the chill air.

Vanessa pitched forward. I opened my arms to catch her and saw an evil void where her left eye had once been. The warm, red-and-gray eruption from the ghastly wound blinded me. I grabbed Vanessa, rolled us to the ground, and covered her with my body as a second shot tore through the morning silence.

From a shadowy perch hidden beyond the silvery, weathered boards of a derelict and graffiti-smeared lakeside cottage, the shooter focused on the drama playing out in the perfect circle of the scope's eyepiece. The reddish mist from the lawyer's head appeared as a silent cloud of dust and created the familiar calming satisfaction that ran warm in the shooter's veins.

The shooter paused to get the first real-life glimpse of the famed Dr. Bradford Stone, legendary Marine recon operative turned healer and scientist. He was such a big man—six foot five, 230 pounds—that he filled the scope's field of view and made it hard for the shooter not to take him out instead of the intended target. Before the first shot, the shooter had canvassed his face, looked into the deep green eyes and compassed the lines of his face and the arrow-straight part in his short, graying hair, and knew she could have taken him out in another split second, but her employer had other plans for him.

The dossier they had given her on Stone tracked him through every country in Southeast Asia and included fitness reports that described a friendly, congenial, well-mannered, ethical, and deeply moral man with an outstanding record of killing those who were enemies of his country.

Stone's lengthy and highly classified record of his service both as an active-duty Marine and a government contractor afterward showed an unusual proficiency for killing, whether at close range with bare hands, knife, garrote, or at the farthest distances as one of the best snipers ever to graduate Camp Pendleton.

Then one day, he filed a request to train as his unit's medical officer. After Stone's request was approved, he became a gifted healer who could staunch a bleeding wound with one hand and kill an attacker with the other. Killing became preventive medicine.

The dossier contained extensive psychological evaluations indicating that Stone still had no moral issues with killing in the service of his country or his own self defense, but that he had grown weary of dealing with his postbattle regrets of killing other humans. And that he was afraid that he'd stop having those regrets and begin to enjoy the process.

The shooter remembered a time when she had had to struggle with the personal nature of reaching out and touching her targets, seeing their faces and regretting the deaths as a necessity of war. But that regret ended with her own wounds. Now, killing brought her profound joy. Other soldiers killed to live, but she lived to kill.

"Bang," the shooter whispered faintly as the crosshairs of the Leupold 6X scope tracked Stone and the dead lawyer as they rolled to the ground.

Then she heard the reports of a small-caliber weapon, a handgun from the sounds. She played the Leupold around the cemetery and quickly spotted a man with a shaved head firing in her general direction.

"Good-bye, motherfucker," the shooter said as she steadied her breathing and caressed the trigger like the lover it had become.

It was too damned cold to be Thailand or Vietnam, but in the next split second, my body reacted with the old combat reflexes my brain had developed there and in a variety of other warm, humid places where I was officially not supposed to be. Slugs thumped into graves around me as I gave Vanessa a great bear hug and rolled with her into a pale protective penumbra in the lee of a polished marble monument.

Slugs tracked us as I rolled, peppering my face with the sharp, stinging shrapnel of frozen earth. When the timbre of the slugs changed key and chewed at the soft stone of the marble monument, I knew we were safe, if only for a moment. I paused then to think, to plot a path of escape, or barring that, better shelter. I didn't want to die in a cemetery, although it did suggest a certain ironic propriety.

Then, a second firearm weighed in from my left flank with a higher, shorter pitch. I looked over and watched Rex shooting from the safety of Mama's headstone. His return fire silenced our unknown assailant. In the brief lull, people yelled into cell phones for help. An instant later, rapid semiautomatic weapons fire from somewhere beyond the magnolia plowed the earth around Rex into potting soil, shredded the green canvas canopy, and ricocheted off the heavy steel of the backhoe. There was an instant of silence, the distant snick and clatter of a magazine being ejected, a fresh one inserted, followed by a volley coming as fast as our assailant could pull the trigger.

An instant later, the shots ceased. I focused my thoughts and stilled my ragged breath into the calm, steady rhythms that had served my survival so well in the past. I looked over at Rex. He gave me a thumbs-up and made a questioning nod toward Vanessa.

I wiped at the tissue that covered my face, then examined her closely. As the medical specialist for small, agile detachments of highly mobile combat teams, I had seen wounds like hers before and had never seen anyone survive. Regardless, I laid her gently on the cold earth, ignored the hideous wound, and searched all the usual locations for some signs of a pulse.

Finding none, I pulled back the lid on the intact eye and found the pupil wide, flat, and totally unresponsive even when I raked a fingernail firmly across her forehead. So dilated was the pupil that I had to close my eyes to remember the deep wisteria that had once made her gaze so compelling for me. I looked over at Rex and shook my head. From somewhere beyond the magnolia and, to my ears, farther down Lakeside Drive toward town came the high-pitched whine of an electrical starter, then the growl of a powerful motorcycle engine. It idled for only an instant, then accelerated swiftly into the distance.

As the sirens regained the upper hand over the receding motorcycle noise, Rex made his way over to me in quick, erratic lunges, using the headstones and monuments for cover in a practiced manner far too accomplished to be self-taught. One more mystery. As he crouched beside me, he tucked a palm-sized, nine-millimeter automatic into an ankle holster.

"Catch you later." He looked about with a quick, precise scan as the sirens grew louder. "Can't hang around." He gave me an enigmatic smile. "All those warrants, you know."

Then he was gone, all swift, fluid moves and secure, confident steps. I was even more convinced than before that I would not want him as an adversary.

With the immediate threat certainly gone, the great survival gate in my mind imploded beneath a flood tide of dark, biting grief. As I looked down at Vanessa—not really her, but at the deceptively dead sack of organic remains of what once had been her—I searched for a thought to tag this feeling with, a dust-to-dust sentiment or maybe something about remembering people as they had lived and not as they had died. But where I had remembered Psalms and sorrow and guilt with Mama, Nietzsche came to me now. Words I had not remembered since college filled my head and with the same dark emotional entourage that had accompanied my postadolescent Herman Hesse *Steppenwolf* phase. "Many die too late, and a few die too soon. . . . Die at the right time! . . . Die at the right time—thus teaches Zarathustra."

I shook my head, trying to shed the words. But it was all too clear to me Vanessa had not died at the right time, and that made me angry. I held my hand close to my face and looked intently at the bits of gray matter clinging there. Fractions of a second before, the tissue had held Vanessa's mind. I had devoted my life to figuring out how this biological jelly mysteriously orchestrated itself into the phenomenon of consciousness, how it defined who we were and how it gave us the unique human consciousness of being conscious, our awareness of being aware of being aware.

I sat back on my haunches, transfixed by tissue that had once sustained genius and goodness, a sense of humor and one of outrage. Now the shards of Vanessa's mind were just sticky, dying bits of organic dust-to-be thanks to the simple transfer of kinetic energy from a few grams of lead.

"Where are you?" I tried to imagine where her thoughts had gone.

Sirens pulled me back into the cold, bitter day as first one, then a second squad car came flying into the cemetery showering gravel over the nearby graves. A big, white, boxy ambulance followed a few seconds behind. The driver's-side door of an Itta Bena PD squad car opened, and a moment later a defensive-tackle-sized black man in a police uniform climbed out. He reached deliberately into the car and pulled from it a large black cowboy hat, which he carefully placed on his head. Only then did he look slowly around the cemetery and pull a large automatic pistol from its holster and hold it along his thigh, index finger resting ready outside the trigger guard. Shouts echoed through the cemetery. Everyone pointed toward me.

The cemetery grew silent again as the giant cop looked at me. His face was as broad and expressive as a cast-iron skillet as he took in my embrace of Vanessa. Something like disapproval rippled beneath his gaze, then turned to horror as he took in Vanessa's bloody, gaping wound.

I saw recognition make its way across his face. Despair, then anger, and finally sadness played across his face in cinematically swift flashes as he recognized Vanessa. During all this, the ambulance attendants stayed close to their vehicle, looking to the giant cop for directions. Finally, he holstered the automatic and made his way slowly toward me. The paramedics came running behind; the contents of their kits rattled in the stillness. I thought to tell them they could take their time, but my words found no voice.

9

Once across the Roebuck Lake bridge at the east end of Itta Bena, the motorcyclist settled into a breakneck pace that would have been suicide for a less experienced rider, especially when the blacktop ran out southeast of Runnymede and fed into a wide, rutted lane of still-frozen gravel, sand, and mud. She wore a black helmet and was androgynously clad entirely in the woodland camouflage favored by local deer hunters. With her rifle slung crosswise over her back she looked pretty much like most any other hunter that time of the year.

The warmth glowed in her belly. Relaxed. Satisfied. At peace. The tingles of the orgasmic release crackled about her skin and warmed her thighs and groin where she hugged the saddle. She liked killing when it was quick and cold, but loved it like this morning, when she could expel every bit of anger and frustration from her body with just the right shot. Head shots were the best.

Behind the helmet's face shield, her face was a smooth postcoital mask that did not change as she blew quickly past groups of black people, walking along the road in twos and threes. She gave no thought to them or the groups of old black men with old cynical eyes sitting on the steps of cheap mobile homes, which had replaced the gray, weathered wood shacks in which they had grown up. Their old eyes had watched the world change from one of poverty, official segregation, and legal inequality to one of poverty, de facto segregation, and de facto inequality. This was progress as good as they expected in this life.

The unpaved road cut through a winter Delta sameness as flat and featureless as an empty table. The motorcyclist glanced frequently in the rearview mirrors. Ragged tatters of bolls left behind by mechanical pickers clung to the sepia-black skeletons of last year's cotton crop and raced past her on both sides. In every direction, the fields gave way only to rows of winter-bare trees bordering water and marshy areas too wet to farm. The land was flat as a still pond, owing to the Yazoo and Talla-hatchie rivers, the Big Sunflower and the Little Sunflower and the Yalobusha and a score of other tributaries of the Mississippi, which had meandered across the Delta for thousands of years, leaving behind countless oxbow lakes like Roebuck and depositing layer after layer of rich, black soil that still made for the best cotton growing in the world. The Delta's fetidly omnipresent moist smells were absent on this day, frozen to sleep by the winter cold.

There were unseen and mostly unimagined hills beyond the cinched-down horizon. That much she knew: southeast of her at Yazoo City and east at Carroll County. But here, a lid of haze squatted atop the land, creating an artificially close horizon cutting off visions of what might exist a few miles beyond. The grinding flat sameness threw a blanket of myopia over Delta culture. Geography became destiny as the flat topographic conformity imposed its two-dimensional will on the people, rolling their ambitions as flat and thin as cheap grits.

Some found the Delta inspirational in its adversity, especially those who had found their way to the hills and beyond.

In moments, she had left behind the last of the mobile homes and pedestrians, then began to slow as she strained to discern the overgrown dirt ruts leading down to the lake where she had left her truck. She downshifted as the road made a gentle arc toward the gray-green canopies of the cypress trees she knew grew only submerged in the silty waters of the old Yazoo River oxbow.

She found the frozen mud ruts easily enough, but less than twenty yards off the main road, the first complication of the day arose. Calmly, she rolled to a stop, stretched her left leg, and killed the engine. Options ran through her head as she took in the rusting Chevy Monte Carlo with a missing rear bumper and cardboard taped over one rear passenger-side window. The fabric of the landau roof had almost finished peeling off; a coat hanger emerged from a broken antenna. The loud, clear tones of a black gospel station reverberated from the car's radio. Her older, tan Ford 150 pickup truck sat less than ten feet away.

She dismounted, rested the bike on its kickstand, and made her way down the path on foot, unslinging the M25 sniper rifle as she walked. The gospel music masked her steps as she made her way down a steep slope ending at the edge of the brown, still water where a stooped, gray-haired black woman stood patiently holding on to a long bamboo fishing pole, which had been patched with gray duct tape. In the water, a large red-and-white float bobbed with the faint movement of the water. Nearby, two small children, warmly bundled into roughly the same shape as two tan hush puppies, played with some sort of yellow, blue, and red plastic toy. Grandma and her daughter's kids, the motorcyclist assumed.

Nailed high on a tree right next to the grandmother, a brilliant white sign with bright red letters warned of pesticide runoff from the adjacent cotton fields. The sign prohibited commercial fishing and cautioned individuals not to eat more than two meals per month of carp, gar, catfish longer than twenty-two inches, and no buffalo fish at all.

The cyclist thought about this neutrally as she raised the M25 and squeezed off two quick rounds, neatly taking out the two mobile targets first. Grandma dropped her fishing pole and turned, her face wide with fear and confusion. Then the cyclist shot her too. The slug went neatly through the round O of the grandmother's surprised lips and showered fragments of her cervical vertebrae into the water. The woman staggered and fell backward into the lake.

With quick, precise moves, the cyclist went back to her bike and drove it down to where the slope began. Then she dismounted and with the aid of a little throttle, ran the bike down the slope and into the water. The bike slowed, slewed, sank. The cyclist nodded, satisfied when the last inch of handlebar sank beneath the brown water.

Next, she took the time to administer confirmation rounds to each of her three targets, then hurled the rifle high over the lake. She felt a moment of regret as the rifle and its Leupold 6X sight rotored lazily out over the brown water.

The M25 had been tuned by one of the world's best gunsmiths, a man who had been her spotter when they'd picked off Taliban ragheads in the Shah-e-Kot Valley in eastern Afghanistan. She remembered sitting up in a notch of rocks on the border and dropping those crazy fucks who thought they were safe once they hit the Pakistan side of things. She'd been loosely connected with the Army's 187th Rakkasan brigade in March of 2002, part of the fierce combat of Operation Anaconda. She had a contest going with one of the Canadians and dropped her eighty-third confirmed kill at 2,420 meters, a record for a combat sniper until one of the Canadians dropped his target at 2,430 meters.

He got a medal and the next day she got an Al Qaeda round right through her forehead and out the top of her scalp. Her medical discharge had left her in a deep depression until the medicine and the new opportunities arrived at her door unexpectedly just nine months ago. The thought brought a faint smile to her face. Unconsciously she touched the bottom of the nearly invisible scar the plastic surgeons had left and followed it to her hairline. There had been problems until she got the experimental drugs.

She cleared her mind and made her way calmly over to the pickup, opened the tailgate, pulled out the motorcycle ramp, and hurled it into the lake. Without watching it sink, she turned back and pulled a red, plastic, one-gallon gasoline container from the truck bed and set it on the ground about twenty feet from the truck. Blond hair cascaded onto her shoulders as she pulled off the crash helmet. She set it upside down on the ground, then stripped off all her outer clothes, leaving her in jeans, a Pendleton shirt, and the surgical gloves she always wore when she was working. She stuffed the helmet with her camouflage overalls.

Next, the motoryclist unlaced her boots, purchased at the same Goodwill store in Jackson as the outerwear, and set them next to the helmet. Standing there now in thick ragg wool socks, she emptied the gasoline on the boots and helmet and set the container down next to them. Finally, she stripped off the rubber gloves, set them on top of the pile of camouflage, and set the entire ensemble afire with a wooden kitchen match.

Checking off the items in her head, she nodded to herself, then quickly made her way to the pickup's cab, exchanged her ragg socks for a fresh pair of white athletic socks, and slipped on her well-worn Nike cross-trainers. She scratched another wooden match on the steering column and waited while it flared off the sulfur and phosphorus before using it to light a Marlboro. She drew deeply on the cigarette as the fire established itself. When she was certain the fire had eaten any latent prints, she put the pickup in gear and drove away. She watched the smoke recede in her rearview mirror as she drove along, dragging furiously on the Marlboro. Finally, she tossed the lit butt out the window, reached for her cell phone, and hit the number one speed dial.

The morning sun struggled up over Napa Valley and glowed off the vast quilt of wine-grape trellises carpeting the valley floor. Southeast of Rutherford, retired general Clark Braxton raised his face to take in the brushy seismic mountains that rose steeply to bound the east and west flanks of the valley. A small scattering of long-extinct volcano cones studded the table-flat valley floor and rose a hundred feet or more above the surrounding vineyards like carefully placed stones in a raked-gravel Zen garden. Their scarcity turned the old volcanoes into objects of intense desire and envy, coveted as trophy home sites by the very wealthy who inflicted their architectural whims on the general public.

Braxton ran swiftly into the westernmost shadows of one such cone, finishing a ten-mile run in and through St. Helena. A hundred yards behind him, Dan Gabriel's steady, even breathing grew louder. Braxton picked up his pace around the red-and-white-striped road barrier leading onto his fortified estate and saluted the guard inside the stone and bulletproof-glass hut. The guard, charged with making sure only the proper vehicles were allowed beyond, returned the salute.

A tastefully landscaped visitors' parking lot shaded by scores of olive trees lay to the right, mostly empty save for a black Lincoln Town Car and a dowdy plain blue sedan with U.S. government license plates. Neither of the cars' occupants were visible, and they had obviously taken the small, well-appointed aerial tram that conveyed privileged guests up the precipitous slope to Castello Da Vinci, the General's massive Renaissance palace atop the old volcanic cone commanding a 360-degree view of the valley.

Deliveries and tradespeople used a massive freight elevator running from the wine caves at the base of the old volcanic cone up to the mansion's service entrance. A smaller, parallel shaft housed a cylindrical and opulently appointed, glass-sided elevator that granted an elite subset of his guests access to marvel at the General's massive ten-thousand-square-foot wine cellar, filled with a multimillion-dollar collection from the world's premier châteaus and wineries.

Clark Braxton was renowned for the intensity of his passion for collecting—wine, historical military medals, cigars, stamps, coins, among many. The press had written extensively about his near-maniacal obsession with making sure his collections were complete at all costs. He never collected art, he had told *Fortune*, because it was impossible ever to have a complete collection. "All it takes is one empty spot to ruin the whole thing, like a single drop of vinegar in a fine claret."

Fortune had concluded, "General Clark Braxton brings the same sort of intense passion to wine as that which made him famous as a combat field commander. He is known in the esoteric world of wine as a collector's collector and a man who will make no compromises in his near-maniacal quest to fill empty slots in his collection."

Braxton picked up his pace as he approached the steep cobblestone drive where only the General's private vehicles and those of his armed guards were allowed. In front of the gate and again another ten yards inside sat twin retractable, steel vehicle barriers sturdy enough to resist the impact of a fully loaded semi at more than fifty miles per hour.

Flanking the gate now, two armed outriders sat astride idling trail bikes, whose exhaust systems had been extensively engineered to provide maximum power despite their whispering quietness, which assured the General tranquillity during his famous early-morning runs. In their earpieces the men listened to the terse reports from their counterparts on identical bikes bringing up the rear.

The outriders, along with the sentries behind the greenish blue armored glass of the guard huts, were only a handful of the extensive, well-trained, and heavily armed security staff paid by Defense Therapeutics to make sure their chairman met with no harm from the legions of religious fanatics, kidnappers, terrorists, antiglobalization protesters, extortionists, white militia groups, and other assorted mentally marginal groups who viewed him as the distilled essence of everything they hated about the United States. Security was always paramount for a company like Defense Therapeutics, which developed and manufactured biowarfare vaccines, nerve gas antidotes, battle-hardened diagnostic devices, electronic dog tags, and other military medical supplies.

One cycle rider put a hand over the microphone at his throat and leaned over to his comrade.

"The old man's an inspiration," he said.

"Fucking unbelievable," the second rider agreed. There was no disguising the admiration in both men's voices.

Braxton turned around and ran backward. "Come on, Dan!" His voice boomed now as loud and unwavering as it had been in combat.

"You're getting soft, soldier!" Despite the chronic pain from half a dozen action-related wounds and injuries, including the head wound that had nearly killed him, Braxton prided himself on being as fit and physically capable at sixty-four as he had been at thirty-four. That, along with his legendary heroism in battle, had propelled him to the very top of the presidential polls.

"I'll still beat you to the top, sir!" Gabriel yelled.

Braxton laughed as he turned and launched his sprint up the 15 percent grade. The driveway spiraled counterclockwise up the weathered volcanic cone for a quarter of a mile. Braxton called it "a real man's 440."

Along the left side of the drive ran a sheer wall of fractured, red volcanic tuft. Olive trees defined the perimeter of the outer curb, teasing sightseers with lacy glimpses of the valley floor.

Gabriel audibly picked up his pace now. He was a sharp, tough man who had been Braxton's capable sword arm during his endlessly trying political years as chairman of the Joint Chiefs. Gabriel later became head of West Point when Braxton resigned to become chairman of Defense Therapeutics.

Braxton bent forward into the steep slope, challenging gravity as if he were heading back up Hamburger Hill.

"I imagine the incoming slugs," he told the interviewer from *Forbes*. "You never forget that battle separates the quick from the dead, and I always wanted to be the quickest. It's amazing how light your boots can be when you're trying to outrun the devil."

Behind them, the cycle-mounted armed guards paced the duo at a distance.

Ironically, his near-fatal head wound had not come from a hill but from a griddle-flat rice paddy in the Mekong Delta when a Vietcong ambush wiped out most of his Ranger unit. The initial VC attack with RPG-7s tore through their two Hueys. Braxton saw the first one go off like a bomb in midair. Braxton, then a freshly minted major and less than a month in country, hung on to his surviving chopper as they pancaked hard into the paddy and came under withering AK-47 fire. Braxton pulled his remaining men together and charged their attackers.

"Did you see the videotape of that old CBS footage?" the first armed outrider asked.

"Who hasn't?" said the second man. "I mean, all that footage with Cronkite's voice showed the American people a real giant. A genuine hero."

The first man nodded. "I never get tired of watching it. Talk about inspiring."

On the VHS tape, now copied to scores of DVDs and streamed from the Web sites of Clark Braxton's most admiring supporters, viewers watched Cronkite call it "the aftermath of hell": four wounded GIs thigh deep in mud surrounded by black-clad bodies floating in the nearby water. But the image that found an immediate place in the American heart and its mythology was the close-up on Major Clark Braxton's face, particularly the scorched, twisted, foot-long rod of Huey fuselage that had entered his forehead a hairbreadth away from his right eye and emerged from the top of his head. From his hospital bed in Saigon, a rank second lieutenant among the survivors, Dan Gabriel, had told the CBS war correspondent that the sight of Braxton, a man with a hideous wound who should have been dead, broke the nerve of the Vietcong, who were gunned down as they fled.

"He never even lost consciousness," the first outrider said as they moved stealthily up the steep drive. "Jesus! He never even hesitated a second!"

"And that look of surprise on his face when the cameraman pointed out the fucking metal sticking out of his head," said the second outrider. "Fucking amazing!"

When he received his Congressional Medal of Honor, Braxton still wore a bandage over his postsurgical wounds. Postsurgical evaluation of Braxton indicated no physical or neurological impairment, a finding consistent with a small number of similar wounds carefully cataloged by medical science. Interviews with his instructors at West Point indicated his actions that day in the Mekong Delta had demonstrated far more courage under fire than expected from a student whom they had once considered better suited for logistical and administrative command. Clearly, they said, battle was where the true man had emerged.

Braxton's legend grew through two more tours in Vietnam. He became the frontline commander the army called on when things got tough. Hanoi considered him so effective they marked him for assassination with a $1 million bounty on his head.

Army psychologists noted that Braxton's mania for collecting began about this time.

Now, as Dan Gabriel's footsteps grew closer, the General picked a memory to sustain himself. This time it was the charge he'd led to rescue a trapped squad of Marines at Hue. He felt his body respond as he visualized the terrain, recalled the clash of weapons, and smelled the stench of spent ordnance and open abdominal wounds. But Gabriel's ten more years of relative youth started to show as the men neared their finish line, another red-and-white barrier laid across the road with a guard hut beside it. Discreetly disappearing into the landscaping on both flanks of the gate was a double row of electrified metal fencing crowned with concertina wire.

At that moment, Braxton's wireless phone vibrated on his belt. With Gabriel's footsteps pounding in his ears, Braxton ignored the phone and urged his burning quadriceps into a final burst of energy, carrying him past the finish line inches ahead of Gabriel.

Braxton broke his pace then and allowed Gabriel to shoot past him.

"You peaked a bit too late," Braxton said as he searched for the precisely sportsmanlike tone the situation demanded. He kept the gloating to himself: it offered nothing to be gained.

Gabriel fell in beside the General. "Thanks, sir."

"Soon," Braxton said as he grabbed his phone and looked at the caller ID, "you'll be beating me." He smiled as a short message scrolled across his screen. The rules he had established with her required no voice mails, no trails. "VT86D," read the short text message.

Braxton worked on suppressing the broad smile he felt within. Vanessa Thompson was dead, and along with her, one more of the few remaining barriers capable of derailing his presidential run. He looked at his Rolex. "Okay, we have twenty-five minutes before your briefing."

Gabriel looked at the Swiss Army sports watch on his own wrist. The altimeter function he had selected at the bottom of the hill indicated they had climbed a little more than two hundred feet straight up since passing the gate at the bottom of the driveway. He pressed the watch's time button, then said, "Roger that, General."

They returned salutes from the guards who buzzed them through the last set of gates, which gave on to a Tuscan courtyard filled with exquisitely tended landscaping. The entire complex, named Castello Da Vinci by wealthy financier Kincaid Carothers, had once sat atop a hill overlooking Siena and, according to painstakingly preserved historical records, had been designed in 1502 by Leonardo da Vinci as a fortified sanctuary for his patron Cesare Borgia.

Leonardo's talents as a military architect have received little attention, but he had designed fortifications and invented weapons far ahead of their time. Borgia worried there might come a time when he would need a Renaissance bunker of sorts, and naturally he turned to Leonardo for help.

Carothers, whose company once exercised hegemony over the issuance of American Treasury bonds, had the entire structure disassembled in 1936, stripped, shipped to America, and reassembled. A briefly wealthy dot-com CEO bought the villa from one of the Carothers heirs before the first Internet meltdown. Defense Therapeutics had purchased it out of bankruptcy for a song equivalent to a coda and two arias. The corporation then signed the deed over to Braxton as a bonus. Framed copies of magazine articles about Castello Da Vinci lined many of the hallways. They appeared mostly in extravagantly snotty home and architectural magazines, and some dated back to the 1930s. One even detailed how Carothers had spent lavishly to prepare the site exactly as it had existed in Tuscany, duplicating many of the tunnels and underground safe-room chambers, leading to speculation that Carothers had once feared a workers' or domestic Communist uprising.

"Okay then, let's hit the showers. You know how I hate to be late." Braxton broke into a slow jog.

Gabriel smiled faintly. The General never arrived late

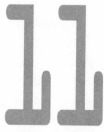

Twenty minutes later, Gabriel carried his notepad and the folder of materials the General had left in his room and made his way to the only new structure in the compound, a marble-sided pool house outfitted as Braxton's private office and conference room. A tall, beefy man with a discreetly shouldered sidearm stood by the multipaned glass doors of the pool house, saluted Gabriel, then opened the door for him. Braxton tried to hire the best of former military, including those from the Special Forces. Gabriel learned the General had even hired several veterans of Task Force 86M, Gabriel's old command. The most elite of the elite, 86M was a small, tight group of specialists.

Gabriel returned the salute. "Good morning."

"Morning, sir."

Inside, the door to the women's room opened as Gabriel stepped inside. He recognized Brigadier General Laura LaHaye as she emerged.

"Hey, Dan," she said as she offered her hand. She was a tall, lean woman in her late forties with a long, pointed jaw, permanent scowl lines, heavy eyebrows, and three Ph.D.'s. Gabriel knew her as the non-communicative head of an extensive, black-funded operation about which he'd learned very little even when he worked for the Joint Chiefs.

LaHaye controlled several supersecret operations attached to the Army's Research, Development, and Engineering Command, but like himself, even those at the top of RDECOM did not know the full extent of her operations even as they were required to provide support and logistics for her work. Gabriel's access at the Pentagon allowed him to learn that she had significant operations at the Edgewood Chemical Biological Center at Aberdeen Proving Ground in Maryland and, strangely, at the DOD Combat Feeding Program at the Natick, Massachusetts, Soldier Systems Center.

"Laura." He shook her warm, dust-dry hand. "Good to see you again."

"It's been too long," she said, returning his handshake. "How's life up there on the Hudson?"

He caught her insinuation immediately: "up there" meant ivory tower, out of touch with reality, and too far away from the orbits of military power circling the Pentagon.

"Surprisingly stimulating," he replied, then made an obvious show of checking his watch. "Three minutes. We better get moving."

She nodded and the two of them followed the aroma of freshly brewed coffee to the conference room. When they entered, Gabriel spotted Clark Braxton in conversation with Defense Therapeutics CEO Walter Bentley and Wim Baaker, who was a top official with the NATO Pharma Lab in the Netherlands. With them was a short, round man Gabriel did not recognize. The men stood by an antique mahogany sideboard covered with a lavishly arrayed continental breakfast heavy on yogurt, freshly sliced fruit, and cheese. A single table had been set for them, its white tablecloth laid with gleaming silver flatware. An overhead projector sat on a metal projection stand next to the table.

"Dan, Laura!" Braxton called out. He gave his watch a faint glance before smiling. "Come on in and get some coffee before we start."

LaHaye and Gabriel nodded their greetings.

"You're looking well this morning Greg," LaHaye said to the pudgy man.

"Thank you, Laura," the man said.

At the sideboard, all six people swapped handshakes and greetings.

"Dan, I don't think you've met Greg McGovern," Braxton said of the short, round man. "Greg is the head of research and development at Defense Therapeutics." Pastry crumbs clung to the corner of McGovern's mouth. He reeked of an overdose of expensive cologne. Braxton spoke often about this man, expressing his exasperation over the scientist's slovenly ways, but always conceding this as an acceptable trade-off for McGovern's near-Hawking-like genius in molecular pharmacology.

"Pleasure," Gabriel lied as he shook McGovern's clammy hand slick with pastry butter. Gabriel resisted the immediate impulse to wipe his hand on the thigh of his pants.

"Good," Braxton said as he picked up a plate and loaded it from the breakfast buffet. "Let's move along. We have a lot to cover this morning."

Gabriel made a pretense of spilling the first couple of pieces of fruit, which offered the opportunity to wipe off his hand as he cleaned up the convenient mess.

Two audiovisual functionaries pulled down blackout shades over the numerous windows and lowered the screen in front of the overhead projector.

"Your standing in the polls has certainly skyrocketed," said CEO Walter Bentley.

"My campaign people are awfully talented," Braxton said modestly. "They've been working very, very hard."

"The Democrats and Republicans seem to be working hard for you as well," Bentley said with a chuckle. "The more mud their candidates sling, the better you look."

"Well, it's still early in the primary season," said Braxton. "We have a long way to go to maintain our lead so we can lance the abscess which threatens our way of life."

Braxton stood up, holding his coffee cup in one hand. The lights dimmed immediately, and from high up in the rear of the room came the whir of a projector fan. In front of the table, a simple graph filled the screen.

"Thank you very much for interrupting your tight schedules, but as you know, the elections are approaching, and because—God willing—Dan Gabriel's probably going to be the next secretary of defense, it's vital to bring him up to speed on the significant progress you're making."

Braxton looked at each one and, in turn, got their nods of appreciation. "I have a series of briefings arranged for Dan, but I want him to have as much time as possible for him to get to know you all after this formal session is over."

Again, nods all around. Then Braxton addressed Gabriel. "Dan, I know you're familiar with some of what I have to say, but bear with me because it's vital for establishing the context for addressing the single most serious problem facing American armed forces today: overextension and underfunding." With his free hand, he pulled from his pocket a custom-made laser pointer, which had been built into a .50-caliber round.

"This data clearly shows that for the past thirty years, the number of personnel under arms and the net present value of defense appropriations, adjusted for inflation, have both been falling." His pointer emphasized the decline, then moved on to the bottom part of the slide. "At this very same time, global demands for U.S. military intervention have been rising." He paused for effect and took a sip from his cup.

"In short, every year we get more to do and less to do it with."

A new slide appeared.

"Technology leverages our effectiveness. Computers allow a single Apache attack helicopter pilot to deliver the firepower of an artillery battalion; advanced guidance systems mean one precision bomb can do the work that hundreds used to do; satellite and other electronic surveillance can give us usable data like never before."

He drained his coffee cup and set it on the table.

"The most recent Iraq war clearly proved the power of light, fast, smart troops. But it also demonstrated that the soldier has become the weak link now that gains from technology have plateaued."

Another slide appeared.

"Facing us with the necessity to improve the only part of our fighting force which has eluded efficiency so far: the soldier on the ground."

A new slide.

"You're all too familiar with the ultimate conundrum of victory: it can't be done from the air or from a ship; it can only be achieved by troops on the ground. But troops are not only financially costly, they can be politically disastrous when feet on the street turn into bodies on the ground. The relatively brittle nature of the average ground soldier complicates this mightily."

A bar chart appeared, showing every major conflict from the past 150 years.

Braxton motioned for a refill of his coffee cup. When the white-uniformed waiter failed to respond instantly, Gabriel felt, rather than saw, the nano-glint of near-incandescent anger flash across Braxton's face. From long years beside the general, Gabriel recognized it for what it was. But for most others, the burst of fury was so brief it fell below the limits of conscious perception like a single motion-picture frame, leaving them only with a vague sense of danger and insecurity that compelled them to do what the General commanded. Braxton exploited it ruthlessly to his advantage.

The waiter appeared in the projector's light and apologized as he re-filled Braxton's cup. The General sipped from his cup and gave the waiter a warm, magnanimous nod. The waiter responded with a bow of respect and a broad, relieved smile.

Braxton turned to his small audience. "Again, I know you're familiar with these facts. But it is critical to maintain focus on the problem." His laser pointer lingered on 1945. "The heart of our new initiative has roots during World War Two. You're all familiar with the pivotal study by General S.L.A. Marshall, who found that only about fifteen percent of American troops actually fired their weapons at the enemy, even when attacked. Fortunately for us, the German and Japanese troops exhibited identical firing rates, otherwise the conflict would have had a far darker outcome.

"We all know that Marshall has had his detractors over the years, but his conclusions have been verified over and over," Braxton continued. "We know that humans innately hesitate to kill other humans. This is good for the overall survival of the species, but awfully bad when you're trying to win a war."

He nodded and looked around the room to make sure he had every attendee's total attention. "It's critical to remember that heroism is not just about killing," Braxton continued. "We should remember that the vast, vast majority of those soldiers who did not shoot their own weapons nevertheless performed bravely. Some rescued wounded comrades, others valiantly transported ammunition for the fifteen percent who pulled their triggers.

"New infantry training instituted after WW Two tried to address this firing-rate issue. But while we increased the firing rate dramatically by Vietnam, we did not improve the kill rate because soldiers shot to miss."

He shook his head. "The majority of average infantry troops still shoot to miss. I'm not, repeat, *not* talking Special Ops here or first-wave invasion forces like Marines or Airborne, but the average grunt who constitutes a vast majority of military personnel. Think about it: if we can produce a grunt who shoots to kill every time, we'd need only about one-fourth of the number of troops."

Gabriel nodded. This metric was well-known among those assembled and thus drew no reaction.

The General paused for effect. "Do the math: it means we can deploy an efficient killing machine and need only one-fourth the tents, supplies, meals, hospitals, helicopters, doctors, and other logistical supply-chain expenses. A one hundred percent shoot-to-kill ratio will save billions!" He sipped from his cup. Then in a far softer voice he said, "I also don't need to tell you how much that decreases the political costs of war here at home. Fewer bodies mean less opposition.

"But to enhance the killing power of this leaner force, we need something else." Braxton nodded; the slide changed. "Call it battle fatigue or something more scientific, but in a modern ground war, some forty to fifty percent of casualties will be the psychiatric. Only about two percent of troops are psychologically built to withstand sustained combat beyond about three weeks." He looked at Gabriel and nodded with a faint smile. "Today, thanks to some significant research and testing pioneered by Dr. LaHaye and her staff, we're pretty good at determining who those people are and steering them into one Special Forces unit or another.

"The armed forces are thus faced with the seemingly impossible task of turning the other ninety-eight percent of ground troops into a smaller, more lethal Special Forces operation."

The screen went blank. "I say 'seemingly' because over the past ten years, Drs. LaHaye and McGovern have focused their considerable intellectual power on the human pharmacological and psychological engineering aspect of this issue and have produced surprising results. Significantly, Wim's laboratory has been able to develop the final pieces which will allow us to fully implement Laura and Greg's discoveries on a combat operations level."

The slide projector went dark.

"A new era of combat effectiveness will begin in just a handful of days," Braxton said as he walked back to his table. "We have found the formula for creating the perfect killing machine."

When the General seated himself, Laura LaHaye and Greg McGovern took up positions by the overhead projector. LaHaye turned it on, filling the screen with a map showing the Central Russian steppes. McGovern then stepped into the projected light and held a small glass jar sloshing with yellow liquid.

"About two millennia before the rise of Rome, the Koyak and Wiros tribes of the steppes found an extract of *Amanita muscaria*—a mushroom very closely related to the so-called angel of death—produced a powerful combat-enhancing effect which almost totally eliminated pain, generated phenomenal stamina and bravery, and did it all without reducing mental alertness."

McGovern waved the liquid-filled jar over his head. "The shamans of the tribe fed the mushrooms to their reindeer to concentrate the important psychoactive ingredients in the animals' urine." He shook the jar again. "Warriors who drank reindeer urine were unstoppable in battle." McGovern smiled, sloshed the yellow liquid again, and looked at his small audience.

"This is one of the more effective chemical concoctions in the history of attempts to enhance the combat performance of troops," McGovern continued. "The Crusaders were terrified by the stealthy fearlessness of the Muslim *hashshashin*, who smoked hashish before killing. And let's not forget Pizarro, whose men were nearly overwhelmed by Inca warriors chewing on coca leaves. More recently, the British gave their soldiers rum and the Russians got vodka and the soldiers from our teetotaling nation, amphetamines."

He nodded toward LaHaye, who stepped up to the overhead projector, replaced the slide of the steppes with a clear sheet of acetate, and began to write on it.

"The psychochemical mood alterants Dr. McGovern mentioned have two functions: decrease anxiety and increase stamina. Our new, smaller, deadlier military must have these because frightened, tired soldiers don't kill well. Conversely, if we control anxiety in three-quarters of the troops on the battlefield, killing efficiency soars by at least four hundred percent!" She sketched a bar chart in red and colored it in.

"But controlling anxiety by itself can't do it all because the sustained use of today's drugs eventually impairs other functions like stamina or mental acuity. Some cause psychotic or toxic side effects, and most produce a hangover once the dosage wears off. Harris Lieberman's team at the Army's Research Institute of Environmental Medicine studied Navy Seals and Army Rangers and found that combat stress and lack of sleep made them perform worse than if they had been drunk or blitzed on narcotics.

"Contrary to those effects, the ideal pharmaceutical, which we call the nondepleting neurotrop, produces a warfighter resistant to out-of-control emotions, who will kill on command, logically, methodically, and without hesitation—perfect killers.

"We have seen this behavior in natural two-percenters and, on a rare basis, in people who have made dramatic personality shifts following specific and limited combat head wounds. The study of those personality-altering head wounds eventually grew into a pharmaceutical-based program as surgical intervention to produce better warfighters was abandoned as too imprecise and, of course, too permanent.

"Thus, as becomes clear, the search for a perfect, controllable, and totally reversible pharmaceutical enhancement to produce the perfect killer is the Holy Grail of combat psychiatry. My operations command and Dr. McGovern's laboratory in cooperation with Defense Therapeutics down in Los Angeles have achieved those goals with Xantaeus. We have succeeded where others failed because we have created a drug which functions more like a subtle hallucinogen, reshaping the patient's perception of reality rather than overloading them with crude compounds which eventually overwhelm the brain's natural chemical environment."

"And this doesn't produce flashbacks like LSD?" Gabriel asked.

LaHaye shook her head. "When administered correctly. Proper dosage control and time-based administration is vital, and that is where Mr. Baaker comes in."

Across the table, Wim Baaker unfolded his cranelike frame and approached the small podium.

"It's good to see you again, General Gabriel," Baaker began as the title slide featuring a massive laboratory building appeared on the screen. "I believe we met at the NATO subcommittee meeting on combat nutrition prior to Desert Storm."

Gabriel nodded.

"Well, to refresh your memory, the NATO Combat Pharmaceutical

Lab is located in Rijswijk, near Den Haag, and employs more than five thousand people." Baaker's voice was dull, flat, and deep from the back of his throat. "We were founded in 1930 and charged with conducting applied research for the Dutch government, including her military forces, to whom we provide advice and consultation in areas such as protection against chemical weapons, munitions technology, and weapons system and platforms technology.

"One of our subsidiaries, which provides support services to my classified operations, is TNO Pharma, which has developed, among other things, highly effective, microprocessor-controlled, transdermal delivery systems for appropriate molecules. We have expanded upon the pioneering products such as nicotine patches and those containing nitroglycerin for angina patients and developed more precise delivery methods for a wide variety of pharmaceuticals such as Xantaeus, which must be applied precisely to avoid the unfortunate side effects of previous drugs."

Baaker paused and looked at each person in turn.

Gabriel felt the ghosts of My Lai, Thanh Phong, and a host of more successfully covered-up incidents. He could almost see the near disasters hovering in the projector's vague penumbra.

Baaker cleared his throat. "Indeed, the first of our new devices is currently undergoing testing by RDECOM under the guise of the Transdermal Nutrient Delivery System. We are exploiting advances in nutritional sciences, microminiaturized physiological sensors, and molecular delivery to make this possible. We hope to deploy this within the next year."

The slide changed.

"Here is how the system works: Biosensors currently in development monitor the warfighter's metabolism, then send information to a microchip processor. This processor might then activate a microelectrical mechanical system that transmits the appropriate chemicals either through skin pores or pumped directly into blood capillaries."

The slides changed to show, in succession, a diagram of the patchlike device, a close-up photo of it, and a shot of the device installed on a heavily muscled man stripped to the waist.

"For now, we are developing and testing this system as a nutrient delivery system, which serves a real need while also serving as solid cover for the Xantaeus project." Baaker paused. "Please understand this is not a sham cover. The TDNDS will undoubtedly provide significant benefits delivering vitamins, micronutrients, and nutraceuticals to warfighters with limited access to normal meals either because of protective garments or sustained combat.

"However, the TDNDS's real beauty comes with an ability allowing us to administer—along with nutritional supplements—precisely controlled amounts of Xantaeus or other drugs.

"We've tested three generations of the TDNDS system, all controlled by a microprocessor, and based on a number of inputs, including simple periodic timing, triggers transmitted by encrypted radio signals, and/or from real-time personal biosensors monitoring the individual warfighter's metabolism and blood chemistry. This latter control structure will develop as the technology advances to make sure we can wirelessly connect each individual warfighter's biometry with field command by extending the same GPS, identification, and data-connection technology currently used on the battlefield. This highly secret research gives us the power to shape the most lethally effective military force the world has ever experienced."

The implications of Baaker's presentation and those of LaHaye, McGovern, and the General twisted like a knife slash in Dan Gabriel's gut. He had heard vague rumors of dissenters, including his distant cousin Rick Gabriel, who warned that unspeakable horrors lurked beneath the growing enthusiasm for drugs like Xantaeus. The Pentagon establishment had done an effective job at silencing those voices who accused the drug of issuing in the era of the "chemical soldier," and creating a form of warfare that would turn every battle into its own holocaust and destroy the very essence of what it means to be human.

But like others in the military, Gabriel had paid scant attention and given no real thought to those critics, preferring to believe the day of the nondepleting neurotrop would never come and decisions would never need to be made. But the day had clearly come, and he would now have to decide what was right.

I had died, gone to hell, and was doomed to spend an eternity attending funerals in the freezing cold.

This time I stood far from center stage, out toward the edge of a crowd that jammed Little Zion Missionary Baptist Church's ragged little cemetery north of Greenwood. A brilliant sun had chased away the winter frost and loosened the buttons on overcoats and jackets. Among the hundreds of people there to say good-bye to Vanessa Thompson, some wore $5,000 suits and arrived on private jets. Others mourned in their Wal-Mart Sunday best worn so often the elbows shone when the sun hit them just right. I watched expensively coiffed celebrities with their surgically enhanced beauty literally rubbing elbows with entire families of tough, enduring people whose hard-won wisdom was sculpted in the deeply lined geography of timeworn faces. Despite the multitude, people spoke so quietly I could clearly hear the distant sounds of an old "Popping Johnny" John Deere tractor and the slamming of a screen door in some distant house.

I turned toward the sun and squinted as I held up my face to its light, trying to let it into the winter darkness that clouded my heart and chilled my soul. It failed miserably.

Here I stood as a footnote in the crowd, a grain of salt amid the pepper, relegated to the fringe less for my pale complexion than for my lack of familial, personal, political, or professional standing.

I had been to this cemetery once before, to visit the grave of blues legend Robert Johnson, who, myth has it, met the devil on a Delta crossroads somewhere nearby and sold his soul in exchange for his unholy excellence on the guitar.

As the final hymn drifted over the heads of Vanessa's mourners, I heard the low murmur of a single-engine prop biplane that resurrected a distant memory of riding in the back of Al Thompson's pickup down some dusty road at Mossy Plantation when the crop dusters would fly right over our heads and leave us lightly frosted with DDT powder.

Faces in the crowd turned expectantly upward as one, toward a vintage, fabric-covered Stearman PT-17 Kaydet biplane painted bright red. The old military trainers from the mid-1920s had been all over the Delta when I was a child. From a lengthy *New York Times* article, we all knew the Stearman was owned and piloted by Vanessa's daughter, Jasmine, who had almost become a commercial airline pilot before being pulled into her mother's irresistible orbit of law and power.

The *Times* article noted that even as a child, Jasmine had been something of an aviation prodigy, winning competitions and the respect of adults many decades her senior by designing and building advanced radio-controlled model aircraft that enabled her to obtain three patents by the time she was thirteen. But by then, she had moved on to earning a license to fly real aircraft.

Because her mother's offer of financial assistance with college came with law school strings attached, Jasmine—having inherited her mother's headstrong temperament—refused the money and had put herself through school by flying a news helicopter for a series of Los Angeles television stringers and freelancers before finally landing a slot with one of the network affiliates.

All of this came back clearly and easily as the biplane emerged over the treetops so low and slow I was certain it would simply fall out of the sky. Instead it made a lazy, tight circle as only a biplane can do in the hands of an expert pilot, then loosed a dense shower of rose petals, filling the sky with color and the air with fragrance. The Stearman dipped its wings, then vanished as the brilliant petals drifted to earth.

No one moved until long after the sound of the Stearman's engine had faded, such was the shock, the depth of loss, and the reluctance to leave a wonderful woman behind. Then we all began to drift reluctantly away.

I thought I had said good-bye to Vanessa and the past. I was wrong.

Standing at the wheel of my sailboat, I marveled at the smoky orange remains of a late June sun as it sank beneath the horizon, leaving behind a hazy Southern California sky painted with shifting pastels of peach, terra-cotta, and a strange smoky rose that worked its way through violet into the black approach of night.

The deck of the sloop *Jambalaya* hummed smoothly beneath my feet as I steered her on a port tack, heading straight toward the beach at Playa Del Rey. Night sifted down swiftly now, filling in all the spaces between the shadows. I reached through the spokes of the wheel and turned on the running lights. I kept a close eye for the idiots who had no clue about lights and for the legitimate Sunday-evening traffic as well. As the traffic to my port side opened up, I eased the *Jambalaya's* bow through the eye of the gentle wind. When the big 135 Genoa headsail began luffing, I hauled in on the port jib sheet, wrapped three coils around the self-tailing winch, and trimmed it in. The main brought the boom around and filled itself with the air coming over the starboard bow.

On my new tack, roughly northwest, the lights marking the breakwater protecting the main channel into Marina del Rey made faint halos in the evening haze. The chatter on the VHF grew louder and more urgent as a jam of private watercraft clotted at the narrow harbor entrance.

As the *Jambalaya* gathered speed on its new tack away from the traffic, urgent, angry shouts echoed from the harbor entrance, shouts so loud they carried across the water, arriving like an echo moments after the same sound on the radio. Instants later, the sound of crumpling fiberglass made it across the distance. Repairmen and insurance adjusters always had plenty of work on Mondays in Southern California, where the benign summer weather enticed too many Trafalgar wannabes into water way over their heads.

With my course steady for a moment and no traffic ahead, I gazed back toward Catalina and tried to recall the memories of Camilla and of the weekends we had spent there. In the beginning, it was the two of us, lazy weekends anchored at Fourth of July Cove, with walks in the hills and steaks at Bombard's at the Isthmus. Nate's birth and Lindsey's two years later changed all that, and as they grew older, there was snorkeling, swimming, and hiking around the Catalina hills, chasing after wild pigs and feral dreams. But as I squinted into the gathering night, Catalina's Bactrian hills were darkly indistinct against the flatness of dusk. Much like my memories.

I tried to recall other Sunday nights like this one, filled with songs and jokes delighting us during the six or eight hours' upwind return sail. In the first few months after the accident, memories of these return trips and the weekends preceding them came to me all too clearly and brightly, because throughout our marriage—but especially after the kids were born—Camilla had endlessly implored me to "make a memory." She'd hit me with this especially when we'd watch the children at play or as they slept and we realized they would grow up fast and one day leave the child—and us—behind.

Make a memory. How could Camilla know it would become a curse? The memory I once made of Lindsey haunted me most of all. One afternoon shortly before she turned five, she was dancing by herself in her bedroom in the little bungalow we had in Playa Del Rey. I don't remember the music now, but when I went in and picked her up and danced with her in my arms, I saw the most transcendent, undiluted joy in her eyes and a steady gaze of absolutely trusting love, which rocked my heart down to my soul. As we danced and I hugged her tight in my arms, a bittersweet revelation shook me that one day, some young man would see the same look and feel the same irresistible attraction in her eyes. I remembered praying then that this young man would treasure Lindsey's gaze and trust as much as I had, and when he took her away, he would protect her as I wanted so much to do. But I had failed. There would be no young men for Lindsey nor pretty young women for her older brother, Nate, whose trust in my ability to protect him from all the world's harms had been equally as strong as his sister's.

They'd invested me with that unbounded love and trust right up to the moment they died.

Make a memory, Camilla had said. Damn the memories! Those precious heart-rending, frightening, wonderful, awful neuronal circuits whose actual workings eluded the best efforts of philosophers and of scientists like me.

We feel these memories in solitude and share them badly in the flat, sloppy medium of words and gestures that do little to re-create the fleeting snapshots of reality in our heads.

Then we die.

Where do the memories go? Were they attached to a soul? Or just cheap synaptic Kodak moments stored in a fragile biological medium destined for decay? I wiped at the moisture in my eyes and checked my watch. Vanessa's daughter would be arriving at the airport in less than two hours. I focused on this to take my mind off the memories.

I turned the ignition key for the *Jambalaya*'s auxiliary diesel and counted to myself. At ten, I pressed the starter and the diesel fired up on the first crank. Next I flipped on the white light at the top of the mast, signaling my transition from sailboat to power vessel, eased the transmission lever forward, and steered gently into the wind to help me drop the sails. Then I set course to avoid colliding with the great clueless hordes at the harbor entrance.

With my portable air horn and emergency flare gun with extra rounds within reach, I steered a wide counterclockwise circle toward the south entrance, hoping to find a gap in the incoming traffic. Only in L.A., I thought, could boating be so damn much like jockeying for position on a freeway on-ramp.

With my attention riveted ahead, the bullet-fast approach of a dark inflatable with no lights and a well-muffled outboard motor startled me when it appeared on my stern. I stopped my gradual circle and held a steady course, expecting it to notice my lights and speed by. Other than for my wonder at the scarcity of brain cells that would set someone off at great speed at night with no lights, the inflatable did not concern me. Even if it hit the *Jambalaya* at speed, the small, soft craft could do little serious damage to a thirty-five-foot sailboat.

I was right about the boat, wrong about the people inside.

Instead of shooting past me, the inflatable slowed and closed in on the *Jambalaya*'s port side. I grabbed my handheld halogen spotlight. The half-million-candlepower light revealed three men, all dressed in black clothing and balaclavas, all holding elegantly misshapen weapons that, to my experienced eyes, were clearly Heckler & Koch MP5SD submachine guns with their long, tubular suppressors.

The men cursed at my light. The helmsman jammed the tiller to the right and spun his craft into a sharp counterclockwise spin. I tracked the craft with my light long enough to spot one of the men raise his weapon and aim it at me. I fell to the deck and turned off the light as a long burst of full-auto weapons fire punctuated the darkness with muzzle flashes.

One slug slammed into the *Jambalaya*'s mast, ringing like the peal of a dull bell.

An angry shout followed: "Stop it! We want him alive."

Then the snick-click of a fresh magazine being seated.

I got to my knees and peered into the darkness as the outboard motor grew louder again. The beams of their flashlights cast shadows on the *Jambalaya*'s deck and rigging.

I grabbed the flare pistol and popped up long enough to fire a round straight at the inflatable. As I hit the deck again, I broke the pistol down, pulled out the spent .12-gauge cartridge, reloaded, and fired a round straight up. In an instant, the illuminating parachute flare hung above, painting the scene with its flat blue-white magnesium glowlight.

"Get him! Get him now!"

Why? Why me? A drug gang raiding what they thought was a rival's shipment? But the expensive H&Ks they carried weren't the usual drug-gang firearm. I knew it, instead, as the choice of professionals ranging from urban SWAT teams to military Special Forces in close-quarter situations.

The flare-lit seascape, urgent shouts, and the lingering smell of cordite pulled the rip cord on a pack of long-buried memories that arced through my head, activating old reflexes that had often saved my life. I unsnapped the carabiner attaching my lifeline to the harness, reloaded the flare pistol, and fired. New illumination brightened the sky as I sensed my assailants' inflatable boat thumping against the port stern quarter. From my crouched position in the cockpit, I shoved the *Jambalaya*'s throttle full forward, steered the *Jambalaya* straight into oncoming traffic, then set the autopilot to hold the course.

I was reaching for the VHF to radio in a Mayday when the first man came over the gunwale. I focused on his shadow, coiled myself tight, and waited. The man had a single tipsy moment as he stepped on deck. I lunged for him then in one long, taut step, focusing all the strength in my legs and torso and arms and shoulders into the single forearm of my right elbow, which I slammed into the side of the man's head right behind his ear. His head snapped unnaturally to the left accompanied by a dull snap of cracked vertebrae. Sweat flew from his face and arced like tiny glowing beads through the stark flarelight. Experience taught me that the higher the vertebrae in his neck, the faster he'd die.

The man crumpled into the cockpit like a sack of melons. He looked at me as his uncontrolled bladder and bowels darkened his pants. Regret passed through me like a quick shadow as I watched the recognition and panic ricochet in his eyes before the lids fluttered shut.

Scrambling to the cabin below, I flicked the VHF to Channel 16.

"Mayday, Mayday, Mayday. This is the vessel *Jambalaya* and am being attacked by armed assailants. Request immediate assistance." I read off my coordinates from the GPS screen on the panel next to the VHF.

I was still radioing my Mayday as I dialed 911 on my cell phone and got the inevitable recording.

"Hell," I muttered. I had barely finished stuffing the phone back in my Windbreaker's cargo pocket when the *Jambalaya* rocked gently, letting me know someone had stepped on deck. With the *Jambalaya*'s diesel laboring away at full rpms, I rushed forward to the head, threw open the door, and yanked out a strategic piece of teak paneling to reveal a small void between the hull and the interior lining. From it, I pulled out a heavy waterproof bag containing an old friend—a Colt .45 Model 1911 semiautomatic pistol—and three clips of ammunition.

I slid a clip in the handle of the Colt, worked the slide to chamber a round, and made sure the safety was off. As I stepped from the head into the cabin, I spotted a man descending the steps from the cockpit, silhouetted by the trapezoidal opening of the companionway and the dimming flarelight beyond. I shot him.

The slug spun him around with his finger on the trigger of his weapon. I dived away from the long-full-auto burst that hosed the *Jambalaya*'s interior. Before the last shot faded, I sprang toward him and nailed his head to the deck with a second shot. Never shoot once. Good training never died.

I was facing the stern when I heard the door to the bow stateroom slam open behind me, followed by the voice of command.

"Don't move, Dr. Stone. Don't even twitch or I'll blow your kidneys right out the front of your belly."

I stood with the *Jambalaya*'s galley on my right as I faced the stern. My hip touched the corner of the counter that jutted about three feet toward the centerline of the cabin creating a small alcove, but it was little cover. The fixtures had deliberately been designed as light as possible to avoid flotation and balance issues. The H&K's slugs could readily parse the flimsy paneling I was using for cover and dissect me with ease.

"Toss your weapon outside," the voice commanded me. I set the safety and sent it flying into the cockpit.

In the moment of ensuing silence, my ears took in the loud hammering from the *Jambalaya*'s diesel and, just barely detectable through the noise, frantic shouts, voices, air horns. The VHF squawked a verbal collage of sudden traffic, none of it intelligible as one transmission after another sank beneath the frantic verbal hash.

"Dr. Stone, hand over the Palm Vanessa Thompson gave you."

"I have no idea—"

In the next instant, a pinpoint of red laser light shone remarkably steady on the teak bulkhead immediately to my right, then vanished through a hole with remarkably clean edges. The shot passed so close to my head I heard the slug's high ripping whine.

"I can shoot to wound you all night long, Mr. Stone. If you play games, it will cost you a great deal of pain."

I ransacked every memory of the past year.

"I can't remember—"

I didn't see the laser dance this time and realized what had happened only after I heard the gunshot and felt the warm stickiness flowing down the left side of my head. I touched the top of my earlobe and found the wound slight and the pain faint.

"That's my last warning," he yelled above the din from the VHF and the urgent voices outside.

In the next few fractions of a millisecond, I replayed the short scene in the graveyard and felt the pleasure as Vanessa slipped a hand inside my suit coat. The pleasure of her touch had overshadowed anything cognitive, especially because she was killed a second or so later. I had no idea about a Palm, but I needed a story to buy time.

"I have it in a safe at my office. I can get it for you."

"No." The laser dot danced again. "No. Give me the combination and I'll get it." The laser dot disappeared again, undoubtedly illuminating some part of my body that I had grown fond of.

Before he could shoot, the *Jambalaya* pitched forward with a thunderous deceleration that sent her rolling and yawing. My assailant cursed; I heard the deep thump of him colliding with something stationary. I lunged up into the cockpit. Gasoline fumes filled the air. I looked forward toward an epicenter of screams and curses and saw the *Jambalaya*'s bow impaled in a flashy Cigarette boat.

I grabbed my Colt and almost fired at my attacker before my nose stopped me. I lunged topside and jumped overboard. The water geysered all around me as the H&K's slugs stitched into the sea. I dove under the surface just as the full-automatic muzzle blasts ignited the spilled gasoline from the Cigarette boat's ruptured tanks.

Darryl Talmadge sat up in the hospital bed with its chipped enamel paint and threw back the pilled polyester blanket with its cigarette burns and medicinal smells. He took as deep a breath as his emphysema would allow, then struggled through a coughing fit that rattled through his bone-and-beef-jerky frame.

The air-conditioning blew hard and chill, cutting through the baggy pajamas he lived in. When the last of his seismic coughs had faded, he swung his legs over the side and stood up, ignoring the battered aluminum walker the Veterans Administration hospital had issued him. He didn't need it, and besides, the damn thing was too short for his rangy six-foot-six frame—just like the bed—but that was the Army for you. He'd told all this to Jay Shanker, his court-assigned lawyer, nearly six months ago, the last time he had been allowed an outside visitor.

Talmadge craned his head up to the corner of the room and glared at the closed-circuit video camera attached to the wall above the television. He focused right on the camera's little red LED, and despite the arthritis from the partial shoulder separation he'd got at Chosin Reservoir more than half a century before, Talmadge raised his arm with an extended bird finger.

"Fuck you!"

It pleased him to know the camera captured his unvarnished opinion for posterity and scientific scrutiny. One day, somebody honest would find the tapes. The truth would come out then and heads would roll.

The truth was why they had jerked Talmadge out of Leflore County Court on the second day of sentencing hearings. Before that, his lame court-appointed lawyer had kept him shut up and drugged out during the murder trial, not even letting him speak up in his own defense. The trial took less than a week and the jury less than an hour to convict him of murder.

Everybody, especially Talmadge, knew the conviction was a greased rail to the gas chamber, which is why he secretly flushed his medicine down the toilet before the sentencing hearings.

There, his mind freed from the chemical handcuffs that had kept him silent for so long, he stood up in open court and declared it a frame-up to keep him quiet about Project Enduring Valor and began to rattle off names and dates and places he had mostly forgotten until the seizures started.

A contingent of Army officers and MPs conveniently in court that day hustled him out of the courtroom in record time, then bundled him off to the mental ward at the VA hospital, where he had remained ever since. The judge sentenced Talmadge to death in the gas chamber at Parchman, then sealed the court records and threatened anyone present with serious jail time if they talked about what had proceeded.

"Y'all got a tough row to hoe, now don'tcha?" Talmadge addressed the camera. "Y'all want me dead so I can't remem-buh things no mo'." He looked up at the camera and nodded his head for good measure.

Then he gingerly increased the weight on both legs. Despite the arthritis pain in his knees and hips that had ended his career as a hunting guide, Talmadge ignored the walker and shuffled over to the window. He parted the curtains and squinted through his reflection in the window glass. Southwest through the darkness he caught a glimpse of the very top of the Capitol dome above the trees. Talmadge imagined himself free out there with real fresh air to breath and grass and dog shit to avoid stepping in. Anger filtered into his chest, dark, hot, and sharp.

Then he turned back toward the camera and the red light that never went out.

"Fuck you all, 'specially you, Mr. High-and-Mighty, General dog-fucker Braxton and all them clap-rotten horses you rode in on."

Sweat beaded up on Talmadge's face and his pulse throbbed along the neat surgical scar that ran like railroad tracks from the bridge of his nose up past his right eyebrow and into his thinning hairline. Then his vision faded the way it always did when his medication wore off. A scintillating crescent of multicolored neon obliterated his peripheral vision, then spread.

The damn lights had started it all. That first day, he'd bent over a cup of coffee at the Delta Café in Itta Bena, talking with Dud Shackleford and Dooney Clark about how fishing at Mossy Lake had gone right to hell, and they all agreed it was thanks to all the crowds from as far away as Jackson with their fancy bass boats and million-dollar tackle that made too damn much noise for real fishermen to catch anything.

On the first day when the lights in his head had shattered his vision, Darryl Talmadge had dropped his coffee cup and spilled coffee all over the table. Dooney called 911. Talmadge was sure he was having a stroke, but when he got to the hospital in Greenwood, the emergency room doctors diagnosed it as some sort of migraine aura, perhaps a reaction to the stress of his wife's death and the need to sell his house to pay her medical expenses. The doctor said the aura probably didn't mean anything serious, but if it came again, perhaps he needed to go to Jackson or Memphis to have his head scanned.

Then the flashbacks came cascading from his head right after Dud and Dooney settled him into his room at the Tallahatchie Manor Assisted Care Facility, where he'd lived since his wife, Dora, had died of cancer from all the cigarettes, right after his knees had gotten too arthritic for him to care for their little place on Highway 7, north of the Episcopal chapel outside Itta Bena. He still felt guilty for the relief that had mixed with his sorrow when Dora died. She had begun to slip into the cranky stages of Alzheimer's and was running him ragged when the cancer killed her. His depression had hit right after the Alzheimer's, back when he'd realized the woman he loved no longer lived inside the body he tended. Yet he used every shred of his swiftly eroding energy and money to do the best he could for her. Talmadge figured out a few months later that he had done it all to honor Dora's memory; it had been like living with a fresh gravesite in the house where feeding her and bathing her and keeping her from wandering off and getting hit by a tractor filled the same emotional need as placing flowers on a grave. He felt gratefully ashamed when the cancer finally took Dora.

But the really bad memories that landed him in hot water flooded from his head not long after Dooney and Dud had dropped him off at his room. The scintillating lights came back with a vengeance. As the neon rainbow crescendoed towards climax, he fumbled out the old cassette recorder and filled up all the tapes he could find with an avalanche of memories that had never scrolled through his consciousness before. He'd always thought the mortar shell that had separated his shoulder in Korea and laced his head with shrapnel had forever erased memories from those days. But here, to his astonishment, they flooded back, and along with them, memories of white coats and hypodermics and Project Enduring Valor. He babbled into the microphone until he lost consciousness.

The next day, after the lights had gone, he played the tapes and heard his voice as if for the first time and listened to his words relating strange tales of which he had no memory. Now certain this was the beginning of Alzheimer's like Dora's, he pulled out his old .12-gauge, the Remington automatic built on the Browning patent that had once made him a legendary wing shot in any season, loaded three cartridges with number four shot—the largest he had since duck hunting was his favorite—then with an old cassette of Dora singing in the background, he danced with the .12-gauge for the entire morning before calling Dooney.

Two hours later at the VA hospital in Jackson, they sat in the waiting room almost all day until a harried physician came out, listened to his story, pried the shoebox with the cassettes away from Talmadge, and arranged for his admittance.

If only he had left the freaking tapes at home, things would be so different now, as he shifted his focus to the television screen where one of CNN's artlessly untalented but sensuously full-lipped news girls filled the screen, droning on about some flood in Europe washing away priceless art treasures. She wore a sly smile on her face as she read this tragic story. Then she read something that cut through Talmadge's latest light storm.

"Eight Russian soldiers were gunned down and three others wounded yesterday by one of their comrades in the Caucasus Mountains on a remote crossing post on the border with Georgia," she said with that sly cynical smirk just below the surface. "A regional duty officer with Russia's branch of the Emergency Situations Ministry said the shooter was under the influence of some sort of hallucinogenic mushroom popular with conscripts in the remote border region. This is the second such shooting in the same region within the past four months as desertions, violence, and suicides continue to plague Russia's deteriorating military establishment. . . . And now with entertainment news about Paris, J.Lo, and Britney . . ."

Through the scintillating lights that dominated his vision now, Talmadge concentrated all his anger on the video camera. "Russians're tryin' y'own damn shit, ain't they?" he began. "Fucking mushroom story makes a damn good cover-up, huh? Huh! Well, it's a shitload bettuh than that fuckin' combat stress crap y'all trotted out after all those killin's at Ft. Bragg when the boys came home from Afghanistan." His anger and the electrical storm in his brain began to merge. "You limp-dicked cocksuckuhs hung those boys out t'dry ovuh My Lai an' all those other times when it was th' fucking drugs, y'drugs, y'fuckin' drugs, y'fuckin' drugs, y'fuckin' drugs, fuggingdrugs! Fuggingdrugs!"

He raged at the camera until the arcing neon rainbow filled his vision and his mind, clutched at the deepest parts of his entrails, and squeezed the breath from his chest.

Then Darryl Talmadge buckled face-first to the floor.

I sat on the guano-frosted concrete riprap jetty and field-stripped my .45 and my cell phone. Either might save my life if my assailants had friends around. Shaking the water out of the gun and phone, drying off the .45 cartridges and battery, took me less than five minutes, about as long as it took the L.A. County Sheriff's Department Harbor Patrol to show up with two fiberglass-hulled boats and a bright orange inflatable. Behind came the Coast Guard's forty-foot multipurpose rescue and fire-suppression vessel. County Fire Department trucks made their way along the jetty running between Ballona Creek and the Marina's main jetty.

The Coast Guard vessel technically wasn't supposed to respond to incidents here in the sheriff's jurisdiction inside the marina. But tonight, the sheriff had obviously requested assistance under their mutual aid pact. I knew this because I had spent more than twelve years as a reserve with the Sheriff's Search and Rescue team and almost as long with the Coast Guard Auxiliary. I didn't get paid for any of that, and in fact, equipping the *Jambalaya* to serve as a Coast Guard Auxiliary facility took a fair amount of my personal cash. But I didn't mind. I told most people it was my way of giving back to the community, which was mostly true. Only, I could never decide whether that counterbalanced the sheer fun of testing myself against the ocean when no sane person would be out on it (those being the ones we usually had to rescue) or dangling from a line beneath a helicopter to rescue the equivalent fools in the mountains.

I thought about this as I sat on the stinking rocks and watched the *Jambalaya* and the Cigarette boat melt into one crumpling mass of gasoline, diesel fuel, and burning fiberglass resin that had gone up far quicker than I had ever seen before. I guessed it was the enormous amount of gasoline in the Cigarette boat's tanks.

The Harbor Patrol and the Coast Guard spotlights supplemented the already ample light from private watercraft, blasting the scene with stark, flat illumination from so many directions it bleached out shadows and washed away colors with a blue-white gesso that made it look like a virgin paint-by-numbers canvas. I squinted into the light, grateful to see all three passengers aboard the Cigarette boat being pulled aboard other boats.

The *Jambalaya*'s aluminum mast softened from the heat, then wilted, sending the masthead anemometer and other instruments plunging into the water.

The Coast Guard vessel maneuvered gingerly in close to the wreckage to allow the crew to spray fire-suppressing foam. Abruptly the two burning boats made a noise oddly reminiscent of a flushing toilet, then sank immediately, propelled to the bottom, no doubt, by the massive lead weight in the *Jambalaya*'s finned, torpedo-shaped keel.

Watching the *Jambalaya*'s rigging disappear beneath the water sucked me under my own surface for a moment. Like the individual frames of a motion picture flashing by too quickly to focus on any single one, the images of what I had lost aboard the *Jambalaya* created a deep, unified sense of loss.

I stood up straight and tall and tried to shake off the sadness. I focused instead on the Coast Guard scattering foam to quell the remaining fire on the surface; I teased the scene apart with my eyes, desperate to spot someone thrashing about. But as one of the Harbor Patrol's inflatables made its way toward me, I grew increasingly comfortable that my assailant had not made it out before the burning mass sizzled beneath the waves.

"What in hell've you gotten yourself into this time, Doc?" I recognized sheriff's sergeant Vince Sloane's gruff Brooklyn accent before I actually recognized his face through the glare. "It looked like the freaking Fourth of July out there." He was a beefy, powerful man with no tolerance for BS and an amazing capacity to keep his temper under control. He was a perp's nightmare, hell on wheels with a heart for the innocent that knew no natural bounds.

Sloane knelt amidships as the helmsman feathered the throttle and brought the craft within inches of the jetty and kept it there without actually touching the riprap. That had to be Lexus Guzman. She was the only deputy with such a deft hand on the helm.

"Hell if I can figure it out," I replied to Sloane as I climbed aboard the inflatable.

"Doc, you smell like manure," Lexus said as she moved the inflatable away from the jetty.

"Good evening to you too, Lexus," I replied. Her real name was Carolina; she'd come from a well-to-do family with a vineyard down near Ensenada and had shown up for work the first day in a bright, shiny new Lexus convertible. And while she had gone on to newer and fancier cars, the nickname Lexus stuck.

We made our way north in the main channel and I filled them in. Overhead, a sheriff's helicopter passed us heading west, then settled into a rock-solid hover above the accident scene at the mouth of the harbor.

"I should give you this," I said as I tugged the Colt .45 automatic from my Windbreaker, pulled out the magazine, and ejected the cartridge in the chamber. I held the .45 upside down dangling with one finger in the trigger guard. Vince made a question with his face.

"I think when they finally pull the wreckage up, they're going to find three bodies and one of them is going to be carrying a slug from this."

Sloane frowned deeply as he took all this in. Even without pay, I served as a sworn peace officer, which meant I would be placed on administrative leave while Internal Affairs investigated this officer-involved shooting.

"Okay," Sloane said, his voice heavy with resignation. "Tell me everything before I have to write it down officially." He nodded to Lexus, who slowed the inflatable and made a broad, sweeping circle. As I began, a television helicopter thwacked past overhead, the station's call letters prominently illuminated on the tail for maximum marketing impact. The door was open with the cameraman strapped in the opening. Another TV chopper followed close on its tail as we made lazy circles in the channel. Soon, the sky above and around the harbor breakwater looked like an aerial parking lot for giant mechanical dragonflies.

Ignoring the circus in the sky, I spilled everything, especially the part about how I thought it had been a botched drug rip-off and how professional my assailants had been.

"But not professional enough for *you*, eh, Doc?" Sloane gave me the same curiously wary look he wore whenever my military service came up. He had seen my DD214, the official discharge document issued by the Department of Defense summarizing my military service. A lot of stuff was too classified to put on it. I didn't talk about it and Sloane was too smart to pry. Guzman steered the craft slowly to the sheriff's dock.

"Just lucky," I said, and shrugged.

"Lucky!" Sloane scoffed. "If you'd've been lucky, the bastards would've hit the right boat and not yours." He mumbled, "You have any idea how much freaking paperwork this is going to be? Not to mention that bozo season is here and I can't afford to lose a good reserve officer."

I was about to make a sarcastic wisecrack about how sorry I was for his terrible evening when my cell made a fuzzy buzzing sound. The wet speaker had a hard time with Robert's Johnson's "Crossroad Blues," which I used as my ring tone, but I was amazed the phone still worked.

I answered and froze at the sound of a full, melodic, and all too familiar voice.

"Mr. Stone?"

I checked my watch. "Jasmine?"

"It's me. My flight was one of those very rare creatures that arrived early."

"Oh, jeez!" I blurted. "No, don't . . . I didn't mean that the way it sounded. It's just . . . I've been . . . my boat's been in an accident and—"

"You okay?"

"For now. But there's going to be a lot of paperwork and the usual hassles."

"Okay. Look, I booked a room at the Crown Plaza right near LAX. Why don't I check in and call you in the morning?"

Guzman brought the inflatable to soft landing at the dock. Sloane grabbed the inflatable's bow line, jumped out, and tied it to the nearest cleat. He took the stern line from Guzman and did the same.

"Look, it's okay." Jasmine's voice was warm and confident, like her mother's. "I'm not a tourist here."

I had once clipped a *Newsweek* article on Vanessa with a sidebar on Jasmine. She'd graduated from USC, then Stanford law school, clerked for a justice on the Fifth Circuit Court of Appeals, then went to work with her mother in New York. When Vanessa moved to Mississippi, Jasmine stayed up North with a multimegaton Manhattan law firm. I manipulated the dates of the articles in my head and figured that Jasmine was in her mid- or maybe late thirties.

Then six months ago, after Vanessa's murder, Jasmine had come home to continue her mother's legacy at the Advocacy Foundation for Mississippi Justice, a Delta powerhouse inspired by Martha Bergmark's Mississippi Center for Justice down in Jackson.

"Still—" I stuttered.

"Still nothing. Take care of business and call me in the morning." The confidence and generosity in her voice amazed me and fooled me again into believing for an instant that I was talking to Vanessa. The daughter's genes had fallen right close the source, I thought, at least the DNA from Vanessa had. No one actually knew about the other half.

I stood there with the phone in my hand, thinking about the mystery of DNA and how it encapsulated the strong and independent thinking that had made Vanessa so incorruptibly autonomous. I wondered whether Jasmine had the same stuff.

Most of what I knew about both of them came from magazine and newspaper articles about Vanessa I had occasionally clipped and thrown into an expandable file. Some I had read and reread until the edges frayed and carried the smudges of my fingers.

When I married Camilla, I put the file in storage, a symbolic putting away of all others.

After the accident, when we knew Camilla's coma had no end and I could no longer face the ghosts in our house, I took to living aboard the *Jambalaya* three or four nights a week and the rest at a cot in my office. I dragged Vanessa's old file down to the *Jambalaya*. At first, I'd sit belowdecks and simply touch the file. Every time I tried to open it, I'd see Camilla wasting away on her motorized hospital bed with the panoramic view of the Pacific, which no one could tell if she saw or not. Legally we remained husband and wife, but the coma had evicted the real Camilla from the body. Still, I remained faithful to the *memory* of Camilla, to the *idea* of who she had been. My nondecision to remain poised without action haunted every part of my life.

The day Vanessa was buried, my heart told me I could read her file without the spirits of adultery reaching out for me. From that cold winter day until this very morning, I'd sit aboard the *Jambalaya*—in the cockpit on warm sunny days and down below in the main cabin at night—and reread the pieces written about her. I was surprised at how complete a record I had collected, going back almost thirty years. Sometimes I felt guilty when I read the pieces, wondering at first, then knowing in my heart that Camilla had always been my second choice.

With Jasmine's voice echoing in my head, I remembered a *New York Times* article that emphasized that Jasmine had never met her father. She had been conceived during a one-night stand back in the licentious 1970s when Vanessa was a volunteer at a San Francisco law firm representing Native Americans arrested in the occupation of Alcatraz.

Vanessa's quote from the article struck me now as I listened to her daughter: "Good breeding material doesn't necessarily make for a good parent. Too damn many black children grow up with episodic and unreliable fathers who create expectations of love and trust that rank several steps below the family dog. I also didn't like the way abortion felt for me, so I raised her myself."

All of this hurtled through my mind as I struggled to say something intelligent to Vanessa's daughter. I came off inarticulate and banal, then said good-bye.

"Daughter of an old friend," I said to Sloane as he stood on the dock looking down at me. He raised the eyebrow that said he had questions that could wait. When he extended his hand, I accepted it.

"Thanks, Sarge."

He grunted something I took as a "You're welcome."

We walked toward the Coast Guard and sheriff's building, but it no longer felt familiar and secure to me. Now it loomed alien and full of unknown menace as we pushed through the doors and headed for the suspect-interview rooms where the doors locked from the outside.

Vince grabbed a first-aid kit on the way in. "Technically, we oughta have the paramedics look at this," he mumbled as he wiped at my ear-lobe with an alcohol pad, which burned worse than the original wound.

"Hell, that's not even big enough to put a Band-Aid on," Vince said.

He slapped me on the shoulder, then left me alone to wrestle with life, death, murder, and salvation. Little did I know that the enormity of what had just happened would pale into insignificance within just a few hours.

19

Fifteen minutes later, two plainclothes officers I had hoped never to see walked in. Internal Affairs was a lot like the Internal Revenue Service: necessary for the proper functioning of the organization, but best if never actually experienced firsthand. They interviewed me until nearly midnight. They had a job to do, but their assumption I was guilty pissed me off.

I told my story three times, first with both the investigators, then, by turns, with each of them alone. They asked me about my military background and tried to pry into the classified stuff. I told them they should talk to Vince or to call the Pentagon. I gave them the number.

They left the room by turns, and from the follow-up questions they asked after returning, I surmised they had called the Pentagon and interviewed Vince. Clearly they had also interviewed witnesses on the other boats, obtained copies of the duty logs from the Coast Guard and sheriff's dispatchers, and listened to the radio tapes of my Mayday calls. Their swift professionalism made me feel a lot less like an Inquisition victim.

They didn't know what to make of the reference one of the men had made to the "Palm" and at first were skeptical that I also had no clue. But over time, their attitudes mellowed; softened, I assumed, by the consistency of my story and its concurrence with the other witnesses, my radio calls, the gunshots, flares, and their discovery of a military-style inflatable drifting west of the breakwater.

They constructed a timeline and eventually wound things up by telling me I should be available at any time for more interviews. They also explained that releasing me was not an exoneration for my killing the men.

I finally grabbed my Windbreaker and walked from the interview room, toward the locker room and a quick shower. Trudging through a grinding fatigue where fluorescent lights glared way too bright and normal sounds hit my ears as too loud and brittle, I recognized the adrenaline hangover that always accompanied every life-or-death battle. I half-closed my eyes as I made my way down the familiar corridors, through a quick rinse in the shower, and back toward the main office, dressed in a ratty pair of old cargo shorts and Café Pacifico T-shirt that had been stuffed in the back of my locker.

I made my way through a mostly deserted warren of desks and offices and spotted Vince at the doorway leading to the visitors' reception area.

"How you feeling?" He searched my face.

"Okay, I suppose. Internal Affairs has a job to do."

"Uh-uh."

When he shook his head at my words, then nodded back toward the breakwater where the firefight had happened, I knew what he was trying to say.

"They started it, Sarge," I said. "Whoever they were, they deserved what they got. It was them or me. That part doesn't bother me a bit." I paused. "Having my boat sunk bothers me."

Vince looked at me strangely, cocking his head and focusing on my eyes as if he could see something mysterious there. Unlike others, I never experienced guilt or remorse after killing an assailant.

As a neuroscientist, I cognitively understood why about 98 percent of the population had trouble with killing in self-defense, but I had never grasped the emotional sense of it. Decades ago, that combination of personal characteristics had once allowed me to keep effectively soldiering along while combat fatigue claimed people around me. But on this night, age and a lack of practice had taken their toll; fatigue hit me a lot harder than it would have twenty-five years before.

"Uh-huh," Vince said doubtfully. "Regardless of how you *feel*, you still *look* like shit, Doc, even if you don't smell like it anymore."

"And you *sound* like an echo."

"Well, you may want to perk up a little. You have a visitor." Cocked his head toward the reception area.

"Who?"

He shook his head.

"See for yourself."

I combed my fingers through my still-wet hair.

"Go on in," Vince said impatiently. "The young lady has been waiting patiently."

In the brightly lit reception area, a murmuring entourage of uniforms jammed the front: three or four khaki-clad sheriff's deputies, two LAPD partners in navy blue, and a CHP motorcycle cop in knee-length leather boots holding his helmet in his left hand. In the next moment they parted like a curtain, framing Jasmine Thompson, who made her entrance. She looked more like her mother than she sounded. The similarity took me by surprise and made me wonder if she had her mother's intellect and sense of humor as well. The whole package would be astonishing.

As Jasmine made her way to me, I got a collective glare from the assembled audience, equal parts displeasure and envy.

"Mr. Stone!" I picked up on the sly winks and nudges among the cops flanking her. Most were half my age and looked palpably relieved at her formal greeting.

As Jasmine drew near, she appeared to be Vanessa reincarnate. I felt the faint stir of old, faded memories. Jasmine had her mother's generous, almost Lane Bryant figure, which amply filled out her jeans and knit top in a way that guaranteed the undivided attention of the appreciative audience around her.

I recognized differences in Jasmine as she approached. Jasmine stood a head taller than Vanessa. She was nearly as tall as me, making it necessary for most of the cops to look up at her face. A wild halo of ringlet curls surrounded her face and cascaded nearly to her shoulders. Her intensely black hair dazzled with rainbows. And where her mother's skin reminded me of creamy mocha, Jasmine's glowed more warmly like maple sugar. Her lips were fashionably full even without makeup, and her nose looked more American Indian than African-American. Two small diamond studs on one of her ears dazzled intensely even under the fluorescent lights.

But her eyes dominated everything else: large, intense, with the pale luminescence of wisteria blooms accentuated by the warm, dusky hues of her high, aristocratic cheekbones. If these were the window to her soul, then I swear I could see Vanessa shining through.

I remembered Vanessa in the next minute and swallowed against the constriction in my throat. Jasmine held out her arms as she approached; I followed automatically, accepting a brief, polite, concerned family-variety hug.

For an instant, the minor notes of Mississippi funerals played in my head. Then those dark, anxious emotions vanished as her scent, blissfully different from Vanessa's, made a direct connection with my innermost thoughts.

Jasmine's scent moved my heart before my mind could grasp it. In one instant, it made me sorry the hug was so chaste; then the next instant, guilt hit me for feeling that. The human mind is a strange amalgam of deep-seated, foundational Darwinian impulses and rational centers of higher control. The first govern basic animal survival and land people in prison when the second doesn't take control. Impulses happen physically, spontaneously. They are hormone-driven and totally without thought. Free will can either surrender or control the chemicals. In an instant, I knew then my reaction was physical, the impulse all wrong. I worked at thinking with my big head and not the small one.

"How are you?" she asked as she stood back a step, and I saw concern make its way across her face as she took in my face and head. "Are you all right?"

"A scratch," I said gently, touching the top of my ear. "I got lucky."
She frowned.
"You should see the other guy." I smiled.
She shook her head.
I said, "I thought you—how did you find me?"
"Television. Every local channel has a helicopter."
I nodded slowly. "But you really shouldn't have—"
"Do you really think I'd miss the action this close to my hotel?"
"You really *are* your mother's child."
A quick shadow of loss momentarily eclipsed the smile in her eyes

and made me regret my words. Jasmine had had six months of getting on with life to ease her pain, but I knew that the loss of someone so close would leave a wound that would never quite heal. I also knew I had to be careful, because open psychological wounds leave us all emotionally vulnerable, irrational, apt to go with the flow of our natural steroids. I thought of people who get divorced and marry on the rebound, or Stockholm-syndrome hostages who fall in love with their captors.

"Awright, awright! Quit the gawking!" Vince Sloane's voice boomed as he made his way in front of us toward the assembly of law enforcement personnel. "Don't you guys have a report to file or something?" When the clot of uniforms failed to give way, he bulled his way through and motioned Jasmine and me to follow. "C'mon, c'mon! I hear your mother calling you. Step aside; there's nothing to see here; gimme some air," he barked like the Marine gunnery sergeant he had once been.

We followed Vince out of the building and into a night that had turned crisp and clean with a light breeze off Santa Monica Bay. I followed Jasmine to a Mercedes two-seater glowing bright red under the streetlights. Vince gave a low whistle as he looked admiringly at the car's polished shine that reflected every streetlight in the vicinity back at us. The chrome dazzled, the top was down.

"I didn't know you could rent these," I said.

"You can rent *anything* in L.A." She hit the alarm release. "Anything." She gave me a Mona Lisa smile that hid more than it revealed. "All it takes is money."

Jasmine looked good next to the Mercedes. She wore style without looking flashy and pretentious. Vince had stopped a good ten yards from the car. I turned back to look at him. He gave me a wink and a nod of approval, then turned back toward the building, where the uniformed officers still crowded behind the broad plate-glass windows. Vince slowly shook his head as he advanced on them.

Jasmine opened her door and nodded at me. "Hop in."

I obeyed as she cranked the engine and backed out of the space. "Where to?"

I thought for a moment as she headed slowly toward the cop controlling traffic into the lot. Beyond, a jam of television trucks with their satellite dishes worshiping the southern sky crowded both shoulders.

"Just around the marina," I said as we cleared the checkpoint and made our way toward Fisherman's Village. The mob of television functionaries instantly spotted the flashy convertible, then recognized me. Shoulder-cam lights burst out of the darkness like magnesium flares. Jasmine muttered some low derogatory curse about leeches or roaches as she hit the accelerator and sent both production crews and the well-coiffed talking heads lurching for safety. In an instant, we were through the corridor of inquisition and into the freedom of early-morning darkness.

Jasmine looked in her rearview mirror and smiled; a sly satisfaction lit up her eyes. My heart filled with trouble when I studied Jasmine's eyes and felt Vanessa's irresistible gravity that had never let me go. I looked quickly away and struggled against memories I dared not recall.

"They'll follow us," she said as she pressed on the Mercedes's accelerator.

"Not much chance the way you're driving."

She looked over at me and raised her eyebrows. "Too fast?"

The g-forces pulled me toward her as she steered the car through a sweeping curve.

"Nope," I said. When her face made that ambiguous Mona Lisa smile again, I wondered what she was thinking and worked diligently on not caring.

Our trajectory straightened out parallel to the H Basin; ahead of us, the light at the intersection at Admiralty Way turned red.

She braked hard. "Which way?"

"Left," I said. "My truck is over near my slip."

"Truck?" She raised her eyebrows again and eased through the red. "I didn't know brain surgeons drove trucks. Next you'll be telling me you wear Fruit Of The Loom briefs and watch television wrestling."

I did wear Fruit Of The Loom briefs, bought in twelve-packs at Target, and almost said I was a neurophysiologist and hadn't performed brain surgery since the accident, but it all played in my head as too stuffy, too fussy . . . too *old*, and something in me wanted very much not to sound too old for Jasmine. But in fact, I thought of nothing that didn't sound old or lame, so I said nothing at all.

I closed my eyes and we rode in silence for several long moments. The scene on the *Jambalaya* played in my head.

"The guy said, 'I want the Palm.' That's what he said," I mumbled to myself.

"Pardon?"

I opened my eyes and caught Jasmine looking at me.

"The guy on the boat. He said he wanted the Palm your mother gave me." I shook my head. "I don't remember a Palm.

"What could be so important about a PDA that people are willing to kill for it?"

While I pondered the mysterious missing Palm, Jasmine sped past the turnoff.

"That was our turn," I said, pointing behind us to the left.

"No problem." She slowed for a turn lane, then hit the brakes hard enough for my shoulder belt's inertial catch to grab as she steered the Mercedes through a 180 and headed back.

"What Palm?"

She reached the turnoff and I pointed toward the parking lot next to *Jambalaya*'s berth. We pulled into the lot and found a parking space next to my battered three-quarter-ton Chevy pickup with the off-road roll bar and sheet metal sculpted by a decade's worth of encounters with a wide assortment of near misses and tight squeezes with high-Sierra trees and granite boulders.

"Impressive," she said, looking up at my truck. "Perfect for L.A. freeways."

"Nobody tries to crowd me when I merge."

She nodded and turned off the ignition. "Nothing to lose."

"Pardon?"

"They take one look and know you've got nothing to lose and they let you in, right?"

"Something like that."

"That's such a totally contra-L.A. thing."

I shrugged.

"No, really." She leaned over and placed her hand on my forearm; her touch felt electric. "That's very cool." She paused, and in the silence the sounds of engines and tortured tires grew louder.

"The jackals are coming," she said. "Give me a ride and tell me about the Palm."

We transferred everything to my pickup. I cranked up the big-block V-8 and pulled out of the parking lot. The light was red at Admiralty Way.

"Duck down." I faced away from the onrushing surge of television vehicles as Jasmine slumped down in her seat. Nobody gave my battered truck a second glance. I didn't have a plan yet, so I took the easy path and turned south on Lincoln.

"Could Mom have slipped something in your pocket there in the cemetery and you didn't remember?"

"I suppose. Everything happened really quickly and I could have easily missed something. Our brains can only handle focusing on one thing at a time. We switch back and forth between things so fast we think we're multitasking, but it's an illusion."

"Mom always told me it was impossible to have a conversation with you without learning something."

I looked over at her.

"Mom was right," she said.

Jasmine gave me her mother's smile again and, with no warning, opened up an epic blockbuster of a memory. The vision nailed me with fine holographic details like one of those incredible black-and-white Ansel Adams photos where you can see the needles on a Jeffrey pine all the way across Lake Tahoe way up on the top of the distant Sierra ridges.

Jasmine's smile did that. It brought me face-to-face with that fateful Christmas party so long ago. Vanessa opened the door as if she had watched me come up the walk, and when I stepped in, she stood so close I felt the heat from her face and savored the aroma of Doublemint gum on her breath. I recalled the fine variegated color detail in her eyes as she focused on mine, holding my gaze right down to the last instant, when I had to turn away from the moment that would have been our first kiss had the house not been jammed with people.

This memory struck me now, as I drove my truck and Vanessa's daughter across the Ballona Creek bridge. All of this seized my thoughts so completely that I ran the stoplight at Jefferson.

"Oh, hell." I slowed down, half-expecting to see the lights of a police car, then realizing it was unlikely in the dead of night.

Emotions careered wildly about in my head, then suddenly distilled themselves; I visualized the heap of bloody clothes I had stuffed into a plastic bag in my Mississippi motel room after Mama's funeral.

"Hold on," I said quietly at first.

Jasmine looked at me expectantly.

"Whoa! That's got to be it."

I slammed on the brakes and hung a U-turn.

"If it's anywhere, it'll be in the suit I wore at my mother's funeral."

"The Palm?"

I nodded. "It's the only possible thing."

I replayed the scene in Itta Bena once again. Only this time I had trouble focusing on Vanessa's face. It came to me now as one of those hyperpixelated images you get when you enlarge a digital photo too much.

Excitedly, I described things to Jasmine, slowly struggling to relate every detail as I drove north along Lincoln, making most of the green lights and easing through the reds. I visualized the cracked concrete in the garage of our little stucco beach house in Playa Del Rey a block from the ocean where the music of the surf rode the ocean breezes through the open windows on warm summer evenings. My mind saw the washer and dryer and the kids' bicycles and my workbench and the tools and the stacks of boxes I had packed when I had briefly thought of selling the place after the accident. But mostly I fixed on the plastic bag from the hotel room in Jackson all knotted up around the bloody new suit.

"How could you possibly have hung on to that?"

I shrugged. "Memories. Why does the Catholic Church hang on to the bones and other relics of saints?"

"Perversity?"

I laughed. "Okay, that's why I didn't toss it."

When I pulled the truck into the driveway of the white, 1930s, art deco bungalow with the giant jade plants and the white picket fence guarding the little postage stamp of fescue in front, I knew at once everything was all wrong.

"Porch light's on." I sat in the truck and tried to decipher the shadows around my house.

"So?" Jasmine asked.

"So it's on a heat and motion sensor." I killed the engine.

"Maybe we triggered it."

I shook my head. "It was on when we were half a block away."

"A dog?"

Again, I shook my head. "I adjusted the sensitivity so that doesn't happen. It used to wake us up all the time."

I yanked the keys from the ignition, shouldered open my door, and got out. "Wait here."

I climbed into the truck bed and opened the big metal box bolted to the truck right behind the cab. The box held a few tools, chains for snowy Sierra roads, and a lot of gear for sailing, hiking, and mountain biking. And shooting.

Jasmine got out and made her way to the side of the truck bed, where she watched me pull out a sturdy metal box, locked with a case-hardened padlock and secured by a thick security cable to a bracket welded to the truck bed. I unlocked the box and pulled out the Beretta Model 92F 9mm semiautomatic pistol I used for duty as a reserve sheriff's deputy. With another key on my chain, I unlatched the trigger lock, pulled a fifteen-round magazine from the box, slid it into the handle, and worked the slide to chamber a round. I grabbed two more fifteen-round magazines and shoved them in the pockets of my shorts.

"I thought you were going to wait there." I nodded toward the front seat.

"I never said that." She gave me that wry Mona Lisa smile again.

"Whatever." I slipped a spare ammunition clip in my pocket and climbed down. "They might still be here." I motioned toward the house.

Jasmine gave me a "So what?" look.

"You might want to wait in the truck."

She rolled her eyes, then pulled her cell phone off its belt clip and waved it at me. "Isn't this one of those times when you're supposed to call for backup or something?"

That stopped me. I took a deep breath and held it for a long moment against the tension wringing my guts like a high-C piano string gone sharp. The palms of my hands tingled.

Was I overreacting? There was no sign of movement. I thought about the hours I had already spent with Internal Affairs and the probability that dialing 911 would mean more bureaucratic hassles and paperwork, and the reality that calling the LAPD for help usually meant waiting on hold.

"Well, I think the guys who attacked my boat wouldn't have done it if they'd found what they were looking for here."

"Maybe," she said. "Or not."

"Well, we can debate it all night or find out." I turned and made my way up the short walk to the porch and found the front door ajar. I motioned Jasmine to stay back, but she ignored me again. I reached inside the front door, turned on the entryway light, and stepped in.

We made our way to the living room. I went first, following the Beretta, then turned on the overhead lights.

"Oh, hell."

My home, which I had lovingly saved from the wrecking ball with my own sweat, muscle, and considerable money, had been expertly tossed, drawers emptied, cushions slashed open, fixtures ripped out, heating-duct grills pulled and thrown about. With a gathering sense of dread, and Jasmine right behind, I made my way from room to room. In the bedroom I had once shared with Camilla, the snapshots of her and the children lay scattered on the hardwood floors amid the fragments of glass and remnants of frames.

The devastation hit me hardest in the children's room. Untouched since the accident, the toys lay scattered, broken and shattered open with venality beyond professional thoroughness. I froze when my eye caught sight of a tiny stuffed tiger, my daughter's constant companion and sleep partner. It lay disemboweled on the floor, the stuffing probed and discarded. This ripped my heart like rusty barbed wire.

"Motherfuckers." I bent over and picked up the tiger. The touch brought memories and tears. Then I stepped through the debris and placed the tiger gently on the lower bunk where my daughter's head used to lie, so perfectly beautiful in her sleep.

I swallowed hard against the tears, and when I turned away, my heart was hard again and filled with the momentum of revenge.

"Come on," I said.

We headed through the kitchen and made our way toward the garage door, stepping carefully through the mess of broken glass, spilled flour, and broken mustard jars. A couple of feet before we got to the door leading down the two concrete steps to the garage door, we came to the walk-in pantry on the right. I laid my hand on the knob and paused.

"The suit should be in a plastic bag." I nodded toward the garage. "Next to the washer and dryer. I never got around to doing anything about it, but I couldn't throw it away."

The image flooded back vividly so I turned from the pantry and went to the garage door, opened to reveal a new scene of chaos.

It stank like a stale beer joint. The reason became clear when I turned on the light and smashed on the concrete floor lay the remains of a full case of Lagunitas IPA. Foam still adorned the puddles. I drew a quick mental sketch of the cluttered one-car garage: my tool bench on the wall to the right with nothing disturbed, the old refrigerator-freezer used for beer, wine, and Costco overflow, piles of boxes stacked nearly to the ceiling, mounds of sailing and sporting gear. I spotted the shreds of the plastic bag from the hotel room in Jackson, scattered about the floor amid the articles of wrinkled, bloodstained clothing. In the split second it took me to comprehend this, the door to the walk-in pantry burst open.

"Hey!" Jasmine yelled as the door slammed into her. Then a single gunshot and the voice of a man cursing.

I whirled, Beretta at the ready. Jasmine stumbled sideways as the pantry door swung open again, slammed into my foot, and stopped instantly. The top twisted forward as if someone was shoving it with his shoulder. The upper hinge complained as the screws holding it in the casing began to splinter.

A gun muzzle emerged at the edge of the door, followed by the rest of a large-caliber revolver gripped by an even larger left hand overgrown with thick brambles of black hair. Jasmine threw herself to the floor as the muzzle found her. I fired two shots through the hollow-core door; the pistol dropped to the floor and clattered away. Pressure on the pantry door ceased immediately. I jumped back, pulling the door with me. There, bent double on the floor, a tall, muscular man clad in Levi's and a navy blue T-shirt cradled his arms around his belly and moaned softly. He rocked himself gently as a severed artery siphoned the life from his body and flooded it across my terra-cotta tiles. Blood filled a small crater dug by the solitary round the man had accidentally fired when the opening door hit Jasmine. He had obviously assumed we had continued on into the garage when he'd sprung his ambush and run into us instead.

Jasmine stood up and joined me, her face oddly composed and her eyes working to take in everything.

"Get his gun," I said.

Jasmine followed my gaze and picked it up.

"Forty-four Magnum," she said, holding it with an easy familiarity.

"Know how to use that?"

"I'm a civil rights lawyer from Mississippi. What do you think?"

"Good point."

I looked down at the man on the floor. "He could have a friend. Shoot anybody that's not me." I moved cautiously toward the garage with the

Beretta ready. The garage was small, cramped, and left few places to hide. I cleared it quickly, checking behind the towers of boxes and even inside the refrigerator.

"Okay, time for 911," I said reluctantly when I got back to the kitchen.

"Done already." Jasmine plucked a tiny cell phone off her belt with her left hand and waved it at me. A think black wire snaked from the phone to her ear. "On hold." She reclipped the phone to her belt. "Like you promised."

The big man lay still now, his skin whiter than a kosher chicken and surrounded by an enormous pool of blood that no longer expanded.

"He's gone," I said.

"But you're a doctor."

"Even if I gave a damn, he's a goner. A severed aorta empties a body faster than you can count seconds on one hand. Come on." I clicked the safety on the Beretta and headed for the garage. "Let's see if we can find anything in my suit they missed."

I made my way through the mess to the cabinet holding sandpaper and painting supplies and grabbed a box of latex gloves. I pulled out a pair, then offered the box to Jasmine.

She shook her head. "It's my mother's blood. I don't mind touching it."

The way she said it made me feel guilty for getting the gloves in the first place. Jasmine placed the .44 Magnum on my workbench, then picked up the bloody suit coat. I couldn't think of anything to say so I slipped on the gloves and went to the kitchen. I leaned way over the pool of blood, not wanting to step in it, not wanting it on me or my clothes. The body lay on its left side, which made it easy for me to pat down both rear pockets and the right side.

Nothing. I struggled him over on his back and found the left-side pocket empty as well. The man was a cipher.

"Brad!" Jasmine's voice reached me loud and excited. I turned. She stood at the garage door holding up what looked like a thick postage stamp.

"It's an SD card," she said, walking over to me.

"What?"

"Secure digital flash memory. Mom's Palm used these for data storage."

Into my hand, she dropped something slightly more substantial than a postage stamp. Small wonder I had overlooked it and so had my assailants.

"How did you find it so fast?"

"I knew what to look for. Mom wouldn't give you the whole Palm. So I—" She cocked her head like a person listening to unheard voices.

"One moment, please," she said into the small cylindrical microphone hanging from the cell phone wire. Then she unclipped the phone from her belt, disconnected the earbud cord, and handed the phone to me.

"It's for you," she said.

Darryl Talmadge's collapse on the VA hospital floor dominated Clark Braxton's flat-panel computer monitor. The General pushed his Aeron chair back from his black granite slab desk to give Frank Harper a better look.

Harper studied the image, leaning one bony hand on the brilliantly polished desk and the other on his polished briar cane with the brass knob cast from melted shell casings he had collected from the sands at Juno Beach. Braxton resisted the impulse to remove the old doctor's hand from his desk and polish away the residue left behind. He loathed having other people's bodily oils on his belongings.

Instead, the General studied Harper's faint trembling. Secretly, Braxton had learned Harper's new palsy had lately begun to overwhelm the Parkinson's medication. Despite this, Harper's back was straight and his bearing sufficiently military and his intellectual capacities still useful enough to warrant Braxton's continued association.

"Would you like a chair?" Braxton made sure not to sound overly solicitous. When Harper shook his head, his sparse, down-fine, white hair swayed, then landed in disarray. Chaos irritated Braxton and he turned toward the window. The General stared at his own well-crafted image in the glass, mirrored by the darkness beyond. His frown deepened as he visualized the well-remembered view down the hill—*his hill*. Braxton's frown embraced the small brushy patch at the base that belonged to a stubborn son of a bitch in the ersatz Spanish stucco McMansion on Oakville Crossroad who kept jacking up the asking price.

That brushy patch remained the sole piece of his hill he had not been able to acquire. The arrogant bastard had let the land go to hell, didn't even have the decency to plant grapes on it. The parcel left a breach in security and posed a severe brush-fire hazard.

A recurring fantasy visited him now, replaying images of a solitary jog through vineyards glowing with the faint green haze of spring. Coming round a row, he confronts the stubborn landowner and settles the dispute with a lethally honed grape knife, crescent-curved and wicked with serrations. Braxton's frown vanished as he unzipped the man from sternum to scrotum. Then the General smiled, visualizing the first sip of wine made from the grapes fattened on the man's blood.

"That happened awfully fast."

Reluctantly, Braxton turned back toward Harper. On the flat-panel display, a burst of white coats and scrubs exploded into Talmadge's room. The phone on Braxton's desk rang then; Braxton hit the pause button on the video stream, freezing two uniformed MPs in midlunge.

"Braxton," the General barked into the mouthpiece. He tilted his head as he listened.

"Ben, how many times do I have to tell you, price is not the issue?" Braxton closed his eyes for a moment and squeezed the bridge of his nose.

Harper watched the microtremors ripple across Braxton's jaw that indicated he needed to adjust the General's medication. Harper had trained himself to see the symptoms where others couldn't. That's why he and he alone treated the General. The speed with which the tremors intensified now alarmed him.

"Just get me the fucking wine, Ben!" Braxton's voice carried a deep, honed menace few ever cared to provoke. "This is my *collection* and it is incomplete. Incomplete! Do you know what that means? It means this collection is worthless—worthless—without that 1870s solera vertical. . . ."

"Yes, I know I've already spent millions, but this is not about the money; this is about having a complete collection. Complete!"

Braxton listened for a few more seconds. "Ben, I am paying you for results. Get me the collection or get the hell out of my life!"

Harper looked discreetly out the window as Braxton struggled not to slam down the receiver. The dosage and formula of the General's drug cocktail had become increasingly complicated with week-to-week and sometimes daily adjustments needed. Neither the General nor any other person knew how much effort Harper put into keeping one of his oldest surviving patients on an even keel.

After hanging up the phone, Braxton restarted the Talmadge video.

After Braxton's microtremors subsided, Harper said, "I still don't understand why you didn't have Talmadge killed like the others."

Braxton offered the old Army physician another question: "Well, for one thing, have you recovered the old microfilmed files *you* left in Belzoni?"

Harper sighed and, with considerable effort, straightened up and faced Braxton. He was taller than the General and more than two decades older. When he spoke, his voice failed to hide his own lack of patience.

"Obviously I would have told you if I had. Why do you keep giving me that question instead of an answer?"

"Because you keep asking me that very obvious question." Braxton worked to maintain a neutral tone. "You know darned well our Mr. Talmadge got his hands on those records and his do-gooder lawyer burned them all on CDs. For all we know, lawyer Shanker or an ally made arrangements to have the CDs turned over to the press if Talmadge dies in our hands." Braxton paused to select a tone of voice conveying the appropriately serious edge. "The problem with old men is that time and guilt loosens their lips. When consequences disappear, people do things that we can't tolerate."

"Clark, you know that without the microfilm of the documents, or your testimony, the CD copies can be dismissed as forgeries," Harper responded. "Something concocted by desperate people who want to block your election." He paused. "Besides, the real dynamite is still here." He tapped his head.

Braxton shook his head. "Frank, with all due respect"—*which is rapidly diminishing, you old fool,* Braxton thought—"you simply don't understand the process. All those ankle-biting Chihuahuas in the media have to do is release the CD a couple of weeks before the election and I've lost."

Harper shrugged.

"Until we find those documents—and any copies which might be out there—we cannot be sure, and until we are sure, my bid to rescue this great country from its own sloppy foolishness is in grave danger."

"Yes, yes." Harper waved his free hand about. Braxton noted that Harper had, indeed, left a handprint on the black granite. "But don't you think the longer he continues this"—Harper pointed toward the screen—"this repeating drama, the greater the danger?"

Damn! The old fool was losing it. And he's wasting my time as well, Braxton thought as his eyes strayed to his desk and the two unread hardcover thrillers by David Baldacci and Dale Brown. They were his favorite authors and he'd much rather be reading them rather than nursemaiding a broken-down old sawbones.

"Frank, you're a brilliant physician, a gifted researcher, and a loyal, patriotic soldier who has served his country well." Braxton turned toward Harper and placed his hand on the old man's shoulder and felt the bones. "You understand the inner workings of the human body, and I, for one, am grateful for your work." Braxton paused as he shifted from the richly warm congratulatory tone that had brought a smile to Harper's face, to one now of wisdom and caution.

"But, Doctor, dealing with these sorts of situations is not your expertise. The Good Lord didn't bless me with the immensity of your intellectual gifts, but he did give me an operational sense of how to handle things such as this, and I think you should let me worry about that. It's worked well so far—this division of labor—for damned close to forty years, hasn't it?"

Braxton paused. "Think about it: How many from your original program are left?"

"Only Talmadge and you," Harper said without hesitation. "We have a few more recent head-wound veterans using the medications, but those are administered indirectly."

"And who knows the whole story from beginning to end?"

"Just you and I."

"There," Braxton said. "See? I've done all right with that part of things, have I not?"

Harper offered an uneasy smile. "I only wish I had been as successful with the others." He nodded toward the screen.

Braxton was disappointed at Harper's swift concession. Not long ago, Harper had been a formidable intellectual opponent. They had enjoyed sparring and Braxton didn't always win. But, the General knew, it was time for being graceful.

"Frank, I admit we failed by not taking Talmadge out before he fell into the hands of people we don't yet control. But by the time we found out, he was spilling the beans to the shrinks in Jackson. You know as well as I do, we can't do anything while he's in custody. That would only invite more questions. Things will change after my election, but until then we need to work with what we have.

"But you have to admit his mental condition and the nature of his crime pretty much destroyed his credibility. Nobody wants to believe a man like that."

Harper shrugged and made his way to the window. "Except for Jay Shanker and the nosy bitches at the legal foundation." He looked over at

Braxton. "And of course we still have the daughter to contend with and she's as bad as her mother. And there's Stone."

"I disagree. She's not half the lawyer her mother was. And we're well on the way to taking care of Stone."

"Oh, yes, your crack teams have taken very good care of him so far."

"Stone's a capable man," Braxton said evenly enough to keep the brief flare of anger from showing on his face.

"He's a natural two-percenter—and not one of ours," Harper said.

"We have ways to handle him."

"How—"

Braxton shook his head. "You don't want to know." He nodded. "And the gas chamber will take care of Talmadge. Either that or the cancer. That's my bet." Braxton faced his old comrade. "Frank, things will be fine so long as *your* records don't emerge from the grave *you* were supposed to put them in."

Jasmine's head rested on my right shoulder. We leaned against each other in adjoining plastic chairs in an unoccupied office at the LAPD's Pacific Division Headquarters. She slept lightly, wrapped in a borrowed blanket.

The open door gave on to a fluorescent-lit deskscape of paper, phones, and tired people winding down their watch. At the far corner, two uniformed officers and a plainclothes detective escorted a handcuffed man tagged with prison tattoos out of an interview room, the same one I had occupied for almost two hours. Events before then had been predictable: first there was one black-and-white, then a Smokey-and-the-bandits parade populated by backup uniforms, plainclothes detectives, scene supervisors, crime scene vans, forensic techs, then finally the coroner and a meat wagon.

Jasmine and I had made things as easy for them as possible. We bagged my gun and our assailant's in separate Ziplocs, labeled them properly, and set them on the kitchen counter before going outside to wait.

Then they brought us here to the architecturally undistinguished building on Culver Boulevard just off Centinela in a nondescript neighborhood filled with two- and three-story stucco apartment buildings, strip malls, gas stations, and dueling gang graffiti.

Across the big squad room, Darius Jones, the detective sergeant who had driven us here, emerged from the watch commander's office shaking his head. I heard nothing, but someone in the office must have spoken because the detective stopped in the doorframe and turned around. He stood a couple of inches taller than me, nearly as broad in the shoulders, a lot sloppier at the waist, and nearly filled up the doorframe. He'd played defensive tackle for USC until he'd blown out his right knee at the end of his senior year.

Darius Jones shrugged and continued to shake his head as he headed toward the main reception area. My stomach growled; I rubbed at the stubble on my jaw with my free hand and checked my watch. Again.

Hours had dragged by after detectives had interviewed Jasmine and me and then quickly agreed it was self-defense. But because there had been a homicide, Jones needed his supervisor's okay to let us go. Approval took a lot longer than expected thanks to a platoon of Oakwood boys who showed up in rival gang turf a couple of blocks away with Molotov cocktails and large-caliber weapons.

I tried now to enjoy the feeling of Jasmine's head against my shoulder, but the intractable fatigue and adrenaline hangover of the past twelve hours had left me drained, distracted, and dwelling on death. In a previous life, I had seen a lot more than the average person and had frequently been on the dealing end of it in service to my government.

During that time I had casually ridden a ballistic path of workaday death and risk that I accepted as an inevitable part of my personal trajectory. My acceptance didn't change until the day I realized death wasn't only for the other guy. My finger grew more reluctant on the trigger then. I started to wonder where people went when they turned into one more seeping sack of organic soup waiting for the cell walls to burst and feed the waiting bacteria. I struggled with the durability of consciousness and realized it was the only thing that mattered. If you're unaware of being alive, then dying's not all that different. Did death represent the irrevocable loss of that individual or could a disembodied mind prevail? If it prevailed, was it our soul? Questions led to more questions. Was consciousness our soul peeking dimly through the meatware of the human body? Did bad people have good souls sabotaged by bad meatware?

No memorable epiphany stands out; no discrete single event redirected me from killing to healing. The process ran more like dust accreting on one side of a balance scale until one day it tipped, propelling me out of one life into another. Medical school turned me into a better than competent but less than brilliant neurosurgeon. Nevertheless, I reveled when I opened a cranium and moved my fingers and instruments among the living stuff that made someone who he was. Making him well felt even better, especially when I had cut away a tumor or relieved a pressure and had returned a profane, vile patient back to the congenial, likable person he had once been.

The most poignant cases came from the families of patients accused of the most hideous crimes, criminals whose malevolent creativity produced horror that seemed to verify the existence of evil.

"Please tell us it's a brain tumor," the families would plead. "Or an artery blockage or some sort of lightning storm in the brain cells." Something, *anything* that could be seen, touched, treated, removed, that would confirm that this loved person was not evil, only suffering from a merely physical lesion, which would absolve them of crime and guilt.

On occasion, surgery located such a physical epicenter, but even more often, I suspected a physical cause I could not prove. Locating a physical cause often allowed the sort of treatment that frequently led to normal lives. The lack of an identifiable, biological lesion was a shortcut to jail terms or execution. This bothered me because in many of the successful cases I located physical causes that would have gone undetected fifty years ago. Will people we jail and execute today be saved fifty years from now by more advanced diagnostic technology that will find the physical evidence?

Of course, taken to its logical absurdity, this led to the speculation that no one was ever guilty of anything since every act had a purely biological origin that precluded free will. Despite the lack of answers, the questions fed my notion of good souls trapped in bad meatware.

As I built an astoundingly lucrative surgery practice alongside my teaching and research at UCLA, I began to consider the tissue beneath my hands as a philosophical duality—spirit and flesh—which threw me into conflict with the scientific mainstream, which believed—with faith as absolute as that of the most ardent Bible-thumping Baptist—that consciousness came solely from the brain's electrical activity, all matter, nothing transcendent, which they couldn't *prove* any better than the average Baptist could *prove* the virgin birth.

What did it mean? Even more significantly, did it mean anything at all? I had worried this issue around and around for years, confusing myself half the time and often coming back to things I had written about it and realizing I did not quite understand my own words.

Instead, I tried to make sense of the attacks on my boat and at my house and finally fell asleep concluding that it all pointed straight back to Mississippi, to Vanessa and Darryl Talmadge. A convicted white racist murderer sentenced to die in the gas chamber. I certainly hoped Jasmine knew why in hell her mother would want to save a man like that.

24

I awoke to Vince Sloane's worst scowl.

"Up! C'mon, wake up!"

Sloane shook my shoulder.

I struggled to remain in a significant dream, desperate for its fleeting epiphany where answers outnumbered questions.

"Shit." I opened my eyes.

"Glad to see you too," Sloane said.

Jasmine stirred.

Looming over us, Sloane offered two large Styrofoam cups glaring with the orange-and-black logo of a small convenience store a block away we called the "Shop and Rob" because of the way crooks frequently used it as their personal ATM.

"Time to go home," Sloane said as he shoved a cup at me. "Wherever the hell that is for you these days."

I took the cup and caught his disapproval. Vince was a solid, trustworthy man with a time-honored and still-admirable set of ethics and personal principles that he always hoped others would live up to, while recognizing most would not. He reminded me of that Marine division motto: "Your best friend, your worst enemy."

Beyond Sloane, Detective Darius Jones obscured the doorway like a walking roadblock. His deep black skin trended toward blue; sweat beads glistened on his forehead and a murderous stare distorted his face. He avoided my eyes, looking first at Jasmine, then back toward me. Back and forth, pendulum regular. When I finally caught his gaze, Jones glanced away and made a perfect poker face.

What the hell was that all about? I looked over at Jasmine, who sat up straight in her chair, leaving a warm spot on my shoulder. She had obviously read a message on the big detective's face. I thought better of asking her about it, for now.

I pried the plastic top off the coffee and took a gulp. A palsied shudder ran down my spine and cinched my scrotum tight like a drum. The coffee was everything I expected. I took another gulp, then stood up and stretched.

"You and I need to have a little chat." Vince looked toward the door, then back at me. "Alone. I'll drive you home."

"But—" I looked over at Jasmine, who struggled to throw off the fatigue and jet lag. She shivered for a moment, then tugged the blanket tighter around her shoulders. Vince caught her eye, waved the coffee about, then set it down next to her.

"No buts." Vince gave me his authoritative sergeant's tone and I almost returned a "Yes sir," but knew no matter how I said it, he'd hear sarcasm. I nodded.

"Good." He nodded toward Jones, who stepped forward and addressed Jasmine.

"I'll give you a ride to your hotel, Ms. Thompson," the big detective said, his voice deep, formal, and professional. His assassinating stare had vanished, which made me wonder if I had imagined things in waking up.

Jasmine stood, let the blanket slip into the plastic chair, then combed her fingers through her tight curls.

"Thank you for the coffee," she told Vince. "And thank you," she said to Jones. Then, to me: "Call me after you get some sleep." My gaze held her face, but my peripheral vision caught anger flashing across the big detective's face again, quick and bright like fractured shards of sun glinting off polished chrome.

"Count on it," I told her, and felt all sorts of regret when she picked up her purse and left the room with Jones.

Vince made his way over to me, picked up the blanket from the chair, and folded it. I took that moment to drink as deeply as I dared of the Shop and Rob coffee.

"You know I don't mess in people's business," he spoke so softly I had to strain to hear him.

"Sorry?"

He cocked his head to the now empty doorway and continued to fold the blanket. He always took care of equipment. Put things where they belong and you'll know where to go in an emergency.

"Your friend." He finished the blanket. "Look, you've known me long enough to know I don't care what color a person is or any of that."

This bewildered me.

"It makes no difference to me, but it makes a *lot* of difference to some other people, a big, big difference."

A queasy recognition blossomed in my gut.

"And it's not just your Aryan Nation bozos and Klanners who think birds of a feather should stick with their own kind."

"That's just freaking wonderful," I mumbled. Darius Jones's visual daggers added up.

"Ducky." He bent and placed the folded blanket with its perfectly aligned corners and perfect right angles on the chair. "Now, if you don't mind . . ." He motioned toward the door with his head. "The LAPD gives me the creeps; I'm running a severe sleep deficit, and quite frankly I am truly weary of following the trail of bodies you've left behind you."

Without waiting, Vince left the room. I spilled hot coffee down the front of my pants following behind. We exited into a bright new day and crossed the parking lot, lined with trees and populated by a variety of temporary buildings. We zigged through a jam of cruisers, RVs, personal vehicles, and brown temporary buildings until we came to a battered Dodge pickup parked under a spreading eucalyptus tree. Vince used the truck for his house-painting business, one of those side ventures cops need either for financial reasons or for the psychological satisfaction coming from a job not connected with drug dealers, casual killers, gangbangers, rich celebrity drunk drivers, hormone-crazed teenagers, and an aggressively disappreciative public who rarely had anything good to say about their public safety officers. I experienced enough of that on my reserve duty to realize why some cops retreated into their "cops versus civilians" world.

We walked silently and got in. Vince started the truck's engine and backed out of the space.

"Remember what I said back there. Jones is a terrific detective, closes a lot of his cases without all the BS you get from others." Vince headed for the exit. "He's a lot smarter than he is big, but he's got this *thing* about *his* black women and white guys."

My fingers tingled with anger and caffeine.

He paused at the Culver Boulevard exit. "Where to? Where the hell you gonna sleep now that your boat's sunk and your house is trashed?"

I shrugged. "My lab's pretty much it." I looked at my watch. "Besides, it's time for work."

Vince smiled, then pulled carefully into traffic.

"I thought Jones's kind of thinking was for Archie Bunker," I said.

"Bigots come in all colors." Vince turned north on Centinela. "Watch yourself."

I opened my mouth to reply, but he cut me off.

"Look, Doc, we could talk forever about why it's not right. But we can't change it and we don't have all day because I need to tell you a few things which are a lot more important."

"Ooh-kay," I said slowly.

"Chris Nellis—you remember him, the reserve guy who dives?"

"Uh-huh, he's got an ad agency or something. I've trained with him."

"We had Chris in the water right after we pulled you off the rocks, down to check to make sure there wasn't anybody still alive. He retrieves some debris and a few pieces of a guy left after the explosion. Then out beyond the breakwater, one of the Harbor Patrol guys finds an inflatable idling around in a circle, and nearby a floater with a very broken neck.

"So, while the suits at Internal Affairs are working you over, they haul all this stuff to the dock, and they're not there half an hour when this Army chopper lands on the jetty and farts out some pretty pushy guys in fatigues flashing heavy-duty military ID and firepower."

Vince stopped at the light by the east end of the Santa Monica airport where Centinela turns into Bundy Drive. A small single-engine plane on final approach coasted across the road above the stoplight.

"To make things short, these military guys check out. Then they take everything. Raft, body, body parts, debris." The light turned green, and a nanosecond later a horn sounded behind us. I turned around and spotted a blond in a black BMW, one of those California clichés that plays on the worst of both worlds. Vince looked in the rearview mirror as she honked again. He pressed on the accelerator more slowly than usual.

"She's very important, I guess." He smiled. She wore a snarl on her face as she weaved the Beemer back and forth in the lane. She had nice, shiny nails on the hand used for her Anglo-Saxon salute.

"Anyway, these Army jerks are gone almost as fast as they arrive, only they leave behind a tight-assed, full-bird colonel, who tells us there's not going to be a report on this incident because it involves national security and it's a training exercise that got out of hand with some new men who were way too gung ho."

"Whoa! No report? What about my boat?"

"He said the check would be in the mail."

My jaw dropped.

"No, really." Vince gave me a smile. "That's what he said. Checks would go out to everybody today. He made a point of saying that you would be a lot better off without insurance, not filing a claim."

"It doesn't add up. My attackers told me exactly what they came for and that they came looking for *me* to give it to them."

"That's what *you* say, *Officer*," Vince said.

"What the hell's that supposed to mean, *sergeant*?"

"It's their story and your word against theirs." He fell silent. Then: "Look, Doc. I know you did some classified work before. And if this is connected, you'll need to sort it out."

"This has nothing to do with my past life and everything to do with Vanessa Thompson's killing."

"Uh-huh. They have a different story. And firepower to make their version stick." He turned right on Olympic. "Not that I believe a word of it, which is why I am telling you what they told me not to. It's not a lot, mostly what Chris pulled together before the chopper arrived—that the people you killed were from an elite unit attached to the Army Technical Escort Unit, which is a one-of-a-kind, battalion-level organization headquartered at the Edgewood facility at Aberdeen Proving Ground in Maryland. They were reorganized a while back into something called the Guardian Brigade, and when that happened, some of their command structure went covert and untraceable. They're all good soldiers is my understanding, but the covert part of things offers some opportunities for abuse, especially those who're supposed to be secretly supporting Homeland Security operations.

"In the words of the tight-assed colonel who did all the speaking, most of their missions are 'no notice, hazardous, and classified,' which means no damn thing to me. Does it to you?"

It did. Dread gathered in my gut. "What else?"

"Nothing, unless Chris has something."

We drove the rest of the way in silence, up Westwood Boulevard, past the medical school and right toward my lab's entrance, where Vince stopped at the curb.

"Watch your back. These guys may be assholes, but they're powerful, dangerous assholes and they're holding enough cards to make you play whatever game they want."

"They think." I got out.

"No hero stuff," Vince said. "What you're doing in there means a lot more to the world than you getting killed." He paused. "Call me if you need help."

"Thanks, Vince," I said. "I will."

Former general and president-to-be Clark Braxton held the telephone handset to his ear and struggled with the hot and ready rage seething in his guts. He glared at the night-mirrored windows in his private study, watching the anger play across his face. But when he spoke, his voice carried the cool, even authority of command.

"Colonel, I comprehend the situation report, but I hope you realize what a bind the events of this evening puts you in." Braxton emphasized the *you* and allowed himself a thin smile in the ensuing silence. The colonel was one of an elite corps of devoted loyalists on active duty who owed their lives or careers—or both—to him. Obedience to Braxton outranked other loyalties and commitments because they believed only Clark Braxton's presidency could save the United States.

"Of course, sir. I fully recognize the gravity, which is why we've moved as quickly to neutralize the consequences and collateral damage. With all the military and Special Forces exercises we perform out here in the West, law enforcement cooperates with us pretty well."

"Law enforcement's not the concern," Braxton said. "Stone's a natural two-percenter."

"Yes, sir. I've reviewed his record, active-duty and his covert service. He's unusually capable."

"Better than six of your elite so far."

Braxton let the awkward silence work on the colonel.

"Sir—uh, we . . . well, I have an operational situation."

Braxton said nothing.

"Sir?"

"Go on."

"Sir, I've committed as many of my resources as I have for this operation. I, uh . . . I've got quite a mess to clean up. Mounting another operation now would produce issues I would not be able to successfully contain."

Braxton watched the second hand of his Rolex sweep smoothly through another ten seconds of silence.

"I understand your predicament and appreciate the effort and risk you have undertaken," Braxton said finally, his voice calibrated with firm, sympathetic authority. "You contain things there. I may be able to help."

Braxton smiled broadly as the colonel exhaled a faint shudder of relief.

"I will contact a combat-tested operative I already have on the ground," Braxton continued. "I want you to go back to the sheriff and to the LAPD. Just you. Find some politically ambitious blabbermouth way up in the chain of command. Meet them at a coffee shop or some other neutral territory. Before you go, shape Stone's record to fit what I am about to tell you. Make sure you give them a hard copy with all the right classified stamps on it so it'll have maximum credibility when they leak it to the press. You with me so far?"

"Yes, sir. It might take a little time to create the document, set up the meeting."

"Make it fast. Now listen carefully, this is what you're going to tell them."

As I made my way out of the stairwell on the fourth floor and down the polished linoleum-tiled corridor, Sonia Braverman, all of four foot eleven, and maybe a hundred pounds on a heavy day, stepped out of the break room in front of me. She wore one of those dark faux-silk dresses with the tiny, light print and the matching belt that women of a certain era like so much. Sonia served as my office manager, as she had for many previous directors of Neurosurgery. She was way past retirement age, but I didn't mind the annual bureaucratic torture trial to keep her there. Sonia looked at me for several moments before the recognition dawned in her eyes.

"Dr. Stone! Just look at you!" She scanned me up and down more thoroughly than an MRI. "Oy!" For her, that syllable had about a hundred shades of meaning. I understood about seventy-seven of those meanings and was all too familiar with this particular one. I was busted.

"For a brilliant man you have no sense at all, not a bit." Sonia's voice carried a high-pitched timbre, something like that of a songbird raised in Queens. "Look at you! Getting shot at and having your boat sink out from under you? Oy! You know what that does to the people who care about you? My hiatial hernia flared up with the television news this morning, and you know what that does to me. This dangling from helicopters, you have got to stop! And walking around with a loaded gun and boating around at all hours of the night and dragging in here for work looking like a derelict and smelling twice as bad." She finally paused.

"Just look at you!" She shook her head. "What I am going to do with you I do not know. You will never live to be an *alter kocker* if you keep on like this!"

Sonia herded me toward my office.

"Your face is all sleepy. And that ear!" Then Sonia shifted her voice from surrogate Jewish mother to efficient scheduler and office boss. "You have a busy day already. In addition to your appointments this morning, you promised to lecture to that visiting group of postdocs from Toronto, and your friend at Pacific Hills has a conflict with your usual weekly appointment and needs to do this afternoon instead. I've cleared your schedule already for that."

The mention of Camilla's extended-care facility northwest of Malibu took my breath away as I realized that I had thought of her so seldom in the past twelve hours, mostly not at all. I had once believed that our souls had touched and that we represented something eternal.

In the six years since the accident, I had danced around the naïveté of that belief, uncomfortable with its significance and unwilling to let it go. And while the orbits of my life had become eccentric over the years since—drawing me nearer to her at some times and farther at others—she maintained her gravitational hold on my heart and kept my emotions circling around her.

"Let's get you some sleep," Sonia said. "I'll reschedule your morning appointments and cancel the lecture."

I shook my head as I walked through the reception area. "Only the morning. I'll be okay after a couple hours' sleep."

She tsked her partial approval as I shuffled through my office toward the door to a small room I called home when I worked late at the lab. I stopped with one hand on the doorknob. "Can you make sure I am up by eleven?"

"We'll see."

"Yes, ma'am." I turned around and went through the door, closing it softly behind me.

I sagged onto the folding cot and fell asleep with my clothes on.

In the gray half-world we transit before sleep takes us, I thought about Camilla and who she was, who I was, and how Jasmine threatened that.

It struck me then that we can never be who we *are* because the actual moment of being in the present is an infinitely small moment sandwiched between the constantly shifting memories of who we *have been* and the thoughts and fantasies of who we *will be*. My research, and that of many others, indicated that consciousness perceives events in the world about one-fifth of a second after they have actually happened. That means any time we think of the present, we are already looking at the past. The reality we perceive never coincides with the reality that exists.

Who we *are* is never the same from instant to instant because the *present* we perceive is continually reshaped by the *past*. Thus our hopes and dreams for the *future* propel us through an illusory *present* to a fourth state of time: our state of being that is simultaneously neither past nor present nor future and yet all of those combined. It had something to do with space-time, which made me wonder if that had anything to do with the soul and where Camilla's mind lived.

Camilla had no future in this world; no one had ever recovered from her level of profound brain injuries. While she occupied a physical presence in the present that I perceived, her brain showed no indication of consciousness or directed neurological activity above the brain stem, which indicated she lacked a present of her own.

I often worried if an internal life played in her head beyond our scientific ability to detect it. Physicians not so long ago lacked the instruments to detect brain waves, which made me realize that merely because we failed to detect something did not prove its absence. I fell deeply asleep then, wondering what this meant. And whether it meant any damn thing at all.

My fine, dreamless sleep ended with Robert John-
son's raspy voice and gifted guitar.

I tried to ignore it, but "Crossroads Blues" persisted. Finally I woke up enough to recognize it as
my cell phone. I grabbed the Motorola handset as
the song stopped, read the display, saw it was shortly
before 11:00 A.M., and watched the voice-mail indicator blink at the
bottom.

The canvas-and-wood folding cot creaked as I sat up, rubbed at the
fatigue on my face. As I stood, my muscles and joints painfully reminded
me that, even though I was in damn good shape for a guy on the upside
of fifty, the unaccustomed gymnastics of staying alive had carved a load
of new aches into my body. I stretched everything to the pain limit and
found nothing indicating serious injury.

Only then did I shuffle over to the coffeemaker near the shower.
Bless Sonia, I thought as I flipped on the switch. She had filled it up
ready to go. While the coffee brewed, I shaved, then stumbled into the
shower to see if the stinging-hot water could jump-start my brain. By
the time I got out and toweled off, my cell phone went off again. I
picked it up, recognized the same number, and answered it.

"Stone."

"Brad! Sorry to be so persistent, but I thought you would want to
know you received a wire transfer a few minutes ago for three hundred
and fifty thousand dollars." The voice belonged to Juan Hernandez, president of Simi First Bank, a small, solid, and profitable institution run by
top-quality executives who treated customers as people rather than cattle.

"Jeez." I reached over to pour coffee into a John Deere mug.

"You weren't expecting it?"

I sipped at the coffee for a moment. Vince's comments about the of-
ficious colonel came to mind, the part about no report, better off without the insurance. The *Jambalaya* had cost me only about $100,000. I'd
bought it in bad shape out of a bankruptcy, put in another $50,000, and
saved a bundle by doing most of the refurbishing myself. It might have
been worth $200,000 the day I finished the work, but given the depre-
ciation since then, I doubted she would have fetched more than about
$130,000 yesterday morning.

"Uh-huh, it's the . . . insurance on my boat. I wasn't expecting it so quickly."

"I caught the news. It said you were okay," Martinez said. "Did they get that right?"

"Just bruises."

"Good. Well, I wanted you to know the payment arrived." He paused. "Take care of yourself."

"Doing my best." I started to say good-bye, then a thought came to me.

"Juan, can you print out a copy of the transaction record and fax it to me? It'll remind me to deal with it when I get time."

"Done."

"Thanks."

After I hung up, I turned on my laptop and worried about where the funds had actually come from. I slipped into a softly worn pair of khaki cargo pants and pulled the laundry plastic off a blue, oxford-cloth, button-down shirt. I refilled my coffee mug as I slipped on socks and my spare pair of walking shoes before settling down in front of my laptop. I felt a memory rising from unremembered dreams. These came from time to time; some might call it inspiration and others a message from the divine.

As the ideas coalesced, I double-clicked StarOffice and slipped a Mozart piano concerto into the laptop's CD drive. Finally, I slipped on headphones and sat still, eyes closed. The music cleared my head and I began to write. Soon, everything else vanished.

Eventually, the music ended and left me looking at new words for the first time. I often felt like a conduit rather than a creator. This would make for a provocative presentation to the postdocs from Toronto.

Sonia walked in with a grilled-cheese sandwich and a large mug of chicken soup.

"Not to disturb you, but your postdocs will want you in about half an hour." She set lunch on the table.

The wiring spell faded and the rest of my life raced toward me: the J2 icon on my laptop screen told me Juan's fax had arrived with my e-mail; my cell phone whined its low-battery plea; the time startled me. I looked my watch.

"Wow!" The writing had consumed my morning and the beginning of the afternoon. An urgent rush rippled through me.

Sonia waited until I had sampled the chicken soup before retreating from the room. I printed a hard copy of what I had written, then pulled up the fax image on-screen and tried to decipher the banking gibberish as I wolfed down lunch.

The money came from an insurance company in the Isle of Man, as-set playground for spooks, terrorists, tax evaders, and others with enough money and motivation to play international three-card monte with their cash. I had received wire transfers in my other life that had originated from places like this. I did not want that part of my past creeping up on me again.

With time running out, I grabbed the pages from the printer and re-trieved my still-damp wallet from my shorts along with a Space pen, a small blue Leatherman tool attached to one of my old military service dog tags, and a tiny, thin LED light that shone bright blue when you squeezed the sides. I slapped a fresh battery in my phone and headed out with Sonia's good wishes echoing behind.

As I rushed along the corridor, I pulled up Chris Nellis on my speed-dial list and got his answering machine.

"Chris, I had an interesting conversation about what you found in and around the *Jambalaya*. Call me on my cell when you can." I left the number, hung up, and set the phone's ringer to vibrate. When I reached the enclosed bridge to the next building, I began a jog toward the con-ference room. Inside, the half dozen postdoctoral students from Toronto were sitting around a long, elliptical plastic-laminate table, drinking cof-fee from a variety of disposable cups. The rest of the seats around the table along with the standing room around the windowless walls were jammed with a collection of my current students, colleagues, and a sprinkling of faculty members and graduate students I vaguely recog-nized but whose names I could not recall.

The conversation lulled when I entered the room and made my way to the big white board at the front.

"Good afternoon," I greeted them. "Before we get started, I want you to know that if today's lecture is interesting and you want more, you can find my notes and other data at my Web site: ConsciousnessStudies.org." I turned and wrote the address on the white board.

"Okay." I turned to face them. "Let's begin with a question: Did you *really* decide to attend this seminar today, or are you here because of some unremembered incident last year or maybe during your infancy?"

The attendees unanimously gave me the confused stares I wanted.

"Or maybe you're here because of some artifact lurking in your DNA?"

Their befuddlement deepened.

"Some among us today believe everything you do is predestined. These reductionists and determinists whose dogma dominate brain science today think free will is an illusion and consciousness an accidental by-product of synaptic electricity."

A couple of the faculty members present, acolytes of the orthodox, frowned deeply at this.

I tapped an index finger against my temple. " 'One hundred percent in the meatware,' they say. 'Inspiration, meditation, right and wrong, eloquence, philosophy, do not exist; transcendence is a fantasy and everything's just the meat talking.' "

Most heads shook their disagreement.

"This issue transcends science because free will underpins our relationships with others and forms the philosophical foundations of law and society. Genuine accidents carry a different reaction than intentional injury or insult. Courts treat two people convicted of identical crimes very differently if one's insane or visibly, provably brain-damaged.

"Sadly, the scientific mainstream has mishandled free will. They have a vested intellectual interest in promoting politically correct science over reality, just as the Renaissance Vatican favored the religiously correct over provably factual heresy.

"They conveniently forget Albert Einstein when he said that 'science without religion is lame; religion without science is blind.' "

I ignored an assassinating frown from a slight man sitting toward the back of the room. The man, Jean-Claude Bouvet, had a lot to lose if I was right. A widely published author and leader of the "consciousness as meatware" movement, Bouvet was a pompous, brilliant man who received lavish research funding from large pharmaceutical companies.

"We will speak heresy today," I continued. "Because like Copernicus, our search for truth requires that we see things as they are, rather than as we would like for them to be. This means setting aside politics, social engineering, and corporate profits to accept the unwelcome pain of unexpected discoveries. Unlike our reductionist colleagues"—I singled out Bouvet with a glance—"we will deal with science rather than fantasy."

Bouvet mumbled something derogatory, and I continued without acknowledging him.

"Our quest for the truth begins with three important steps:

"One, free will derives from consciousness. Two, consciousness is our perception of reality. Three, reality is weird."

This produced a titter of nervous laughter.

"There's no real argument over the first two steps," I continued. "Because without the awareness provided by consciousness, there can be no exercise of free will. And even the most orthodox priests of reductionism agree that consciousness is perception. But the nature of reality divides us bitterly.

"The reductionists believe we live in a classical, clockwork universe as defined by Sir Isaac Newton where any future action can be predicted by knowing all the data about its starting point and every starting point can be determined by reversing the process.

"The classicists also believe that all action must be local. But entanglement—the foundation of quantum cryptography now being tested by banks for money transfers—proves that actions on a particle here can instantaneously affect an entangled particle anywhere else in the universe.

"Uncertainty and entanglement mean that biological reductionism is about as right as the Vatican was about astronomy in Copernican days. Quantum physics has trumped Newton's classical physics in everything from semiconductors, global-positioning satellites, and nuclear bombs. Despite this, classicists cling to predictability despite quantum physics' proof that uncertainty rules the universe.

"In our quantum world, we cannot even predict the behavior of a single electron or proton in any atom of your body. We can calculate probabilities of its behavior, but nothing is certain—not even whether that particle will exist a nanosecond from there. Thus, classical reductionism falls short because quantum reality prevents it from determining starting conditions, and this means they cannot forecast actions based on those conditions. In place of their fantasy clockwork, reality consists of infinitely nonpredictable sets of mathematical probabilities. In other words, uncertainty is the only thing of which we can be certain."

"I can't sit here and let you mislead these people." Bouvet's angry interjection riveted the room. "Your theory is misleading because quantum physics determines science at the very small levels of atomic and subatomic particles, whereas people and the cellular structures that govern life and our behavior are many times larger. A biological system is too large, too warm and messy, for any sort of coherence or quantum phenomenon to govern it."

He jutted his jaw at me like the tip of a spear. Eyes flitted from him to me and finally fixed me with expectations.

"An excellent recitation of the current dogma," I said, nodding evenly at Bouvet. "But one rooted in the erroneous belief that biology and physics operate by different rules."

Bouvet snorted.

"Biology is not immune to the laws of physics," I responded. "Every atom in our bodies obeys the same rules, adheres to the same quantum mechanical properties as every other atom in the universe.

"Biology is chemistry; chemistry is physics; and quantum mechanics rules physics," I said. "Biology may seem like the study of large, messy systems, but all life depends on chemical reactions: metabolism, cell division, DNA replication—you name it. Chemical reactions depend on electron bonding orbits, and those are entirely quantum-based. What's more, every atom in your body is composed of the very same subatomic particles as those in a doorknob or a distant star.

"Let's do an experiment. Imagine your head, then visualize your brain." I saw some eyes close. "Pick a neuron, any neuron. Then select a random molecule, and from that molecule, single out one atom." I paused to let people focus as more eyes closed.

"Okay, focus on a particle in the atom—proton, neutron, electron—doesn't matter. Particle physics tells us that particle is a wave and a particle at the same time, which says that even though the results of our experiments allow us to *perceive* it as one or the other, it is in *reality* probably neither. Superstring theory indicates that energy and matter are just different patterns of vibration from space-time, the basic fabric of the universe. *That* is the ultimate weird nature of the reality we must understand in order to comprehend consciousness and, through that process, come to grips with free will."

"But you're still confusing the rules!" Bouvet interrupted. "Quantum mechanics applies to the very small, not to biology."

I gave Bouvet an indulgent smile. "If you'll allow me, Doctor?"

He slid sullenly into his seat without replying.

"Quantum effects underlie all processes, even those with large, observable effects which—"

"Name one!" Bouvet's temper burned down toward the limits of my patience.

"Well, Doctor, a nuclear bomb fits pretty well. Hard to miss one of those, and yet quantum processes underlie the whole thing."

"But—"

"Every biological process including consciousness is rooted in quantum physics, which carries the inherent uncertainty that makes it impossible to determine the fixed starting point you and other reductionists and behaviorists need to predict anything at all. Doctor, classical physics is dead. You need to get a grip on that."

In the front, a slight young man with thinning sandy brown hair tentatively raised his hand. I nodded at him.

"Doesn't that just shift the issue of free will around from the tyranny of biological predestination to the chaos of rolling dice?"

Bouvet smiled at the young man, then shot me a challenging look.

"You might think so," I said, "if not for some very good published studies into cognitive behavior therapy—CBT—showing that people with various problems—depression for example—can create new interneuronal connections through directed thought. What's more, the research proves these people overcome their psychological problems in far more significant and lasting ways than those who pop a pill."

I looked around the room and, for the first time, saw Jasmine inside the door, leaning against the far wall nearly hidden in the standing-room crowd. I took a deep breath and desperately scanned my notes for an intelligent thought. Her hair framed her face like an aura and created the perfect backdrop for the dazzling diamond studs in her ears. Her eye shadow sparkled faintly violet, and she wore a bright cornflower-blue polo shirt and khaki slacks with lots of pleats. A large leather bag hung over her shoulder.

"CBT upsets the reductionists because classical physics offers no provision for something as ethereal as the mind to act on the physical world. In other words, their dogma rests on matter creating thoughts, but they have absolutely no intellectual explanation for thought-creating matter."

Bouvet squirmed and fidgeted. He was beside himself now, barely able to contain his growing indignation. Orthodoxy fed such incredible anger, I thought, and it didn't matter whether the beloved dogma was religious or scientific.

"How's this possible?" asked the brown-haired man in front. "Is this your fantasy or is there a plausible scientific explanation?"

"As a matter of fact, new work in this centers on a small set of nano-capable structures in every neuron called microtubules. These work on a quantum-level scale, possibly through a biological variant of a Bose-Einstein condensate in surrounding water molecules, which enables them to achieve a quantum coherence. World-renowned physicist Roger Penrose and his colleague Stuart Hameroff theorize that quantum consciousness may entangle itself in space-time, which means our thoughts may even permanently alter this basic fabric of reality."

"So, why don't we read more about CBT?" The question came from a crowd near Jasmine. I smiled at her, then said, "Mainly because the multibillion-dollar drug industry has a vested interest in keeping the truth covered up. CBT research fails to get research funding because the pharmaceutical companies can't afford for the world to know their products are a poor chemical Band-Aid that does not fix the underlying problem and that their science is based on the buggy-whip science of classical reductionists who do get funded by these megacorporations. In a real sense, those who are addicted to the big research bucks are not seekers of the truth, but seekers of grants. And you don't get grants by challenging the establishment's dogma even if it is provably wrong."

"Bullshit!" Bouvet's anger finally overran his self-control. "I've had enough of your insupportable, insulting, and completely unscientific speculation!"

I watched him search the assembled faces for some support. Finding none, Bouvet elbowed his way toward the door.

Jasmine shifted slightly and nudged Bouvet off-balance. The pompous Frenchman ricocheted awkwardly off the doorjamb, then disappeared.

I couldn't tell if she had done it on purpose. Then she offered the room a faint conspiratorial smile. Mona Lisa again for an instant. Then applause resonated in the small conference room and spilled from the doorway.

The heels of Jasmine's open-toed pumps drummed a light tattoo on the polished linoleum as we hurried toward my office. I checked my watch.

"I thought they'd never let me go," I muttered. "We're going to be way late. I hate being late. Really hate it."

"You gave a remarkable presentation."

"You think so?" I checked my watch again.

"It's no wonder Mom talked about you so much."

"She did?" Surprise, joy, and the old regrets about the path not taken set me off balance.

Jasmine gave me a curious smile and nodded as we rounded the last corner. She seemed to have as many enigmatic ways of smiling as Sonia did for saying "Oy!"

"All the time. Mom said you were the smartest human being she had ever met."

"She must have met a lot fewer people than I would have imagined." Sonia stood in the office doorway.

"Mom kept a file of articles about you."

I nearly stumbled over my own feet.

"You okay?"

"Fine," I lied. I visualized my Vanessa clip file, waterlogged at the bottom of the channel. "I need more sleep."

"You do know she was wildly in love with you."

"Oh, jeez . . ." My voice cracked. "You're kidding, right?"

Jasmine gave me a penetrating gaze that spun through me like a giant electrical armature.

"God's truth." She paused and I saw the puzzle pieces of some decision falling into place behind her eyes. "I'm pretty sure I understand why now."

As we approached my office, a small dark shadow passed over Sonia's face as she connected my expression with the fond look on Jasmine's face.

"I called Pacific Hills already for you and told them you would be a bit late," Sonia said. I was about to introduce Jasmine, but Sonia turned too quickly and stepped inside the door.

"A couple of the people who work with that nice Mr. Sloane brought your truck for you."

I stepped through the door as Sonia sat behind her desk. "He left it in your spot." She pulled open the middle drawer and pulled out a set of keys. I walked over while Jasmine hovered outside in the corridor.

"You need to hurry. The doctor won't be able to wait for long."

"Is everything okay?"

Sonia paused. Her eyes went to Jasmine, then back to me.

"She's beautiful. Be careful."

I had no good reply. "Of course," I said, and left.

Jasmine and I quickly found my truck and drove in silence, through campus and up to Sunset, where I headed west. Jasmine gazed up at the Getty Museum as we crossed the 405, which, even this early in the day, was already clotted with vehicles creeping to the beat of their own mysterious rush-hour drummer.

From the corner of my eye, I admired the strong, lithe muscles of her neck as she craned her head up. It was the first time I had seen her up close in the sunlight. The warm sheen of her skin and the way it tautly wrapped her elevated cheekbones and classic jawline captivated me.

Jasmine turned to me. "Where are we going?"

The realization hit me that we were rushing to visit my comatose wife and I had not told Jasmine anything. It also struck me as significant that Jasmine had not asked.

"Pacific Hills," I said, stalling to arrange my thoughts. "It's a . . . long-term care facility."

The light at Barrington remained green as we came around the curve.

"Your wife," Jasmine said with no notes of a question in her voice. "I read about it in Mom's scrapbook."

"Amazing."

She nodded and retreated into a far-off gaze I recognized as grief and remembrance. She caught me looking and offered a small, understanding smile.

I concentrated on my driving then, guiding the big truck along Sunset Boulevard's infamously serpentine course.

"Do you want to talk about it?" Jasmine said finally.

I didn't, but instead of shaking my head, I surprised myself when my own words reached my ears, words I had not spoken since I'd related them to the policeman who had taken the accident report.

"Six years ago," I said. "Another life."

I concentrated on the road for a bit, easing off on the gas as the lateral g-forces urged us toward the outside of a clockwise turn.

"Around ten on a Saturday night; coming back from a birthday party in Westwood for a programmer who works for me. I drove Camilla's minivan. She sat next to me. Lindsey and Nate were strapped in their car seats behind us. We had the green heading south on Westwood Boulevard. I drove across Wilshire and up the hill when this big Lexus came out of nowhere heading north."

I shook my head and struggled with the emotions. For an instant, I saw the Lexus crest the hill and actually leave the ground. Witnesses testified that the Lexus's driver lost control when the car landed. It happened fast enough for me to see, too fast for me to react.

"The Lexus veered away, ricocheted off a parked car, and slammed into Camilla."

I remembered the Lexus again and the look of joy on the well-publicized face behind the wheel. I took a deep breath against the angry riptide that memory always triggered.

"The impact tore the minivan in half, killed my kids instantly."

Jasmine said nothing as I drove silently for a long time through the tunnel of the trees that lined Sunset, past the Riviera Country Club, and finally to the final steep hill that slinked down to Pacific Coast Highway.

"The Lexus driver, a famous producer tanked up on some outrageously trendy Napa Valley cabernet, gets a bruise or two." I used all my willpower then to loosen my white-knuckle grip on the steering wheel.

"So then, Mr. Studio Exec spends a wad on an entire law firm and a battalion of expert witnesses to fabricate this obscure metabolic disorder to explain his intoxication. It doesn't matter that he killed my family as long as his defense team can convince the jury he really didn't mean to and he couldn't help himself because he had this questionable physical syndrome supported by a bunch of quacks and expert trial whores. It also didn't help that half the jury had a talent agent or a screenplay in their desk drawer, so they suck up to this guy and he gets off despite a drunk-driving rap sheet longer than Pinocchio's nose."

"Hard to believe."

I nodded as I turned right onto Pacific Coast Highway.

"Didn't I read that he died in another accident a couple of years later?"

I nodded again and could not hide my smile.

We navigated the strip of gas stations, shabby convenience stores, and odd, timeworn retail stores and made pretty good time before getting snarled a couple of miles later in a line of traffic oozing past a Caltrans road repair crew shoring up a concrete and metal-mesh rockslide barrier.

Jasmine looked up the steep slope, then over at the beach, then at the Pacific, and finally over at me.

"I don't know what to say."

I shook my head. "No need to say anything."

The deep growls of heavy machinery grew louder as we trickled past the work site and picked up speed. Behind me a black Audi two-seater flashed its brights, then pulled out across the double yellow lines, tailgated by a motorcycle, its rider clad in black leather. Blond hair trailed from the back of her helmet.

"So what do we do next?" Jasmine asked. "I mean, after you see your wife?"

Wife. She said it so casually, but it rekindled all the guilt and indecision that had kept me orbiting the body of a woman I had once loved.

"I'd like to drop in on a friend of mine who lives down toward the end of Topanga Canyon." I told her about Chris Nellis and what he had found during his short dive. Without worrying about her discretion, I replayed everything Vince had said, overlaid with my opinions and fears and confusion over what was happening.

"That fits," Jasmine said.

"It does?"

"I took a look at the SD memory chip from Mom's Palm last night." She pulled her own Palm from her bag and turned it on.

"I have the same model as she does"—her face lost its composure for an instant—"as she did." Jasmine concentrated on the screen for a moment. "From what I can tell, the SD chip contains a test dossier of some sort, and I think it came from Darryl Talmadge's former defense lawyer, the one who got booted after the military claimed national defense jurisdiction and Patriot Act violations. Or it might have come from someone working with the lawyer."

"A test dossier?"

"Bait. Bona fides."

"I don't get it."

I slowed as we made our way into the southern end of Malibu.

"I think this is what got Mom interested in Talmadge's case. I think the lawyer promised her a taste of bigger things to come, something explosive that would make her commit to a deal and throw our legal foundation's muscle behind Talmadge's defense."

"Far-fetched, wouldn't you say? I mean, given the crime?"

"Not so far-fetched. Mom's been pretty out front about opposing the death penalty, especially in places like Mississippi where white people still get jail time for the exact same crimes that send blacks to the gas chamber. So, no—it's not all that far-fetched, especially if he didn't do it."

"Well, there is that." I stopped for a squad of surfers in wet suits heading for one of the few public access spots not already illegally blocked off by wealthy Hollywood scofflaws. "Or there is the issue of whether Talmadge was insane or suffering from some sort of detectable physical problem with his brain—the reason your mom first contacted me."

"Exactly. But I think it runs a lot deeper and reaches into some scary places that somebody will kill to keep us out of."

We passed a gas station, where I spotted the motorcyclist filling the bike's tank. The helmet was off and I saw the insane rider was female. If

Jasmine had not been in the truck, I would have flipped the rider a middle finger, but concentrated instead on what Jasmine had told me.

"Like what?"

Jasmine bent her head and looked at her Palm. "Well, Clark Braxton's name keeps coming up, and—"

"Whoa! Heavy-duty stuff. With the Democrats still out in the political ozone, he's gonna be the next president for sure unless . . ." My voice trailed off as the implication hit me.

"Unless something comes along to screw it up."

I glanced over at Jasmine.

"Whoa," I said quietly.

29

The shock stunned us speechless for a solid minute. Then Jasmine tapped the Palm with a manicured, but not flashy, index finger.

"It's about Braxton," she said. "Talmadge's lawyer, Jay Shanker, put the files together showing that Braxton served as a lab rat for some secret medical research program at one of the old POW camps in the Delta."

I nodded. During World War II, the United States had a problem with Southern-ported cargo ships returning empty from Europe. On top of that, there were European food shortages and huge troop resources needed to guard POWs over there. Somebody looked at the situation and solved them all by loading captured German soldiers on the empty ships and sending them to rural Mississippi with its plentiful food and cheap land and open spaces where escapees had no place to run and few spoke German.

The Army located most POW camps near Delta farming communities like Belzoni and Greenwood. After the war, most prison camps deteriorated, although as a child I heard talk of continuing activities at the camp in Belzoni, southwest of one of the Judge's plantations.

"Belzoni."

"What? How did you know?"

"Educated guess."

"You're right. The SD card Mama gave you says the Army conducted some sort of secret medical experiments there, something not quite kosher—like the Tuskegee syphilis thing."

An uncomfortable vision of my previous life burrowed toward the surface. As a new recruit, I participated in the end of Project 112 and later, Project SHAD, experiments that tested nerve gas and bacteria on more than five thousand military personnel from 1962 to 1973. Scores of soldiers closer to the release site than I had suffered permanent disabilities. These tests leaked into the media in 2003 with little interest.

Instead of mentioning this, I said, "Or like all the atomic tests on soldiers in the 1950s."

Jasmine gave a rueful shake of her head.

"Jesus, it hurts me to think of things like that," I said. "Here we have brave men and women who're willing to die to protect their country and they get betrayed by the fat-assed, political paper-pushers in the Pentagon."

I felt the anger rise as we finally cleared the Malibu congestion and started making some speed up the hill.

"Anyway, the stuff on the SD chip contains excerpts from Braxton's medical records. They indicate he underwent brain surgery in Belzoni as treatment for a head wound he received in Vietnam."

"That's pretty famous."

"Uh-huh, but these records say Army doctors experimented on him and others with head wounds in order to make them more aggressive. In their words, they wanted 'perfect killers' for the Army."

I whistled. "That's political dynamite."

"More like a nuke."

"On the other hand, maybe it helps: brave, mortally wounded hero gets taken advantage of by the military he so bravely served."

"I doubt it," she said. "Nobody wants a head case for president."

"Why not? They've all been head cases since JFK."

"Good point."

The road dipped toward a broad expanse of beach and ocean.

"What else is in the file?"

Jasmine shook her head. "A lot of vague stuff, intended to tease Mom and get her involved."

"It worked."

"Jay Shanker promised her the microfiche archives of all the Belzoni medical records on a CD, including name, rank, serial numbers, dates, procedures, doctors, and chain-of-command approvals authorizing the whole thing."

I whistled. "Any number of people would kill to keep that quiet."

A few miles past Point Dume, I slowed for a small, discreet sign designed to attract only the attention of people already looking for it. As I had twice a week for the past six years, I turned into a narrow, cobbled lane bounded with lavish landscaping; a sculpture-quality steel gate fixed to stone columns loomed ahead. I stopped next to an intercom/keypad pedestal and punched in my code.

"Talmadge ties everything together," I said as the gate opened. "Which means the answers are back home."

"Home?" Jasmine gave me that Mona Lisa smile again. "I thought California's your home."

I accelerated slowly through the gate as I thought about this.

"Camilla used to catch me saying that. She told me it made her sad."

"The Delta never lets loose."

"Yeah, it's got my heart, but I can't imagine living there again."

We drove in silence for a bit more, then I said, "Why now? Why bring Talmadge to trial now after so many years? And why kill Vanessa?"

"Well, the leading theory for the killing—at least among the cops—is that Mom was assassinated by someone in the African-American community who didn't want her helping Talmadge."

"Blame the victim?"

"Old story. She got a lot of hate mail. Some pretty angry voices among big African-American groups condemned her for helping the white devil."

Jasmine stared silently out the side window. "It had a race thing about it. And a personal thing. Some of them were the same voices which slammed her years ago for being a traitor to her race when she dated a couple of white guys in New York."

She said it evenly, but my pulse stumbled anyway. Her ability to talk so casually about the incendiary topic of race astonished me. I had friends of every race and tried to ignore skin color, which seemed to strengthen the friendships because I considered each as a surgeon, an entrepreneur, a talented artist, first, rather than as a Pakistani, Asian, black, whatever. But then, I was white and could afford to ignore race since it was not constantly thrown in my face by those who were incapable of seeing past skin color.

"So," I said, and hesitated. "So *could* it be that?"

"It's always possible, but I doubt it. Doubt it very seriously. Convincing the police is another matter."

"But why prosecute Talmadge now? The man's old and coming apart

at the seams. His awful seizures tear him apart and he's got terminal lar-
ynx cancer from cigarettes. Why doesn't somebody just let him die. The
cancer's its own punishment."

"Punishment is not always justice," Jasmine said. "Do you think the
Nuremberg trials were only about punishment and the culpability of
those being tried?"

She paused for an answer I did not have, then shook her head.

"Justice outranks punishment. It brings a cultural repudiation of
criminal behavior and that act brings justice—to the individual directly
wronged and to society as a whole."

"But why Talmadge and why now?"

"What's happening now began in 1990, a couple of weeks before
Christmas when a grand jury in Jackson indicted Byron De La Beckwith
for the murder of Medgar Evers."

I was familiar with the case. Evers had been gunned down in front of
his home in 1963. An ambitious young district attorney in Hinds
County, Bill Waller, brought De La Beckwith to trial and endured abuse
and anonymous death threats to see justice done. Waller also resisted intense pressure from the racists who controlled the state—the Sten-
nis/Eastland Democrats who had made their careers standing in the
schoolhouse door and who thought good race relations was providing
new paint to freshen up the Colored Only signs smeared across the Mississippi landscape like ugly cultural graffiti. In this atmosphere, Waller
got hung juries in two separate trials. I suppose that, given the all-white
juries back then, the verdicts stood as a partial victory, and indicated
that not all white people were behind Mississippi's brutal apartheid.

Less than ten years later, Mississippi elected "nigger lover" Waller as
governor thanks in large part to the FBI backed up by the guns and steel
of the federal government and National Guard troops. Many think the
Reverend Martin Luther King Jr.'s nonviolent protests did the whole
job. True enough, Dr. King and his protesters had to be the first wave to
show the nation their dedication, their suffering, and to help Americans
understand the evil. But they could never have succeeded without the
federal muscle even the Klan had to respect.

"Bobby DeLaughter got a conviction in the Evers case," Jasmine continued. "And produced more than simple justice for Myrlie Evers and
her children. It sent a tremendous signal that Mississippi had changed,
and if we got a conviction here, it might happen everywhere. Lightbulbs
went off all over the South, and pretty soon we had convictions in the

Birmingham church bombings and in a whole lot of other Klan killings. All the way up to Indianapolis and Pennsylvania."

"A compelling case, counselor," I said.

"Feed one person's hunger for justice and you can feed a whole people. It's a fish-and-loaves thing."

We came out of the dense landscaping at the top of the hill to find a rambling, three-story building with extensive porticoes, a red-tiled roof, and simulated adobe walls designed to evoke the Spanish missions to the north and south along El Camino Real.

"Impressive." She stretched the word out over several seconds.

"I wanted the best for her." I let my eyes follow along with Jasmine's. "And I'm fortunate enough to afford it."

A uniformed man waved us past a small guardhouse, and I continued on into the guest parking lot and pulled into an empty space.

"There's one problem," Jasmine said.

I put the truck into park and turned off the ignition.

"With this place?"

Jasmine shook her head. "With the Talmadge case."

"Which would be?"

"It's what bothered Mom." She looked up thoughtfully, gnawing on her lower lip as she searched for the words. "Talmadge wasn't a known hate crime gone unsolved. It had been long forgotten as an old Balance Due homicide.

"Then one day last year, an anonymous file arrives at the Greenwood PD, the evidence and information all lined up, almost too perfect to be real. Mom suspected something and started asking questions."

"Then they killed her?"

She nodded.

We sat quietly listening to the metallic ticks and creaks of the truck's engine cooling off. Then Camilla's primary physician, Jeff Flowers, walked out of the building, his white coat trailing behind and an arm extended in a broad wave.

"That's my appointment." I pulled the keys from the ignition. "Come on in and wait for a while."

"Okay," she said, then followed me across the lot.

"Professor," Flowers said with a smile as he extended his hand. "You don't look any worse for wear for a man up all night making news."

I took his hand. "Well, I *feel* a lot worse than I look."

I turned to Jasmine. "Jeff's the medical director and CEO here. This is his baby." I introduced him to Jasmine.

"Very pleased," Flowers said warmly as he shook her hand. "Come on in. It's nicer inside."

"Nicer?" Jasmine made a show of taking in the building and grounds, then said, "This I *have* to see."

We followed Flowers into the building, where he settled Jasmine in one of the private reception rooms.

"The phone there has my cell and pager number and my assistant marked on the speed dial," he told her. "Make sure to call one if you need anything."

"Thank you."

Flowers gave her a little bow, then held the door for me. I stepped into the corridor.

"Sorry to be so harried, Professor," Flowers said to me as he took the lead, heading toward Camilla's suite. The days had long passed when he had been the bright student in the front row of my neurophysiology class at UCLA, but he still insisted on calling me professor in an honorific way that made me uncomfortable.

"It happens to me as well."

He picked up his pace. "Your wife is not doing well. In the past fourteen hours, she's acquired a nasty inflammation around the enteral site of the transgastric jejunostomy. We began immediate and aggressive antibiotic treatment, but there's no sign of a response so far."

I nodded as we detoured around a housekeeping cart and made a right-hand turn into a stairwell leading up to the front wing with the ocean-view rooms.

The transgastric jejunostomy feeding tube entered an incision in Camilla's abdomen and threaded though her stomach into the upper part of her small intestine. Acidic gastric fluids can leak outward from the incision and erode the tissue; bacteria can infiltrate from outside.

"Not surprising," I said. "It's actually hard to believe she's gone six years without this."

"That's not all, Professor," Flowers said seriously. "Her renal function has declined noticeably and there are signs of developing pneumonia. We don't know yet whether those are connected to the wound infection, but the lab is working on it as their top priority."

My hopes rose and fell with his prognosis. For six years I had wrestled with the fatigue and resentment tied to Camilla's endless hover between life and death. Years ago, Flowers had discussed removing Camilla's feeding tube. But I loved her deeply despite the evidence that the Camilla I had known no longer inhabited the still-breathing body she had left behind. Also, in the back of my mind, loomed the AMA's ethical statement that "there is no ethical distinction between withdrawing and withholding life-sustaining treatment."

The feeding tube had been installed in the relatively early days when there was hope Camilla might recover. But once installed, removing made me executioner . . . or murderer. Other things restrained me as well. Before Camilla, I had lived like a kite without a string, soaring and diving wildly, hitting enormous heights and knowing the terror and pain of watching the earth rush up at me, all jagged, hard, and sharp. Camilla had been the string to my kite. Even the idea of Camilla had allowed me the same discipline for the past six years. Living without her terrified me.

"We've also seen changes in her EEGs I don't understand," Flowers continued as we reached the top of the stairs and made directly to Camilla's suite. "I'm hoping you can shed some light on them."

We entered the door leading into the suite's sitting room. The Pacific Ocean glowed through the broad windows, showing a top-heavy container ship on the distant horizon heading toward Point Conception. Closer in, I made out the brilliant geometry of a red-and-white sailboat spinnaker and, nearer still, a squad of surfers astride their boards waiting for a good wave.

I followed Flowers to the door leading to Camilla's room. He opened the door, then turned back to me.

"I'm afraid she also looks worse than last week." He turned and I followed him into the room.

As always, Camilla's bed was inclined toward the window. We detected no cognitive control over her eyes, but knowing how much she loved the ocean, I wanted to make sure, if there was any spark in her brain connecting her to this world, she could spend her time as pleasantly as possible.

Research showed we had no way of *proving* she lacked consciousness, only that we could not detect it. So I paid for the best DVDs and music and for people to come and read to her. I don't know whether it did any good for her, but it did a little for me.

When I approached the bed, my heart fell. Camilla had shrunk from the woman I'd visited less than a week before. Her skin trended toward gray and I became acutely aware of the additional IV rack with the antibiotic drip.

"I'm sorry," Flowers said as he read my face.

I moved to Camilla's side and held a cool, dry hand so inordinately small in mine. Behind me, the door clicked discreetly as Flowers quietly excused himself.

Camilla's eyes held steady at the ocean as I held her hand. Then careful not to disturb the network of tubes and monitor leads, I put my head near hers and looked out the window, trying to see what she saw. I recalled a time when our thoughts and emotions and imaginations synchronized with a rare coherence that kept our two lives utterly in step. I looked away from the ocean and into her eyes. They did not change, did not find my own gaze, did not look away from a distant vision I knew extended beyond any horizon visible to me. My heart told me she was not aware of me, that she was no longer there, that she was no longer Camilla.

But I wasn't sure.

I bent over and kissed her on the cheek.

"I love you," I whispered. "I love you."

Jasmine left me with my thoughts as I collected her from the sitting room. Flowers said he would e-mail me the files of Camilla's EEGs so I might have a look at the odd patterns.

I thought little of Jasmine or Flowers as we retraced our path south along Pacific Coast Highway and I let the weight of sadness fill me. Experience had taught me that surrender to the pain reminded me of the futility of human ambition. When measured against eternity, wealth, power, fame, status, all passed away in a blink amounting to nothing. The pain always scrubbed away ambition, then faded, leaving me to wonder what enduring thing I should dedicate my life to.

These moments brought images of God, souls, the human spirit, love, the endurance of consciousness beyond the death of the human body—the evanescent territory beyond science and proof, provinces of faith beyond human certainty. I never reached a bankable conclusion, but yielding to the process eventually left me with a peaceful sense of well-being.

Calm had finally begun to sift into my heart when, right past the big slide area south of Malibu, I pulled over to let two CHP motorcycle officers and a sheriff's car pass with their sirens and lights at full attack. I drove on and made the left-hand turnoff to Topanga Canyon, where Chris Nellis lived.

"I have a bad feeling."

Jasmine sat silent as I continued northeast. We crested a gentle rise. In the distance, police vehicles and an ambulance crowded in front of a small A-frame house. Closer, CHP worked traffic control.

"Oh, hell."

"What?" Jasmine asked.

I accelerated slowly down the hill toward the CHiPs.

"That's Chris Nellis's house."

At the traffic control point, I showed my sheriff's reserve ID to the CHP officers and they informed me then that Chris Nellis had been killed. Shot multiple times, apparently by a sniper. They waved me on through, but I turned around instead.

"You have got to get out of here," I told Jasmine as we drove back to PCH.

"Take me back to the hotel. I'll pack and get the next flight to Jackson."

I thought about this as I made the left at the beach, suddenly convinced someone was watching us, certain now my phone call to Chris was what had killed him.

Suddenly I realized there could be a tail among any number of vehicles in the surrounding traffic, that my truck might even have a tracker.

I shook my head at Jasmine and put my index finger over my lips.

"Good idea." I shook my head.

We drove in silence for another minute. I turned into a beachside parking lot, watching for a tail.

"But before you go, you need to experience the beach at least once."

Jasmine gave me a questioning look, but followed me out of the truck.

At the water's edge we walked the firm, moist sand, and I told her my suspicions.

"No time for you to go back to the hotel. They'll be expecting you to do that. I'm taking you straight to the airport."

"But my clothes, my—"

"Give me your key. I'll take care of it, pay the bill. Ship your stuff back."

"Are you sure . . ."

"You may be in as much danger as your mother. Get on the first plane out of terminal one. It doesn't matter where . . . Phoenix, Sacramento—wherever. Just so you're gone faster than they can track you. Work your way home on whatever flights you can get."

We walked through the sand toward a concrete bench beneath twin palm trees, then made a U-turn back to my truck.

"I'll get there myself by tomorrow," I promised.

"But your practice, your work."

"Unless you and I can get to the bottom of this, those won't be worth a damn . . . not to mention your life and mine."

Once the largest building in the world, the Pentagon hunkers down in a former Virginia swamp always in sight of Arlington National Cemetery, a constant reminder, too seldom heeded.

As he always did, Lieutenant General Dan Gabriel paused at the top of the north Pentagon steps, looked toward Arlington's graves, and said a silent prayer of thanks to the men and women buried there and around the world. Then he pushed his way through the heavy brass-and-glass doors into the lobby.

The sergeant at the duty desk snapped to attention when he spotted the three stars on Gabriel's shoulders.

"Sir!" The noncom issued a swift, precise salute. Gabriel returned the sergeant's salute with a great deal less formality. Despite his rank, Dan Gabriel no longer had an office here and needed to show his identification and sign in with his intended destination. Three-star generals didn't simply just drop in for a visit. This created a flurry of phone calls, consultations, and the appearance of little beads of sweat on the sergeant's upper lip and forehead. Gabriel noted the man's campaign ribbons from Vietnam, Afghanistan, and the Middle East and realized this decorated vet was a lot more comfortable facing incoming RPGs than an unannounced general.

"No sweat, Sarge," Gabriel said. "I'm not in a hurry."

The sergeant gave him a look of disbelief. Generals were always in a very important hurry.

Less than five minutes later, Gabriel made his way into the claustrophobically cramped, linoleum-tiled corridor of the Pentagon's outer ring, heading for Laura LaHaye's office.

As he made his familiar way toward LaHaye's office, linoleum floors, metal and plastic furnishings, and walls covered with GI-issue paint gradually gave way to hardwood paneling, thick carpet, and expensive furnishings for people of rank and importance who believed others should bleed instead of them. A corrosive atmosphere of personal power and ambition corrupted these corridors and reviled those who came to serve their country and not themselves.

Gabriel's refusal to accommodate this political snake pit had propelled him into what many viewed as career suicide when he headed to West Point. But their opinions held no water; he knew that living up to the ambitions and expectations of others led only to misery.

Predictably, Gabriel found Laura LaHaye's office on the third floor of the inner ring with ankle-deep carpet and designer lighting. He opened the polished solid-mahogany door and found himself face-to-face with LaHaye, bent over the reception desk in conversation with a uniformed woman sitting behind it.

LaHaye looked up. "Dan!" She tried unsuccessfully to hide her annoyance. "We were rearranging my schedule to accommodate your unexpected visit." She stepped from behind the desk and extended her hand.

"Sorry." Gabriel shook her cold, dry hand. "I can come back another time if that's better."

LaHaye shook her head. "No. No, that's not necessary. Jenna's used to the dynamic state of my schedule." LaHaye nodded toward the tall, blond woman behind the desk. Gabriel noted she wore the rank of an Army chief warrant officer.

"Thank you," Gabriel said to the receptionist, and to LaHaye, who had already turned and headed for her office. Gabriel followed her.

Bright sunlight flooded into an office sized like a handball court, filled with highly polished dark wood furnishings and carpeted with plush navy-blue pile embossed with the U.S. Army seal. The Stars and Stripes, along with other service and regimental flags, stood behind her massive desk. Expensively framed photos covered the walls, all with LaHaye alongside presidents, senators, congressmen, and a scattering of world leaders, Nobel Prize winners, and a lot of military brass Gabriel recognized as mediocre soldiers and superb political manipulators.

A conference room table dominated the corner to his right. LaHaye made straight for a sofa in the left corner by the windows.

"Have a seat." She directed him to a chair facing the window glare and sat on the sofa. Gabriel seated himself at the nearest chair instead, facing away from the glare.

"What can I help you with?"

"I was in town tying up the loose ends, briefing the new Academy superintendent, that sort of thing."

"I read about it in the *Post*," she said. "Quite a talk you gave to the House Armed Services Committee." Gabriel detected political envy in her voice. "The General is fortunate to have you on his team." She might be envious and annoyed, but she knew when to kiss a politically important arse. "You'd have quite a career in politics if you set your mind to it."

He shook his head. "Only the General could drag me back into politics."

"So what can I do for the next secretary of defense?"

Gabriel found LaHaye's remarks pretentious and off-putting but figured he'd play along.

"The excellent briefing you and Dr. McGovern gave in Napa made quite an impression on me."

LaHaye smiled at the compliment.

"The more I struggle with budget projections, the more I have grown to appreciate the significance of your work."

"Bang for buck," she said.

"It's always bang for buck," he agreed. "And because Project Enduring Valor promises to reshape the military's future, I'd like to know a little more about it—you know, some of the history, how it came about—you know what a history buff I am."

She nodded enthusiastically. "I'm a big fan of your most recent book." She pointed to a set of shelves near the door. Gabriel quickly spotted the red-and-gold-foil dust cover of his latest book on American Special Forces operations beginning with Revolutionary War guerrilla tactics. He also noted the raw ambition on LaHaye's face, no doubt sizing up her role in one of his future books.

"So, how did it begin?" he asked again. "Who got the idea? It would make a great new book." Gabriel waited for the pieces to shift beneath her gaze, for the blocks of ego to topple her caution.

"Would you like coffee or something else to drink?" she said, reaching for the phone on the end table beside the sofa.

"Please."

After she hung up, she gave him a big ass-kissing smile.

"You're very perceptive," LaHaye said. "Dr. Frank Harper started it all."

"I remember him," Gabriel said. "The doctor who got Braxton back on his feet."

"We owe Frank a heavy debt of gratitude. Think of what the future would look like had the Fates clipped the General's cord back then."

In the ensuing silence, the muffled corrugated hiss of a commercial jet on final approach to Reagan National Airport filtered in. When it faded, the distinctive thwack of a Blackhawk chopper thumped persistently against the window.

LaHaye broke the silence. "Enduring Valor's genesis began in the late 1930s when Frank trained as a neurosurgeon. Back then, opening up the cranium led to death as often as not. Like many aspiring physicians interested in the nervous system, Frank learned about Phineas Gage in med school. But unlike most of them, the implications obsessed him."

"Gage? Who's that?"

"A twenty-five-year-old railroad construction foreman transformed by an industrial accident in 1848. Gage's employers, coworkers, friends, and family unanimously praised him as an intelligent, responsible, honest, polite, disciplined—moral—man. Then late one hot summer afternoon in Vermont, Gage made a near-fatal mistake using a four-foot steel pike to tamp explosives into a drilled rock hole. The powder exploded, driving the steel pike into his left cheek, through his eye socket, and the frontal lobes before shooting out the top of his head."

A polite knock came at the door.

"Come in," LaHaye answered, and moments later the blond warrant officer entered the room, all six-foot-plus of her, carrying a tray with a coffee carafe, cups, saucers, sugar, and cream. She was a big woman who carried herself with a strong physical assurance. Gabriel was ambivalent about lowering physical standards to allow women in certain military units. They were fine for fighter pilots and other positions where they were unlikely to be called upon to perform with any degree of raw physical strength. But, he thought, as the warrant officer placed the coffee tray on the table between him and LaHaye, he'd certainly feel comfortable having this one covering his backside.

"I'll take it from here, Jenna," LaHaye said of the tray.

"Sir," the warrant officer said, then retreated to the reception area.

LaHaye sat down and sipped at her cup before continuing.

"After having the steel pike blasted through his head, Phineas Gage recovered, remarkable given the state of medical care at the time. After his recovery, doctors found his intelligence unaffected and no physical incapacitation other than losing his left eye. But the steel pike changed his entire personality. Instead of the former Sunday-school teacher, the physically healed body housed a profane, venal, violent brute with no self-control or sense of responsibility. Call it self-control or free will, Gage had become a victim of his new biological configuration. The 'bad' Gage had evicted the 'good' Gage."

She took another sip, then held the saucer and cup in her left hand.

"Gage fascinated Frank Harper, who had treated more than his share of head wounds, so he kept a notebook containing the names and serial numbers of the patients he treated along with fairly precise descriptions of the wounds and treatment. The War Department funded him to follow up on these men, to interview friends, family, and work associates on personalities before the war and after.

"He found many unchanged." She gazed out the window. "But he also found some startling differences in those who had specific wounds in the frontal lobes. Some had became violent like Gage and wound up in jail." LaHaye turned back toward Gabriel. "I know of at least two cases where Harper's notes and medical records and testimony kept men from being executed for murders they committed.

"Harper's work prompted the Army to fund a major research effort and essentially gave Harper a recently vacated POW camp in Mississippi. From about 1947 and well into the 1960s, Harper's people brought in patients for study and sent out teams to prisons and mental hospitals to treat those who were confined and unable to travel."

"General Braxton was one of these?"

LaHaye nodded. "One of Frank's biggest successes."

"Thank God."

"Absolutely. Anyway, Harper's biggest successes came after he abandoned the surgical route and began experimenting with psychoactive drugs. Harper structured joint development ventures with private pharmaceutical companies—with some success, I might add.

"At any rate, Harper's public-private partnership evolved into the operation I now head. Harper's people and a core of researchers who founded Defense Therapeutics looked at the mechanisms of treating 'Bad Gage' injuries, and as they developed new formulas, they realized it might be possible to produce a nondepleting neurotrop which temporarily produces useful combat behavior modifications in warfighters to increase battle efficiency and performance. In addition to the focus and stamina, the ideal nondepleting neurotrop induces the warfighter to surrender a large portion of their free will to the command structure, allowing them to better function in a cohesive fighting unit rather than as an individual."

Gabriel frowned.

"Imagine the huge time and cost savings," LaHaye offered. "Instead of weeks and months to create units out of individuals, we can accomplish the same thing pharmaceutically almost overnight and at a tiny fraction of the cost. As long as they're in the zone, they're perfect killers."

Perfect killers. In the zone. Gabriel saw killing zombies in his mind and struggled to keep his horror from showing on his face.

"You talk about the *ideal* nondepleting neurotrop," Gabriel said. "That makes it sound like there are a lot of them."

LaHaye nodded. "There are. We thought we had the perfect one back during the first Gulf War."

"You mean you actually tested one?"

"Not officially. But just in a few units. We deployed buspirone II in a few units and it worked brilliantly for combat effectiveness." She hesitated.

"But?"

"Gulf War syndrome. I would think you'd know about that given the writings of your cousin."

"Rick Gabriel's a fairly distant cousin," Gabriel said. "I've not read much of his work. Should I?"

"He does strike a lot closer to the truth than I'd prefer." She paused, then changed the subject. "Anyway, we've built on the buspirone work and hit pay dirt."

"How do you know?"

"We've done tests with perfectly adjusted doses and formulations," she said vaguely. "We've had none of the long-term side effects from Iraq, unlike the Gulf War syndrome, which continues to plague us, or the rash of murders and assaults by special ops after returning from Afghanistan."

Gabriel worked to control the unease squirming in his belly and sensed this was not the time to ask further probing questions because he guessed she had already told him more than she should have.

"Have you been reading about that old murder case down in Mississippi? Talmadge, I believe."

"Who hasn't? It's been a running sore on the national news for months now."

"Does it have anything to do with your work? Or Harper's?"

"Not that I know."

"Right. That's good enough for me." Gabriel paused. "But, you know, it's truly amazing that we as a people and our justice system can look at two men who committed identically horrible crimes and send one to execution and spare the other because there is a physical scar we can see."

LaHaye frowned. "Maybe, but I fail to see how it matters."

"Well, it does raise some interesting philosophical implications about right and wrong and free will. The religious views of 'good' versus 'evil' take on new meanings if good or bad behaviors are controlled *not* by some sort of extrahuman spiritual realm, but by the physical world of neurons, brain physiology, and neurotransmitter molecules," Gabriel said. "Perhaps of relevance to your research?"

Her frown deepened as the lines in her face branched into a mask of annoyance.

"Really," Gabriel persisted. "Seeing the scar, knowing about the wound which turned a 'good' person into a 'bad' one, motivates us to treat that person differently than another person without the wound. Presumably we do that because we recognize the person with the visible wound has a physical impairment to their free will. So, for one we have treatment, and for the other we have punishment. But suppose the punished person actually has a physical wound in the brain we can't detect—perhaps genetic or from some sort of development problem in the brain. How can we tell? Suppose there are physical wounds resulting from DNA damage? Shouldn't society treat them the same as one who has a scar that can be touched? Do we have to touch the scars to believe? Don't you see? Your research has great philosophical implications for the military, and society as a whole."

She shook her head aggressively. "It's not my table." LaHaye waved her right hand dismissively. "It has no operational significance."

"Of course you are right." He nodded sagely. "But that's precisely the sort of speculation obviously a book author would be interested in." He smiled as engagingly as he could muster.

Her face brightened. "Of course! It will make for some fascinating reading."

Gabriel stood up. "Thank you for your time and patience with me dropping in unannounced. I definitely see the beginning of a new book here."

LaHaye's face beamed. She stood up and walked him through the reception area to the door. They shook hands. Gabriel opened the door to the corridor, then suddenly stopped and turned back to LaHaye.

"Do you have Frank Harper's contact information? I think he would be a good place to begin the history."

"Of course." LaHaye said pleasantly. Gabriel let the door close as she turned to the chief warrant officer behind the reception desk.

"Jenna, please make General Gabriel a copy of all my contact information for Dr. Frank Harper."

I stood away from the crowd in the Jackson airport's baggage claim area and dialed Vince Sloane's cell number. He picked up on the fourth ring.

"Where the hell are you, Doc? All hell's breaking loose here."

There were times when I longed for the old, anonymous pre-caller-ID days.

"Mississippi. Jackson." I tried to shake the fatigue from my head.

"Figures."

"What kind of hell?"

"Jeez, it's hard to know where to start."

"How about with Chris? How is he?"

"Dead."

All during the flight I had hoped the cop at the roadblock had been wrong.

"It's all over the media and they're connecting it to the crap with your boat."

"Wonderful."

"That's not all. The Army spooks did a walk-through of your house and got LAPD looking for angles."

"Angles?"

"You know how cops think. All this stuff coming down one thing after another doesn't just happen to innocent people."

Dread sifted down into my gut like lead shot.

"You're the only link they can find connecting all the dots. And you've fled the scene."

"Fled!"

"Whoa! Whoa! It's not me saying that; it's them. Take off your victim hat and look at it from the viewpoint of a detective."

Luggage thudded into the pickup area. I realized he was right.

"You have now become a person of interest," Vince continued.

"A person of—"

"They're taking your place apart with tweezers. I imagine they'll have people over to UCLA pretty soon."

"Oh, hell." I slumped against the wall.

"I also imagine that pretty soon they'll be contacting the local cops in Mississippi about the death of your young lady's mother."

"But that was my mother's funeral! I had no idea Vanessa was even coming."

"I know that, and you do. But their theory is that the slug which killed Vanessa Thompson was meant for you."

"For me? Why do they think someone wanted to kill me?"

"They don't know, but they're fabricating a theory about some sort of drug operation—you know, your boat, the attack—"

"That's insane!"

Silence hung heavy between us.

"Vince? You still there?"

"Still here." He cleared his throat. "If I didn't know you . . . really *know* you, I'd probably connect the dots the same way."

"Oh, man," I said quietly. "I agree something's wrong and none of this is coincidence, but it's tied to this Talmadge thing."

"I hope you can make your case . . . fast."

Jasmine's bag and my duffel thudded into view. I made my way through the crowd toward them.

"Me too."

"Keep in touch."

"Roger."

. . .

Jael St. Clair pulled her rented Ford Explorer into an empty slot in the short-term parking lot at the Jackson airport terminal where she could watch traffic exiting the rental-car lot. She swept the blond hair from her face with one hand, then stretched her arms and untangled the knots in her back that had accumulated during the flight from Los Angeles. The Citation was an okay corporate jet, she thought, but as a bedroom, it left a lot to be desired.

She reached over to the substantial saddlebag purse on the seat and, without taking her eyes off the rental lot, sorted through the bag's contents. Her fingers quickly found her cell phone, then the Heckler & Koch, HK4 semiautomatic pistol with the .380 ACP barrel and seven-round magazine, the Garmin, and finally the powerful, compact Zeiss binoculars. She pulled the binoculars out, raised them to her eyes, and adjusted the focus.

Bradford Stone made his way toward a white Ford pickup truck in the rental car lot. He had used a credit card for his flight from L.A. to Jackson, his vehicle here, and his hotel in Greenwood. He might as well be wearing a strobe on his head. Stone put his bags in the jump seat of the truck and got into the driver's seat. After several moments of adjusting mirrors and seats, he drove out of the rental lot.

Stone drove past her. Jael waited for a moment, allowing a battered Chevy truck and a midsixties Toronado listing from a broken suspension to pass, then pulled into traffic behind them, heading toward I-20.

Robert Johnson's artfully unadorned guitar notes filled the cab of my rented pickup as I raced north along Highway 49 through the kudzu-smothered hills south of Yazoo City.

The CD had been on sale cheap at the airport gift shop on my stopover. I loved the genius of Johnson's blues guitar and the transcendent depth of the lyrics. Blues masters like Johnson and Mississippi John Hurt had a way of owning my imagination.

"There's a hellhound on my trail," I thought.

The hellhound had killed Vanessa and laid waste to my life in California. No name to this hound, no breed, no face, all fangs and death without form. In my mind, I walked through the pieces of the puzzle:

Mama's funeral, my boat, the attack at home. I ransacked every thought, desperate for some dim, unremembered key to the deadly puzzle placing me as the only logical suspect.

Outside, the kudzu shrouded utility poles, abandoned barns and houses, and everything in between, even the tallest of trees. The trees looked like giant undead mummies trailing their scattered rags slowly over the hills.

I listened to the beginning of Robert Johnson's "Me and the Devil Blues" and imagined evil making its way through the landscape here. Even though Johnson was a man of the Delta's flatness, his words and music spoke to more universal fears.

It had been decades since the last time I had driven this road, and back then it had been a narrow, two-lane patchwork of cracked, tar-sealed concrete with no shoulder that slashed through the kudzu jungle, abruptly ascending and dropping like a cheap roller coaster as the highway's thick expansion joints thwapped an endless iambic *k-dunk, k-dunk, k-dunk* against the tires.

Highway 49 was four lanes now, bordered by a broad demilitarized zone cleared of the aggressive imported Asian vine that grew up to a foot per day. Kudzu had been widely planted to control soil erosion back in the 1930s and could invade a farm and occupy it in a single growing season. Poet James Dickey called it a "green, mindless, unkillable ghost," and there were legends of unwary farmers found strangled in their beds because they fell asleep with the windows open. I had read once kudzu was actually a useful plant—a source of Asian medicines and a nutritious forage for livestock, which enriched the soil with nitrogen-fixing roots. Many useful things become toxic when transplanted out of their native environments.

All of these characteristics no doubt contributed to the way kudzu had grown into a cultural metaphor for Southern society, although no one agreed on the meaning. Maybe it had to do with manners and sugar-sweet hospitality gone wild or because it proved a relentless adversary much like poverty and racism. Probably these things more.

Johnson's raspy voice scratched out "Crossroad Blues," supposedly his lament after selling his soul to the devil in exchange for his supernaturally superb guitar ability.

Mmm, the sun goin' down, boy
Dark gon' catch me here

On the southern outskirts of Yazoo City, signs pointed to 49E veering off to northeast. The bifurcated Highway 49s would almost parallel each other for another eighty miles, describing a long, thin diamond sliver that bounded much of my early life.

Staying on 49 would take me through Midnight, Silver City, and Belzonio to Indianola at the western point of the diamond, where Saints' Rest, one of the Judge's plantations, was located. A little farther on, 49 passed through Ruleville, where my mother's sister had lived and died, and up through Parchman Prison, the Devil's Island of the Delta. Finally, Highway 49 healed itself with 49E up in Tutwiler, north of Summer, where an all-white jury back in the mid-1950s had acquitted the killers of Emmett Till, who had been tortured to death for the crime of being a black teenager. I was about six years old at the time, but I don't remember much specific about all this other than visits from a lot of strangers and hushed conversations behind the closed doors to the breakfast room in the Judge's house in Itta Bena.

Back then, my mother and I lived in a small apartment attached to the main house the Judge had built for us during the first divorce. Mama and Papa divorced and married each other three times before ultimately each marrying someone else for the fourth time. What Papa and I did together was rare and episodic. I went on trips with him to New Orleans exactly four times, twice when he was working and twice to watch Ole Miss win the Sugar Bowl. We went dove hunting three times and once for ducks. I remember those eight events primarily because they were so very special but also because eight things are not hard to keep in mind.

Despite that, I loved Papa deeply whenever I was with him. I can remember to this day how he always smelled of Old Spice and Camels. The cigarettes railroaded him into a series of long, dark, painful, and humiliating final days living mutely with a tracheotomy where the cancer had eaten his lungs away.

I would like to have known my father better, but he died first.

While it never made up for not having Papa to hug, I enjoyed the run of the Judge's big house and yard with the giant sycamores along the street in front, the massive pecan tree out back, the tulips blazing along the driveway in the spring, a pen full of bluetick hounds, and of course Lena Grayson and Al Thompson, who served as cook/housekeeper and chauffeur/gardener. I owed my life to Al Thompson. As the story goes, after going to a cowboy-movie matinee, I decided to hang myself. I took apart the rope swing on the pecan tree, tied a damn good noose for a five-year-old, stood on my tricycle, and nearly choked to death.

Al Thompson observed the entire thing from the screened-in back porch next to the Judge's kitchen. He called Lena out to watch and she told him to stop me. Al waited until I started to choke. "If I stop the boy before he gets a taste for things, he'll just try it again some other time when nobody's watching."

To this day, I fight panic when cinching up a necktie.

Not long after I turned onto 49E in Yazoo City, the four lanes narrowed to two, then plunged from the textured land of kudzu-covered hills to the table-flat elevations of a hundred merging flood plains of the Delta.

Train tracks heavy with long snakes of hoppers, boxcars, flatbeds, and log carriers paralleled the curvy, tree-lined two-lane with no shoulders and barely wide enough for two pickups to pass without taking off the side mirrors. The highway and tracks flirted with the base of the hills until we got to Eden, where 49E ricocheted north-northeast, off toward the heart of the Delta. My new trajectory ran atop a steep berm, which would usually keep the road surface above the waters of creeks and rivers that escaped their banks every winter and spring. Beyond lay cotton in various stages of development.

Water stood in many of the fields, testament to a period of unusually high rainfall this year. The rice and catfish farmers had no trouble, but I saw this would be a horrible year otherwise if the fields didn't dry out. In the higher, drier fields, cotton grew thigh-high and colorful with flowers. As a child, I had marveled how cotton blossoms opened white one day, closed up that night, and reopened the next day all deep reddish pink for the next day or so until they dropped off.

Everywhere I looked, the landscape was the same: fields of developing cotton punctuated by rows of trees marking streams, sloughs, and oxbow lakes that could not be cleared for crops. Ironically, in the distance, I saw the dust pointing to vehicles in the higher spots, places where the brutally hot sun baked the surface dry and left the standing water around it a warm, perfect incubator for mosquito larvae.

One of Mama's favorite stories she told so often was how, during her early childhood in the late teens and 1920s, Mr. Durham, who owned one of the two drugstores in town, would mix quinine with Coca-Cola and chocolate syrup as a "spring tonic" for her and the other children in town as a prophylactic against mosquito-borne disease. The best attempts at mosquito abatement must not have been very successful, because by the time I was a kid, I remember getting vaccination shots for yellow fever, a barely better behaved but still nasty hemorrhagic cousin of Ebola.

The first time Highway 49E straightened out, a pickup filled my rearview mirror, then accelerated past me and quickly disappeared around the next curve, leaving me alone with my thoughts and the gathering thunderheads to the northeast reaching for the stratosphere even though it was not quite noon. More storms, more rain, more misery.

When the highway broke free of the trees, I was struck by how the thunderheads resembled great angry Confederate privateers with storm-bellied sails and armed with lightning, tornadoes, and hail. I remembered hikes in the woods when the storms would announce themselves first with the distant low rumble of thunder that said, "Head home." Then came a blast of cool air like opening God's own icebox, hurtling me into a dead run for home. I'd sprint to escape the march of heavy rain, which sounded like a giant pushing through the leaves and brush. I ran faster and faster, especially when the interval between the lightning and thunder came like my racing heartbeat.

Sometimes I beat the rain, sometimes not. One time when lightning took out a dead tree less than fifty yards away, I almost urinated in my pants. When I was about sixteen, I huddled in a gully as a tornado passed overhead and sounded like every B-52 in the world charging down the runway toward takeoff with a full load and every engine straining. I'm fine if I never hear that again.

With the past ringing in my head, I spotted a small settlement ahead scattered on both sides of the highway with a water tower, a gas station, and a store with a driveway of loose beige gravel. I slowed as my truck passed old black men in blue overalls sitting still on the sagging porches of gray, weather-bleached shacks with rusty tin roofs. Three gray-brown pigs rooted along the road shoulder. In the distance, a dust contrail plumed across a field, pointing at the pickup that had passed me.

Once past the settlement, I drove like a drunk dodging dead possums, dogs, skunks, raccoons—passing more red meat in the highway than you'd find at the Piggly Wiggly's butcher case. Even with the air-conditioning on recirculate, I could tell some of the animals had been fermenting in the hot sun for days.

I was making good time up 49E, chasing heat mirages that looked like fleeing desert ponds in the road ahead and thinking about how Talmadge was most likely the key to this whole mess, when my cell phone rang. I hoped it was Jasmine, but when I looked at the caller ID, I recognized it as Rex's. I turned the CD's volume down.

"Hey, man," I said.

"Hey y'own damn self, asshole. What's the big idea of coming to my town and not stopping by? What am I going to tell Anita?"

As tense as I felt, I couldn't help but smile. They had to be the oddest couple. Rex's wife, Anita, originally from India, was an accomplished physician from a royal family that still lived in the old country. Rex was a genius with ready hands, one of the smartest people I had ever met, who managed to hide his intelligence behind a rough physical style that, outwardly at least, favored fists over philosophy.

"Tell her I'm buying y'all a big fancy dinner when I get back to Jackson."

"That'll be a start." Rex laughed.

Static filled an awkward silence.

"So what can I do for you?" Rex said finally.

"Well, for one thing, I have just gone through the strangest seventy-two hours of my life and it's made me think I badly need a man of your, uh, talents."

"You need some drywall installed?" Rex laughed. In the background other people yelled amid the whine of screw guns. When Rex spoke again, his voice was low, serious, and all business. "Let me step outside."

Newly paved asphalt hissed beneath my pickup's tires. The sun baked my face through the windshield as I passed a cotton gin with a dozen rusty, wire-sided trailers beside it with lint tangled in the mesh.

"Talk to me," Rex said finally. "Don't leave anything out."

So I started with the attack on my boat and made my way past the shock at Chris Nellis's house in Topanga Canyon to LAX with Jasmine.

"I've got all her stuff in the back," I concluded as I neared Tchula, one of those grinding third-world poverty pockets in the Delta.

"I'm headed to Greenwood to meet Jasmine at her office."

"Watch your back there, my man."

"How so?"

"The Mississippi Justice center sits right in the crosshairs of the Snowden-Jones housing project; that whole area's a drive-by shooting gallery."

"How'd you know that?"

"You don't think I've got turnips for brains, do you? Of course I know where the office is. It was one of the first places I scoped out after the shooting at your mama's funeral. And Snowden-Jones is infamous; it's always in the news. Makes Oakland look like Beverly Hills."

"I should have figured—"

"Yep, you should have. Did you think the shooting at the cemetery was a fluke?"

"The cops think so."

Rex snorted. "Of *course* they do! Those poor bastards have their hands full. A bunch of country boys and they've got more crack and drug murders per capita than the pros in the big city. They *have* to think that because they haven't got time to think of anything else."

"But you have, right?"

"That's right, pod-nah."

I slowed for a light as I got into Tchula proper.

"And?" I prompted him as the light turned and I followed traffic through the main part of town.

"Well, for one thing, all the people who usually know everything about everything don't know jack about nuthin' here."

"Well, that's helpful," I said as I hit the brakes. Immediately in front of me, a battered midsixties land yacht painted in twelve shades of rust and primer came to a sudden stop right in the middle of Highway 49 as the four occupants spotted a young black man walking along the shoulder they wanted to chat with. The pedestrian's face went wide with fear until he recognized the Pontiac's occupants as friends and not drive-by assailants. I steered around the Pontiac.

"So did you ever piss off anybody in the military?"

"Every day."

"Well, look who's helpful now."

"Meaning?"

"Meaning, the word is Vanessa Thompson was *not* killed by anybody in the community. And there are people around there asking questions about you."

The skein of dread in my gut yanked another knot tighter. I told him about my conversation with Vince Sloane.

"That's bad my friend, but it gets worse."

"Hard to imagine."

"Yeah, but get this: from what I can gather, the people asking the questions are military types."

I thought back to the helicopter and the military inflatables.

"This really makes no sense, no sense at all."

"Like your last three days make sense?"

I let that sink in as the road sign for Egypt plantation came up.

"So what do we do?" I asked.

"What do you mean 'we,' kemo sabe?" Rex laughed, then said, "Keep your head down; keep asking questions. I'll finish up this drywall job here in Eastover by tomorrow, and I'll put all my time into helping you."

I thanked him, said I needed a good wingman more than ever, then said good-bye.

I checked my various voice-mail boxes and found multiple, increasingly hostile message from the LAPD, and a raft of messages from Sonia, increasingly frightened and indignant. I thought of nothing reasonable to say to either of them and decided to think first instead.

Greenwood loomed quickly ahead, and according to the map I had printed off the Internet, Jasmine's office was on Main Street, straight ahead at the looming cloverleaf. But Rex's warning about the dangerous neighborhood made me worry about parking there because stealing my laptop—which had my life on it—would be child's play.

So I took the ramp for west 82 instead and followed it over the steep viaduct spanning the mainline railroad tracks. I dialed Jasmine's cell phone as I came down to a red light where the highway made its way through a congested strip area lined with motels, fast-food restaurants, muffler shops, and other outskirts establishments.

Again she didn't answer, so I left another voice mail. The light turned green and I pressed on. The local newspaper, the *Greenwood Commonwealth*, passed by on the left and, next to it, the EZ-Sleep Suites.

I turned toward the EZ-Sleep and drove past a small brick building whose sign identified it as a cancer treatment outpatient clinic. The building was surrounded by people scattered in ones and twos smoking cigarettes.

I entered a lobby alive with the faint spicy fragrances of ginger, turmeric, cumin, and lime, which made my mouth water and reminded me it was after noon and I had eaten nothing in the past eighteen hours of travel other than Lilliputian bags of peanuts and pretzels. A middle-aged Indian man checked me in and directed me around the corner to my room.

As I parked near the stairs and got out, I noted a line of white panel vans with ladders on the roof and signs on the side marking them with the name of a large national contractor that laid and installed fiber-optic cables. Down at the far end of the building, people in orange shirts gathered in conversation, obviously the contractor's people here on extended assignment.

I lugged my laptop bag and duffel up to my room on the second floor and dumped them on the nearest bed, cleared off a table for my computer, connected it to the phone's data port, and turned it on. I entered the BIOS-level password, then plugged in a USB flash drive that governed the automatic encryption and decryption of everything on the hard drive. Without the flash drive plugged in, the hard drive was impenetrable to anyone save those with access to a supercomputer and advanced code-breaking software.

With this done, I dialed into the local EarthLink number and launched Eudora, which began downloading all the spam and e-mail. Next, I knelt beneath the desk, unscrewed the plastic faceplate from the electrical outlet, and replaced it with an invention of my own: a sturdy metal faceplate with an attachment point for a hefty security cable, which I secured to my laptop and set the combination. To steal my laptop, a thief would have to rip the entire electrical outlet junction box from the wall. Then I plugged in the laptop's AC power supply.

E-mail was still downloading by the time I finished settling in, so I stood in the door of my room for a moment looking out at the field behind the hotel. The heat of the day blushed at my cheeks like staring into an open oven. Over to my left, next to the stairs, big red wasps with plump bellies filled with sting and pain hovered near a cranny under the eaves. Experience told me if I risked a closer look, I'd find a big paper nest filled with fat white larvae waiting to be more red wasps. I remembered long ago as a child using the garden hose nozzle at full blast to knock the nests off from under the eaves of our house and running like hell after about a dozen blasts until the nest finally fell and I could toss some gasoline on it to finish the job.

The vivid, painful memories of being stung replayed themselves now with an amazingly clear image of how a sting grew into perfectly round red welt with a little hole surrounded by white skin at the very center. With this memory vivid in mind, I closed the door and stood there uncertainly. I wanted something to eat. I wanted to talk to Jasmine. I didn't want to look at my e-mail, but I did, all 307 new messages.

My head spun bright and dizzy with travel fatigue and sleep deprivation. I didn't want to deal with the spam, so I went into the cramped little bathroom, stripped, and took a shower instead. Afterward, I put on the least-wrinkled blue, oxford-cloth, button-down shirt, tucked it into a clean pair of khakis, and sat down to deal with the e-mail vomit fouling my in-box.

Not needing to add a full cup size to my breasts and being comfortable with the size of my penis, I deleted large stretches of spam, including those from Tiffany, Brianna, and others who promised me a good time and had attached explicit photos. I quickly winnowed things down to about a dozen that really mattered, then focused on two from Jeff Flowers.

Flowers's first e-mail told me Camilla had not changed significantly. He had enclosed the links and account access information for me to access EEG scans on one of Pacific Hills' Web servers. In the second e-mail, sent about four hours later, he said her EEGs had taken a turn toward the bizarre, which had prompted them to conduct a PET scan. He enclosed another set of links for those files.

I leaned back in the chair and let out my breath in a loud, heavy rush. Again guilt wrestled with feelings of relief. I did not want to look at the EEGs and scans. I really wanted to let Camilla's condition take its course without any further intervention. But my heart told me that if she simply slipped away without me doing all I could, I'd never get rid of the guilt. Regrets were always for the living.

So I launched Netscape, double-clicked on the links Flowers had sent, and logged in to the server using the user name and password he had sent. The EEG scans would download on this dial-up connection in half an hour or so, but the PET scan files were huge, multimegabyte monsters. I realized I needed to make contact with someone at the Greenwood Hospital who would allow me to use their broadband connection.

I stood up, looked at my watch, and found the time creeping up on 1:00 P.M. Jasmine's failure to return my calls nagged at me, but I decided I had left enough voice mails. I pulled out the small notebook I always carried with me and scribbled in it the necessary information from Flowers's e-mails and shut down my laptop.

Next, I pulled two small Targus motion detectors from my laptop bag and locked one to the laptop and the other to the security cable where it attached to the wall. Then I pulled out a laminated Day-Glo orange placard in English and Spanish warning people not to touch or the alarms would go off. I armed the laptop's motion alarms, made sure their blinking red LEDs were immediately visible to anyone who might enter, and left a light on so the warning note was clearly visible.

In the far corner of the EZ-Sleep Suites' parking lot, hidden among the cable vans, Jael St. Clair sat behind the wheel of her white rented SUV, took a deep hit off a fresh cigarette, and watched the door to Brad Stone's room open. He walked out, empty-handed, closed the door, then headed toward the stairs.

St. Clair smiled as Stone turned back to check the door, then got into his truck and drove away.

"Surprise, asshole," she said quietly, thinking about how nice it would be to watch the reception she had arranged for him and his black beauty. But there was work to be done. St. Clair opened her door, stood up, and took another drag on the cigarette. Then she ground it out on the pavement with her shoe and made her way to Stone's room, pulling on a pair of latex gloves as she walked. At his door, she wiggled a plastic shim in the lock; the door opened in the blink of an eye. Jael closed the door behind her and turned on the lights. The multiple flashing lights on Stone's laptop drew her attention.

Her anger rose as she examined the cables and alarms. She'd need cutters and a way to muffle the alarms. The heavy, braided steel cable meant a bolt cutter wouldn't work. She'd need a Dremel with an abrasive cutoff disk.

And fast-setting acoustic foam for the alarms. What a mess.

"You pig-fucking shit-bird."

She walked to the bathroom, where her frown softened as her eyes fell on the short, graying-brown hairs gathered at the drain. St. Clair gathered the strands and put them in one of the Ziploc snack bags she had brought just for this. Running her hand across the cigarette-scarred fake-marble counter, she found another half dozen hairs.

Then she left.

About a mile northwest of my hotel, Highway 82 crossed a wide stretch of railroad tracks. Moments later, I turned right on Strong Avenue and caught sight of the hospital in which I had been born. According to Mama, lightning from a passing thunderstorm had hit the building pretty near to the time I had been born.

The hospital was a pale yellow brick affair towering over the street and the green, green levee that ran behind it along the Yazoo River. Suddenly, I looked through a seven-year-old's eyes at my grandmother, Mamie, the Judge's wife, lying in one of the hospital's darkened rooms under a plastic oxygen tent that looked pieced together from dry-cleaner suit bags. A cerebral hemorrhage had nailed her like a stroke of lightning and sent her there to drift out of our lives for a terminal day or so. Mamie slept so peacefully to my young eyes.

This vision washed over me like muddy floodwaters from a breached levee. Something like this happened every time I visited Mississippi, home no matter how long I lived elsewhere. I shook my head and tried to focus on my mission. I decided to start with the emergency room, which always had sharp people able to deal with the unexpected—such as some California doctor coming and asking to use their computer system. I put the truck in gear and pulled into sparse eastbound traffic.

As I neared the emergency room entrance, I spotted a prominent sign at the road's edge for Giles Claiborne, M.D., and the past lurched in front of me again. Claiborne had to be as old as the hills because he had been my family physician in Itta Bena not long after Uncle Doc had died. Uncle Doc was the husband of Mamie's sister and took care of everyone regardless of color or their ability to pay. I remembered shots, stitches, and the back entrance that led to a separate waiting room for Negroes Only. I do remember getting entirely unsatisfactory answers about this from Al Thompson and Mama.

As I parked next to Claiborne's office, my cell phone rang.

"Stone."

"Where you at, boy?" I recognized Rex's voice.

"Greenwood. Camilla's in a really bad way. I'm at the hospital seeing if there's a way to have them pull up her scans."

"Y'mama said a prayer for her every damned day."

"I know."

"I'da said some myself, but God'n me, we don't get along."

I wanted to laugh, but Camilla's shadow chilled my heart.

"Okay, look. I've been doing some checking," Rex said. "Nothing for sure. I just wanted to say you better watch your back. I—"

My phone beeped its familiar "no service" tone and lapsed into analog roam. The signal meter hovered at the low end of the scale. I tried to call Rex back, but got nothing.

"Nuts." I got out and made my way into the clinic. A young woman with intensely dark skin in a white uniform sat behind the receptionist's desk and gave me a smile filled with brilliant, even teeth set in gums the color of blueberries. I introduced myself and asked for Dr. Claiborne.

"Across the street in the little broom closet he calls an office," she said. "I'll call him"

As soon as she finished punching in the numbers, she looked up at me. "You one of his old patients?"

"I think maybe his father's." I smiled. "A long time ago."

She gave me a warm laugh and shook her head. "Dr. Claiborne has three daughters, no sons."

The surprise played across my face.

"He retired once, back when my mother worked for him. It didn't take so—" She stopped to leave a voice mail to tell Dr. Claiborne about me, then she drew me a map to his office.

I thanked her, took the map, and hurried across the street, where a uniformed security officer directed me straight on back. I passed through a set of double doors guarded by another security officer and followed the hand-drawn map's zigzag along the fluorescent-lighted, tiled corridor to the first landmark, a lighted sign for radiology. Across the hall sat an unmarked wooden door with louvered vents in the lower panel. I stopped by the door and raised my hand to knock when it opened, leaving me to stare straight into the timeworn face of Dr. Giles Claiborne.

The wrinkled familiarity of the past froze me for another instant. I figured he must be at least eighty-five, but his cool, glacial blue eyes lit up his face and made him appear decades younger. Claiborne stood imperially straight and unbent by time and crowned with a full shock of white hair.

He wore a cotton broadcloth shirt with a weave as fine as silk and a three-letter script monogram instead of a pocket. A gold collar bar made sure the knot in his silk, regimental stripe tie remained perfect. His khakis had knife creases, where mine resembled tired aluminum foil someone had tried to press into respectability. The knife creases broke perfectly above stylishly comfortable and obviously expensive burnished leather loafers.

My old feelings of social insecurity rebounded with a vengeance. Even though I had been wellborn into a family with a distinguished Mississippi heritage, I had come along at a time when the family fortunes had slipped away in a latter-day Faulknerian crisis that had left too many of my relatives clinging to nothing more substantial than ancestral bloodlines. As a result, I had grown up uneasily among the privileged classes from the planter culture of the Delta and, later, the moneyed movers of Jackson.

I had always felt *from* those classes but never *of* them. I tried to belong to those classes as a child, but never found a comfort level with their patrician attitudes and their casual, nonreflective acceptance of superior entitlement granted by the natural order of things. I'm sure that played no small role in my ultimate rebellion and rejection of my heritage.

Despite my professional and financial achievements, I had never completely exorcised my desire to be accepted by them. I didn't understand that flaw, but it played a major role in my avoidance of my home state and most of those with whom I had grown up. Clearly, I had rejected this culture but had not escaped it.

"Bradford! What an unanticipated pleasure!" Giles Claiborne extended his hand. I took his powerful, warm grip. It subtracted yet more years from my perception of him and made me feel almost like his child patient again.

"Dr. Claiborne," I managed as I returned his handshake.

"Please call me Clay. You're an accomplished physician yourself now; I've run across your papers in the literature any number of times now, and I have to confess, a lot of what you have written sails right over the head of this old country doctor."

His broad, self-deprecating smile further rattled my emotional equilibrium.

"Of course . . . Clay."

"Well, then, come on in." He motioned me into a small, windowless room overstuffed with an Oriental rug, dark mahogany furnishings, and all the professionally decorated accoutrements that went with the look.

Broom closet indeed. I saw from a quick glance at the walls that he was on the hospital board and had been for a several decades.

"Here." He motioned me in the direction of his desk, to an armchair upholstered in burgundy leather and studded with brass. "Have a seat." He closed the door and followed me, settling his tall, lanky frame into an identical chair facing me.

Claiborne gave me an intense silent stare that made me feel like a patient again. Then he leaned closer to me, studied my face, then sat back in his own leather-upholstered chair.

"Lordy, Bradford, you *do* have the Judge's eyes," he said finally. "You have that *look*, that . . . *demeanor* he had which made people do what he told them to, made them instantly believe he was right about most anything." He nodded to himself as he continued to fix my face with his gaze. "Call it charisma or presence if you like, but it clearly made him such a successful lawyer and a political force that lives on today."

Given the Judge's political leanings and the ways he enforced his power, I did not want to say "Thank you," so I nodded and asked, "You really think so?"

I knew my noncommittal, equivocal response fell right in with how good people could stand by and let evil things like segregation happen. I reminded myself, I had not come to refight the Civil War, but to find a way to look at my comatose wife's brain scans.

"Lordy," Claiborne said again. "Why, I remember the last time I saw you, you were about this high." He raised his left hand about three or four feet off the floor. I caught the gold Piaget on his wrist. "Yes, yes," he mused to himself. "That would have been about the time you were in the first grade and we were giving everybody Salk vaccines. I remember one other time your mama brought you in bleeding like a stuck hog where you had stepped on some glass barefoot." His eyes went distant for a moment and I sensed he was watching some version of the same memory in my own head where I'd played in tall grass down by Riverside Drive near Eddie Stanton's house. I thought for sure I had been bitten by a water moccasin and was going to die right there.

"Your mama had a cute little Nash Rambler and you lived in the Judge's house then. Lordy, your mama sure was proud of you." His face went blank for a moment and showed me his professionally sympathetic gaze. "I sure mourned her passing." He nodded again, then returned to studying my face.

"Yes, yes, you certainly do have the Judge's eyes." Then he laughed.

"Fortunately for you, you don't have his hairline." He combed his aristocratic fingers through his white thatch. The Judge had been cue-ball bald.

Claiborne mined this particular historical vein for another eternal ten minutes before finally asking me what had brought me into his office.

"Got just the thing."

I followed Claiborne to the radiology department.

"We've got a terrific system allowing us to send digitized X-rays and scans down to the medical school in Jackson for consultation, or Ocshners or anywhere else for that matter."

I followed him through the waiting room, smiling and nodding politely as he introduced me in glowing terms as a local boy made good, all the while letting everybody know I was the Judge's grandson and he had been my physician. Somehow that seemed to matter, and once again it astounded me how eagerly people here allowed their lives to be shaped by dead men.

We made our way to the back corner of a long, claustrophobic supply closet, where we found a young man in a white coat intently tapping at a keyboard. A giant, high-resolution, flat-panel plasma screen dominated the room.

Claiborne cleared his throat. "Tyrone?"

The young man turned toward us.

"Tyrone Freedman, this is Dr. Stone. He's one of my old patients, but he's from California now." Claiborne said nothing about the Judge this time.

When Freedman stood up and shook my hand, I tried not to look at a ragged scar that puckered its way from the corner of his left eye and made it across his temple before disappearing into his hair above his ear.

"Tyrone here is a surgical resident from the University Medical School, a local boy who proves Valley State can produce more than famous NFL stars. He wants to be a trauma surgeon." Claiborne paused. "We have plenty of practice for him unfortunately."

"Pleased to meet you," I said.

"Likewise," the young man said.

"Dr. Stone wants to know if we can help him view some scans from back in California."

A smile broadened Freedman's face. "Of course we can."

"Tyrone's something of a computer genius," Claiborne said. "He was actually a programmer before premed."

Freedman nodded.

"Well, that's beyond this old country doctor," Claiborne said as he sidled his way out of the confined space. "Tyrone, you take good care of Dr. Stone so he'll have nice things to say about us when he gets back to Los Angeles."

Tyrone turned to me. "Okay, Dr.—"

"Please call me Brad."

The young man gave me an odd raised-eyebrow look, then nodded. "All right, uh, Brad. Let's get down to it. What site do we head to first?"

"Head to ConsciousnessStudies.org—three *s*'s in the middle—and click on the *private data* link."

Instants later, my Web site appeared. Tyrone brought up the account entry box when he clicked on the data link.

"My user name is *bstone*, password, *jambalaya*."

"Those are way too obvious," Tyrone said. "I mean, my apologies, but anybody who wants into your private data would be deterred by like . . . seconds."

"You're right," I said as the scan files began downloading.

"You want me to change it for you?"

"Let's wait."

Tyrone shook his head. "What do you want first, the MRIs, the PET, or the EEG?"

"Let's do the EEG."

"If you want privacy, I can show you what to do and leave."

I thought about this for a moment. "I can walk you through things if you're interested."

"Wow! Really?" He turned and looked up at me. The scar presented itself again. He caught my glance.

"Drive-by shooting," he said casually. "My own damn fault. I fell in with some older gang members, hacked bank accounts and school grades for them. When the police caught me, the trails all led to the gang. I needed to be zeroed out . . . fourteen years old and sitting on my uncle's front porch in Balance Due when it happened."

Balance Due had been the black section of Itta Bena. I had been a small child the last time I'd visited there, but I still remembered the smell of raw sewage, which raised sulfurous bubbles in the stagnant, scum-carpeted ditches alongside muddy, unpaved roads lined with weathered wood shacks, rusted corrugated metal roofs, and wood-fire smoke coming out of battered tin stovepipes.

"Killed my uncle and aunt," Tyrone said. "Left me with this souvenir." He swept his index finger casually across the scar. "Made me want to be a trauma surgeon."

"I thought drive-bys were a big-city thing."

He shook his head and returned to the keyboard and display, talking as he worked. "Every small town in the Delta has got its Crips and Bloods, or a bunch of drug-thug wannabes who are half as smart and twice as dangerous." He paused. "That's why I live way out in the country, at the end of a dirt road." He nodded to himself.

"What happened to the people who shot you?"

"Dead," Tyrone said without emotion. "They crossed somebody. Somebody zeroed them out. End of story."

An instant later, the EEG appeared on the screen.

"Okay, that's the new one," I said. "Can you display the reference file for comparison?"

An instant later, we had the two files on-screen.

"The reference EEG's been consistent for almost six years, consistent with a persistent vegetative state in this subject, a forty-four-year-old female suffering from profound brain damage resulting from a motor vehicle accident." It felt odd to describe Camilla in the dry, impersonal language of grand rounds, but it focused my objectivity and made me reach deeper for details than I might otherwise have.

"Okay, you can see the new EEG from yesterday differs significantly, indicating a substantial increase in higher brain function."

"How do you know it's higher brain function from looking at this and not brain stem or something else?"

"Good question." I traced the jagged-line patterns with the cursor. "Notice the P15 peak absent on one side and markedly prolonged in latency on the other." He nodded. "And here, BAEPs show neither wave IV nor V on either side."

"Meaning?"

"I have an idea, but let's see what the scans tell us," I said uneasily. An increase in higher brain might mean an end to her coma.

"Why would things be the same for six years, then suddenly change?" Tyrone asked. "I thought once you got this far into PVS, nothing ever improved."

I recalled my last conversation with Flowers.

"Well, the patient recently suffered from a severe, antibiotic-resistant bacterial infection resulting in temperature spikes over one hundred and five degrees. Sustained high fever can dramatically affect the brain."

Tyrone nodded. "PET or MRI now?"

"MRI."

I grew increasingly uncomfortable as we went through the MRI and, later, PET scans.

"It looks familiar, the pattern here," I told Freedman when we had gone over the scans for the third time.

When I finally recognized the pattern, the significance hit me like a hammer.

"Oh, Jesus," I whispered. Freedman turned in his chair, his face full of startled concern. I grabbed the back of the chair for support.

"Dr.—uh, Brad? You okay?"

I shook my head. Freedman got up quickly and helped me sag into his chair. We remained like that as I struggled to calm my breathing. Finally, I regained control, took a deep breath, and let it out slowly.

"Can you pull up the recent EEG and PET?"

"Sure." Freedman leaned over the keyboard and brought the scans on-screen.

"Here." I tapped at the monitor. "And here . . . while higher brain functions are increasing, there's no change in the activity of the lower brain and brain stem. Remember that MRI of the ventral part of the rostral pons?" As my horror grew, I struggled to keep my focus on presenting Camilla like a grand rounds patient.

"Uh-huh."

"Okay, now look over here, and there's clear evidence of recovery of higher brain function, especially in areas associated with awareness and consciousness."

"So this patient is coming out of the coma?"

"It appears so."

"Induced by the fever or the bacterial infection?"

I nodded dully at the implications.

"That's good."

"Maybe," I said.

Tyrone started to ask another question. I stopped him with a raised index finger as I grabbed my cell phone and hit Jeff Flowers's speed dial. I turned to Tyrone as the phone rang.

"The scan patterns are a variation on what is known as locked-in syndrome."

"Locked in?"

"Usually from auto accident trauma and strokes, sometimes by pontine lesions, which damage specific portions of the lower brain and brain stem while leaving little or no damage to the upper brain."

Flowers answered.

"Jeff, it's Brad Stone," I said urgently. "We may have a situation."

"Let me get to a place where I can talk," he replied.

As I waited, I pointed at the MRI image on the monitor display. "Look closely at this area and the pattern of hypodensity where the tissue has been destroyed. The pattern of damage leads to quadriplegia and, depending on the extent of damage, easily leads to death without artificial ventilation. This patient's death—ah, case, I mean—did not require ventilation, but all voluntary muscle function was lost as well as higher brain functions—until yesterday."

Flowers's voice came back on the line. "Sorry, Brad, I was in a staff meeting."

"Thanks for taking the call. Look, Jeff, I think we have a case of locked-in syndrome developing."

"Dear God."

"Yeah. Can you do some tests to make sure."

"Anything you need."

"Thanks. As you may remember, a lot, if not most, people with locked-in syndrome retain some small degree of voluntary control over eye movement or eyelid function. We know Camilla has had neither of those. We need to determine if that's changed. Additionally, we need a functional PET to determine if she's experiencing sensory perceptions—vision, hearing, touch—the whole gamut."

"Any specific tests or protocol?"

"You pick it. We need to know whether she is aware and conscious even if she is unable to communicate."

Flowers's breath caught, echoing my own of a few minutes ago. "I never imagined in my worst nightmare it could come to this."

"I know the feeling."

"Okay. I'm on it now. Should I call you back on your cell?"

"Uh-huh. And could you upload the new scans as soon as you can." I explained my ability to retrieve them. "If for some reason you can't get hold of me, you can call Dr. Tyrone Freedman here at Greenwood Hospital." I read the number and extension off the phone. Tyrone also offered his cell number, which I passed along before ringing off.

"This is really deep," Freedman said.

I turned slowly and looked up at Freedman. "People with locked-in syndrome usually retain their ability to see, hear, feel emotions, understand spoken language, analyze complex thoughts—everything cognitively and emotionally, but all the wiring to their muscles that allows them to interact with their environment doesn't work. I'm terrified this patient's consciousness has awakened inside a black void without sight, sound, or other senses, perhaps feeling pain without any ability to express the feeling or do anything to decrease it. Something like being buried alive, but without the compassion of death to look forward to."

"Oh, man." Freedman's voice was dull, flat, and low as the implications played across his face. "I imagine hell would be a lot like that."

He opened his mouth, but before he spoke, his pager went off. He plucked it off his belt.

"Oh, great," he said as he read the text message. "All hands on deck. We've got all our ambulances filled with incoming gunshot wounds, but we don't usually staff up until after it's dark."

He turned and headed for the far end of the narrow, cramped room.

"We can use all the help we can get," he said. "If you're up for it, follow me to the scrub room and I'll introduce you to the chief."

I rushed along behind him.

The wail of approaching sirens quickly disappeared beneath the urgent conversations in the scrub room. Freedman introduced me to trauma unit chief Clifford Scarborough, a tall, dark-haired man built like an NFL linebacker.

"I've read some of your stuff," Scarborough said as we soaped up to our elbows. "We're likely to have head wounds."

"I'm up for it."

"Good. It's been a bad day for serious trauma," Scarborough said. "Normally, we stabilize the most serious and chopper them down to University Med Center in Jackson, but the whole damn region's had rash of incidents. There's not a free helicopter available. You may need to do more than help me get these people ready to ship."

"Whatever I can do."

"Okay then, suit up." He pointed toward a pile of fresh folded scrubs.

I changed, and scrubbed at my hands, forearms, and elbows. I had my gloves on by the time the triage nurse stuck her head in and said she had two she thought were DOA and six more in a hurry to get there. I took a full-face splatter shield from the scrub room nurse and adjusted it to my head as I pushed through the double doors leading to the emergency room.

The corridor beyond was packed with police and paramedics. Along the wall, two young men lay on gurneys: tall, heavily muscled, and way too young to be so completely inert. Blood dripped significantly onto the tiled floor. Uniforms filled the corridor with a blue hover as police and EMTs in latex gloves moved among their charges, working to keep more life from leaking out and on guard for violence and escape.

The doors by the ambulance dock exploded inward with two more gurneys, followed by Jasmine in a white silk blouse blossoming red with fresh blood, which covered her face and arms and matted her hair.

Thirty-eight thousand feet over the unremarkable to-pography of South Dakota, Braxton's chartered 737 anonymously sketched contrails on a cornflower sky. In the front of the aircraft, tousled and rumpled re-porters slumped in the forward seats and spoke wearily among themselves. The predawn takeoff from Reagan National and the three lightning-quick campaign stops in Buffalo, Duluth, and Fargo had exacted their toll.

At the rear of the aircraft in the off-limits area outside the General's private compartment, Daniel Gabriel looked down at the towering storm clouds and chaffed at putting "retired" after the *lieutenant general* in his title.

He had devoted his life to the Army. His only marriage had lasted less than a year when his wife realized the military was a mistress with which she could not compete. Now, with his retirement papers grinding through the DOD bureaucracy, the change in his life gathered like the same thunderstorms assembling themselves over the prairie below.

"Retirement getting to you?" Gabriel turned as Braxton settled into a seat across the aisle. "Yes, it disturbed me as well, for months."

Gabriel felt half-dressed under Braxton's gaze.

"Yes, sir," Gabriel said. "That's most of it."

"I thought so." The General paused. "What's the rest of it?"

Gabriel looked back out the window for a thoughtful moment before returning his gaze to Braxton.

"When I was making some last rounds at the Pentagon, I paid a visit to Laura LaHaye."

"I know."

"Well, sir, I'm, uh"—Gabriel searched for the correct word—"not entirely comfortable with all the implications of the Enduring Valor project."

"What bothers you most?"

"The disclosure part, mostly, I suppose."

"Disclosure?"

"To the men. The soldiers." Gabriel searched Braxton's face for a clue, but found nothing there but encouragement. "Doesn't giving them medication without telling them leave us open to charges we're performing medical experiments on people without their informed consent?"

Braxton nodded slowly. "Dan, we have a life-and-death struggle to make sure our forces win every battle. If we had to have a public debate on every damned thing we do, getting a signed disclosure on every damn vitamin formula we hand out to the troops, we'd never get anything done, and whatever we accomplished would be out there for all our enemies to copy. Informed consent works fine for civilians, but when it comes to war, it would only cost the lives of a lot of brave men and women."

"But—"

"But nothing. Look, do you suppose we're telling everybody the nerve-gas antidotes we pass out contain a lot more than atropine? Or that MREs in a combat zone contain top-secret formulations designed to get the best possible performance from our boys? Which is why we don't sell those particular formulations to the public."

Gabriel nodded. "But I understand Enduring Valor has a history of side effects."

Braxton's face tightened for a single frame of reality, then smoothed out so fast Gabriel didn't really see it happen; it still made him anxious.

"Side effects?" Braxton said. "I can tell you about side effects." His hand traced the famous scar on his face. "Before God gave me this, artillery fire made me urinate on myself, son. But God struck me and changed me and left a mark telling others they can triumph over their shortcomings as well. Now *that's* a side effect of being wounded, and I am grateful for it every day I get up and look at myself in the mirror."

"But, sir—"

Braxton raised his hand. "Hold on. I'm taking you somewhere with this."

Gabriel nodded.

"Frank Harper saved my life twice," Braxton said. "First on the battlefield and later in a little clinic he set up in an old POW camp in the Godforsaken swamps of the Mississippi Delta. He took a look at me then, studied me along with others who had received head wounds of one sort or another. He helped me to understand what had happened to me and explained I had apparently received the perfect wound. I received a surgical incision so precise only the hand of God could have wielded the scalpel.

"Harper studied me and tried to perfect an operation on others with head wounds that could duplicate my success. Some got better, some worse, and most were unchanged."

"Harper's work?" Gabriel ventured. "Was this some sort of official military experiment?"

"Of course not!" Braxton shook his head. "It was *treatment*! A new treatment. As hard as he tried and as many operations as he performed, Harper and his team of crack brain surgeons could never duplicate with the scalpel what God had done for me with a twisted piece of metal."

The warrior who would be president leaned back and shook his head. Gabriel saw in his face the satisfaction of being the unique success.

"That's a side effect," Braxton said again. "Harper and his people had a lot better success with the new drugs. Those *treatments* eventually inaugurated what is, today, Enduring Valor."

Anxiety coiled tighter in Gabriel's chest.

"Yes, there have been undesirable side effects in Harper's work and in Enduring Valor," Braxton conceded. "Think of it as friendly fire of another stripe."

"Friendly fire."

"My Lai. Almost the right formula, wrong dose."

"You mean My Lai—"

Braxton nodded. "We never did get formula perfected in 'Nam. Fortunately the side effects looked similar enough to Agent Orange problems that it never got picked up."

"I'm not sure I want to know these things."

"It's time." Braxton looked up at the front of the aircraft to make sure the press remained obediently out of earshot. "Time to get your feet wet, soldier, wet with things you'll need to handle as SecDef."

Gabriel's anxiety gained new weight.

"Same thing with the new drugs we used in the first Gulf War," Braxton continued. "An almost perfect formula that did its job, but in a very small number of cases it caused permanent brain modifications, Gulf War syndrome, blamed it on accidental exposure to low levels of Iraqi nerve gas.

"We thought we had things worked out in Afghanistan."

Gabriel heard Braxton only distantly as his anxiety became the cuckold's shock and anger at proof of the betrayal.

"Then we had all those murders by troops who had returned from combat. Fortunately the test samples were small. But by then, LaHaye and McGovern had the right formula but realized the drug needed to be released in continuous, sustained concentrations to avoid complications. That's what our allies in Holland have perfected."

Gabriel let the drone of the aircraft wash through an emptiness in his soul he had not experienced since the death of his father.

"Son, war is for keeps," Braxton said as he laid a practiced hand on Gabriel's shoulder. "War is hell. People in American society can sustain their delicate ethical sensitivities only when people like you and me clearly grasp the reality of winning."

You and me. Gabriel thought about this. He recognized the horrors of war, and he certainly knew the arrogant hypocrisy of the antimilitary, anti-any-war people who were willing to take advantage of freedoms that could be maintained only by the very force and establishment they defamed and despised.

You and me.

Gabriel encountered a new line here and worried about stepping across. He wished Braxton had never told him about this. The knowledge burned like acid, ticked like a bomb.

You and me.

The General had made good points about necessity. War was a messy ethical morass that usually rewarded action over contemplation.

You and me.

Gabriel considered resigning. Walking away before he learned any more. But he had nowhere to go, no career, no job. He had left his wife— the Army—and he had nothing, no one to rely on. The press would also have a field day with the resignation. It was something he would never live down; he'd live the rest of his life in shame.

You and me.

Perhaps the General was right. He had seen a lot more action, had needed to make more tough decisions, and had more experience weighing them all. *You and me.*

Gabriel knew he had to cross the line with the General. It would just take some time to come to grips with this new reality.

Relief arced through me in a great electrifying wave when I realized the blood on Jasmine's white silk blouse had come from someone else.

Jasmine didn't see me at first, as I studied her holding the hand of a woman with a severe head wound lying on the gurney. From all the blood on Jasmine's blouse, it appeared to me she had cradled the wounded woman's head in her lap. My ears picked up the strong, calm tones of Jasmine's voice as she tried to reassure the woman on the gurney. The woman blinked her eyes and looked to Jasmine for strength.

More police and EMTs came through the double doors bringing more casualties. One casualty had both hands cuffed to the gurney and his feet bound with shackles. The echoes of too many excited voices jammed the corridor. I followed Claiborne and Tyrone Freedman as they headed for one of the young men dripping blood onto the floor. I pressed the thumb and middle finger of my right hand to his neck and found no pulse.

"Quiet!" Clifford Scarborough's deep, authoritative voice resonated in the corridor. "Heads up, people!" Talking ceased as if a switch had been flipped. A sucking chest wound filled the brief acoustic vacuum with ragged wet noises; the woman next to Jasmine groaned quietly.

Scarborough looked around and asked for a triage roll call along with an injury assessment from each of the medical personnel surrounding the wounded. The presentations were quick, concise, professional, and, sadly, reflected the extensive practice all the medical personnel had, even those not formally assigned to the emergency room. I did not remember Greenwood as being a dangerous place and wondered when it had become so.

There were seven cases in all. When it came time, Tyrone Freedman spoke for our patient. When Jasmine's eyes met mine, her jaw dropped and her gaze widened. I offered her my best smile.

Scarborough and the triage nurse then directed patients and trauma teams into treatment bays.

"Dr. Stone," Scarborough called. "I'd like very much if you'd take a look at the head wound in C-2."

I doubted "Good Samaritan" laws would protect me for treating this woman. I had no license to practice medicine in the state of Mississippi and knew the trial lawyers who had the entire country by the gonads would surely sue the hell out of me for the slightest and most irrelevant of provocations regardless of whether I was volunteering to save this woman's life or not.

But a life was in the balance here. I'd worry about the lawyers later.

"Yessir," I said.

Scarborough gave me a smile, then turned to a rotund woman with short brown hair. "Helen, please find another nurse and assist Dr. Stone."

"Right away." Helen pulled another woman over and wheeled the gurney into the treatment area. When a policeman tried to pry Jasmine away, the woman on the gurney launched into terrified hysterics. Scarborough shook his head at the cop, then nodded at Jasmine.

"Don't worry," Jasmine said as she bent over the woman's head. "I won't leave you." The wounded woman calmed immediately. "And don't you worry. The best brain surgeon on the planet is going to take care of you." Jasmine turned her head toward me and smiled.

Scarborough glanced at Jasmine, then gave me a questioning look. I shrugged as we all made our way into the treatment area proper. "What happened?" I asked Jasmine as we made our way into the treatment bay.

"Lashonna—" She looked down at the woman on the gurney. "Lashonna's my paralegal, my right hand, my right arm. She's my main contact with Talmadge's lawyer. The guy won't talk to anyone else." Jasmine stopped and fixed my eyes with hers. "We're sunk without her. Anyway, she was outside the office taking a cigarette break with the others when the shooting started." Jasmine's voice carried a case-hardened toughness.

". . . felt like a hammer," said Lashonna. Her voice slurred more than just moments before, and her gaze flickered like a bad television signal.

"Then I fell . . . hit head." She closed her eyes. I bent over and saw that above and to the right of her eye was a pronounced depression roughly shaped like an inverse pyramid.

"Did she hit her head on the corner of something?" I asked.

"Uh-huh. Brick planter."

"Nuts." I gently opened each of Lashonna's eyelids in turn and found her right pupil more dilated than the left.

"Okay, folks, let's get her relaxed and intubated," I said as I bent over Lashonna's head and moved her long hair around to get a look at her wounds. "Helen, what do you think about her weight?" The woman looked surprised to have someone ask her opinion.

"About fifty kilos."

I nodded. "What do you think about giving her about five milligrams of pancuronium for the endotrach and two milligrams of morphine sulfate in her IV?"

Helen smiled. "I'd say you were right on."

"Then let's do it."

She and the other nurse moved swiftly to sedate Lashonna.

While they prepared the anesthetics, I examined Lashonna and located a long, horizontal scalp laceration running through the hairline over her left eye and disappearing into a small, almost invisible hole above her ear. I felt Lashonna relax beneath my probing fingers as the drugs worked quickly. Jasmine stepped out of the way and stood with her back to the wall.

Helen announced that Lashonna's heart rate and blood pressure were steady; her breathing was steady. She was stable. For now.

When I looked up, Tyrone stood there with an endotracheal tube. "I came to watch the master work his magic," Tyrone said. "We called the other guy about a minute ago."

"I don't think you'll find any magic, but I'm happy to have help." I stepped back to let him do the work. "The gunshot was tangential and appears to have penetrated the cranial cavity. There is no exit wound."

Tyrone expertly worked the plastic airway tube into the woman's throat.

"Nice," I said quietly to him, then louder, "We'll need a CT to determine the extent of the projectile's damage, but I think the immediate issue is this parietotemporal injury." I looked at Tyrone, then pointed to the indentation in the woman's forehead. "Since her arrival, the patient has deteriorated from a group one prognosis to group two, which lowers her survival rate from about ninety percent to maybe sixty-six percent. I think her condition is clearly indicative of significant mesencephalic compression, likely from herniation of the ipsilateral uncus of the temporal lobe through the tentorium."

I looked at Tyrone. "Is there an OR ready?"

"All of them. Standard procedure for a big trauma call like this."

"Cool." I looked over at Helen. "Can we get a quick CT on the way to the OR?"

"Sure we can," Helen said. "I'll get her prepped and up there in a jiffy." She nodded toward the other nurse and set about shaving the area around Lashonna's wounds and painting everything with Betadine. The ominous wounds stood out.

I pointed at the slug's entry wound, then looked at Tyrone. "The problem with a tangential wound penetrating the cranium is that a slug with enough momentum will follow the interior wall of the cranial cavity, orbiting around inside, doing more damage as it goes."

Tyrone made a tsking sound as Helen unlocked the gurney wheels and pushed it toward the doors.

"Yeah." Tyrone and I followed the gurney. "But as bad as that is, I suspect the blunt trauma will be the one to watch."

"Brad?" I turned toward Jasmine. "Is she going to make it?"

I hesitated. "I'll do my best. I'll know better after we get the CT."

Jasmine nodded slowly as moisture gathered in her eyes.

I scurried to catch up with the gurney and followed it from CT scan to OR, where we first set about reversing the pyramidal depression above her eye.

"Okay, this is good," I said as I pulled the broken pieces of her cranium back from the wound. "See here: the dura is intact, and since the CT didn't show a significant herniation, we'll leave the skull pieces folded out and give the brain room to expand. Nothing more we can do for this wound but pray."

"Pray," Tyrone said. "That's a pretty odd thing for a surgeon to say."

I shrugged, then bent over to look closely at the bullet wound. I put my finger on the hole, then traced it back.

"Now, according to the CT, the slug'll be about here." I rested my index finger on Lashonna's shaved head. "Right here, a couple of centimeters down. We'll need to open her up along the entire path and debride the damaged tissue."

With Tyrone's assistance, I performed a circumferential craniotomy, which exposed a large, oval portion of Lashonna's brain along the bullet's trajectory.

"To start with, remove all the debris you can find here"—I traced a gloved finger along the slug's trajectory—"pulpified brain tissue, bone fragments, clots, and other crap." I looked over at Helen. "I need to irrigate the missile track with saline, something that'll sustain a moderate pressure."

"Will a squeeze bottle do?"

I nodded as I bent over and began to clean up the wound with a pair of forceps. When nurse Helen returned with the plastic squeeze bottle, I showed Tyrone how to use it to rinse out tissue as I debrided it.

"We want to debride all the necrotic tissue as well as about a half centimeter of healthy tissue around it. A bullet can contuse a substantial area around the path, and while it may look normal to us now, it could deteriorate and leave us with a problem on our hands later."

We worked methodically toward the slug.

"It's awesome," Tyrone said as he looked down at the surface of the brain beneath our hands. The blood vessels pulsed. "I mean . . . this is her, what makes her who she is."

I nodded and tried to suppress a smile.

"Do you still feel that? That . . . awe?"

"Every time I open up a skull."

"It never gets routine?"

"Some people get blasé about the time they start thinking they're God with a scalpel." I shook my head. "But it still gives me chills."

"No lie, man."

We worked silently for a long while. Cutting, trimming, washing, cleaning, as best our human hands could work, and yet at a cellular level, we were a crude, dull, chipped flint blade scraping through.

"How do you know what tissue *not* to take? How do you make sure you don't scrape away something she needs?"

"You don't. Just take all the dead stuff and a little around it. It's all you can do."

He paused to think for a moment. "You might be debriding a memory there, or the ability to do math or make an important decision."

"Right. Only sometimes I wonder if we're debriding the memory or just the ability to access it."

"What's the difference?"

"No practical difference. That's why I told you there wouldn't be any magic here. We're like a couple of Neanderthals looking at the insides of a supercomputer. We can't directly repair any of the trillions of synapses or rewire any of the live neurons to bypass the ones we had to remove. Even if we magically saw the connections, we're still screwed because all the synapses and neuron patterns are different for everyone, the product of genes, environment, education, experience. There are an infinite number of possible connections among a trillion cells. Only an infinite intellect could possibly know all the infinite permutations and combinations."

"God?"

"I believe so."

"Caveman."

"Uh-huh."

We worked steadily to the end of the bullet track.

"I need a pair of bayonet forceps, please."

Helen handed me the tool, and moments later I pulled the slug from Lashonna's brain. "We need to rinse and secure it for the police," I said. Helen held out a stainless steel kidney pan and I dropped it in and gave it a quick squirt from the saline bottle.

"We'll need a clear evidence trail, Helen. Let's make sure it doesn't leave your sight or mine until the police take possession."

We finished the debridement moments later.

"Okay, let's clean this up and cover the wounds with sterile dressings."

"You're going to leave the wounds open?" Tyrone asked.

"The brain is going to swell," I said. "If the tissue can expand out of the openings, there's less chance of intracranial pressure buildup." Tyrone nodded slowly. I looked at Helen.

"If we can't get a chopper, I think she should start to Jackson in an ambulance. One that can maintain a program of controlled hyperventilation to reduce the $PaCO_2$ to twenty-five to thirty torr. This should give us enough cerebral vasoconstriction to help reduce intracranial pressure. I'd also like you to start mannitol at half a gram per kilo and dexamethasone at point three. Make sure the ambulance crew has diazepam in case she has convulsions. Make up a couple of hypodermics for them ahead of time at point two grams per kilo."

"Right."

"Also, if you have fresh frozen plasma, send it along. It could help with thromboplastin releases."

"I'll check."

"Go ahead and do it now," I said. "We'll finish up while you handle the ambulance and the medications."

She headed for the door.

"The bullet?" I asked after her. She stopped. "Why not take it down to the police when you go?"

She nodded, then retrieved the crumbled mass of lead from the pan, dried it out on her scrubs, then tucked it in her pocket.

As she pushed through the stainless-steel OR doors, I looked back down at Lashonna's brain and knew then that the shooting had not merely been another routine drive-by but had been designed to look like it.

I felt old and in desperate need of sleep by the time Tyrone and I finished with Lashonna. What little sleep I had snatched between connecting flights on the red-eye from Los Angeles hadn't done much to erase the deficit I had been running since the sinking of the *Jambalaya*. The wound to my ear was minor,  but still it throbbed with every heartbeat, my lower back ached from standing over the operating table, and my feet slogged as if mired in the red, slickery goo of wet Yazoo clay.

Wordlessly, Tyrone and I ditched our gloves, masks, and splatter guards and followed Lashonna's gurney toward the ambulance dock. Outside, heat and humidity smothered us in a steaming blanket. Warm afternoon light painted the street with deep, oblique shadows. We crossed the concrete platform and made for the open doors of an ambulance, where Helen huddled with two EMTs.

Cigarette smoke carried the essence of burning horse manure from the backlit silhouettes of two uniformed police officers and a man in plainclothes to my right. Fear squirmed in my gut. Drive-by shooting investigators or LAPD? My hands turned cold and my heart warmed up for a race.

Jasmine stood upwind from the police, avoiding their smoke. Seeing her cleared my head, shook the mud off my feet, and leavened my fear. She waved at me, then detached herself from the smoking men.

A deep voice boomed behind me, "Nice work, Doctor!"

I turned as Clifford Scarborough ambled through the ER's double doors. He examined Lashonna on the gurney and inspected the dressings on her head.

"No doubt your fine work gives her the best possible chance," he said.

"Thank the whole team," I said, looking at Tyrone, Helen, and the nameless nurse who had assisted. I looked at Lashonna. "As you can see, there's a lot more for the folks in Jackson to do."

"Will she make it?" Jasmine's voice reached over my shoulder.

I turned toward her and squinted as the sun dazzled my eyes and bathed her face in shadows. Beyond her, the policemen took deep, terminal drags off their smokes, then tossed them on the platform. They ground the butts under their shoes and walked toward us. I wrestled with an irrational impulse to run and instead watched Jasmine go to Lashonna and place the tips of her middle fingers on the wounded young woman's forearm. With her head bent reverently, her face reflected a deep inner tincture of sorrow, fear, and concern. Jasmine looked like a Madonna urging a miracle to flow from her touch. Then she straightened up and looked at me.

"Is she going to make it?"

Fatigue lined Jasmine's face. Lashonna's blood had dried brown and puckered on her white silk blouse and trailed onto her dark skirt. It struck me then that Lashonna had also been dressed in a white blouse and dark skirt. The cops drew within earshot but without crowding our space.

"Well? Will she make it?"

"She could."

"Could?"

"I think she stands a good chance but—"

Jasmine's composure imploded. Her arms locked around me as she buried her face in the warm shelter of my right shoulder and sobbed quietly. I returned her embrace, patting her gently on the back.

The moment froze, statues caught in the uneasy creeping shadows of a hot Delta afternoon. Wet, heavy air pressed on us like a hand. After a respectful moment, Tyrone caught my eye. He pointed toward Lashonna. I nodded. When the gurney wheels rattled, Jasmine straightened up and stepped back half a step. She wiped at her face.

"Hold on a moment," I said to Jasmine. She raised her head and squared her shoulders.

As the EMTs secured the gurney and Lashonna's IV rack in the ambulance, I huddled with Tyrone, Helen, and Scarborough about the medications and the preparations in Jackson. When we finished, I eavesdropped as Tyrone and Helen briefed the ambulance crew. Jasmine took a last peek as the ambulance doors closed, then stood silently as the lights and sirens launched the big boxy truck off into the glare of the setting sun, where it turned left on Highway 82 and wailed its way toward Jackson. From the corner of my eye, I caught the tops of another thundercloud armada sailing our way.

With the ambulance gone, tension vanished like spit on a hot sidewalk. Scarborough shook my hand and left; Helen gave me her business card. The other nurse said she appreciated the recognition. Most of my fear evaporated as two of the cops made their way toward a Greenwood PD squad car.

"That was one helluva ride, man," Tyrone told me with wonder still in his eyes. "You may have just derailed my specialty."

"Think long and hard before you do that," I said.

He shook his head. "Today turned me around, man. You did." Sirens sounded in the distance. "Damn. Gotta get ready for the next wave."

I nodded as he shook my hand and rushed away.

"Dr. Stone?"

I turned toward a deep, resonant voice and found myself facing a lean, muscular man of medium height with café-au-lait skin and a tightly trimmed mustache. His uniform identified him as a deputy with the Leflore County Sheriff's Department, the three stripes on his sleeve indicated he was a sergeant, and his nameplate said he was John Myers. I feared LAPD had finally caught up with me.

Jasmine moved close.

"Sergeant," I said, extending my hand.

"Call me John," he said, accepting the handshake.

"John."

The deputy looked me over for a moment, sizing me up as cops did.

"How's the boy doing?" He nodded to the emergency room doors.

"The suspect?"

Myers shook his head. "Uh-uh. Tyrone. What do you think about him? You know, with your reputation and all? Has he got it?"

"Clearly."

Myers smiled broadly.

"John mentored Tyrone," Jasmine said. "Took him under his wing after all the trouble."

"Just tried to help the boy develop his God-given talent."

"John also arrested Darryl Talmadge," Jasmine said. "He thinks today is related."

"Don't forget that Lashonna wore clothes almost identical to yours? And her role on the Talmadge case?"

They nodded.

"Of course, Greenwood PD doesn't want any of that," John said.

"You got the shooter, right?" I asked. "The guy cuffed to the gurney?"

"One of 'em. But he ain't talking 'cause he's dead."

"Oh, boy."

"Uh-huh. Why don't you get some sleep and let's us all talk about Talmadge tomorrow."

"Thanks again, JM," Jasmine said.

"'S my job." He turned and headed toward his squad car.

My stomach loosed a kettledrum roll.

"We need to get you something to eat. There's a Sonic not too far away."

I'd been there, over on a busy commercial strip across the Yazoo, right after Mama's funeral. Sonic was a 1950s-theme drive-in with awnings and carhops to deliver your burgers.

"And we need to get you in some clothes that won't have the carhops dialing 911 when they see you."

She glanced down at the blood on her blouse as if she were seeing it for the first time.

"Good point."

We thought about that as shadows crept up the street from the superstructure of the old cottonseed-oil mill to the west. Beyond it, thunderheads tacked across the setting sun.

"Got it!" I said. "Follow me." I made my way to the emergency room doors, pushed one open for Jasmine, then followed her inside.

Ten minutes later, we reemerged in fresh, clean green scrubs. Jasmine carried her blood-soaked clothing in one of the ER's plastic personal-effects bags. I carried my shirt and slacks hung on a hanger along with a plastic bag containing my wallet, Palm, and the rest of the contents of my pockets.

"Now all you have to do is avoid requests for medical advice," I told her.

She gave me an easy laugh and a gentle touch on my shoulder. For as long as her fingers lingered against me, I forgot how tired and how old I felt.

Wasps the color of burnished cherrywood loitered among the Sonic's covered stalls. I pulled the pickup into the only empty space and let the engine idle in park while the wasps danced in quickening breezes that foretold evening thunder and rain.

"Wicked little creatures," Jasmine said.

I recalled the pain again as a squadron traversed the narrow space between my closed window and the ordering speaker.

We scanned the menu beyond the speaker, listening to the air-conditioning whirr.

"Number two, Diet Coke," Jasmine said.

I waited for the wasps to clear, but as soon as I rolled the window down, they seemed to gather. I swatted at them, hastily ordered two number twos with diet Cokes, then rolled the window up. A wasp darted for the last bit of opening. The glass crushed it into the window channel, leaving the long, dangling legs to spasm outside.

"They don't give up, do they?" Jasmine said.

"Evolutionary fitness."

"Word." She paused. "You acquitted yourself well back there." She nodded vaguely in the direction of the hospital.

I shrugged. "Just trying to help."

"No. Not just that." She chewed on a corner of her lower lip and gazed past me in thought. "You were so calm; you had a presence in the middle of the chaos, like you've done this before." When she looked at me, her eyes made me believe they saw into my heart, and I knew I would not, could not, lie to her.

"That's what I did before I became a neurosurgeon."

She looked expectantly at me.

"Another time?" I asked. "It's a long story. I'd rather not talk about it right now."

"Sure."

Disappointment shadowed her voice and raised a guilty burn in my chest. I badly wanted to make her feel good.

"I'm tired," I tried to explain, but my words fell lamely even on my ears. "The whole story takes energy, and I'd like to spend what I have left to figure out what's happening to you."

"Us."

Us created a personal proximity filling me with a boiling emotional gumbo of guilt, fear, fatigue, and frustration.

"Uhm . . . so do *you* really think I was the real target today instead of Lashonna?"

"It has a certain amount of logic," I said slowly. "But please realize she's a logical target because of the work she's doing for you."

Without preamble, Jasmine burst into tears and covered her face with her hands. "I killed her," she sobbed. "I should have done everything by myself like Mom."

"She could make it."

"Could, could . . . if it weren't for me—damn!"

Her tears felt so out of character for the rock-solid, nerves-of-steel woman I had seen to this point. Jasmine wedged herself into a knot, back against the door. I wanted to reach over and comfort her, but sat helplessly in my seat instead.

I tried to give her some privacy by pointedly looking out my side window, but I could not look away for long. I watched her so closely I could almost see her picking up the scattered bricks of her shattered composure and fixing them solidly back into place. In the compressed space of those few moments, she recomposed herself, wiping finally at her eyes with the floppy sleeve of the surgical scrubs. I looked quickly away before she caught me.

Then, from behind us, gangsta rap lyrics spilled out of a mid-1970s Chevy Monte Carlo loud enough to vibrate the pickup's seats and force the lyrics on us whether we wanted them or not.

I just wanna fuck bad bitches . . .

"Charming," Jasmine said darkly as anger took away her tears.

Chicken-head, chicken-fed, with a dick in your mouth . . .

She shook her head. "Dr. Dre." She shook her head. "All women are bitches and whores, lower forms of life to be raped, beaten, and abused."

I had never paid any attention to rap lyrics before. The heat of Jasmine's reaction took me by suprise.

"All testosterone and no impulse control," Jasmine said after a while. "Hip-hop's about young men not stopping to think about consequences.

When society says this music is okay with all the violence, the crime, sex as brutality, then that says, 'This stuff about rape and murder is okay. Listen to it; sing it; act it out.'" She shook her head ruefully. "Then they wring their hands and wonder why violence is so rampant."

The volume faded as the Monte Carlo reached Park Street and turned right.

"So. What the *hell* do we do next?" Jasmine asked.

"Hell if I know," I said. "Things are a lot more complicated than we thought twenty-four hours ago."

"Hard to believe."

A tapping on my window startled me. I turned to see the carhop with our food standing outside warding off wasps with a rolled-up newspaper. I rolled down the window, pulled in the food, and rolled up the window before the wasps zeroed in on us. The aroma made my mouth water.

"Vince Sloane said this morning that I'm the LAPD's main suspect," I said as I handed Jasmine her burger, drink, and fries.

"What? How could they even think that?" She placed her meal on the opened glove-compartment door. I used the center console and cup holder.

"Lack of imagination for one thing." Between bites, I told Jasmine everything.

"Well, judging from the reactions of JM and the cops from Greenwood PD, it doesn't look like they've gotten any word from L.A.," she said.

"Not yet, but I think it gets a lot worse."

Jasmine frowned.

"I spoke with Rex on the drive up and he tells me the military's asking questions."

"Why would the military . . ." She paused for a moment as her mind assembled the pieces. "Okay, first we have Darryl Talmadge held in a military hospital—the VA—in Jackson. Then we have the supposedly mistaken attack on your boat." She searched my face and found confirmation. "Finally, I suppose we should factor in your military service."

She looked at me expectantly. "I miss anything?"

"Nope. Which is not to say I haven't missed some important connection myself." I sipped at the diet Coke. "But in the place we're living now, what you don't know can kill you."

"That's encouraging," she said darkly, and turned to her half-eaten burger.

I attacked my own food as well. We sat there silently, chewing on food and on the facts as we had them.

"It makes me very, very uncomfortable to point fingers at the military," I said finally. "I owe my life and my career to the military, and this country owes its very survival and success to people who risk their lives for us."

"Like you did."

I shrugged. "I did my job."

"You did and so do lots of other good soldiers. But you know as well as I do there are a few power-hungry people in the military who will do anything for their own personal agendas. They'll destroy you—or Darryl Talmadge—if it gets them what they want."

"You're too right," I said. "But the military's got too many powerful enemies who think we can love our enemies into submission."

"Well"—Jasmine's face subtly reflected the parade of thoughts behind her eyes—"solving that won't help us much."

I pulled the straw out of my soft-drink cup and drained the last of the cola.

"Absolutely right," I said finally. "That's not our mission. Not right now."

"So what is the mission?"

"Staying alive's number one." I finished off my fries and thought about repeating the entire order.

"Here. Have mine." Jasmine handed me her mostly untouched fries.

"Thanks."

"Keeping you out of jail's a top priority too," she said. "We'll never get to the bottom of this without you." Jasmine shook her head. "I can't believe they'd suspect you."

"Look, given the circumstances, *I'd* suspect me if I was in charge of the investigation." I tried to laugh, but the attempt fell flat on my ears.

"It's all about Talmadge," Jasmine said. "On the flight back I had more time to study the information on the SD memory chip Mom got to you."

"And?"

"In addition to the stuff about Braxton, Talmadge's attorney says Talmadge acted on Army orders, and the man he killed had escaped from the same secret military medical-experiment program that treated Braxton."

"Sounds like the tactics of a desperate defense attorney," I said.

"Without the events of the past few days, I might agree. But Shanker's an honest man. I do believe he has a trove of documents to trade us."

"What's he asking in return?"

"You."

"Me?"

"If Mom got you on Talmadge's defense team for the appeal, Shanker promised to turn over the microfilm."

"Why me?"

"You've got a certain reputation." Jasmine smiled broadly. "You've gotten a lot of headlines as a guy at the top of neuroscience."

"But there are a lot—"

"And as a guy with gold-standard military service, you have the credibility to take on the defense establishment."

"Hmph," I grunted. "I may have had my problems with the bureaucracy, but I'm hardly an antimilitary tool of the flaky left."

"No kidding." She paused for effect. "Which means what you say carries water."

"Meaning we have to connect with Shanker stat."

"Lashonna—" Jasmine's voice cracked. "Lashonna met with him yesterday."

"She write anything down?"

"I don't know. I hadn't really talked with her since getting back from L.A. We planned to do that after her smoke break. In fact, I had promised to go outside with her, but the wind was swirling from every direction and I couldn't find any place to stand without breathing in the smoke. I'd gone inside a few seconds before the shooting."

"Which means you were a target too."

"Yeah."

"Okay," I said. "Where do we go? There's obviously Shanker. And John Myers. Two solid places to start." I turned my head to follow the source of a siren and watched an ambulance wail by out on Park Avenue. Distant lightning flashes illuminated vast cliffs of approaching thunderheads.

"Do the court records have anything helpful?" I said as the siren faded. "You know, autopsy report, interviews, etc.?"

"Sealed," Jasmine said. "Homeland defense. National security."

My cell phone filled the cab with Robert Johnson.

" 'Crossroad Blues.' " Jasmine smiled. "Sweet."

I checked the incoming number and recognized Flowers's cell.

"Hey, Jeff," I said.

"Brad, it's bad. Horrible," Flowers said. "All of Camilla's scans and the other exams are fully consistent with locked-in syndrome; there's absolutely no doubt about it. Her fPETs indicate a virtual typhoon of metabolic activity in the areas we associate with consciousness."

"Oh, God."

An fPET—functional positron-emission tomography—a new method I had helped pioneer—was a method for real-time observation of the brain's metabolic activity.

Jasmine gave me a concerned look of curiosity as I spoke with Flowers.

"You're sure there's a total disconnect? Not a finger or an eyelid, no connection to the outside world."

"Nothing. Absolutely nothing," Flowers replied. "I've FTPed the latest scans up for you, but I think it's pretty clear that Camilla's regained consciousness but she's totally locked in . . . her mind is in hell, Brad. She's in hell."

"She's in hell."

Flowers's words hit me like a chain-mail fist.

"Oh, man." I rested my forehead on the steering wheel.

"I've never seen anything like it," Flowers said.

I sat up and shouldered my way through the darkness. "We have to do something."

"I recommend anesthesia," Flowers said. "A Hameroff thing."

"Makes sense." Anesthesiologist Stuart Hameroff and cosmologist Roger Penrose theorized that consciousness arose from the quantum mechanisms of microtubules inside the brain's neurons. Other research showed anesthesia terminates consciousness by binding to specific proteins on those microtubules. Did this mean consciousness really terminates under anesthesia, or do our brains just fail to record the memories? If we die under anesthesia, does consciousness rekindle itself?

"It's a delicate balance," I said finally. "Enough to suppress consciousness without affecting vital functions."

"I've thought about that."

An off tone laced Flowers's words, and I wondered if he planned "accidentally" to take her over the edge with the anesthesia. I thought to tell him to be careful, not to take her over the edge.

The cell connection crackled and faded beneath my silence.

"Go ahead," I said, and tried not to feel the guilt and relief cutting at me.

"You're dropping out."

"I'm going to call my attorney to determine if we can legally terminate life support."

The connection crackled. I think Flowers understood me because his voice came through strong and clear when he said, "I can't understand a word you're saying."

Then he hung up.

I thought about this for a moment, then pressed the "end" button.

"Camilla," I said. "She's regained consciousness deep in the recesses of her brain." As I explained locked-in-syndrome to her, Jasmine's face passed through confusion, understanding, horror, and finally sorrow.

"She can't communicate," I reiterated. "Not a finger, not an eyelid. If she's uncomfortable or in pain or afraid, we have no way of knowing. There's no indication anything we say or do can get to her either."

"That's . . . like a recurring nightmare I've had all my life," Jasmine said. "I'm walking along and everything is fine, then suddenly I'm flying through a black void where I can't see anything and I can't smell or touch. The void's filled with an evil laughter I don't really hear but feel in my mind, and there's a horrible"—she struggled for a word—"horrible groping. Like an unseen hand reaching inside my body which's no longer there, but the hand rips everything out and squeezes me, hurts my soul." A small shiver animated her shoulders. "It takes the most effort I can muster, but eventually I wake myself up."

She looked at me and eventually the sorrow settled in her eyes. "Camilla can't wake up, can she?" The terrible realization blossomed in Jasmine's eyes. "Or finally go to sleep."

"Not without our help."

"A fate worse than death."

"There is something I can do." I flipped open my cell phone, hit the speed dial for my attorney. "We've got to get the court to approve ending life support." The receptionist recognized my voice when she answered and connected me immediately.

"Jesus, Brad! Where the hell are you?"

"I'm pleased to talk to you too."

"What have you gotten yourself into? I've got enough subpoenas and search warrants to wallpaper my office. LAPD's got people sifting through your house and your office and your lab. And I just met with a real prick, a tight-assed colonel who tried to muscle me around. And he's in addition to the Feds."

"Oh, man."

"Don't freaking 'oh man' me, Brad. What the hell is up? They all want to know where you are and so do I."

I thought of the police, the military, the Patriot Act, and wiretaps, which is when I ended the call.

"We've gotta move," I said as I released the parking brake and put the truck in reverse.

"What now?"

I concentrated on backing the truck out into the narrow space. "If they're searching my home and office, and they have all these subpoenas and warrants, then it's only a matter of not much time before it leads here. I'm in a box and it looks like the only way out is through Talmadge."

"What are you going to do?"

"Get my stuff out of the hotel and disappear. I used credit cards for the truck and room. They don't have to look far for me. I know enough about police and military to give us a fighting chance." I paused to think. "Do you have a gun?"

Jasmine gave me a condescending glare as she pulled a snub-nosed revolver out of her handbag. She unsnapped the hammer strap of a black nylon clip-on holster and produced a Ruger Speed Six .357 magnum revolver with the short, 2¾" barrel.

"That's a serious piece."

"Look, I'm a black civil—"

"—rights lawyer in Mississippi," I finished her sentence for her, and we laughed. Then she surprised me by pulling out two speed loaders filled with six rounds each. I whistled softly as I backed the truck out of the stall and made a right-hand turn onto Park. From the corner of my eye, I saw her slide the revolver back into the clip holster, snap the strap, and put it back in her purse.

"I don't suppose you have another one of those?" I asked as we slowed for the light at Grand Avenue.

"Lashonna has one exactly like this." Her voice caught for a beat. "I bought it for her; it should be in her purse at the office."

"Mind if we go get it?"

"Sure." The light changed and I turned right on Grand, a lush boulevard lined with large expensive mansions elegantly lighted to show off their pricey landscaping and architecture. This was still an all-white part of town.

We rode past the grandeur in silence as I tried to sort out the thoughts that would keep us alive and discard those that would surely get us killed. Jasmine had obviously tuned in to this process because she sat there, looking straight ahead, absorbed with her own thoughts. An idea came to me as we came off the Keesler bridge where Grand turned into Fulton. I slowed for the red light.

"Can we use your car?" I asked. "They'll be looking for this truck."

"I'm driving Mom's big red Mercedes; that's not much better."

"It is for now."

"It's in the hospital parking lot."

I turned right on West Washington.

Just off Fulton Street and immediately south of the Keesler Bridge, the Leflore County Courthouse is a grand piece of old architecture surrounded by magnolia trees and the ghosts of racial injustice meted out before the shift of power brought by the civil rights movement of the 1960s.

It still houses the sheriff's department and the jail, which gives the building and parking lot a 24/7 buzz of activity that does little to suppress the drug dealing and companion violence plaguing the mostly black city beyond.

On this evening, two dark, unmarked federal government sedans sat among the sheriff's cruisers, their engines ticking away the heat of their swift journeys, one from Jackson, the other from Memphis. The highway patrol cars that had accompanied them on their high-speed trips on I-55 sat nearby next to the personal vehicles of the sheriff himself and the chief of the Greenwood Police Department.

The occupants of those vehicles and a host of others jammed a third-floor conference room. A tall, lean federal agent with close-cropped, gunmetal-gray hair and a thin, red birthmark slashing into the hairline on the left side of his forehead addressed the group. He wore pinstripes with knife-sharp creases, an immaculately knotted red power tie. He had declined to tell the gathering much at all about his position or precisely whom he worked for, only that he had been sent by Homeland Security.

John Myers stood in the back of the room next to the sheriff, a fit, linebacker-like man with "high-yellow" skin and deep freckles that took an edge off the menace of his otherwise impressive presence.

"Check out how the Fibbies and the brass from the Pentagon defer to him," the sheriff whispered to Myers.

"Doesn't bode well."

"We should have a tactical unit in place by noon," said the man from Homeland Security. "If any of your personnel make contact with this man, do not—repeat *do not*—take any action whatsoever. Bradford Stone is a deadly capable man and has shown his ability by killing at least seven people in the past forty-eight hours, six of them highly trained Special Forces members, and one man from his own search-and-rescue team.

"This is the cover legend you need to remember: Stone was involved in a drug-smuggling operation with a vicious cartel headquartered in Guadalajara. Our personnel attempted to apprehend him and he killed them all. We do not want a general alert. We will not be issuing mug shots, and our operation here should be restricted to the personnel in this room. We will take all the risk."

Myers raised his hand. "Sir?"

The man from Homeland Security frowned at the interruption. "Yes?"

"As you know, I talked to this man not two hours ago. He'd just saved the life of a gunshot victim and appeared pretty normal."

The man from Homeland Security smiled indulgently. "Yes, Stone can seem normal. But we believe he's cracked after six years of dealing with his wife's injury and coma. He's like a serial killer, only he's a serial thriller. The rush from the danger associated with the drug running gives him a release allowing him to lead a normal life. Until it builds up."

He looked around the room, tried to meet every set of eyes, then focused on Myers.

"Does that make better sense, Sergeant?"

Myers glanced at the sheriff, who raised a skeptical eyebrow only his subordinate could see. Myers put on the "Yassuh, Mr. White Man" mask he had perfected as a young child, looked at the man from Homeland Security, and lied.

"Yes."

Cedric Valentine eased his bronze Monte Carlo to an industrial-park turnout along southbound Highway 49 north of the Rising Sun crossroads and cranked up the volume on Dr. Dre's "Some L.A. Niggas" and sang along with lyrics he knew by heart.

L.A. niggaz rule the world nigga! . . .

He'd been to Compton once, a visit with his uncle two summers before, and hung with some Bloods. They'd sold him a Glock 9 one of them said he'd taken right out of the dying hand of a pig he'd shot while the sucker sat in his black-and-white on Slauson.

He remembered driving through South Central and using the Glock packed with hollow-points to peel the cap off a Rolling 60s ricket. The rush still stirred him when he remembered how the Crip's brains came out the holes in a reddish gray splatter all over the concrete wall behind him. "Yeah!" he yelled to the world. "We L.A. niggaz rule! Fuck all the fuckin' muth'fuckers!"

They called him Dr. Glock after that. He made damn sho' the pissant niggas in Snowden-Jones called him Dr. Glock and not some small-town country-nigga name like Cedric.

He felt a passing flash of guilt when he remembered how it hurt his mama to dump the name she'd given him and how she was always on the rag about him being a player, a baller. Always after him to go to bed at nine, get one of those minimum-wage jobs working for some cracker, go to church, listen to her damned gospel music. She wanted him to rot out from the inside like a fucking Tom, like his uncle—her brother—who lived in Long Beach and spent his life sweating all week for less than an average day's worth of dealing crystal.

"Yassuh! Nosuh! I be fetchin' fo' Mr. Charlie—fuck that!" he said loudly. "Not this nigga!" Cedric shook off the guilt and thumbed the electric controls on his seat. He manipulated himself upright, readjusted the rearview mirror, rolled up the windows, and hit the toggles that adjusted the suspension lifters, raising the chassis now into what he called "country nigrah" mode. It was better for the rougher roads and made him less of a target for the country Jakes and Penelopes. Tonight, he needed to be invisible. First the TEC-9. Then the money. Then the bitch.

He'd bought the TEC-9 off the street in Memphis for the occasion, right after he'd sealed the deal with the bitch with the bucks.

I seal da deal, wid the bitch wid the bucks,
you respect this niggah or you shit outta luck

Cedric tapped on the steering wheel as he rhymed.

This playah gonna take what rightfully mine,
When I start kissin' you wid my Glock and da Nine

He had to remember that because bitches liked gangstas who could rap.

He ejected the Dr. Dre CD and slipped in Snoop Dogg. While the CD player searched for the first track, Cedric put the Monte Carlo into drive and pulled carefully into traffic. He didn't need no Jakes pulling him over for some traffic violation. Not far south of Rising Sun, he turned west toward Quito, across the Yazoo River bridge, and left on a gravel road. He didn't like the dust and the stones chipping his paint, but work was work, and when your work was killin', you needed to do things right and that meant no witnesses.

The "Down 4 My Niggas" cut on the Snoop Dogg CD started. This was the one with C-Murder rappin' wid the Dogg.

Fuck them other niggas, I ride for my niggas, what
I die for my niggas, fuck them other niggas, what

Cedric rapped with the lyrics as he drove roughly southwest toward a tall fucking bridge in the middle of nofuckingwhere where he could ditch the Nine.

"Tha's me, motherfuckuhs," he said. "I'm a nigga with the big balls. I'ma put my fucking name on the wall wid my Dogg! I'ma pound those bitches till they can't even crawl!"

When he crested the top of the bridge northwest of Tchula, he knew he had the right spot. Snoop Dogg was singing about niggas who run but they couldn't hide.

When Cedric slowed to a stop at the top of the bridge, he pulled on a latex glove, reached under the seat for the TEC-9. Not a headlight in sight. He opened the window and let in a stiff, cool wind smelling of approaching rain, maybe hail and a tornado. He tossed the gun over the railing, then drove on into Tchula and back up 49, where he stopped short of the 82 overpass to adjust his seat and lower the suspension. He got out, squinting against the wind as he walked around the Monte Carlo with a flashlight. Satisfied no damage had been done by the gravel, he opened the trunk and grabbed the shoe box his Clarks had come in. He opened the lid and smiled at the stack of hundred-dollar bills rubber-banded together in the trunk. Half a stack, actually. The bitch had cut ten g's worth of C-notes, an even hundred of them, right in half. Federal-fucking-Expressed them to him in a box that arrived at his crib a week to the day after he'd made bail over the drive-by on West Gibbs Street. Wrapped around the money had been a printout of the article about his arrest printed off the *Greenwood Commonwealth*'s Web site.

Cedric smiled now and enjoyed the glow in his belly. He was a true gangsta, famous enough that some woman he had never seen had sent him money to kill for her. She'd called his cell exactly one time to make sure he had the money and understood what to do and when. She told him he'd get the other half of the stack of bills when the two Oreo bitch shysters were in the ground. He'd peeled the cap off one of the bitches so he figured he'd get half the bills tonight and the other half when he took care of the unfinished business. He nodded as he reached under the spare tire and pulled out the Glock.

Back behind the wheel, he looked at the Rolex on his wrist.

"Time to get yo swerve on, Dr. Glock," he said to himself as he went down his checklist: Roly-O, Clarks, bling-bling, and the iced Crissy in back for the bitch. He'd never seen her, but her voice on the phone call gave him some serious bone and he wanted skully from the bitch.

"My dick be stuck up in yo' windpipe," he said. "I be stickin' it up in yo' pie too, bitch."

He merged onto east 82. Just outside of town, he spotted the turnoff they'd agreed on. Cedric pulled to a stop on the road shoulder, waited until there were no headlights from either direction, then made the turn. A hundred yards down, he stopped the Monte Carlo, killed the ignition and stereo, grabbed the Glock, and waited.

Lightning snapped around him and reminded him of the Jakes' helicopter lights. He hoped the bitch would show up before the fucking rain turned the road into fucking gumbo. Cedric thought about pumping the bitch. She was a white bitch, no doubt from her voice, and she sounded snotty and highfalutin. She needed to be fucked within an inch of her life, and he'd be the man to do it. He rubbed at the growing stiffness in his crotch.

Cedric went limp a second later when the cold steel of a gun muzzle pressed behind his left ear.

"Don't move." The woman's voice carried an edge that made him want to wet his pants.

Bitch. Cedric struggled to control his bladder.

"You disappointed me. Jasmine Thompson doesn't have a scratch on her and the other one could live."

Lightning flashed again; thunder came almost immediately.

Warm urine spread across his lap. He'd get the bitch for this.

"You had promise," the woman said. "I could have used you for a long time, paid you big money." She paused. "But no."

He opened his mouth to plead for another chance, then an intense, bright pain filled his head like the flash-bang grenades the cops used. In an instant he knew it was more than mere lightning and thunder.

The thug known as Dr. Glock managed a single last thought and a single last word: "Mama."

Giant balls of rain the size of marbles filled the night as the man-boy who called himself Dr. Glock slumped across the seat. Jael St. Clair emptied the magazine into his head, then made her way to the Monte Carlo's trunk, grabbed Cedric's half of the hundred-dollar bills, and got back in her SUV.

Her cell phone trilled as she turned on the ignition, flicked the wipers on high, and put the SUV in gear. She grabbed the phone and saw it was General Braxton.

"Sir."

"We have a change of plans," Braxton said without preamble. "Stone's beyond redemption. It would be best if you eliminated him and the lawyer immediately."

"Sir!" A long pause crackled softly in the earpiece.

"Sergeant?"

Jael felt her heart catch. The General rarely used her rank.

"This is a mission of vital importance. Until now, your rules of engagement required you to operate via stealth, through other people, and in a manner that minimized the danger to yourself or the chances of being detected."

"Sir," she acknowledged, knowing what was coming.

"Those rules have changed. Use whatever means are necessary to make sure Brad Stone and Jasmine Thompson do not live to enjoy another sunset. Regardless of the risk, regardless of costs."

"Sir."

"Thank you. Go with God." The General ended the connection.

Jael hit the "end" button on her phone. It wasn't the first time the General had given her a suicide mission she had lived to talk about.

By the time Jasmine and I reached my hotel, the night had filled up with rain, thunder, and lightning. An opaque downpour splashed like milk beyond the headlights. The radio announced that tornadoes had hit near Black Bayou.

"Try next to the stairwell." I pointed.

Lightning continued its wicked barrage, followed closely by deep, rolling thunder that stirred memories of night combat. Then came hail the size of cottonseeds, drumming a high-pitched fusillade on the roof as Jasmine backed the Mercedes into a parking space and turned out the headlights.

"Okay, keep the engine on and your eyes open," I said. "I'll be quick."

"You're sure you don't need help?"

"Positive."

Jasmine's face glowed beautiful and strong in the instrument panel's soft light. "If the police show up, ditch your gun and pull out nice and slow like you were just leaving anyway."

"But—"

"No sense both of us getting nailed."

With Lashonna's Ruger in one hand, I started to open the door, then froze as a white Ford Excursion drove into the lot, then continued on to the back corner and parked near the white fiber-optic contractor vans. Moments later the lights flickered off. We waited. Jasmine held her own Ruger in her lap.

From an inside pocket of her big handbag, Jael St. Clair retrieved a thin, paper-sealed packet the size of a large commemorative postage stamp the General's company kept sending her since the head wound in Afghanistan. She peeled off the protective plastic-lined paper wrapper, pulled out a patch resembling a Band-Aid, removed the strips covering the adhesive, and pressed it on the bare skin below her left collarbone.

Then she pressed the electric release for the SUV's rear door and climbed across the backseat into a cargo area half-filled with luggage. Her heart rate steadied and slowed as the warm surge of confidence radiated from the patch, focused her thoughts, and sharpened her senses. Jael located the duffel she had requested with the car. Fumbling in the dark, her practiced hands soon found the familiar shape of a night-vision monocular. Jael smiled when she pulled it out, held it close to her face, and in the dim illumination from the parking lot lights recognized the Night Quest PVS-14. One of the best third-generation devices, weather resistant and highly versatile.

She turned on the Night Quest, held it up to her right eye, and adjusted the gain to accommodate the lights from the parking lot and those illuminating the walkways.

Despite the downpour, the scene around her took on an eerie green clarity, allowing her to see the lawyer sitting in her car talking with Stone.

She put down the Night Quest, located two long, hard-sided gun cases. The first contained an M21 7.62mm NATO sniper's rifle with a Raptor 4x night-vision optical sight nestled in the custom-fitting gray foam.

"Shit."

The second case housed another M21. Jael had specified the M25 and hated to compromise. But having to shoot with someone else's zero bothered her most.

"Play the hand," she said to herself, then pulled a Sionics suppressor from its case and attached it to the muzzle. St. Clair took a moment to check on the red Mercedes with the Night Quest monocular and saw Stone still talking with the lawyer.

She grabbed a twenty-round clip from the duffel and a box of ammunition, noting the rounds were standard M118 Special Ball 173-grain, full-metal-jacket, boat-tailed slugs. She preferred hollow-points for maximum damage over these shorter distances, but she knew the M118 well and had thirty-seven kills with it. She filled the clip, slid it in, and chambered a round, and then the overhead light of the Mercedes went on. Jael picked up the Night Quest monocular and followed Brad Stone as he disappeared up the stairwell.

"Showtime," Jael said softly as she leaned back and pushed the SUV's rear window open. It swung up, and the storm came in. She retreated to the area right behind the rear seat, where she was sheltered from the windblown rain, but where, lying on her side, she could still get a clear shot at the door of Brad Stone's room. She placed her large, folding luggage bag on top of the duffel, pressed everything down into a stable platform for the M21, and finally arranged herself behind it. Not ideal, but she had less than fifty yards for this shot. A piece of cake considering that with an M21 and this ammunition she had never missed a kill at less than eleven hundred yards.

"If anything strange happens, call my cell. It's on vibrate. Make sure yours is too." I kept my eyes on the SUV.

"Already did," Jasmine said.

I looked over toward the white SUV. "Watch that one. Something about it bothers me." I put the Ruger back in its holster and clipped it as best I could to the drawstring waist of my scrubs pants.

"Why?"

"It's way across the lot; they'll get wet heading for their room." I paused. "On the other hand maybe the fiber-optic people all have to park there."

I got out then and dived through the solid sheets of rain, sprinting up the steps two by two through the driving sleet and rain. When I got to my room, light was leaking around the curtain edges from the lamp I had left on so my alarm warning would be visible.

"Shit." The light would make me a perfectly silhouetted target going in.

Jael tracked Stone with the Night Quest monocular as he exited the stairwell. Next, she set down the monocular, picked up the M21, turned on the Raptor, and rested the rifle on the makeshift stand and trained the crosshairs in the middle of Stone's door, right where she figured he'd stand when he put his key card in the slot.

Right on cue the big man appeared in her scope and stopped by the door. But instead of standing in front of the door to put in the key as she expected, he stood to one side and extended his left hand with the card.

Smart, she thought. Avoid being silhouetted by the room lights. Not smart enough for me, she thought as she moved the crosshairs to the right. Then she took a regular breath and exhaled normally, stopping at her usual respiratory pause. She made sure the crosshairs were where she wanted them, then squeezed the trigger ever so gently to take up the free play in the trigger.

What the hell?

Jasmine tightened her grip on the Ruger as she watched the rear window of the white SUV swing gracefully up. This is too strange. She grabbed the Ruger and slipped into the passenger seat. When she started to get out, the night exploded like a bomb.

Lightning lit up the night brighter than day. Reflexively, I dropped into a low crouch, transfixed by a broad arcing river system of electric blue tendrils reaching down. Thunder crackled, then a light stanchion in the newspaper parking lot about fifty yards to the east exploded, sending off flares like white phosphorous.

The rest of the parking lot lights went dark. The air-conditioning in my room faltered, then resumed. I lunged forward then, hoping anyone who might be watching was momentarily blinded and startled by the crash. I put my card in the door lock and got only a red light. I prayed the computer in the front office that controlled the lock had not been fried by the lightning surge.

Damn.

The curse came calmly and quietly as Jael St. Clair continued to follow through with her shot. She held her breath, and the trigger steady, focusing on the crosshairs and spotting the pockmark in the wood siding right where Brad Stone's heart would have been had it not been for the lightning. Never rush a round, she thought as she slowly released her breath and her trigger finger. An indicator light blinked on the motel room door lock.

She trained the crosshairs on Stone again and visualized the slug entering the left side of his rib cage. She was glad then for the full metal jacket because it would penetrate even if it hit a rib. The bone fragments would make more shrapnel.

Jael St. Clair inhaled, breathed out, and held it. She began to squeeze the trigger.

The low rumble of a large truck cut through the maelstrom as I tried the card again without success. Down below, a large white truck with the cable contractor's name on the side came barreling in, pulling a trailer with a giant coil of fiber-optic cable. It lurched to a stop near the rest of the white vehicles.

The approaching headlights lit the edge of Jael's peripheral vision, then washed out the night-vision display. She relaxed her trigger finger, took a breath, and set the M21 down as a truck and trailer blocked her shot.

Jael covered the M21 and crawled into the front seat, quickly running down her options. From her expansive saddlebag purse, she pulled out the HK4 in its leather clip holster, chambered a round, then clipped the HK4 to her belt. Then she reached back into the bag and pulled out a loop of high-C piano wire with two lengths of broom handle on each end and a small collar where the wire crossed to make its loop. It was her own invention. She tucked it into her back pocket.

Male voices from the truck filtered through the open tailgate window; one of them had spotted it and was coming over to be a Good Samaritan. Jael turned the ignition key to its accessory position, rolled down the front passenger-side window. Then, to avoid opening the door and activating the interior lights, she slid out the window and into the storm.

I tried the room access card again and again with no luck. Then lightning and thunder came simultaneously, and this time when the flash faded, there was no light from my room and the air-conditioning had stopped altogether. Time pressed tight around me, so I abandoned stealth and battered the door open with my shoulder, setting off the laptop's alarms. Then I fumbled the locking cables off the computer, snatched the laptop's power supply out of the wall, jammed it in my duffel, and zipped it up. Then, with all the alarms shrieking, I shoved the laptop into its case and sprinted from the room. It had taken just seconds.

Jael crouched in the deep shadows by her SUV's rear wheel and saw the Good Samaritan running toward her, shoulders hunched against the rain.

"Hell if I know," the Good Samaritan called out to the driver. "Call him on his cell. He was supposed to tell us where he wanted the rig."

As the Good Samaritan pushed the tailgate window shut, Jael slipped through the cloak of darkness and rain. She slipped the piano-wire loop over his head and jerked it closed around his neck. The garrote's little ratcheting collar prevented the loop from opening.

Jael stepped back quickly to avoid the man's thrashing and flailing. Seconds later, the lack of blood to the man's brain carried him off into unconsciousness. His head made a ripe-cantaloupe sound as it thudded off the SUV's rear bumper.

In the next instant, she heard a car door slam and the revving of a car engine. Pulling the HK4 from the holster, Jael thumbed off the safety and raced toward the noise. The Mercedes pulled out of the parking space. Jael stopped, crouched into her two-handed shooting stance, and sighted in on the Mercedes as a shout sounded behind her.

"Hey! What's holding you up?"

Jael turned as the truck driver got out. She shot him twice in the head. When she turned around, the Mercedes had reached Highway 82 and turned left into a slow line of westbound traffic. Jael St. Clair sprinted toward Highway 82 with Braxton's orders to get Stone and the lawyer ringing in her ears.

A raw, rasping pain burned her lungs and made Jael St. Clair regret her cigarette addiction. Her legs grew heavy, but she ran on through the pain, closing in on the Mercedes, tangled in a stop-and-go mess. Jael knew she'd have to make a point-blank shot. Her ragged breathing would spoil her aim for anything more.

The windshield wipers struggled against the downpour as Jasmine inched us forward in a long slow snake of cars, pickups, semis, flatbeds, SUVs, and minivans—all clogged by stoplights the storm had blinded.

"You know," I said, "the smartest thing for you to do is to drop me off somewhere and get as far away from the manhunt as possible." I looked over at Jasmine and tried unsuccessfully not to admire the remarkable features of her face, calm with beauty and determination. "I'm the one they're after. If you get out now, you can go back to some semblance of normalcy."

"That's the dumbest thing I have heard in the past ten years," she said. "Mom's dead; Lashonna may or may not be. This has everything to do with Talmadge, and you know as well as I do if I keep pushing his case, they'll come after me. Get a grip."

Jael's lungs burned raw like a cattle brand as she drew abreast of the red Mercedes, now two lanes over to her right. She saw the lawyer behind the wheel, head turned away. An easy shot, but she needed to get Stone, the most dangerous target, first. Traffic surged and stopped, surged and stopped. She needed to time her final move perfectly.

"Then drop the Talmadge thing," I suggested.

"Okay, that's the dumbest thing I've heard in *twenty* years." She laughed, then laid a gaze on me that made me realize I'd rather walk a rotten log over hell than disappoint her.

. . .

Now! Jael told herself. She waited for the vehicle closest to her to come to a stop. She lunged in front of the car; the driver leaned an angry hand on the horn.

Fuck you pal, she thought, focusing on the back of the lawyer's head, one vehicle away. She thumbed off the HK4's safety.

Jasmine concentrated on the side-view mirror on my side of the Mercedes, watching the stream of vehicles heading west along the shoulder. Her lips mouthed something I couldn't hear over the rain thrumming on the roof and the horns of cars on the other side. Suddenly she hit the accelerator and launched us into a space just inches longer than the big old Mercedes.

An incandescent rage rocked Jael as the Mercedes rocketed into the darkness. The impulse to kill shook her. Kill. Anybody. Everybody. A living, molten surge rose in her belly, demanding release. Now.

An impatient horn sounded behind her. She whirled toward the sound and raised the HK-4. The rain broke the night into a streaky impressionistic canvas and stained it with the white, yellow, and red kinetic hues of headlights, running lights, and turn signals. But through it she could make out the vague outlines of the driver's face as his mask of anger and frustration switched to mortal fear. He froze. Jael held her pistol steady, her finger taking slack out of the trigger.

The anger was all wrong, she thought, as she struggled for control. This man was not the mission. But the urge swelled in her belly. Oh, God! She needed the release. Wrong. All wrong.

Then, she lowered the HK-4, raised her left hand like a mock pistol, and aimed it at the man's amazed face.

"Bang," she said softly, then sprinted back to the hotel lot, where she jumped into the cable company truck and pulled it forward to unblock her SUV.

Before Jael drove away, she retrieved a Ziploc from her duffel and scattered its contents on the dead driver's body, making sure they stuck in bloody places where they would not be missed.

The rain began to ease as Jasmine accelerated toward Park Road and turned right.

"That was sweet of you, offering me an out and everything. But this was my fight long before it was yours. Besides, it's too late to turn back. We're in this together."

Jasmine's words connected with my heart and took all my words away. She turned right and pressed on through a shabby section of town.

"Where do we go?" I said finally. "They'll look at every hotel and motel. They'll stake out your house and your office if they haven't already done it."

"I have an idea."

I waited expectantly as she threaded the Mercedes along the cluttered street with an easy familiarity. We reached Main Street, then right, back across the railroad tracks, and past Stone Street.

"So." I looked at her. "You have an idea?"

"Sorry. Years ago, probably twenty or more, Mama bought a two-thousand-acre plantation southwest of Itta Bena out of an IRS lien auction, then donated it to Mississippi Valley State University."

She steered us along frontage roads, industrial driveways, and slushy one-lane gravel paths as only a local can do, bypassing the traffic jam. We were somewhere north of Rising Sun when we hit pavement again.

"Her brother, my uncle Quincy, teaches African-American history at Valley State there, and the donation helped his standing there immensely." Jasmine paused. "Mama was always doing things like that. And not just for family."

Jasmine turned right, crossed a new bridge over the Yazoo River, and headed west on Quito Road. The rain stopped as suddenly as it had started; stars dotted the sky. In the distance, lightning still illuminated the towering spires of more storm cells.

"Anyway, one small part of the deed gave Uncle Quincy the title to a small plot of land containing a collection of old shacks dating from the 1870s. You know, a two-room shotgun with a tin roof, bare wooden floors, and not much else other than a hole in the ground out back to crap in?"

A guilty memory found me as a child riding in the bed of a pickup driven by Al Thompson along the dusty roads through Mossy Plantation. The child almost saw the weathered, unpainted gray-wood shacks always complete with a sagging porch and lots of small naked or nearly naked black children playing outside. To privileged white children, they had been an almost-seen-but-not-quite-noticed element of the landscape, something no more significant than moss in the cypress trees or the green duckweed carpeting stagnant water.

"One of the shacks sat about a hundred yards off in a thicket of oaks and pecan trees. Mama restored it as a retreat, a simple environment outfitted no more elaborately than the original. No phone, no electricity, no indoor plumbing. She said it helped her remember where she came from."

Jasmine looked at me. I nodded that I understood.

"We're headed there. There aren't ten people who know about Mama's cabin, and you and I are two of them."

Around us, the moon found cracks in the clouds and painted pale, high-contrast silhouettes of the landscape.

"Mom always questioned why you turned out so different from the rest of your family."

"Me too."

"Mom said it never made any sense to her," Jasmine continued. "Here you are, born into this enormous position of privilege, a white boy from Delta planter stock, the offspring of a U.S. senator and the chancellor of Ole Miss, a football player, a scholar, and from what I can tell something of a boy genius. That put you about as high on the white Mississippi food chain as you can get."

I chewed on this silently. "Well, Papa was gone most of my life and Mama never realized that a sense of superiority needs careful nurturing," I said tentatively, seeking answers from the moonlit fields rushing by. "Papa's conflict with the Judge always made me like an outsider. I played alone a lot. I learned how to make up my own mind and tell everybody else to go to hell."

"A free will kind of thing?"

"I never thought of it that way before."

"Maybe you should." Mona Lisa smile.

I had thought about this for decades, didn't understand it any better today than I had in 1967.

We chased the moon across the table-flat fields in silence for several minutes. What lessons did God want me to learn from all of this? And if

God really existed and we were supposed to do his will, or hers, why the hell couldn't we get a clue about what it was?

Then I told Jasmine about the social insecurity I had experienced with Giles Claiborne.

"That's silly," she said. "If anything, you should feel superior, given your accomplishments in medicine."

"Whatever." I shook my head. "But it's the biggest reason I could never live here again."

"Never?"

I shook my head emphatically. "No way. Never."

Jasmine slowed for the stop sign at Route 7 and turned north toward Itta Bena.

"So many memories here," I said as the dark past flew by faster than night. "I leave Mississippi, but I can never escape." I squirmed uncomfortably as difficult pieces of my past shifted in my heart, falling into place as they never had before.

Jasmine nodded silently as we drove through the Confederate past. Shortly, she eased off the accelerator as Itta Bena's scattering of lights grew closer, then turned left past a broad, low field. On the field's side, a freight train made its way slowly atop a berm.

West of Itta Bena, Jasmine turned right on Highway 82, toward Valley State, then left to a gravel road through a cotton field. The rear of the Mercedes slewed as she left the gravel for a dirt road through a stand of trees.

"I'm lost," I said.

"Don't worry. I'm not."

The tires thrump-thrumped over a cattle gap, then we broke through a copse of trees into another field of cotton with a group of old sharecropper shacks standing in the moonlight. Jasmine slowed as the road narrowed, entered another wooded area, and went up a short rise, where the mud tracks turned to well-maintained gravel ending at a small house.

"This is it," Jasmine said as she stopped by the house, put the Mercedes in park, and turned off the lights. When she turned off the ignition, the silence sounded like falling into a hole.

The keys jingled as Jasmine pulled them out of the ignition and opened her door. I squinted as the overhead bulb burned overbright.

"Could you get me the flashlight, please?" She pointed toward the glove box. I handed it to her, then stepped out, grabbed her bags, and followed her to the porch. She unlocked the door and ushered me in.

"Wait here," Jasmine said.

She made her way over to a kerosene lamp and lit it. The flame's warm light revealed a Spartanly furnished room with a cast-iron stove and all of the furnishings that established this as a kitchen, living room, bedroom. A patchwork quilt covered the bed, which had probably slept three or four children in its previous life. A facing door led to the shack's other room.

"Go ahead and put my stuff there." She pointed to the bed on the wall opposite the stove. I did as told. The quilt captured my attention. All those little triangles, all those little stitches. All that time.

"Mom made all her quilts here," Jasmine said. "When the pressure would mount, she'd come here and sit on the porch and quilt. She said it kept her sane."

"Amazing," I said. "But it would drive me nuts."

Jasmine gave me a "different strokes" shrug and headed for the other room. I followed her.

"This was her room," Jasmine said.

The room had a bed, a chifforobe, a rough wooden chair, a table made out of odd pieces of lumber, and a door leading outside. This one had a dead bolt as well.

Lacking the quilts everywhere—spread on the bed, hung on the walls, draped over a stand—the shack would have been a stark portrait of poverty. Next to the rough chair sat a large hoop on a floor stand containing an unfinished quilt, heavy with significance. I went to it as Jasmine lit the kerosene lamp on the table next to it.

"I tried to finish it," she said, "but I could never stop sticking the needle in my fingers. And I made these great big, crooked stitches." Her breast pressed into my shoulder blade as she leaned over and stretched out her arm to point to her work. "So I stopped before I ruined it."

We stood there like that for a long moment. With adequate sleep, this could have been an erotic moment, but for now it felt warm, comfortable, secure. Right.

Jasmine sniffed once, then stood up.

"We better get some sleep while we can," she said as she touched her eyes to make sure no tears were showing. "Let's get your stuff and bring it in here."

Minutes later, with everything inside, Jasmine locked the front door, told me good-night, and closed the door to the front room. I took off my shoes, took the Ruger out of the clip holster, and slid it into my right shoe. It took seconds for me to fall asleep in the borrowed hospital scrubs.

Thundering applause rocked the Century Plaza's ballroom so intensely it echoed off itself. Clark Braxton stepped back from the podium and offered a photogenic smile to the standing-room-only crowd, who had paid $5,000 apiece for stylishly mediocre plates of food. Cameras flashed from every table; television lights glared harsh and bright. Then the sound Braxton had grown to love and expect: the gentle scraping sound of chairs when people stood to applaud.

The General stepped back to the microphone. "Thank you." The applause ended as if a switch had been thrown. "Thank you for taking time from your families, from your busy days, to come tonight. I thank you again for the contribution you have made toward America's future. Good night."

The standing ovation erupted anew as he waved, turned around, then stepped from the platform and into the shadowy backstage clutter of cables, folding chairs, and his people waiting to take him to the next engagement. His security detail, scattered strategically about the area, stood at an attentive parade rest. Braxton nodded to them.

Dan Gabriel stepped forward from a shadow. "Another magnificent presentation, sir."

"Thanks, Dan." Braxton adjusted the amount of cuff showing beyond the cuff of his navy-blue pinstripes. "Our next stop's right down the street, if I remember correctly."

"Affirmative. The Beverly Hilton," Gabriel said. "Nanotechnology Entrepreneurs Forum. You're supposed to have dessert and say a few words."

"Beverly Hilton, eh? Not all that far from here. Walking, that is. I've been too damn cramped all day and my legs are giving me trouble."

"You're supposed to be there at ten." Gabriel looked at his watch. "It's nine thirty-five now."

Braxton nodded. "Make sure they have the car ready in case something slows us down. I will not be late."

"Sir." Gabriel walked toward the head of Braxton's security detail.

As the General finished adjusting his shirt, belt buckle, and pants fly to make sure his gig line was straight, his cell phone vibrated. He checked the caller ID before answering.

"Braxton."

"Sir, I need some current intel. The situation's complicated."

"Tell me about it."

Jael St. Clair's words made him angry, made him struggle to smother anger that arced in his head between rational and irrational. He had to take his medication soon. He always needed it more frequently under stress, and this nonstop campaigning affected him worse than combat. He suspected the medication would eventually stop working for Jael St. Clair, as it had for Talmadge. He was grateful to be different from them.

Across the backstage area, he caught his security chief's frown as Gabriel spoke to him. The frown yielded to the man's usual can-do expression.

"I got back to my vehicle in less than half a minute and gave chase," Jael said. "But they vanished."

"Where are you?" Braxton asked.

"On the way to Grenada. I'll check into a motel there, unload things, ditch the vehicle in a shopping center parking lot, and rent another one."

"I assume you need intel on Stone?"

"Sir."

"One moment."

The General used his thumbs to access the address book on his phone. He quickly found what he was looking for.

"Call this number," he said, reading out the digits twice. She read them back to him.

"Good," he said. "It will be picked up on the fifth ring. Hang up if it's any fewer, any more. The person who answers will say, 'Black granite.' If you hear anything else, hang up and call me back."

"Sir."

"You will respond, 'Quarry master.' This person knows about you, not who you are, but that you are mission capable and in the field."

"Affirmative, sir. Five rings. 'Black granite'; 'quarry master.' "

"This person will locate Stone."

Without waiting for a reply he pressed the "end" button as Gabriel walked up.

"Everything's set," Gabriel said. "Security's deploying, but you and I'll need to leave now if we're going to walk the whole way without being late."

Braxton looked at Gabriel for a silent moment, weighing the commitment in the man's eyes, the dedication in his voice. The leading presidential contender scrolled through years of vivid memories, weighed the debits and credits of favors accumulated, and came down on a balance due that added up to loyalty.

"Sir?" Gabriel broke the awkward silence.

"I'm ready," Braxton said. "As it happens, something important has come up I need to talk to you about."

Jael St. Clair drove carefully though darkness. At the speed limit of sixty-five miles per hour, she was the slowest thing on the road, but she didn't need to be stopped by the highway patrol. She pressed the numbers Braxton had given her.

South of her, in a clean, plain, business-budget motel room within sight of the Jackson airport, a cell phone sounded its short, sharp, distinctive tone. Video of the law enforcement briefing in Greenwood played on the motel's television, connected by cables to a laptop computer sitting alongside. The briefing had been captured with a concealed camera and burned onto a DVD.

The phone rang a second time. David Brown, formerly of half a dozen anonymous government agencies whose budgets were laundered through other well-known agencies, completed sit-up number eighty-seven. Brown got to his feet, stretched his tall, lean physique, and ran his hand over his close-cropped, gunmetal-gray hair. He glanced at the mirror at the long, thin strawberry birthmark emerging from his hairline. When he was younger, it had been completely hidden in a dense thicket of hair. The phone, one of three he carried, sat next to the laptop and sounded a third time. For one last second, he focused on the video. He'd watched it the first time on the half-hour helicopter ride south from Greenwood. Something about the black sheriff and his assistant bothered him.

The phone rang again. Brown clicked the pause button on the DVD software control panel and picked up the phone. He waited for the fifth ring, then pressed the green button. "Black granite."

"Quarry master."

"How can I help?"

"Intel."

Still focusing on the paused video of a black sheriff's deputy named Myers, Brown sat on the end of the bed and listened to the woman.

When she finished, Brown said, "I can help you. Call this number back at precisely noon tomorrow."

. . .

"Fuck you!" Jael St. Clair wrestled again with the unrequited anger burning inside her. "Noon! You fucking asshole!"

She struggled to keep the car on the road and her mind locked on reality. She tried controlled breathing. She tried visualizing the last hit, the last release, but that only made the pain worse. She had to kill Stone before the anger got her first.

The anger threatened to tip her over, so she pulled onto the shoulder and fumbled about in her shoulder bag. Finally, she pulled out the amber plastic drug bottle and shook out a capsule and washed it down with a swallow from a plastic bottle of water.

Then she waited. Finally, the heat cooled, and as it did, a plan formed in her head.

There would be someone, she thought as the traffic rocked by on her left. There is always a connection, someone who can always find the quarry. Someone to watch, to follow. It would be in the dossier she had downloaded from them.

She took another sip of water and with calm steady hands pulled back into traffic.

Had this been an ordinary night, the ragged visions that haunted me would have jolted me awake. But even visions of Camilla, Vanessa, Lashonna, and the nightmare of the past days could not break through my desperate need for sleep.

I have no idea how long I had been asleep when I dreamed that Jasmine came in and gave me a gentle kiss. In the dream, she undressed me, threw a quilt over me, then snuggled in beside me and we went to sleep.

Pacific breezes kept Dan Gabriel and Clark Braxton cool as they followed the security detail out to Constellation Boulevard, where armed motorcycle outriders idled near the General's armored limo.

"Project Enduring Valor still concerns me," Gabriel said.

"Go on," Braxton said evenly.

"Xantaeus robs a soldier of free will without their knowledge, overrides their sense of compassion . . . neutralizes the fear of injury."

"Battle can do that all by itself," Braxton said without hesitation. "Natural two-percenters do it all the time. Compassion and fear can kill all the wrong people."

"Maybe I'm not expressing myself very well. One very big issue here deals with free will. Without it, without the ability for soldiers to make moral decisions, we turn them into inhuman, meat-based robots."

"Don't talk to me about free will," Braxton snapped. "Every man who freezes, who doesn't pull the trigger, has had his free will robbed by the irrationality of fear. That, sir, is robbing men of their free will and thwarting the very moral decision to protect themselves, their comrades, and their country. Your argument doesn't hold water."

"I see your point," Gabriel persisted. "But what about the practical issues? You know as well as I do that battles are won when one side breaks the other's spirit. One side surrenders or runs before it's completely destroyed. This preserves lives, talent, knowledge—resources which can be harnessed for reconstruction once a war is over.

"But if both sides have the drug," Gabriel continued, "then neither side breaks, and battles end only when every member of the losing side is killed or wounded so gravely they can no longer pull a trigger. It alters warfare like never before."

Braxton merely nodded as they reached Avenue of the Stars and crossed with the light. Loud traffic moved the two men shoulder to shoulder so they could hear each other.

"It's the reason America needs to keep it for ourselves."

"That didn't last very long with nuclear weapons," Gabriel said.

"That's a good analogy. Because Project Enduring Valor will turn every soldier into the perfect killer, the ultimate weapon more fearsome than nukes. And don't forget: the Cold War's nuclear mutually assured destruction gave the world a longer period of peace than ever before. Now look at all the bloodshed since the fall of the Soviet Union. Controlled Xantaeus proliferation should bring back an era of mutually assured destruction and a return to an enforced global peace.

"Dan, the Russians and the Chinese'll have their own nondepleting neurotrops soon. So too the Indians, Pakistanis, Israelis, and Saudis. Without deploying Xantaeus first, we'll be at their mercy."

"Just like with nukes," Gabriel said. "Get'em or die. Damn."

"Damned if we do, damned if we don't," Braxton agreed. "We're either out front or we're toast."

Gabriel shook his head slowly. They approached Century Park East. "You're right yet again, sir. Absolutely correct. We either have to ride the tiger or get eaten."

"War really is hell. Always has been. Your agony over Xantaeus has been repeated every time a new generation of weapons has come on the scene from bows and arrows to guns and nukes. There is always a new tiger to ride. But the only thing worse than fighting a war—"

"—is losing one," Gabriel finished the General's oft-repeated motto. "You're right again, sir."

Braxton clapped Gabriel across the shoulders. "That's why you'll make a good secretary of defense. You've got the mind of a soldier and the conscience of a philosopher. Don't stop raising the questions."

They stopped for a traffic light as northbound traffic spilled past them, splashing up ahead into a left-turn jam at Santa Monica Boulevard. The signal changed and they followed security across. Around them, the motorcycles and the limo kept pace. Half a dozen paces later, Braxton turned to his long-time adjutant. "Dan, as it happens, I need to chat with you about Enduring Valor as well."

Gabriel gave him a go-head look.

"Mistakes have been made," Braxton said. "Serious mistakes I have learned about just today. Mistakes endangering the program, my presidential campaign, our plans to reshape the military, and quite frankly my entire career.

"I don't have to remind you that without Project Enduring Valor there is no possible way we can build the fighting force the country needs with the shit-pitiful appropriations those clowns on the Hill see fit to give us."

"Yes, sir. The budget and use of proceeds focused my thoughts there. Everything's predicated on Enduring Valor's successful implementation."

"Good. Hold that thought in mind, use it to filter everything I am about to tell you."

They got to Santa Monica Boulevard and turned right.

"By now, you know the complete *official* history of Enduring Valor," Braxton said. "Today I learned Frank Harper committed some very serious mistakes in the early days, some of them prosecutable crimes."

Braxton let that sink in for several steps. Seeing no signs of weakness on Gabriel's face, he continued, "Harper conducted unauthorized surgeries, tampered with his experimental data to make things look more promising, lied to congressional committees, and delivered outright fabrications to his superiors in the Pentagon."

"And this is coming to light now, after all these years?"

Braxton nodded and concentrated on the muscles in his face, working toward a mask of dismay and the shock of betrayal. "I owe my life to his skill, but he's turned out to have a side that threatens everything."

The lights at the intersection of Wilshire and Santa Monica Boulevard came into view.

"How could that be?" Gabriel asked. "His involvement was half a century ago. Isn't there a fire wall of some sort? Isn't Enduring Valor a new program that pays homage to Harper's program but is not a continuation of it?"

"It's not that simple. We have enemies in Congress and elsewhere. They don't give a damn about facts or rational debate. They want to win at all costs, which means finding a 'Gotcha!' for their side of things."

Gabriel made a face. "Right. Make a mistake and it's not an honest error, but evidence of conspiracy and evil intent."

Braxton smiled as Gabriel connected this emotional attachment on his own. He still owned Gabriel's heart.

"Remember that," Braxton said. "Because Frank's mistakes have killed people and more need to die."

Then Braxton told Gabriel about Darryl Talmadge, two black attorneys named Thompson, and a highly decorated veteran and world-renowned neurophysiologist. Then the General connected them all to a string of murders with the dots of a reality he wanted Gabriel to adopt as his own.

"One of the four is dead. We will not be safe until they all are."

Braxton's words landed on Gabriel like a sandbag. He stopped. Braxton took another step, then stopped and turned to face him. Around them, security people, motorcycles, and the gleaming limo came to a slower halt.

"Sir. Please let me get this straight: you're saying we not only have to kill at least three more people, one of them a brilliant and very brave soldier, but we have to keep it all secret?"

Braxton moved close to the man he had handpicked for secretary of defense. "Filter it, Dan. Filter the reality through what we talked about."

"But, sir, we are talking about killing innocent people."

"Innocent people get killed in every war, Dan. Ugly. Evil. Reality."

Braxton stood close and studied Gabriel's face and the movements in his eyes, which reflected the emotions shifting behind them. The General waited for the right moment, the psychological inflection point. When it came, he spoke again, softly.

"Do you remember studying the cases where a ship has taken a torpedo, or a submarine is damaged so seriously, that only sealing off the damaged areas can save the ship? Even if there were sailors still alive in them?"

Gabriel nodded.

"And you realize—you accept—the tragic reality that those lives had to be sacrificed in order to save hundreds of other lives?"

"Sir."

"We must make that decision. If anything derails Project Enduring Valor, millions will eventually die. Perhaps not tomorrow or next year, but when we face an enemy wired on their nondepleting neurotrop and they slaughter our unprotected soldiers. Misguided compassion now for three people will cost us immeasurably more if we wait. If Enduring Valor is sidetracked, we will never get it back on course in time."

"Jesus!" Gabriel exhaled. "Jesus Christ!" He wiped at his face with a cold hand. "There must be another way."

"No. We must act now, just like a ship's captain must make his hard decision immediately."

Braxton followed the despair in Gabriel's eyes, watched his shoulders slump under the weight of the revelations. The time for the kill had come.

"Dan, if I could have handled this by myself, I would never have told you about it all. You understand, don't you?"

"Of course."

"I need your help. I've pushed my own resources to the limits." Braxton paused. "That will change after the election, but for now we have to make the best of what we can cobble together, people we can trust, favors we can call in."

Gabriel felt the dread gathering in his gut.

"I need you to make some calls. Calls to people who are as committed to you as you are to me. People who will take some discreet, out-of-channel action to help us clear this mess up before it destroys us both."

Braxton waited as Gabriel shut his eyes and grimaced.

"This is not right," Gabriel said.

Braxton ignored those qualms. "How about the fellow who took over command of Task Force 86M from you?"

"Maybe," Gabriel said hoarsely as he opened his eyes. "But—"

"But nothing!" Braxton bore down to close the sale. "Think first of America's future. Then think about your future. You've resigned from the Army. You can't go back." He paused. "If you won't do this for America or yourself, do it for me. I will be personally ruined without your help. You've followed me through hell, and together we've come out stronger every time. I've come through for you and I've never once asked you for a thing."

Traffic sounds washed through the long pause that followed. Braxton watched as Gabriel's gaze finally met his own and fixed it with a steely earnestness. A horn sounded; engines accelerated.

"Yes, sir."

"Good. Thank you," Braxton said. "Make some calls for me tomorrow morning. I'm sure you have more than a couple of people who owe you."

"Yes, sir."

"Good man."

Jael St. Clair sucked at the last potent half inch of her Marlboro, then exhaled and watched the smoke join the dense haze surrounding her. Finally, she allowed herself the first smile of the new day. It had taken hours to filter through the names and follow the hidden trails. Now, as she pushed back from her laptop, she knew she had her answer in the minute details of online land records and an archival issue of the *New York Times*. No need to call the arrogant "black granite" asshole back at noon, because by then Stone and the lawyer would be long dead.

She lit a fresh Marlboro off the old one.

The last of the police cars left shortly before dawn. From his reclining position in the back of his pickup, parked at the rear of the cancer clinic, Rex listened to the police scanner through an earbud and waited for signs it was all clear.

He had followed Brad and Jasmine to the Sonic drive-in from the hospital, but decided not to linger in the neighborhood when they went to her law office. Instead, he set up shop where he could watch the EZ-Sleep, figuring Stone would make his way there eventually.

The storm that followed had pounded the camper shell like incoming artillery, and he thought at least once he was surely going to be killed by a tornado.

The storm had really screwed up his surveillance. At times the EZ-Sleep disappeared entirely in the downpour, especially when the power went out. The rest came in spasmodic jerks of time, like an old fuzzy surveillance video with gaps containing the most important parts. He did see Brad Stone, Jasmine, and the red Mercedes, the cable truck, and a white SUV. Then came thunder that sounded like gunshots, a tall blonde with big tits who came running past, and not a whole lot later the police. The police scanner told him cops had an all-points out on Brad and Jasmine.

"Buddy, you are in a heap a trouble," Rex said quietly under his breath. "Y'mama wouldn't like it at all." He crawled over to the tailgate and waited again, looking for any sign of law enforcement. Some people put down his talk of warrants and an unsavory past as bravado. But he knew from experience that once the cops got wind of his warrants and the crimes behind them, they'd shoot first and not bother with questions.

Rex lifted the shell's window and climbed out, unlocked the driver's door, and got in.

"Now where the hell would you two go?" he asked himself as he started the engine and put it in gear. They couldn't go to anybody they knew, nobody they were related to, any place they had ever been before. They had to have a new vehicle and a safe place to hide. And the police knew that as well as he did. Rex hoped he knew Stone better than they did.

He pulled out onto Highway 82 and headed into town. Maybe, he thought, retracing Brad's steps might produce some answers.

"Now, God," he said, looking up through the windshield at the brightening sky, "I know you and I don't have the best of relationships. But I certainly would appreciate any pointers you can spare." It was about as close as Rex ever got to praying. That it was his best bet right now bothered him mightily.

Loud, muffled thuds ripped apart the seams of my solid, dreamless sleep. The thuds came again, louder, faster. Then, a man's voice: "Jasmine!"

I jerked awake then. Hazy light frosted the windows and filled the room with soft quilted colors. Then a key rattled the front dead bolt.

I sat up. Jasmine's exquisitely black hair and the red hues of her brown sugar skin connected with the deepest parts of my heart. Then I remembered my faint dream and realized it had been more than illusion. I wanted to wonder more about this when the front door slammed opened and a man's voice boomed in from the front room.

"Jasmine?"

Her eyelids snapped open wide, revealing bright wisteria eyes that distilled the sunshine and threw it back, deeper and more intense.

"Girl? You here?"

Footsteps thudded closer; old boards creaked.

I sat up and realized I was naked except for my briefs. I stretched over and fumbled around on the floor before locating the Ruger.

"No," Jasmine said as she touched my shoulder. I stopped with my hand still outstretched, fingers curling around the butt of the pistol. I turned my head toward Jasmine and saw she was dressed in an oversize, gray Valley State T-shirt that came down to midthigh. From there down it was all beautiful skin.

"It's okay." She sat up.

I didn't move my hand until she said, "In here, Uncle Quincy."

The door opened. As I sat up in the bed, a man of average height and build with light mocha skin, an embroidered dashiki-style shirt, and matching brimless hat walked in. His facial structure reminded me more of Vanessa and less of Jasmine. His eyes were a pale blue and his face touched a memory I could only feel and not remember.

I had seen this man once before in my life. In Jackson, at the Christmas party that had been the end of a beginning that had not really started for Vanessa and me. Quincy Thompson was Al Thompson's son, Vanessa's brother, Jasmine's uncle.

He looked at Jasmine, then me. His eyes did this three or four times, and with each iteration Quincy's face twisted itself deeper into a mask of rage that made the hair stand up on the back of my neck.

"You gonna be the white man's whore, just like your mama?" he raged at Jasmine. "She always talking black and sleeping white like a brother ain't good enough for the likes of her!"

"Uncle Quincy—"

"Don't uncle me, girl! Don't you have any pride in your race? Any loyalty? You so damned ashamed of being black you want to have a light-skinned baby?"

"You're off base, Uncle Quincy." Jasmine's tone was low, even, and forceful. She got quickly out of bed and stood face-to-face with Quincy Thompson. She was taller by an inch or two, even in her bare feet. She had the strong legs of an ice-skater and well-defined muscles that rippled as she moved.

"You made Mama's life miserable carrying on and I am not going to let you do the same thing to me." Her voice was calm and full of steel and made me pray I would never have to face off against her in court or anywhere else.

"Honey, be true to your race," Quincy said.

"I will be true to myself," Jasmine said, "and not to some prehistoric notion that all black women are the exclusive property of black men."

"You've got a sassy mouth, girl. But it's not going to save you from that white man's jungle fever."

Quincy threw me a white-hot, fastball glare burning with hate. The pitch came high and inside, identical to the one LAPD detective Darius Jones had thrown. Anger rose in my chest, but anything I'd say would only fuel his rage.

"My life is my own, Uncle Quincy." Jasmine's cool voice diluted my anger and helped me understand they had been through this conversation before. "I will not allow black men to own me any more than I will allow white men to tell me what to do. I will not trade one form of oppression for another."

Quincy Thompson opened his mouth, then shut it quickly when nothing came out. He stared at Jasmine for several long moments.

"You're making a big, big mistake letting some white plantation boy come down from the big house and get into your pants," Quincy said. Then he whirled on his heel and headed toward the door. He stopped and fished in his pants pocket and pulled out a bright pink slip of paper.

He paused, and for a long moment all I heard was the man's labored breathing. "Well, this is why I came." He turned, tossed the paper. Then he stomped out of the house, slamming the door so hard it rattled the windows.

Jasmine and I studiously avoided making eye contact as the paper fluttered to the floor. It landed face up, obviously a telephone message. A car started up outside and sprayed gravel in its haste to leave.

With the M21 and a Leupold sight for daytime work slung over her shoulder, Jael St. Clair made her way through the underbrush parallel to the road, steadying her gait with a collapsible aluminum walking staff.

She stopped to take a deep breath and cursed silently when she exhaled. She should have driven the new Toyota SUV rental farther along the narrow, rutted lane, but she worried the 4Runner wouldn't be able to handle the terrain.

She looked back, but through the dense fog could barely make out anything more than fifty yards away. Sometimes less. The 100 percent humidity combined with the cold front that had followed the tornadoes and thunderstorms across the Delta the night before had combined to produce pea soup so thick on the highway she couldn't see more than a car length or two in many places. Highway 82 had been littered with accidents. Fortunately, Quincy Thompson had driven like her grandmother.

Jael cursed the fog. She'd have to get closer to her targets than she preferred. No matter. The mission had to be completed. She pushed on through the brush, grateful the fog thinned some as the woods grew denser.

Her lungs burned again from the cigarettes, and her head spun bright from a lack of sleep. But the new patch was doing its job. And doubling up on the pills had rounded off most of the jagged edges of her anger and brought the usual rock-steadiness back to her hands, her eyes, and her thoughts. The old doctor who worked for the General had been adjusting her dosage continuously over the past six months and told her that was a natural thing and not to worry about it. She'd have to tell him she needed another adjustment.

Jael made her way across the soggy ground thatched with knee-high grasses and saplings, perfect cover for quail and copperheads. She'd already flushed one covey, but snakes didn't concern her. A symphony of birdsongs, mockingbirds, the screeches of jays, filled the morning. Then the sound of Quincy Thompson's car growing louder again, coming from the cabin area.

She knelt low in the bushes and unslung the M21, flipped open the Leupold's covers, and sighted in. Through the hazy shroud of fog, she made out an angry black face. She tracked the face as it drew abreast, then headed off in the distance.

"Bang," she said softly as she closed the sight covers and reslung the M21. She stopped for a moment and concentrated her mind on hearing. She'd heard faint rustles since leaving her SUV. But it lacked any sort of pattern connected to danger. The woods here were filled with birds, deer, possums, raccoons, and every other manner of woodland creature. That's what she heard now as she filtered through the chatter of the trees and brush.

Finally, she opened her eyes and continued on through the woods toward the plot of land and dwelling that had turned up on her Internet search for Quincy Thompson.

Jasmine stood with her back to me, shoulders slumped, staring down at the pink sheet of paper. The fading sound of Quincy's car left us holding on to a brittle silence filled with ancient hurt and modern pain. I wanted to reach out, but Quincy's insults made me second-guess my own motives.

Then, from outside, a mockingbird broke the silence and the tainted mood. Jasmine leaned down and picked up the slip of paper.

"It's from Jay Shanker," Jasmine said as she stood up, her back still to me. "Talmadge's lawyer."

"I remember."

She squared her shoulders and turned to me. "He wants to meet at his office this morning."

Her voice was all business and her gaze had a distance I had not seen before. Quincy had played the enforcer better than he knew.

"He left a number. Said we had to call at precisely eleven A.M." She paused, and when she spoke again, warmth filtered into her words.

"This is weird. The note says under no circumstances should I call his office.

"Strange man." Jasmine shook her head and went into the front room. "And why didn't he call my cell?"

I took the occasion to pull an unadorned, navy blue polo shirt from my bag, along with a fresh pair of cargo shorts.

"Damnation," she mumbled. With my back to the door, I tucked the shirt in and zipped up the shorts. "My cell battery's dead."

I turned as she walked back in. She had pulled on a pair of jeans under the Valley State T-shirt.

"Let me check mine." I went over and excavated the plastic hospital bag from beneath a pile of green surgical scrubs on the floor. I rummaged my phone from the bag and pressed the power button.

"Nada." I held it up and looked at her. Anxiety welled up then as I thought of Camilla and wondered if Flowers had called back. "My charger's in my bag."

Jasmine shook her head. "No good. Mom's authenticity, remember? No electricity, no phone."

"Oh, terrific."

We listened to the mockingbird for a moment before Jasmine spoke.

"I don't know about you, but I can't take much more of this morning without some coffee. You?"

"Yeah. Me."

"Okay, but like everything else here, you're gonna have to work for it." She tossed me a Mona Lisa smile, then headed into the front room. I followed her, jamming my wallet and the rest of my stuff in my cargo shorts pockets. I found her fiddling around with a black cast-iron stove in the corner.

"There should be some dry wood on the front porch."

I went out front and pulled several split pieces of pine from the pile. I grabbed the smallest pieces I could find and made sure a couple of them had nice globs of hardened resin. Pine made for a dirty flame that fouled flues, but it would give us a quick, hot fire for coffee. I pried off a chunk of dried resin the size of a marble and crushed it under my heel. I scraped up the coarse granules, grabbed a fistful of pine twigs for tinder, and carried them in along with the wood.

When I came back in, Jasmine had filled a battered, old steel coffeepot with bottled water. A Starbucks bag sat on the adjacent counter next to a hand-cranked coffee grinder.

"Sure beats muddy creek water and ground-up chicory," I said as I made my way over to the stove and looked it over. I had never lit a fire in one of these.

"In there." Jasmine pointed. "Lift the cover and put the wood in."

"Mama was a coffee snob. It's one of the things I picked up from her." Jasmine placed a conical paper filter in a funnel holder and put it in a thermos. Then I pulled off a heavy cast-iron disk from the top of the stove and bent over the opening to build a fire. I arranged the resin granules over a small bed of pine twigs, then carefully placed the larger pieces.

"Black men really resent successful black women," Jasmine said evenly as I bent over my task. I resisted looking at her. "They come up with every hang-up imaginable. I think Uncle Quincy knows he's off base, but he's too old to shake it off."

I straightened up to grab a large wooden match from a box next to the stove. I carefully avoided looking at her. I did not want her to stop talking.

"My grandmother really liked you," she said as I scratched the match head on the inside of the stove and held my breath against the fumes. "But she was just a woman, and my grandfather and Uncle Quincy hustled Mama away."

"I'll never forget," I said as I touched the match flame to the resin powder. It caught immediately. I stood up and blew out the match.

"Mama told me she always wanted to see you marching through the door to get her."

"Damn." I swallowed hard against the old painful feelings and took a deep breath. "I thought maybe she felt the same way as Quincy and your dad." I shook my head slowly. "I had no idea what to do. Not a clue."

Jasmine smiled and turned her attention to the coffee.

The pine resin, knots, and wood blazed high and hot. I covered the hole in the stove with the black cast-iron disk and Jasmine put the coffeepot on top of it.

"Something to eat?" Jasmine said as she bent over and opened a crude, unpainted cupboard door. She stood up with a box filled with an assortment of foil-wrapped bars: Balance, Power, breakfast, granola. She set the box on a table made of wide pine planks ornamented by decades of use.

"Most everything's past its expiration." She pulled out a Balance bar and pushed the box over toward me. "But I don't think this stuff ever goes bad."

Jasmine unwrapped her bar and took a bite. "Probably not lethal."

I pawed through the box, listening to the coffee water start to tick. I pulled out a bar, unwrapped it.

She walked over to her pile of bags and came back with a legal-size manila folder I recognized as part of Lashonna's files we had retrieved the night before. A CD in a thin plastic jewel case fell out of the bottom of the folder. It landed on a corner and split apart, sending the top of the jewel box and the bottom in different directions and the CD rolling off in a third.

"Damnation!" She dropped the folder and stretched out to pluck the CD off the floor while it was still rolling. "Sometimes I am such a klutz." I helped her gather the jewel box remains, then went to get my laptop.

The mixed woodlot of oak and pine shed the previous night's rain with every breeze, showering Jael St. Clair as she made a broad circle through the brush. She wanted a clear shot to the path between the shack's front door and the red Mercedes.

Jael quickly found the correct angle, then walked a line back from the shack. She found the spot, but when she looked back, banks of fog drifted in and out, totally obscuring the shack as often as not. She moved closer and found a small cove surrounded by pine saplings. She pulled out her laser range finder and specced the distance at thirty-six yards. Not even a proper sniper shot. No matter. Business was business. She adjusted the Leupold for the distance. Then she jammed the aluminum walking staff into the rain-soft dirt. It sank in deep and steady.

Picking up the rifle, she knelt beside the walking pole, grabbed it with her left hand. Then she rested the M21 on that hand, holding it tight against the pole with her thumb. Then she placed her cheek against the M21 and looked through the Leupold, down at the path Stone and the lawyer would eventually walk when they went to the Mercedes.

Then Jael St. Clair sat back on her haunches and waited. She craved a cigarette but knew the smoke could give her away.

Jasmine and I sat at the table and drank coffee, silently scanning record after record off Shanker's CD as I scrolled them down my laptop screen.

"I can't believe this," I said.

"You've said that a hundred times. Maybe more."

The CD contained thousands of images of medical records, administrative documents, experimental protocols, maps, diagrams, photos. The first document on the CD was a memo on Jay Shanker's letterhead that explained that all of the documents had been transferred from microfilm to the CD. The microfilm had been salvaged decades before from the vandalized ruins of a once-secret Army medical facility that had operated on the site of a POW camp built near Belzoni. The memo explained that the records had been salvaged by his client Darryl Talmadge, a hunting guide who had scheduled a duck hunt in a nearby slough. The client had been a no-show and Talmadge had passed a morning digging around in the ruins. Beneath a pile of termite-infested beams and flooring, Talmadge had found a safe that had sunk under its own weight through the decaying floor.

Talmadge concealed his find and returned with an oxyacetylene torch, opened the old, rusty safe, and found that leaking water had destroyed most of the contents. He did recover a number of watertight microfilm canisters, which he tossed in his garage, vowing to read them one day.

The microfilm sat untouched in Talmadge's garage for seventeen years.

In his only private conversation with Talmadge before the military took over, Shanker learned of the microfilm and his client's hunch it might be useful.

Jasmine leaned on my shoulder to better read the laptop's screen as we scanned the documents to get an overview of what we had.

"This Frank Harper starts out like a saint and turns into a monster," Jasmine said.

I shook my head. "I think he's the same person. But he got sucked in by his own insatiable curiosity about what makes us human, good, bad . . . who we are. He was grappling with the big question with some big consequences. I think it's clear, early on, he wanted to explore this Phineas Gage thing firsthand." I paused. "I want to go back when I have time and read that essay he wrote about ethics, free will, crime, and punishment. It's pretty deep."

"So he starts out with a charge of pure scientific curiosity, then someone in Washington gets wind of things and dumps a ton of money on him," Jasmine said. "You think that's what made him cross the line?

Moved him from fixing up people with head wounds and studying them into creating head wounds to make better warriors? Then the chemicals?"

"Clearly," I agreed.

"It doesn't hurt the rationalization process when your own government says it needs your research."

"Big factor. Really big."

The last document on the CD was a memo on Jay Shanker's letterhead summarizing a second CD dealing exclusively with Clark Braxton. That CD and the location of the original supporting documentation for all the information on both CDs would be made available once two conditions were met: if Vanessa Thompson joined in Talmadge's defense and brought me on board.

"Shanker and Mom agreed you're the only expert who could credibly unravel the data in the files."

"I don't understand why Shanker didn't go to the authorities with it," I said.

"He did."

"He did what?"

"He took it to the judge," Jasmine said. "And within hours, the suits showed up at his door and the threats began. That's when he came to Mama. She found it hard to swallow until the next day when Shanker's office and his house and a mini-storage unit, his RV, and even his duck blind had been ransacked."

"How come they didn't find the microfilm?"

"My understanding is, he'd been freaked out by what he had read and had hidden everything before he went to the judge."

"And we don't know where."

As Jasmine opened her mouth to reply, we heard distant sounds of tires on gravel.

"Quincy coming back?" I asked.

Jasmine frowned. "Not likely."

"Who?"

She shook her head. I rushed to the bedroom then and grabbed my Ruger. Jasmine pulled hers from her purse and clipped the holster to her waistband.

"Come on!" She said, heading for the back door. She unbolted it and lunged into a dense wall of green vines, weeds, and saplings. I followed her in my bare feet.

Jael sat on her haunches, waiting. Her instructor had said she had the patience of a spider. The analogy pleased her.

When she heard the motor vehicle, Jael followed the sound and trained her glasses toward the source. Before she spotted the vehicle, Stone and the lawyer bolted from the rear of the shack and plunged into a green drift of kudzu stretching toward the back porch like stop-action surf. Fog frosted the deep green of the kudzu and feathered it into the surrounding green matrix of lush Delta undergrowth.

The vehicle sounds grew louder. Jael compassed the kudzu, methodically teasing it apart. It was hard to separate the movement of the leaves that might be caused by the wind from that which might be from her targets. As Jael toyed with the idea of pursuing them, an older-model, light blue Chevy pickup appeared out of the fog. A motorcycle sat in the bed, held upright by bright yellow straps.

As the truck grew closer, she raised the binoculars and concentrated on the light-skinned black man behind the wheel, noting that he wore the uniform of some law enforcement agency.

"Fuck," she muttered. All she needed was for some county mountie to make an arrest.

Patience, Jael counseled herself. Were more cops on the way? Why had this one come in a civilian vehicle? The truck turned to the far side of the shack and disappeared from view. Jael decided she was too far away from the action to make a good decision. She grabbed the M21, gave a reassuring touch to her HK4, and prepared to shift to a better position. Then Stone and the lawyer emerged from the kudzu. The lawyer kept on moving; Stone stopped. Just like a good target.

Jael knelt, steadied the M21 on the aluminum pole, and settled the crosshairs on Stone's head. The lawyer shouted something that reached Jael's ears too faintly to comprehend. Jael took a breath, let it out, and took up the trigger slack.

"John!" Jasmine ran toward the pickup without hesitation. I hung back, stock-still with indecision.

"Come on!" Jasmine urged me out. "It's okay."

Considering that my only other choice was to run away in my bare feet, I hurried to catch up with Jasmine as she made her way around the corner of the shack.

Jael sucked in a breath through clenched teeth as she eased off the trigger. She closed her eyes and shook her head against the anger boiling up. Shit. Now there were two vehicles to cover. And another armed man.

Jael opened her eyes and tried to hang on to the virtues of patience as she pulled the aluminum staff from the ground and made her way counterclockwise through the underbrush for a better angle.

I shoved Lashonna's Ruger .357 magnum in the deep pocket of my cargo shorts and hung a step behind Jasmine as we approached Myers's pickup. He got out, his face heavy and serious.

"I came to warn you," he looked at me, then back to Jasmine. "The warrants have been sworn out."

"Warrants?" Jasmine said. "Like in more than one?"

Myers's face looked as if he had bad indigestion. "Uh-huh. Like for both of you."

We stood for a long moment, listening to the birds. An odd sound from the woods in front of the cabin caught my attention. I turned in that direction and concentrated. It took me a moment to realize I hadn't noticed a sound, but the lack of one. Birds were not singing there.

"Brad?" Jasmine looked at me.

Then the birds were singing again. I shook my head.

"Thought I heard something," I said. "Probably a deer."

Jasmine looked at Myers. "Coffee?"

"No time," Myers said. "Neither do you."

"We better think real hard now so we make the best use of the time we don't have; don't you think?" Jasmine countered. "The coffee's made." She walked toward the back porch. Myers hesitated for a split second as his mouth worked up a reply. Then his lips went still as he set out behind her. I brought up the rear, lagging behind long enough to give the woods a good scan.

I followed John and Jasmine through the back door. Myers took in the rumpled bed scattered with my clothes and Jasmine's. In the front room, I watched him look at the unslept-in bed there. I braced myself for a replay of the Darius and Quincy show, which did not come.

"The local warrant is for the murder of two fiber-optic cable contractors at the EZ-Sleep," Myers said. He sat at the table with the stiffness of a man with sore muscles . . . or a sore life that had been exercised a mile too much. I stood uneasily across the table from him. Jasmine set her Ruger on the rough cabinet that served as a counter as she got Myers's coffee.

He looked at Jasmine. "There's a warrant for you because your Mercedes was spotted at the EZ-Sleep." He looked at me. "And for you because you had a room there. The detectives also think they have hair evidence linking you."

"Hell."

"Wait." He shook his head. "There's more."

Jasmine filled a cup with coffee and brought it to him. He took a sip and smiled.

"There are federal warrants out of California for both of you." He took a sip of coffee and looked at me. His red eyes and sagging lids begged for sleep. "They're saying you were part of a drug-smuggling operation."

"Do what?"

"I don't believe a damn thing," Myers said.

"But—"

"No time." Myers closed his eyes and shook his head. "I don't need to hear what you have to say." He opened his eyes and looked at Jasmine and me in turn. "But you two need to hear me out because what I can tell you might keep you alive and out of jail long enough to get the truth out."

"Fire away," I said, then walked over to the stove and split the last of the coffee with Jasmine.

Myers's fantastic story took the wind from my sails. I sat down as he told a plausible fairy tale, cleverly crafted to fit the attack on the *Jambalaya*. When he got to the part about my alleged complicity in Chris Nellis's death, it stunned me speechless.

"That's such a load of crap," Jasmine said. Her words carried a passion that went beyond the outrage of a disinterested third party. I picked up on that. Myers did too.

"I understand," he said gently. "But you've got to know what you're up against and maybe you can find a weak spot."

"Why are you doing this?" I asked. "Aren't you putting yourself in danger for helping us?"

Myers's eyes turned inward at my remark and he laughed at something he saw there. His gaze worked my eyes for a very long time. The birds stopped singing again out front.

"Because it's the right thing," he said. "Because I owe it to Vanessa, what she stood for, what she did." He looked at Jasmine. "And because we need Jasmine to carry that on."

He dipped his head for a moment and studied his coffee mug. He took a sip, then looked at me.

"This case has smelled to high heaven from the very first day it fell on my desk," Myers said finally. "It was always too clean, which made me look twice at things. It didn't take me long to conclude Talmadge was being railroaded."

He looked at me. "Here I am, an ole country deputy out in the middle of nowhere when a couple of fancy guys in expensive suits drop a thick file on my desk. Hate-crime cold cases make good headlines these days. Good publicity for everybody. Feel good. Justice wins." He shook his head. "They brought it to me because I'd nailed an old Ku Kluxer a couple of years ago.

"But the case they brought me was too airtight. It had no holes. That simply doesn't happen unless somebody's done some creative evidence gathering . . . like that Nathan Bedford Forrest Brigade BS. No such organization. It existed on some paper in the file they handed me and nowhere else." He sighed and drained his coffee.

"I can make more," Jasmine offered.

"Uh-uh." He stood up and looked out the side window toward his truck. "The higher-ups took this and ran with it. I wanted to look deeper. They said no; they wanted the conviction and the publicity." He turned toward us. "I held my nose until the Feds stopped the trial, then I sat down and wrote a letter to Vanessa Thompson describing everything I thought was rotten with the case."

"Fourteen pages' worth," Jasmine said. "Single-spaced."

I whistled.

He waved his arm in dismissal. "It was just an opinion. Mine. Didn't count for a damn thing." He walked to the front window.

"You're going to need something other than your fire engine to drive," he said. "They're looking for it." He turned around and looked at me. "Your rental's at the impound."

He caught my questioning look.

"In the back of my truck," he said. "A bike. Plain, good on gas, easy to conceal." He looked at his watch, then stood up and moved toward the front door and opened it.

"I've got a ramp. Help me get it out."

Jasmine and I caught up with him as he opened the passenger side of his truck and pulled out a plastic grocery bag and handed it to me. Inside were two deli sandwiches in white paper, two cartons of chocolate milk, and two cell phones.

"Can't run if you get hungry," he said. "Phones are prepaid, untraceable. Already activated. Drug dealers love them. The Feds are camped out on your old cell numbers waiting for you to make a call."

"You're a helluva guy," I said.

Jasmine gave him a hug.

From the edge of the clearing, about where the road entered it, Jael crawled flat on her belly in the grass. The trees had given way to scrubby underbrush way short of the distance she needed to see them well through the fog. She moved, stopped, listened. The shack's door creaked open, voices leaked out. Slowly, she raised her head and watched the black sheriff cross the porch toward his truck.

She stepped forward, then a pair of quail came racing through the grass and stopped inches from her face. Jael froze and held her breath. The moment stretched out. In a morning as quiet as this one, if the birds took to wing, they'd set up a racket pointing right at her. Quail didn't like to fly; they walked unless threatened. She assumed Stone knew that.

Then came a rustling, a bang and rattle that sounded like a tailgate opening. Jael was ready to charge when the quail turned and scurried away through the grass.

She gave the quail time, then raised up for a look. Tufts of fog drifted across the clearing, offering first a clear shot, then no shot at all. She moved forward with the fog and hunkered down when it cleared, watching the three of them at the back of the truck positioning a ramp for the bike.

The view now was consistently good enough for a shot. The three of them concentrated on the bike, shoulder to shoulder, their backs to her. They moved back and forth, almost in unison with Stone in the middle. Jael decided to make him her first shot. She quickly sat up, one leg under her, the other bent, knee-up in front of her. She steadied the M21 with her elbow on her knee. With the crosshairs centered between the lower part of Stone's shoulder blades—in a position to blow the tatters of his heart right out the front—she took a breath, exhaled, held it, took up the trigger slack, and squeezed off the first round.

"Damn!"

Myers cursed as the motorcycle ramp shifted, then gave way, suddenly hurling Myers into me. I staggered left into Jasmine. She grabbed my arm and I caught the tailgate support cable for balance. Equilibrium hadn't begun to settle in my head when a gunshot thundered through the morning stillness.

To my right, Myers stood approximately where I had been a split instant before. He let out a loud, pain-filled "Hoof!" as if the wind had been knocked out of him. He ricocheted off the tailgate and slumped to the ground.

Simultaneous with this, another gunshot cracked through the clearing. The pickup's left rear taillight exploded inches from my hand. I laid a wicked body check on Jasmine and sent the two of us flying into the leaves and mud alongside the truck.

Another shot followed. The slug thumped into the shack's wooden siding.

Then came shots from another gun.

"Stay down!" I told Jasmine as I got to my knees and struggled to free the Ruger tangled in my cargo pocket. I peered around the rear fender and saw Myers crouched in an academy firing position, his automatic pointed toward a patch of tall grass at the edge of the clearing. He fired twice, adjusted his aim, then twice more. Tatters of ripped fabric fluttered near his far shoulder blade showing pale, straw-colored tufts of Kevlar fabric from his body armor, laid open by the oblique trajectory of a powerful slug.

The Ruger refused to come free of my shorts pocket. I cursed the pistol, the pocket, life, God himself, but mostly my own damn self for leaving the holster behind.

I yanked desperately now and tried to see where Myers was aiming.

Through the rolling fog and gloom, I thought I spotted something in shadowy camouflage. I finally ripped the Ruger out along with the pocket's fabric as Myers's gun fell silent. Myers ejected his spent clip and expertly, quickly loaded a new one. I jerked at the cloth tangled up with the revolver's hammer.

In the few seconds it took the sheriff to reload, the camouflage patch in the tall grass grew a rifle barrel. The cloth finally let go of the Ruger's hammer. I raised the Ruger, aimed, and fired. Wide.

I saw the rifle's muzzle flash before I heard its sound, and I heard the sound right as John went down again, a lot harder this time.

The muzzle of the rifle arced toward me. As I aimed, an explosive *whump!* resonated in my chest like the beat of bass drums in a parade. Before I could wonder whether I had been hit and how long I would remain conscious, my peripheral vision registered a long, bright tongue of fire to my right followed by the tremendous acoustic overpressure from Jasmine's .357 magnum.

Gratefully, I saw the rifle muzzle dip, heard it fire again. A mud crater erupted less than a foot away from Myers, who rolled himself toward a wide hickory tree. Across the clearing, the rifle's muzzle remained still. I looked over at Jasmine, crouched and ever so exposed.

"Take cover by your car." I pointed as I lunged left, scrambled past Myers, and took cover at the base of a nearby hackberry tree. When I next looked toward Jasmine, she was crouched by the rear wheel of her Mercedes. I gave her a thumbs-up, pointed at myself, and gave her a hand signal that I was going to move again. She nodded. As soon as I bolted from cover, she fired a covering shot.

I sprinted my best erratic, broken path to the pile of camouflage, ready to fire if I imagined a twitch. Closer, I made out the inert tangled form of our assailant dressed in deer hunter's camouflage. I slowed; Jasmine jogged closer, her Ruger at the ready.

"On your face!" I shouted.

No movement, no response.

"Hands out to your side!"

Nothing.

I waited until Jasmine took up a position maybe ten feet away to my right. I moved forward and got my first surprise: the body was a woman's. The second was her rifle, an M21. The significance chilled me. As I stared, her blood pooled on the ground, grew, and engulfed a shell casing. I circled her. Still she did not move. In the distance, Myers struggled up and leaned against the rear quarter panel of his truck, gripping his left shoulder with his right hand. Pain lined his face. He held his pistol loosely in his left hand.

"Okay," I said to Jasmine. Her steps grew louder through the grass and diverted my attention to the M21 for an instant. I had trained with this weapon and used it to great effectiveness in another life. With my Ruger vaguely pointed toward the fallen shooter, I bent over to examine the sniper rifle.

At that instant, the camouflaged form sprang up like a horror-house prop. I whirled as a shrieking, blood-soaked blond woman armed with a black automatic pistol sprang up and fired at me. I rolled to one side, and when I came up, I had my Ruger on target, but Jasmine again beat me to the punch. Jasmine's first shot hit our assailant above her right shoulder and spun her around. The second shot nearly decapitated her.

When the Ruger's echo had faded, a dead silence filled the clearing. Finally the din of my own heart subsided, giving way to the whine of mosquitoes, the drip of last night's rain making its way down from leaf to leaf, and finally the buzz of carrion flies arriving to make their unmistakable statements about life and death.

I had witnessed enough scenes like this one to last a lifetime, but I don't know what I expected from Jasmine. Tears maybe. Or perhaps the nausea rising from the realization that you have killed another human being, no matter the circumstances.

When I looked at her, I saw none of this. Jasmine stood motionless for a long time, her Ruger still ready. The deep, flinty determination in her eyes took me by surprise. I'd rarely seen that sort of intense introspective stare beyond the small coterie of men I had trained and served with. Once I recognized Jasmine's gaze for what it was, I was prepared for what followed.

Jasmine lowered the Ruger and deliberately placed it in the clip-on holster at her waistband. Then she stepped toward the mangled body on the ground and examined it in all its mortal detail. When she turned her head in my direction, Jasmine's eyes had a far-away focus that told me she had seen a place far past me, past the current moment, all the way to the province of personal reckoning where reality collides with what-does-it-mean? Traveling there was a Rubicon of the sharpest sort and allowed no ambiguity. I'd met some people who'd gone there and never came back. But even those who returned never came back unchanged. I know I hadn't.

There was never a thing to be said in cases like this, so I held my tongue.

Flies gathered thicker around the body; the coppery fetidness of blood and torn flesh filled my nose. In the distance, a mockingbird tossed out a tentative handful of notes. From way far away the faint staccato putts of an old John Deere tractor made one small part of me feel six years old again.

"Y'all okay?" Myers called from across the clearing, his voice strong but laced with pain.

Jasmine turned. It took a moment for her to process the blood on Myers's shirt and sprint toward him.

"John!"

I knew from the battlefield, she'd get over the dead woman faster given the chance to care for the living. Myers's wound would remind her why she had killed. The anger would more than balance the shock, horror, and mostly the guilt of the kill.

She took the pistol from Myers's left hand and slid it into his holster. I joined them.

"What'cha got there, John?"

"You tell me. You're the doctor."

I grasped the wrist of his right hand and pulled it away from his shoulder, fearing the worst. But when I pulled his hand away, there were no pulsing gouts of blood, no wildly pulsating red tributaries to indicate an artery had been hit.

"Could be worse."

"Easy for you to say, Doc."

"Let's get the shirt off and take a look at the damage."

Jasmine took control and had Myers's shirt off in seconds. He wore a white T-shirt underneath. The left sleeve and shoulder glistened bright red. I wished I had rubber gloves. John must have read my mind.

"Rubber gloves in my right back pocket," he said. "Standard kit for handling suspects these days." I nodded, pulled out a single pair, and snapped them on.

When I pulled the sleeve of his T-shirt up, I discovered a neat puckered hole in the front of a large, well-defined deltoid muscle.

"You work out pretty regularly."

He nodded.

The back of the deltoid showed me what I hoped to see: a modest exit wound oozing blood. I jammed Myers's balled-up T-shirt into the wound as a compress. He sucked in a sharp, painful breath between his clenched teeth. I held my hand over the wound.

"Well, you didn't quite dodge a bullet, but you came awfully damn close."

"Yeah?"

"Uh-huh. It'll take some rehab before you can pump iron again, but it went clean through the belly of the deltoid."

Jasmine and Myers spoke simultaneously, "Thank God!"

"Do you have a first aid kit or anything in your truck?"

Myers shook his head.

"Duct tape?"

"Toolbox in back."

Jasmine quickly retrieved a roll of silver tape and brought it back to me.

"Tear off some strips about a foot long," I said, then bound the makeshift T-shirt compress with the tape strips she handed me.

"Now, make a big loop of tape for a sling."

She nodded.

"Cool. Then tape his forearm securely around his torso and get him a blanket."

She nodded as I went back to the dead woman.

She looked somehow familiar, but I could not figure out why.

Still wearing Myers's rubber gloves, I field-stripped the body, putting the loot in the woman's camouflage hat, which had fallen next to her. Training in my other life taught me to always look for intelligence. Take everything. Its significance might not hit you for a day, maybe longer, but you never knew what might save your life.

As I looted the killer's body, a deep feeling of Camilla's presence filled me suddenly. I suppose the feeling should not have surprised me. Death and close calls can open our minds to the deepest levels of consciousness. I reveled in Camilla's presence; it warmed me. I struggled to feel, not to think.

Then from across the clearing, Myers spoke.

"Sure feels better, girl. You've got the touch."

Camilla vanished.

"We need to get you to a hospital," Jasmine replied.

I stood up to survey my handiwork and used the woman's camouflage pants to wipe her blood from my hands.

"You look like you've done this before."

I turned; Jasmine stood a couple of paces away.

"Long time ago. Another life."

"But that life never lets go of you, does it?"

I shook my head.

"You learn anything here?" She dipped her head toward the now naked blond woman on the ground.

"Nothing which adds up to a conclusion. Her hairline has a nasty scar from a head wound. There's some kind of pharmaceutical patch. I can't place it."

"The head wound might connect her to Braxton," Jasmine said.

"She's too young to be part of his program."

"Braxton's part for sure, but suppose they never stopped? Suppose the patch you don't recognize is part of it?"

"If you're right, we're in more trouble than we think."

"Hard to imagine."

"Been there. Pray you're wrong," I said as I knelt down and rolled the dead woman's rapidly cooling torso over. The head, attached only by the tendons and carotid artery on one side, flopped about and remained nearly faceup. I pointed toward the woman's shoulder.

"The tattoo looks like some I remember from Iraq."

Jasmine leaned over and read the tattoo. "Help a raghead meet Allah." She looked at me. "Profound."

I shrugged.

"So you were in the Gulf War? Which one?"

I shook my head. "Before the Russian invasion."

To keep the conversation from going further, I picked up the hat full of effects, which included a spotting scope, spare clips for the M21 and the H&K, rental car keys, a cell phone, and a single dog tag attached to a small Leatherman tool identical to my own, minus my little LED light. I left a matching dog tag on a ball chain around the remnants of her neck.

"We have a set of keys to a rental car here, and a dog tag that tells us her last name is St. Clair. The first name is odd: Jael."

"It's biblical." I turned and found Myers standing there. "Something from the Old Testament," he said. "She was an Israelite, or from one of the tribes. She tricked an enemy general or king into her tent, and after he fell asleep, she drove a tent stake through his head and nailed him to the ground."

"Nice." Jasmine looked at him. "What kind of mother names her daughter that?"

"Good question."

"Yeah . . . anyway," I said, "we've got her Social Security number and a blank where religious preference goes."

"I can run the Social Security for you," Myers said. "And the cell phone might tell you a lot from speed dials and call records."

"Right," I agreed. "But we need to stick to our mission and get you some medical care."

"I'm in pretty damn good shape for now," Myers said. "Why don't you take my truck? I can call for 911. That'll be equally as fast and you don't risk getting caught."

He pulled his cell from his belt and looked at the LCD display. "Five-by-five signal. And this has the GPS built in."

"We can't just leave you here," Jasmine said.

"Of course you can." He gave her a deep smile. "You get caught, then I got shot for no good reason. I want to be here when my officers arrive so I can give them the whole story before those spooky goons from Homeland Security can steal it away from us."

Jasmine looked uncertain.

"Look at your watch," he said.

She glanced down at her wrist. "Ten thirty-eight."

"You better get ready to call Talmadge's lawyer."

Still, she hesitated.

"Do it for me," he said. "And for your mother."

"I don't understand."

"This is the most interesting case I have ever seen in my entire career," Myers explained. "If you take me to the hospital now, then the case is out of my hands. And if it's out of my hands, I have a feeling we'll never figure out who killed your mother."

California's central coast snakes northward from the missile gantries of Vandenberg Air Force Base to Big Sur's relentlessly beautiful cliffs and surf south of Monterey. In between lies a vast, sparsely populated landscape wedged in between the Pacific Ocean and the fault-line mountains to the east where people  grow grapes, olives, cows, and flowers, make wine and big ideas, dig for pismo clams and occasionally the truth.

Most people either don't know about or studiously ignore the vast tracts of land owned by the U.S. Department of Defense. Some, like the 165,000 acres of Fort Hunter Liggett, appear on maps. Others, like the scores of secret research, communications, and small-unit operational bases, remain blank spots on maps and aerial photographs, phantom installations tucked into arroyos, perched on remote ridgelines, and separated from the curious by miles of forbidding alkali flats, or sitting right over some forgettable rise in the road ahead. San Luis Obispo sits near many of these installations, and when their personnel visit town for dinner, shopping, or a concert, there are no uniforms, no extreme haircuts or overtly military behavior to call them out of a crowd.

As Dan Gabriel jogged along Pecho Valley Road, south of Morro Bay and roughly west of San Luis Obispo, he recalled his command of just such a unit, Task Force 86M, a multiservice counterterrorist unit formed years before September 11. The Army had picked him to create this covert security and intelligence unit and concealed it in the remote, rugged hills northeast of the twin containment domes of the Diablo Canyon nuclear power plant.

The nuke provided good cover because the locals remembered not to remember it despite the emergency warning and evacuation instructions printed in the front of every phone book in the county and pasted on the backs of motel-room doors next to the regulations no one ever read and the prices no one ever paid.

Gabriel rounded the road's final curve down toward the mouth of Hazard Canyon. The morning's cool breezes hung deep with the unique littoral perfumes distilled from the ageless collision of this land and this ocean. He had dreamed on beaches and bluffs overlooking every ocean in the world, but none owned his heart like this; none resurrected in him such profound regrets.

He extended his stride downhill now to maintain the easy, thoughtful pace where the breaths came so easily. He'd begun two or three miles back where he'd parked his rented Taurus in Cuesta-by-the-Sea. Dan left the road, following a seasonal creek that wept softly into the ocean at Hazard Reef. The breezes stiffened, and by the time he reached the beach the wind stiff-armed him to a momentary standstill.

The Pacific Ocean had always incited Dan Gabriel's sense of wonder. He remembered standing with his father on the cliffs at Vandenberg, back in something like 1955 before it became a missile base and some of it still grew cows. He would stand there and let his imagination play hide-and-seek with the horizon, spawning the most remarkable dreams and desires a young boy's thoughts could possibly create.

But the most compelling of all the fantasies came when he traded the endlessly wide spaces of the horizon for the living, pulsing world of the tide pools and the ocean feeding them. Climbing down from the table-flat cliff tops to the ocean, Gabriel would lose himself for hours— days if his parents had ever allowed it—to marvel at the life there and how it thrived. He could not remember a time when he had not marveled at how the waves came in with an almost humanlike pulse, carrying food and oxygen in a salty liquid nearly identical to human blood. Dan wanted to study the sea. But in the mid-1950s few people had heard of marine biology, and even fewer considered the oceans a resource to be studied and preserved.

Gabriel's father was not among the few.

"How can you make a living?" Bill Gabriel asked his son. "You can't afford a wife and a house being a marine biologist. Hell, boy, even the piano player in a whorehouse has got job security and a damn-near guaranteed income."

You had to think about those things, Bill Gabriel told his son over and over. He'd survived both the Great Depression and Japanese war crimes in the Bataan death march. For such a dogmatically prudent man, risk played the same emotional notes as lung cancer.

Gabriel ran faster, harder now, trying to shake the memories grabbing tight against his heart like the coral-colored volcano limpets tiling the rocks below. Regret lingered like a shadow, so he sprinted the dune trail, south toward Spooner's Cove, but the past matched his pace.

Dan's father believed in the Army for security: national and personal. He had reenlisted in the Army after World War II and been assigned to Camp Cooke, an eighty-six-thousand-acre former cattle ranch in the Lompoc–Guadalupe–Santa Maria Triangle north of Santa Barbara. Bill Gabriel rose in the ranks and before retiring made full-bird colonel. Starting in 1957, he played a vital role in Camp Cooke's transition to Vandenberg Air Force Base, the home of ballistic missiles heading to rendezvous in the South Pacific and secret spy satellites.

Against that background, Bill Gabriel would have nothing of his only son's desire to squat with his wet ass in a tide pool watching green sea anemones procreate.

Sweat poured off Dan Gabriel as he made his way down to the small, semicircular beach at Spooner's Cove, now part of the Montaña de Oro State Park, which ran from Morro Bay down to the Diablo Canyon exclusion zone. Dan skirted the cove to avoid the early-morning beachcombers, charged up the hill past the small park headquarters, and set off along the rim of the bluffs above the surf.

He had inherited his father's stubbornness. So it came as no surprise to anyone but Bill Gabriel when Dan enlisted in the Navy right out of high school, despite having stellar grades, all-around athletic ability, and a family mailbox filled with offers of scholarships from prestigious universities on both coasts. Dan saw the Navy as his back door to the ocean and the underwater demolition teams as a way to get a face-to-face view.

South of the park's campground, Gabriel veered off the paved road onto a serpentine dirt track paralleling the bluff's rim.

About the time Dan had completed his basic training and had begun the rigorous physical and mental preparation for what was then known as the Underwater Demolition Teams, Bill Gabriel mounted a campaign to reclaim his son for the Army. Bill secretly used his considerable network of military and political contacts to petition the California congressional delegation for an appointment to the U.S. Military Academy at West Point.

In January 1962, President John F. Kennedy created the Navy's unconventional-warfare unit known as the SEALs. Dan and three of his UDT comrades made the cut for SEAL Team One. Bill Gabriel did not attend the commissioning ceremony. The ceremony to mark a new beginning for the first SEAL unit brought an ending for Dan instead. After the events, the base commander, and a full-blown captain with more scrambled eggs on his hat than a Grand Slam special at Denny's, approached Dan. A full-bird Army colonel accompanied them.

The base commander introduced Dan to the captain, who presented him with honorable discharge documents. The colonel introduced himself as a friend of his father's and handed him the documents for the U.S. Military Academy.

Before Dan could speak, his base commander delivered the finale of the life-changing trifecta: Whether Dan accepted or rejected the appointment to West Point, his Navy discharge was final.

His father had won.

Coming around the rim of the little cove where the rock layers on the beach were tilted nearly vertically, Dan slowed to run his eyes over the narrow battle zone between the waves and the earth and caught sight of a man and a boy of maybe ten, kneeling around a tide pool. His heart snagged on the scene and he slowed first to a jog, then a fast walk.

At that singular moment, he would have given anything to exchange places with the boy on the beach. Or his father.

West Point had turned him out in time to command a Special Forces unit that made a covert grand tour of North Vietnam, Laos, and Cambodia.

Later, he had been assigned to Clark Braxton's regular Army unit to do some training and scouting for potential Special Forces recruits when the now famous shrapnel-through-the-head incident launched Braxton on a trajectory no one could ever have predicted.

The wind buffeted Dan and chilled his sweaty T-shirt as he gazed at the father and his son poking about in the tide pool. Reluctantly, he turned and resumed his run at a jog.

The shrapnel incident made Braxton and him a popular media duo. While Clarke Braxton thrived on the attention, Gabriel found a graceful exit in a command where publicity equaled failure: Task Force 86M.

Pentagon planners originally envisioned TF86M as a covert team designed to challenge security operations at nuclear power plants and military facilities. The job of the small groups of the most highly skilled Special Forces members, pulled together from all the military branches and wired into the intelligence community, had been to play the role of terrorists and enemy special-forces teams and attempt security breaches at high-priority targets.

While Dan's tactics stirred a firestorm among facilities embarrassed by their penetrations, it also improved security in places most in need. It also kept base commanders on their toes because nobody wanted to be Dan Gabriel's latest victim.

Many of those embarrassed by Task Force 86M never forgot, and it earned him enemies in high places. But in the early days of Task Force 86M, it didn't take long for the Pentagon brass to recognize Gabriel's task force as the best-trained covert attack team in the armed forces. Under Gabriel's command, TF86M became the "go to" unit for covert action. More important, the location of the unit's HQ allowed Dan to study the ocean. He took classes at nearby Cal Poly and entertained fantasies of retiring to live as a latter-day Doc Ricketts.

But before the dream could spin itself out, Braxton tapped Dan as chief of staff and launched him on another career in the upper echelons of the Pentagon.

On this warm summer morning he gave his best finish-line sprint, trying to outrun the memories as the fence ahead rushed toward him.

The military had sustained him, nourished him. Braxton became the axis about which Dan's life had revolved for decades. But now Braxton had handed him a corrosive order that ate at Dan Gabriel's heart more caustically and painfully than his father's betrayal: killing Brad Stone.

Nothing felt right. None of Braxton's arguments had found the usual decisive tipping points in his heart: sacrificing for the greater good, closing off the compartments of a sinking ship, the personal obligations, the hell of war. None of those balanced the acids eating at Dan. Things had grown worse when he pulled Stone's records. He shared a lot with Stone. They'd been enlisted men, performed some of the same kinds of missions. Stone would have fit in at Task Force 86M but had followed his medical dream instead.

Nothing Dan clutched at justified ending Stone's dream. But if he didn't follow through with Braxton's order, he was pulling the pin on a grenade with national—international implications—it would leave Braxton's career and his reputation mortally wounded, his presidency dead, the nation with no other choice but to choose one of the intellectual pygmies and sleazy political tools who had run a great country into the ground with rancor and self-dealing.

Failure to follow the General this time would be the ultimate career suicide as well. Dan had no friends outside the military, no colleagues not connected with it, no support mechanism. Even more seriously, doing this would create mortal enemies among those he had served for decades. He'd be completely isolated, and he had little doubt his actions would push some over the edge and they would eventually come after him. He'd spend the rest of his life looking over his shoulder.

Gabriel did not stop when he got to the fence where signs warned of dire consequences for trespassers. Instead, he cut sharply up the hill and redoubled his pace, slowing only when he got to the road near the restrooms.

He broke into a fast walk here and followed the road beyond the fence with his eyes, spotting his favorite trail in the forbidden area, the one south of Coon Creek making its way over the ridgeline. His old unit still trained over there; somebody would eventually shoot at him if he tried running the trail now.

The decision about Stone twisted like a blade in his chest. Duty and loyalty struggled with right and wrong. His entire career had been about subordinating free will to the command structure. You could not win a war by allowing soldiers to act on orders or not, depending on how they felt about the moral implications.

Despite this, Dan realized then he had to stop letting other people make his decisions. And that came down to his life or Stone's. Nothing could alter that no matter how fast he ran.

59

In less than ten minutes, we settled Myers on the front-room bed with a quilt and loaded our gear, the sniper's personal effects, and her pistol into his truck. I wanted the M21 but Myers needed it for his case.

With time fast running out on our call to Shanker, Jasmine and I said good-bye, got in Myers's pickup, and headed away from the shack.

Jasmine stared straight ahead, alone with her thoughts. Somewhere overhead, the sun burned at the fog, turning it into an omnipresent, white, luminous glare that made me squint through the cross-hatching of my own eyelashes. The glare dimmed as the woods closed in on us again. I followed the road through another bright white clearing and back into the trees.

"What time is it?" I asked.

"Ten fifty-nine."

I slowed the truck where the road widened into a flat area, and suddenly a pale silver SUV emerged from the fog way too fast.

"Damn!" I jammed on the brakes and we skidded to a stop inches behind a Toyota 4Runner parked alongside the road.

"Do you suppose . . . ?" Jasmine bent over, pulled the rental car keys from the sniper's hat, and held them up. I waved a hand at them and looked at my watch.

"It's eleven," I said. "Got to stick to our mission."

"The number's already punched in." She handed me one of the prepaid cell phones. I pushed the send button and got voice mail on the first ring.

"Listen carefully, I don't have much time," Shanker's voice quavered. "Forget my office. They're watching. We have to do this now. I don't think they're listening to this, but in case they are, here's what you have to remember: your grandfather, the Judge, used to tell a lot of stories about you. One he told over and over concerns how that cotton gin made you wet your pants. Meet me there at three A.M. The moon should be down by then. Make sure you're not followed. Park somewhere away from the place. Meet me at the wagon pass-through."

I waited for the menu options, selected the one for replay, and handed it to Jasmine. I studied the Toyota SUV and a plan emerged.

"That's it?" she said as she pressed the "end" button.

"It's enough."

"You know what he's talking about?"

I nodded. "It's local legend. I was seven . . . I sneaked off from Al Thompson out at Mossy and climbed into a wagon full of freshly picked cotton. The wagon got hitched up and headed for the gin in Itta Bena with me inside."

"Why Itta Bena? The Morgan City gin's closer."

"The Judge owned part of the Itta Bena gin."

"I get the picture. So, what scared you so badly?"

"Well, I was seven and being all alone in the wagon was bad enough. Then knowing I was in trouble for sneaking away. But when they pulled the cotton wagon under the tin overhang and cranked up the huge suction hose that pulled the cotton into the main ginning section, I wet my pants.

"There was a place, an observation port, showing all the whirling cogs stripping the fibers off the seeds. I had watched it any number of times and seen the workers suck up an entire wagonload of cotton with that giant vacuum hose in what seemed like seconds.

"So, when they got to my wagon, my seven-year-old brain visualized every inch of my doom . . . sucked up through the hose and shredded by the gin."

"Obviously that didn't happen."

"Obviously. The suction hose is probably a foot in diameter and I would never have fit."

"But they played you like a violin."

"Oh, yeah. Made sure I wouldn't do it again. When the Judge found out I had wet my pants, he figured that was punishment enough." I smiled at the memory. "So anyway, we know where to meet Shanker. The big problem is how do we avoid cops until then. They're out there and the fog can't last forever. We can't just park somewhere. We can't call anybody you know, and I don't know anybody here any more."

"Let's think about that while we see if this key fits." Jasmine held up the sniper's rental-car key.

"Remember: John's calling 911. We better be gone before the first vehicles arrive." She nodded. We got out and made our way to the SUV. Jasmine tried the key in the driver's door; it opened easily.

"Start the engine," I said. "If we have gas, let's take this one and leave John's here."

Jasmine got in and started the engine.

"Three-quarters of a tank."

"Okay," I said. "Open the back." I grabbed my duffel and one of Jasmine's bags from the back of the pickup. Jasmine opened the back of the SUV, and when I saw what was inside, I nearly dropped our luggage in the mud.

"Whoa!"

I set the bags on the tailgate and jumped in. The first thing I picked up was a Night Quest PVS-14. I held it up.

"What?"

"This is serious night-vision gear." I put it down, then picked up the Raptor night-vision scope. "This is the civilian version of a heavy-duty night sniper scope." I put the scope down and peeked into the other bags.

"There's a freaking armory here!" An empty hard-sided rifle case lay open, then next to it another one with an M21 rifle and Leupold scope. "She's not working alone. And from the looks of things, she's got military backing.

"We need to move fast," I said.

Jasmine opened her mouth to reply, then the first faint notes of a siren made their way through the fog. She lunged for the driver's seat and put the SUV in gear as I slid in and slammed my door.

Dan Gabriel squinted against the gusting wind and made his way along the tree-lined sidewalk of Higuera Street toward the heart of old San Luis Obispo. Tourists and summer-school students from Cal Poly jammed the sidewalks along with panhandlers trolling for spare change.

The street threw off heat like a griddle. The wind had shifted since his run and howled in now from the east, a Santa Ana wind special-delivering desert heat and Central Valley pollution. A Santa Ana often sparked forest fires and tempers.

Dan felt the dark spots grow around his armpits and soak through the lower back of his knit shirt. He stopped for the light at Osos. At the foot of a shade tree, a battered old man with undisciplined hair and a matted beard coaxed a ragged tune from his guitar. Gabriel hesitated for a moment, then recognized a man in far worse shape than he was. The light changed. Dan pulled a five from his wallet, dropped it in the man's open guitar case, and stepped off the curb to cross the street.

Half a block down, Gabriel pushed open the glass door of the Chinese buffet and made his way to the host's podium. High-backed, leatherette booths, dark walls, dim lighting, and a massive steam table dominated the center of the room. Gabriel needed this dim anonymity for a meeting that didn't happen. He looked at his watch. Noon straight-up.

The host seated a couple of elderly ladies with flowered dresses, refilled the iced tea glass of a lone student with a thick textbook, and finally made his way toward Gabriel. Suddenly, a waving hand emerged from the shadows across the room, then the dim outline of a familiar face.

Dan waved back, nodded his greetings to the host, then made his way to shake Jack Kilgore's outstretched hand.

"You're looking trim these days, General." Kilgore's voice carried a deep, booming authority that inspired fear or confidence depending on whose side you were on.

"Thanks," Gabriel said as he slid into the booth facing Kilgore. "General."

"Yeah, hell, they'll probably take the freaking star if I tell the padded asses at the Pentagon to stuff it one more time, now that I don't have you and Braxton as my point men."

Gabriel's laugh was genuine.

Jack Kilgore had been a member of Task Force 86M for nearly fifteen years and its commander for five. He had been Gabriel's first and only choice for the top slot. Kilgore had a reputation for cutting through BS to get a job done. Right. The first time. But his disdain for paperwork and bureaucracy had earned him enemies among the paper-pushers. His bold operational plans made others nervous and branded him a cowboy.

"It only looks risky when you don't understand the situation," Kilgore explained time and again. "And the upholstered assholes in Washington don't have enough combat experience to understand which end of their freaking M16 gets pointed which way." Kilgore had an enormous capacity to hold every single one of the important elements of a situation in his head all at the same time and to look at things as a whole rather than just piece by piece. Few officers had this gift, and that was one of the two reasons Dan had called on Kilgore. The other was obviously firepower and intel.

"You're right," Gabriel said when the lightness of his laughter gave way to the real reason for the meeting. "But that's not why I called."

"Didn't think so."

"Like I said before, this is a conversation we never had."

"Most of my conversations these days are like that," Kilgore said. "Problem is sometimes I can't remember whether I forgot a conversation because I was supposed to or because I'm getting old." He smiled, but Gabriel didn't pick up on it.

"We have a problem which may need some extracurricular activity."

"Uh-huh. Another training mission?" Kilgore used his fingers to put quotes around *training*.

"Maybe. It's about a secret operation called Project Enduring Valor." Dan waited for a look of recognition, but got only a frown. "It's a high-priority effort. Braxton says it's got some bad history."

"How bad?"

"Enough to blow his presidential bid out of the water."

Kilgore made a low whistle. Then: "You hungry?"

"A little."

"It sounds like you're going to need some time to fill me in."

Dan nodded.

"You paying?"

Gabriel nodded.

"Then I'm hungry too."

Kilgore slid out of his seat and headed for the buffet. Gabriel followed him.

For the next forty-five minutes over food made banal enough for the average middle-American palate, Dan laid out the situation. Kilgore ate quietly, rarely interrupted, as he absorbed the connection between the illegal experiments, My Lai, Frank Harper, and Braxton's head wound.

Kilgore stopped eating entirely when Dan related the details of the soon-to-be-deployed Xantaeus patches.

When Dan ran out of words, Kilgore looked at him in silence for several moments.

"You're sitting right on top of a drum of fuggy old nitroglycerin, aren't you?"

Gabriel nodded. "And I have to make a decision in the next seventy-two hours. There's a huge series of meetings at the General's—"

"He still calling it Castello Da Vinci?"

Gabriel nodded.

Kilgore frowned. "That's awfully pretentious."

"It does look awfully good on a wine label."

"Whoopee-do. Everybody and their yard boy up there has their own wine label."

"Not on a bottle selling for five hundred dollars and up—if you're lucky enough to find one for sale."

"Still—"

"Yeah, I'm with you on all that wine porn crap." Gabriel paused to drain the last sips of his iced tea. When it was gone, he rattled the ice around in the glass before continuing.

"General Braxton's hosting a series of top-level meetings over the next three days. Some relate to the campaign, some are social and fund-raising events. There's one that Braxton has been tight-lipped about, and I'm sure it's about Project Enduring Valor."

Kilgore nodded as he turned his concentration on chasing a chow mein noodle around his plate with his chopsticks. Finally, he gave up and raised his face to met Gabriel's eyes. "Lord, lord." Kilgore shook his head and rubbed at his chin. "My experience has been that the General is rarely wrong about military matters."

"Therein lies the problem."

"On the other hand, I may have heard about this Stone fellow," Kilgore said. "You and I live in a pretty small world. We're talking ancient history, but it's easy enough to check out."

"Soon?"

"This afternoon." Kilgore took a bite of moo shoo pork and washed it down with iced tea. "You've never been this spooked before, old son. You've got to put on your operational hat or you're going to get hurt."

Gabriel nodded.

"Well, besides Stone, the ultimate hard choice we have to make on the usual incomplete information concerns the Xantaeus issue and Braxton's connection." Kilgore paused to study the ceiling. "Genies don't go back into their bottles." He shook his head. "Nukes came out and stayed. CBW. The chemical warrior ain't crawling back inside either. Braxton's right about making sure we win the wars."

Gabriel opened his mouth, but Kilgore held up his hand.

"On the other hand, if the effects are not completely reversible—even if a tenth of one percent never come out of it—we have a national disaster, a whole new class of highly capable killers who can't turn it off. Maybe a lot of them who look normal and act normal, but in the end what we could end up with are bunch of domestic My Lais."

Gabriel nodded.

"But you might be wrong. You could be contravening a decision when you don't have as much data as Braxton has. It's a command thing."

"Braxton's not in the military anymore and neither am I."

"Technically you're correct. But in reality, we're in a war for the soul and security of this country. It's never been in greater danger. And brave, good people like this Stone fellow do get killed in a war, sometimes they have to be sacrificed. It's not right, but sometimes it's the only alternative.

"Now, mind you, I'm not yet convinced the General's right. However, if we play the odds, we both know his judgment has been vindicated so many times I can't think of the last time he was wrong."

"Bothers me too," Gabriel said.

"Good! Absolute certainty's killed more people than informed ambiguity, which means we have to take the ball the General has handed off and run with it until and unless we find we're headed toward the wrong goalposts."

"What if we don't realize it until it's too late?"

Kilgore gave him a broad smile. "You've been pushing a desk way too long, old buddy."

Fog still shrouded the landscape like a gesso wash, robbing the world of depth and color and making close things seem far away. Jasmine and I drove through a few rare spots where the sun had burned completely through, but most everywhere else we looked, a bright, lethal glare left us frowning and squinting.

"Okay, if I remember correctly, we should find a little track leading through that line of trees up there." Jasmine chewed on a corner of her lower lip as she stared intently ahead, steering the pale silver SUV south along a serpentine gravel track paved with ruts and washboard corrugations. A thin selvage of trees and tangled vines along the Tallahatchie River hurtled past on the left. Cotton in full bloom rushed by on the right.

For the best part of an hour, Jasmine had navigated the SUV along a backwoods odyssey of roads—paved, gravel, unpaved—and more than a few dirt and mud tracks that required the SUV's four-wheel drive. She kept us off the main roads and on a mostly northerly course. Occasionally in the distance, we saw police-car light bars strobing in the haze. It didn't take much imagination to interpret those as roadblocks, although the radio made no mention of a manhunt or the shooting of a sheriff's deputy by a mysterious blond woman.

With nothing better to do, I tinkered periodically with the SUV's Global Positioning System navigation unit. According to the GPS, we were nowhere near anything that offered yet another metaphor for the Delta.

Abruptly, I pitched forward as Jasmine stabbed at the brakes.

"There." She pointed. I followed her finger and, right off the tip, saw a break in the trees materialize out of the glare. Slowing to a crawl, she turned the SUV cautiously left and stopped in front of the rusted superstructure of a condemned bridge barricaded with dire warnings. She stopped the SUV nose to nose with a red-and-white-striped barrier.

"Wait here."

She put the SUV in park and got out. To its credit, the GPS display showed us on the Tallahatchie's west bank, south of Ruby. Jasmine strode confidently around the barriers and out onto the bridge. Then she faded to a shadowy cipher on the far side, and a shadow of loss fell across my heart. I turned from the image and tinkered with the GPS for distraction, looking for Tyrone Freedman's house, which, according to the latest technology, existed nowhere except in a native Deltan's head.

While I worried about dragging Tyrone further into this mess and second-guessed my own memories of how well we had connected back at the hospital, I'd called his cell not long after Jasmine had steered us away from John's pickup in the killer's SUV.

"You're lucky I'm in the imaging lab," he'd told me. "Whole hospital's crawling with Feds and some really creepy guys with dead eyes."

He volunteered shelter faster than I could ask. I talked him out of doing more.

Jasmine made her way out of the fog now and, with an easy, swift familiarity, moved the barriers blocking access to the bridge.

"I would have thought those barricades would be a lot more permanent," I said when she got back in.

"They were once, but the locals made some changes, otherwise they have to go down to Money or up to Minter City to cross."

She put the SUV in gear, eased past the barrier, then stopped. Without being asked, I got out and dragged the barrier back in place behind us. As Jasmine drove, I tried not to look at the decrepit, weathered boards covering the bridge's roadway or the storm-roiled brown water below. I also tried to ignore how the bridge swayed and yawed and struggled to ignore the great pancake-sized scabs of rust flaking off the bridge's elderly, anemic girders.

In the swirling silver mist, a lean, fit, muscular man stood at the edge of the thin selvage of trees and brush and followed the pale silver SUV's taillights disappearing across the old Tallahatchie bridge. He pulled the baseball cap off his head and ran his other hand across the top of his head and nodded to himself.

"Good try," he said quietly as he replaced the baseball cap on his head and adjusted the pitch, rotation, and yaw a degree here and there until he got it precisely where he liked it. "But not good enough to lose me."

It was a process of elimination, and from the data he'd gathered and from what he knew about the two, there would be only one place they'd go. He smiled as he walked back to his truck and turned it around and headed south for the Money bridge. No reason to take a chance on this piece-of-shit bridge. His gut told him where he'd find them tonight, and his gut never lied.

The muddy, leaf-matted clearing in front of Jasmine Thompson's sharecropper's shack looked like an all-night doughnut stand at 3:00 A.M. Four sheriff's cruisers were jammed fender to fender with a highway patrol car, two boxy ambulances, the coroner's personal car, a crime scene van, and a hearse.

John Myers stood at the center of the circus, playing ringmaster and repeatedly telling paramedics he wouldn't leave until he was damn well ready. From the moment they'd arrived, they'd poked and prodded at him, attached an EKG, pumped the blood pressure cuff on his good arm time and again, and seemed awfully disappointed to find his blood pressure normal, his EKG solid and healthy, and his heartbeat right at seventy (ten beats faster than normal, but he wasn't about to tell them).

He allowed them to give him an antibiotic but refused the pain medicine. He needed a clear head, for a while at least.

"Yo! Don't walk over there! Evidence, maybe." Myers's voice was as deep, loud, and commanding as ever, and no one at the scene was inclined to mess with his authority.

Before the first vehicles had arrived, Myers had used the camera function on his new cell phone to document the scene. He took closeups and long shots. He took a picture from the sniper's position, then he walked over and took a picture toward the dead sniper from the spot he had been hit, easy enough to spot by the blood on the ground.

He had taken a lot of shots of the dead blond woman, including close-ups of her face, tattoo, and the curious pharmaceutical patch.

Then he had e-mailed all of the photos to himself and his usual cc: list, including a secret Yahoo! mail account he had used since his wife's death to surf Internet chat rooms as a younger, hipper version of himself.

Myers had also taken good shots of the rifle and the scope and, with a great deal of pain, had written down the serial numbers of both. These he had laboriously entered with one hand into an e-mail along with the data off the dog tag and sent to himself and the same recipients as the photos.

Now, Myers watched with satisfaction as the forensics team shot the same images from the same angles with professional, high-resolution cameras, close-up lenses, and tripods. A videographer walked the scene.

With every photo, note, and foot of tape shot by his own people, Myers relaxed. But as the sustaining tide of adrenaline ebbed, the throbbing in his shoulder surged like a red-hot rod. He tried to keep the pain from his face, but instants later an overachieving paramedic appeared at Myers's side.

"You okay, Sarge?"

"Just fine." Myers tried to wave him off, but the sandy-haired young man with pink skin and freckles didn't walk away as earlier.

"Sarge, even if you feel okay right now, the chemicals thrown off from the injury can come back to bite you in the ass. Shock might not be out of the question."

"I'm gonna shock you, son, if you don't leave me alone." But Myers noted his own lack of conviction. Then right when John had decided to sit down, a new sound popped his adrenaline level up a notch. The distant thwack of a helicopter drifted in among the work sounds. As it grew louder, Myers focused on the sound: too deep for the little old bubble-cockpit Sikorskys used for crop dusting. Wrong pitch for the Sheriff Department's Bell JetRanger.

When Myers realized the helicopter sound was growing loud way too fast for any civilian chopper in his memory, the dread settled in on top of his heart. He'd known this would happen even as he'd prayed it would not. An instant later, he looked up as an Army Blackhawk helicopter thundered over the clearing.

Faces turned upward as one. Myers looked around him and thought of hatchlings in a nest expecting to be fed.

The Blackhawk returned and hovered over the clearing. Armed men hung out the side door. One of them held what looked like a video camera. Myers palmed his phone and held it unobtrusively at his side, taking photos as fast as his phone would allow.

Everything else happened in a blur. As soon as Myers looked around, he saw a Humvee come around the curve and into the clearing, the growl of its motor covered by the Blackhawk's powerful engine. The Humvee was the genuine military-issue article, not one of those fake Hot Wheels Hummers favored by wannabes with too much money. Myers took more photos, hit his speed dial, and took more.

Another Humvee followed, and behind them two dark green Suburbans with tinted windows and the all-too-familiar white-and-blue license plates that screamed, "Feds!"

Four combat-ready soldiers complete with body armor and kraut helmets piled out of each Humvee. Simultaneously, the Suburbans disgorged six or seven SWAT-ready Feds each. Myers lost interest in counting.

The soldiers and the Feds fanned out. The Feds pushed their way through Myers's men and shoved them aside. One of them snatched the videographer's camera away. Myers snapped that photo, then e-mailed it and all the others. Then he shoved the phone in his pocket and strode to the Fed with the video camera—*his* damned video camera.

"What the hell you think you're doing?" Myers yelled, and reached over with his good hand.

The hand never got close.

A crushing blow whacked the breath out of his lungs and dropped Myers to the ground. He landed on his wounded shoulder and managed to hear his own scream of pain over the drone of the Blackhawk's rotors.

He rolled off the wounded shoulder and saw the Feds, with soldiers covering their backs, as they relieved all of the law enforcement officers present of their firearms, batons, Mace, and pepper spray. Then, before Myers could focus the pain away from his eyes, a set of knee-length, olive-green rubber boots filled his entire field of vision. He looked up at a tall, lean man with close-cropped gray hair and a birthmark on his left forehead. David Brown, the man from Homeland Security.

Swift as blur, Brown raised one of the muddy boots and planted it right on the wounded shoulder and kicked Myers flat on his back and held it there. John saw the smile on the man's face and was determined not to show any pain. He glared up at Brown. The man's lips moved, but his words were stillborn in the rotor din. The man from Homeland Security took note of this, then moved his foot and bent over.

Myers tried to sit and quickly learned David Brown was as strong as he was tall. The gray-haired man launched a flat-handed sledgehammer blow at John's sternum and slammed the wounded deputy into the ground.

"You are a lot dumber than you look," the man from Homeland Security said as he bent over close to Myers's ear and yelled above the Blackhawk. "Wise up, pal, the Patriot Act allows me to grab your sorry ass and throw you in a fucking cell that few people know about and even fewer could find. I don't have to charge you and I don't need to give you a lawyer or a fucking phone call. I can own your butt if I choose to."

Myers glared up at him and noticed something he had not seen on the man at the courthouse meeting: a small pin with the Customs Service seal on it. That did not bode well. Customs had earned a deserved reputation as a wild posse of loose-cannon cowboys who tried to use force and aggression to make up for what they lacked in intelligence and competence.

"Do you understand me, you worthless cocksucker?" the gray-haired man yelled so loudly his spittle showered Myers's face. Myers shook his head. A brief angry mask played over the gray-haired man's face, and that was reward enough for Myers.

"Are we speaking the same goddamned language here, asshole?" the man asked. "Do I need to use smaller words?"

"Oh, I hear your words, big man," Myers said. "But I clearly do not understand your attitude."

The man from Homeland Security gave him a cynical smile then.

"Pal, it's a new day. September eleventh changed everything, and you don't appear to have gotten the message."

"I—"

"Shut the hell up! I am not interested in your platitudes about the Constitution or due process or any other naïve sermons you have in your head. Look around you and keep the following in mind: You can work with me and probably advance yourself so you can move out of this stinking state. Or you can keep your mouth shut and stay out of my way and your pathetic life will stay the same.

"Or . . ." The man paused. "Or, if you stay on this suicide track, I can—no, I *will*—put you in a place where no one will ever find you and keep you alive long after you wished you were dead."

Myers remained silent.

"Do I make myself clear?"

John Myers looked up at this angry, irrational white face full of power lust and stinking of the ugly past. Then he said, "Yassuh!"

Tyrone Freedman lived in a battered single-wide trailer perched drunkenly on cracked and broken cinder blocks. Blue tarps sagged from the roof. A drunken old hay barn squatted nearby, one corner touching the ground, the rest cleared for storage and garage space. The Yalobusha River levee rose steeply beyond a grove of pecan trees.

"Damn," I said softly.

"I've seen worse," Jasmine said as she steered us into a cleared space in the old barn. "Some people can't afford tarps."

I shook my head, turning to keep the trailer in view.

"But he deserves better?"

I nodded.

"So do a lot of people around here."

As Jasmine turned off the ignition, I spotted a utility pole next to the trailer with the usual phone and electrical wires and at the top, an oval, open-grid dish.

"Check it out." I pointed. "Wireless broadband."

Jasmine laughed. "Looks like something from the old *Max Headroom* series, you know, the weird old couple with the television studio in that decrepit bus."

"I haven't thought about *Max Headroom* in years," I said.

"I loved it."

"Me too."

We looked at each other for a moment, grew uncomfortable way too fast. I bailed out of the moment and opened my door.

Jasmine's door opened as I picked my way through the barn's clutter, located the rusted old Allis-Chalmers tractor, and found the trailer key on top of its engine block right where Tyrone had told me it would be.

Inside the trailer, the floor sagged from piles of books. Tarps draped from the ceiling made it feel like a tent. It was cool inside; the compressors of at least two window air conditioners thrummed unseen. I turned on the lights.

"Check it out." I pointed to a computer cpu in the corner of what passed for the trailer's living room. Behind the cpu, which had no cover, a router and a hub sprouted Cat-5 cable in cable-tied bundles stretching to the ceiling and along the trailer's long hallway.

"You surprised?"

"Nope."

I walked to the computer and pressed the monitor's power button. Instants later the screen gave me a homemade screen saver with logos for Red Hat Fedora Linux and Apache Web server software. A quick look at the hardware showed the computer had been cobbled together from components others had discarded as obsolete.

Jasmine and I followed the overhead cables to another book-jammed room, this one crammed with file cabinets, medical books, and another home-brewed computer. I followed Tyrone's instructions and turned it on. It was another Linux machine.

Jasmine ran her fingers along the open frame of the computer. "It always amazes me how much some people can do with so little." Then she covered her mouth as a broad yawn made its way across her face. "Oh! Sorry."

"Don't be. We need to get some sleep before we leave tonight."

"What time do we need to leave?"

"About eleven thirty, get to Itta Bena around midnight."

"Why so early? We're meeting Shanker at three A.M."

"Going wrong. What a cheery thought."

"Prepare for the worst; pray for the best."

"Uh-hmmmm."

"Three hours seems like a long time, but once we're there, it'll go faster than greased lightning."

As the computer booted, I looked around the room and spotted Arthur Guyton's classic human anatomy book I had used in medical school. One of the keenest intellects on the planet, Guyton had chosen to live in Jackson, taught at the med school there, and mentored too many new physicians to name, me included.

I pulled the text and showed it to Jasmine. "He helped turn my life around."

I opened the book and flipped through the pages. As Jasmine moved closer to see, she rested her left arm on my shoulder. The firmness of her touch warmed my skin.

"If it hadn't been for him . . ."

I remembered Dr. Guyton's kindness and knew I had never thanked him enough.

On the monitor the command line appeared and demanded a password and user name.

"Here goes." I put Guyton's textbook down and entered the account data Tyrone had given me.

"ArrOwcaTCHer666homeINtHEwoods," I mumbled to myself as I entered the characters precisely.

"That's awfully long."

"The longer the sequence the harder it is to crack."

I concentrated even harder on the password: 5149VmB9a65P7ba-DhOmbreNOtXarb.

Instants after hitting the enter key, the KDE graphical user interface appeared, customized with my name and a link, which I clicked.

A long note from Tyrone appeared in OpenOffice.

"There's an alert at the hospital for maximum staffing. It's about you. They think you're one bad dude and they want us ready for casualties. There's even a Life Flight chopper stationed on the roof. What the hell did you do before med school?

"Anyway, because of this, I'll be camping out in the imaging lab. All hell's broken loose. Feds and Army everywhere. John Myers came in to have his shoulder looked at. The paramedics who brought him in looked like they had had a near-death experience. The blond kid with the really pink skin and all the freckles looked even whiter than ever, which is hard to believe. A really creepy guy in SWAT gear stood in the emergency room the whole time. John didn't say a word to me the whole time I worked on John's shoulder. If you click here, you'll see why John was so damned quiet. We debrided things and the paramedics gave him a ride home."

I clicked on the hyperlink that took me to a plain IP address: 216.226.157.157, no domain name, just a twelve-digit IP address that clearly was not Tyrone's server.

"Oh, hell!" Jasmine reacted when a page of thumbnail photos came up. She pointed to one showing an Army Blackhawk helicopter. We skipped over John's documentation of the sniper and shooting scene we had witnessed firsthand and went to images of Humvees, Suburbans, troops, and SWAT-clad Feds. The photos were the typical low-resolution images produced by a camera phone, but the detail was sufficient to show us what had happened. Finally, we read John's text messages Tyrone had posted on the Web page.

I closed Mozilla and immediately a dialogue box appeared: "Please wait: WEBsweeper is permanently removing all cache and history data and permanently sanitizing all associated disc sectors in accordance with NSA and DOD data security standards."

Moments later the box disappeared and we continued reading.

"I've edited the hospital server's access logs to delete my tracks in up-loading this Web page. It and the photos are on a server outside the U.S. and outside its sphere of influence. The servers are totally hidden using a second-generation onion routing system called Tor.

"If you need it, lift the carpet in the hallway directly underneath the furnace's air return and you'll find my firearms. To open the combination to the lock, take the password from this machine. Count backward and pull out the first four digits. There's a little range I set up out back by the levee in case you want to kill some time.

"Good news: Lashonna's conscious and doing better than expected."

"Thank you, God," Jasmine said softly. Then she leaned over and kissed me on the cheek. "And thank you, Doctor."

Her kiss cheered me for a fleeting instant, then I read the next paragraph.

"I wish I had better news for you regarding Camilla, but you should probably click here to check out the new images. The files are on the hospital's server, but don't worry, a series of proxy servers accessed through dark IP addresses sanitizes the access."

My admiration for Tyrone's technical prowess in covering his tracks and hiding Myers's evidence slipped beneath the darkness in my soul that gathered as I paged through the images.

Camilla had died when I wasn't looking.

I cried.

As Dan Gabriel steered his rental car north on Highway 101 north of Paso Robles, his cell phone rang.

"Gabriel," he answered.

"Aren't you going to stop at the In-N-Out Burger there?" Jack Kilgore's voice asked.

"How'd you know where I am?"

"You've got a new wireless phone, with the GPS locator."

"Oh, I forgot. . . . So, did you learn anything?"

"A lot," Kilgore said. "Stone's a real mensch. Plus he's a natural two-percenter, highly lethal, capable, always under control. Back then, if you wanted somebody—or multiple somebodies—dead, you sent Stone. Then he got religion or something, requested and got training for para-medical rescue. Saved a lot of lives. Then he left and becomes a hot-shit doctor."

"Not the kind of person I want to terminate," Gabriel said.

"Roger that. Makes me question the General more than I ever have before."

Silence filled the connection with unspoken doubt.

"And a lot of freaky stuff's going down in Mississippi, not far from the old prison-camp hospital the General was in. I've got some of my guys keeping an eye on things. I structured it as an exercise to assess the operational competence of the Homeland Security screwups driving the show there. A troop of Cub Scouts could do a better job at radio discipline. Operational security's full of holes. It's the usual bullshit in a china shop thing, not surprising since Brown and his Customs bozos are running things. They're the ones who nailed all those innocent Muslims' butts to a tree after 9/11 just to make bureaucratic brownie points. They've now circulated photos of Stone and Jasmine Thompson as wanted fugitives."

"Charged with?"

"Murder and drug running out of L.A."

"Marvelous."

"And, Dan?"

"Yeah?"

"Brown's been calling Clark Braxton's cell phone an awfully lot."

I have no clear idea how long I walked the levee. I know I walked out of Tyrone Freedman's trailer, but I don't remember what or whether I said anything to Jasmine at the time. Camilla's death blew the center out of me like a ton of lead shot through a wet paper bag, and I walked the two-tracked gravel path atop the levee down to the striped metal barrier across the road padlocked to a metal post set in concrete.

I stood for a moment.

Humidity smothered my face as the sun burned it. Sweat dripped everywhere. Around me, the land wobbled and swayed, warped by un-dead water rising from the soil to haunt the Delta with another day of mildew and humidity, which would eventually give life to more thun-derstorms. Horseflies bit at my bare legs, and mosquitoes heavy with someone else's blood blanketed me. My hands moved with a frantic palsy that barely interrupted their bloodlust. Finally, I set off at a dead run toward Tyrone's trailer, leaving the insects behind; guilt, anger, and sorrow paced me relentlessly.

It took me almost fifteen minutes to reach Tyrone's cabin, meaning I had walked two, maybe two and a half miles. As I stumbled down the steep levee bank, I heard the syncopated, guitar-slapping rhythm of Robert Johnson's "Preaching Blues, Up Jumped the Devil" coming from the trailer.

The lyrics reached out for me and I followed them. Despite the heat, the front door was open and I walked in.

"Jasmine?" I called, and when I got no answer, I closed the door.

The desperate urgency of this song set it apart from Johnson's usual cool nasality. So much of Johnson's work moved me to introspection with its sanguine acknowledgment of the evil dogging our lives. But "Preaching Blues" always ripped at me like a scream. I stood at the win-dow and parted the curtains, hoping to catch a glimpse of Jasmine walk-ing back from the SUV.

Johnson's frantic raw emotions cut right through to my own as I lis-tened to the familiar lyrics. The blues behind blues music ate people like heart disease. Hopelessness was the ultimate hell.

When Johnson finished, his voice and guitar trailed off like the last notes of rain after a storm. Then the silence filled with the surf of my heart and the distant drone of a crop duster. A moment later, the floor creaked behind me, followed by Jasmine's fragrance, spicy, earthy, welcome, warm.

"How did you know?" When I turned around, her gaze froze me in place. The wisteria hues of her eyes seemed limitless in their depth and beauty. "The music, I mean?"

In the background, Johnson began "Love in Vain" and my ear recognized this was the same *Hellhound on My Trail* CD from Indigo Recordings I had left in the rental truck.

"I don't know," Jasmine said. "I just knew when I saw it next to Tyrone's stereo." Jasmine and I moved toward each other and embraced in the middle of the living room.

"You okay?"

"Yes," I lied. "No. No, I'm not. Camilla in the middle of all this is . . ."

"Too much?"

"No," I said truthfully. "But damned close."

She put her head on my shoulder. I folded her in my arms and basked in her comfort for a time that stretched comfortably beyond the moment. So much death, so much loss. I wanted the moment to last.

Then, as if a switch had been thrown somewhere far beyond thought and decisions, we held each other tighter, somewhere between desperation and love. The sensuous press of her breasts instantly aroused me. When Jasmine thrust her hips against me, a seismic passion sucker punched me with feelings forgotten in the past six years.

Then everything fast-forwarded. Suddenly we were naked from the waist up and hastening with the rest. Jasmine's elegant abundance of curves beneath the soft, burnished luminosity of her skin stunned me and banished every thought beyond this remarkable moment to a distant and irrelevant horizon.

Then alarms sounded in my head.

Pure, undiluted passion—whether from lust, hate, anger, or fear—terrified me. I'd seen it leave battlefields littered with the bodies of innocent people and derail young lives with unwanted children. Prison cells held legions of basically decent people who'd let passion dump their lives into an endless pit of regret.

As a teenager I ran with a rough crowd, always ready with fists, a phallus, and fast cars. But over the course of less than a year, they all fell by the wayside, snared by police, parents, and unplanned parenthood. Through their mistakes, I realized that unbridled passion could generate an irresistible black hole of unsatisfied regret from which there was no escape. I feared the way it blinded us to consequences and erased everything but the singular urge for release. It was the devil's deal where we traded the future for a blinding spasm of release that always left us hungrier than ever.

Urgent alarms pulsed in my head as Jasmine's hands made their way across my chest and down my belly. As I bent low to kiss her, she slipped her right hand down the front of my partly unzipped shorts. With an effort much like that needed to awaken from particularly horrific nightmares, I struggled back.

Jasmine was startled, astounded. I stood back from her, burning with regret like a death in the family. Perplexity sifted across her face.

"What's wrong?" she said finally. Her voice was husky and tempting.

I wanted to say I needed her more than I had words to express.

"Is it me?" Her face gave me a look of dismay. Then she crossed her arms to hide her breasts.

My heart fell. "No. It's definitely not you."

I wanted to say it was all too common for two people in danger to misinterpret the hormones of fear circulating in their veins for those of love. There was also the issue of Camilla's body, not yet cold.

"So what's the problem?"

I wanted to say the looks and comments from her uncle and the black LAPD detective made me second-guess my own motivations. I also wanted to express unspeakable things like AIDS, condoms, and whether we really wanted to do this without a commitment, marriage whether in the eyes of God or the law. But for reasons I don't understand, I didn't say any of it.

"Oh, yes," I said. "I do so much like you." My voice broke. I cleared my throat. "Jasmine, I . . . I more than like you." I looked at her eyes, her face, and I connected with the most valuable words I knew. "I love you."

The confusion swirled in her eyes.

"Oh, Brad. I love you too." She gave her head a little shake. "But why—"

There were all those things I wanted to say. In the end, I lacked the courage and she began to cry. I stepped forward to give her a hug. When she turned away, it broke my heart.

As she dressed with her back turned toward me, I pulled on my shirt and zipped up my shorts. I prayed for her hurt to go away and hoped this hadn't jinxed our relationship. My brain told me any relationship unable to survive the intelligent exercise of good judgment would not last, but my heart disagreed.

After what seemed like the passing of geological time, Jasmine turned and wiped the remains of a tear from her right cheek. When her face offered me her Mona Lisa smile, I knew it was going to be all right. She accepted my hug this time and gave me one in return.

"That *was* a smart move," she said. "Damn you. One of these days, you'll tell me about it." It wasn't a question.

"Uh-huh," Jasmine said. "Yes, you will. And you know what? I believe you love me. Otherwise you wouldn't have done that. And I love you too."

Fatigue rushed into the calm moment, filling the vacuum left by passion and leaving us desperate for rest. We extended the sofa bed in Tyrone Freedman's makeshift living room. I set the alarm on my watch and we fell asleep in each other's arms.

Without the blare of 50 Cent flooding out the open windows of a slammed Honda with seventeen-inch rims and a rear-window decal declaring the driver a "Bad Ass," shoppers coming out of the grocery store at the west end of the square in Itta Bena might have caught the strains of an acoustic guitar drifting out the open door of the old dry goods store across the street.

They might have heard the nearly on-key voice of a wrinkled, leathery old man who had once gotten drunk with Mississippi John Hurt, singing about pain and betrayal. But the shoppers didn't hear, and had they been able, they wouldn't probably have cared, such is the nadir to which the blues have sunk in the belly of its creation.

The old dry goods store turned juke joint had no signs, no name, no atmospheric old metal chewing-tobacco signs, or any of the other cultural tattoos sought by affluent white tourists. This place was simply known as Lena's, and as soon as some damned tourist stumbled in by accident, she'd shut it down, find some other place for it, and pass the word among the regulars. Vacant buildings were easy to come by.

But for now, Lena's lay in the shadow of the big water tower, kitty-corner from the police station and fire department, and steps west of a bar where patrons rarely let musical appreciation get in the way of serious drinking.

Tonight, Lena's was jammed. Early arrivals sat in folding chairs jammed around card tables, while the rest crowded around the walls, squatted on the worn wooden floor, and leaned against the big folding banquet tables Lena used as a movable bar. Cigarette smog hung in layers and almost chased away the naphthalene pungency of mothballs, which had once protected the dry goods store's wool fabrics.

Oh, Bob shot once and Louis shot too,
shot poor Collins, shot him through and through

The old man sang close enough to the right notes to be enjoyable and far enough off-key to be authentic, none of the perfect-pitch and overorchestrated stuff usually found on CDs that leached out the pain and emotion.

In the far back corner of Lena's, almost to a door marked Restrooms, which actually led outside, John Myers sat at the end of a small rectangular table with Jasmine's uncle, Quincy Thompson, and Pete Mandeville, a high-yellow deputy who had been present at the murder scene when the Feds had arrived. The very end of the folding table groaned under the meaty elbows of the Itta Bena police chief, a giant man with an oversize, black cowboy hat and skin so tight, shiny, and impenetrably dark it reflected like a mirror.

Wedged into the most uncomfortable spot in the room, shoehorned right into the display window behind where the front door opened, sat two thirtysomething white men with tailored suits, $50 haircuts, and perfectly straight, overly bright teeth. They squirmed uncomfortably and nursed the cheap rye Lena had poured for them. Occasionally, one of them would sip at his glass, then grimace. Lena was not about to pour them the good stuff.

The singer everybody called Pap finished with the angels laying Ol' Collins away, then amid a respectful silence, he made his way masterfully through the final bars, and when he finished, the applause would have drowned the loudest of 50 Cent's best.

When the applause trailed off, Quincy Thompson picked up where he had left off.

"I tell you it's all because of that white boy. All his fault for coming here to get in Jasmine's pants." He looked around, expecting confirmation. Nobody met his gaze.

"So, you think those boys're civilian or military?" Mandeville cocked his head toward the front door.

"Civilian. Look at the haircuts," the police chief said, his voice rolling deep like distant thunder. "And the suits; sure ain't military tailoring. You can hardly spot the pieces they carryin'."

"The one on the left followed me to John's," Mandeville said.

"T'other one was cooped in his car out front a my house when Pete arrived," Myers said.

"Our tax dollars at work," the police chief rumbled.

"Yeah, yeah, but you're missing what's going down and it's all that Stone boy's fault," Quincy persisted.

Myers rolled his eyes. The other men concentrated on their sour mash, rattling the remains of the ice and the bourbon.

Quincy tried again. "No, listen to me. It—"

"Oh, yeah, Quince, you must certainly be right," Myers said sarcastically. "That rich ole white boy who lives in the middle of mo' jelly roll and poontang than you ever wet-dreamed about flew umpteen thousand miles just to get yo' niece in bed."

Myers drained his bourbon, then leaned toward Quincy. "Boy, for a damned professor, you can be awfully fugging dumb."

Mandeville stifled a laugh. Quincy glared at him.

"Quincy, Dr. Stone's all right, never mind his grandaddy. He came out here because your sister—God rest her soul—asked him to."

"I know that, John, but I don't trust white people, that boy especially. Look at the blood running through his veins. No way he can get away from that." Quincy paused. "I just won't ever get over my daddy and all the years he worked for the Judge and looked after that boy. And ain'no way to forget Daddy Al sittin' around telling us, 'I ain'no ordinary niggah. I's lawyuh Stone's chauffeur.'" Quincy looked at John expectantly. "Can you forget?"

Quincy looked around the table. "Well, can you forget? Uh-uh. No, suh! White folks just trouble, and we always caught in the shit swirlin' round 'em." He looked around the room and stopped when his gaze fell on another white face in the audience.

"And you been spending so much time on the crackers by the door, you ain'even mentioned the white boy over there." Quincy cocked his head. "Why's he got the pick of the spots? And look at Lena! She's pouring him the same good bourbon we got."

Myers closed his eyes and shook his head, then opened his lids halfway and spoke.

"Quincy, you got a real thing here and we'd all like you to keep those opinions to yourself. It ain't helping a thing. We all got our issues. But we have us here a problem we got to work right or your niece'll have a lot more on her mind than some horny white boy."

The police chief and Pete Mandeville nodded then.

"All right," Quincy Thompson said reluctantly. "But answer me 'bout the white boy Lena's taking such good care of. I've seen him here befo'." They all watched as the leathery old singer went over and greeted the man.

"An' lookit! Even Pap's got to go over and lick the man's boots."

"Cut it out, Quincy!" Pete Mandeville's voice carried a leather-stropped edge. "That's Steve La Vere. If it weren't for him, the rich record companies would've robbed ole Robert Johnson's heirs blind. Man's spent a lot of his money to keep blues alive. The real stuff, not prissified tourist crap."

"Now don't you be knocking B. B. King again," the police chief said. "He's an Itta Bena boy."

"Awright." Myers waved his hands. "Can we be done with this?"

Mandeville and the police chief nodded. Quincy Thompson glared at them all in turn, slumped in his seat, and crossed his arms in front of him.

"Okay, Quincy. So tell us about this phone call," Myers said.

"Yeah, yeah, yeah," Quincy said reluctantly, then sat up. "That's why I went out to the old sharecropper shack. Shanker called me, said I might know where Jasmine would be. I had no idea when I arrived she'd be there in the white boy's bed in her underwear—"

"Let it go, Quincy!" the police chief boomed.

"Uh-huh. Well, they're supposed to meet at Judge Stone's old cotton gin at three in the morning." He inclined his head toward the back of the room. Everybody at the table knew the old shuttered gin in a weed-covered lot about two hundred yards northwest of them.

"Didn't Pap used to work there back in the bad old days?" Myers asked.

The police chief nodded. "Most everybody worked for the Judge back then. I know my papa did." He paused for a moment. "The Holy Rollers got a tent set up across the street, little bit this way from it. They've had a revival there this time of the year for as long as I can remember."

"Why they meeting?" Mandeville asked. "With Shanker."

Quincy shook his head.

"I got an idea or two," Myers said. "Most I picked up from looking into the Talmadge case—and some I learned a lot from Vanessa. I'll tell you what I know and maybe we can figure out what to do."

67

Beneath the fluorescent glare in the Greenwood courthouse offices commandeered by Homeland Security, David Brown sucked another Marlboro down to his fingertips as the encrypted wireless phone rang.

"Brown."

"We got something."

"Go on."

"The tap on Tyrone Freedman's ISP shows a lot of activity; it's encrypted and running through proxy servers outside our jurisdiction."

"Isn't that illegal?"

"No, sir. Not yet."

"Well, we squeeze those bastards on Capitol Hill and make it illegal." Brown grabbed his Marlboro box. It was empty. He ran his finger hopefully inside the box. Nothing. "Shit."

"Sir?"

"Nothing." Brown threw the box toward the wastebasket and missed. The red-and-white flip-top landed on the floor near two other empties. "So, if we can't figure out this guy's net traffic, what the fuck good is it?"

"It's coming from his trailer."

"So?"

"Freedman's at the hospital."

"Bring his black ass to me." Brown smiled.

"Sir! And something else."

"Speak."

"We have a make, model, and license plate for the dead blonde's new rental car."

"APB everything."

"Sir!

By midnight, the full moon had slipped to the horizon as Jasmine brought us into Itta Bena along a one-lane dirt road. She turned the headlights out as soon as we left Highway 7 and navigated by the now-fading moonlight. We navigated an overgrown section where blackberry vines clawed at us. Then she stopped. Ahead lay a patched asphalt road lined with modest houses.

"Where in the world are we?" I asked.

"A little north of the gin."

I rolled my window down. The scent of night blooms and summer flowers rolled in with the moist, cool air. "Let's make a circle to look for bad guys, then find a parking spot."

"No problem." She accelerated slowly, turned left, and clicked the headlights on. Less than a minute later, we intersected the main drag right at the old Turnipseed house and turned right.

Miss Eva's house—I couldn't for the life of me remember her real name—passed by on the left. She had been a widow with a house full of yellow and green parakeets and chickens outside. I remember going through the coop with her often. There were hens sitting on hay nests, and she would collect brown eggs and put them in a straw basket she allowed me to hold the day I turned six. Next to Miss Eva's, someone had built a house on the lot the Judge's wife, Mamie, had used as a vast rose garden.

Shortly after Jasmine turned left by the little brick Presbyterian church, a small car with glaring blue halogen headlights and purple under-the-chassis neon rocketed by in the opposite direction. Moments later, we passed the gin. Instants later, an Itta Bena police car trawled past us in the opposite direction. My heart held still for a moment. I followed it and exhaled when it disappeared without making a U-turn.

"Can you make a circle and bring us by the gin so it's on my side?"

She nodded and made a loop through a modest, well-kept block of houses. It took me a moment to recognize it as Balance Due. Gone were the unpainted, weathered shacks with ditches out front full of excrement and waste water.

"You know, there's a street named for my grandfather not too far from here."

I shook my head. "Al Thompson Street? Really?"

"Really."

I thought about this for a moment. "He deserved a lot more as far as I'm concerned."

A persistent smile brightened Jasmine's face as she drove the SUV back around the gin clockwise. When we slowed for a right-hand turn short of the square, I heard somebody playing "Hard Time Killin' Floor."

And the people are driftin' from door to door
Can't find no heaven, don't care where they go.

Whoever was playing the guitar was doing a damn fine job of emulating the open D-minor licks that had become a trademark for Nehemiah "Skip" James and the rest of the Bentonia bluesmen.

The singer finished off with a single note on the open second string followed by a D7 chord. It was one of James's trademark endings and brought thunderous applause.

"Skip James," I said. "One of my favorites."

"Mine too. The music's coming from Lena's. Real blues."

She turned right and made her way back toward Balance Due without driving past the police station.

"You'll have to take me there sometime."

"Yes, I will." Jasmine offered me her Mona Lisa smile. "I surely will."

Across the street from the gin and about a block down, I spotted a gas station and auto repair shop, closed for the night. Vans, cars, and pickups, obviously left for repair, crowded its parking area and the concrete apron around the pumps.

"How about there?" I asked.

In moments, Jasmine backed the SUV up between two pickup trucks and turned off the lights. The space fit the SUV like a knife sheath, but offered a clear view of the gin.

"Keep the engine going for now."

I scanned the gin and everything around it for maybe a quarter of an hour.

"Okay, kill the engine."

We sat there watching the occasional vehicle pass and listening. I strained to hear sirens or a helicopter thrumming. But the darkness carried only the occasional loud stereo from passing cars along with the distant rumble of thunder. We also enjoyed the blues music carried sporadically by the night air. No sirens. No choppers.

Just before 1:00 A.M., I climbed over my laptop bag, our packed luggage, and the sniper armament and ammo in the back of the SUV and left Jasmine in the SUV with her Ruger in her lap. I headed for the gin with the H&K automatic tucked in the back of my cargo shorts. My cargo pockets were jammed with every spare clip I could find. It was all covered by the tail of one of my blue oxford-cloth shirts left unbuttoned and hanging out. My clothes and white skin made me a good target in the dark, but unlike Jasmine, I had brought no dark clothes and all of Tyrone's were too small.

I carried the small night scope casually in my right hand as I made my way down a weed-covered track toward the old, rusty hulk. A young child's irrational fears of the place stirred in my belly. It took me more than half an hour to make my way around the building and inside it. I couldn't make a full circle because some sort of annex at the back was attached to another block of structures.

Waning moonlight sifted through holes in the tin roof, casting subtle shadows across the vast, vacant space. The shadows rustled. I feared rats, but the night scope showed a mother possum with her young clinging to her underside. I looked around and found the interior crawling with the sluggish and shy marsupials. They crawled over the tall rafters and beams high above the floor and nested almost everywhere I looked.

Snakes undoubtedly lived here as well, feeding off the possums and their young. I feared the copperhead most because, unlike rattlesnakes, it struck without warning. Finally, I walked outside and stood under the wagon-shed overhang, right under the big suction pipe that had once terrified me, and used the small, thin LED light attached to my Leatherman to signal Jasmine. I followed her through the night scope until she was safe next to me.

Shortly before 2:00 A.M., we went inside to wait.

From his vantage point half in a culvert leading under Martin Luther King Jr. Drive close to its intersection with Sunflower Road, the compact, muscular man surveyed the ramshackle cotton gin with his small monocular night-vision scope. Brad Stone had been good with his caution and preparation, but nobody was perfect.

The man bristled with a poised aggressiveness that made his fingertips pulse with every beat of his heart as he crouched in the standing water left by the previous night's rain.

He was as dark as the shadows embracing him, dressed entirely in black from his tightly laced, government-issue, high-top tactical boots to the summer-weight, cotton, ski-style mask never found in retail stores and designed for cool concealment, not warmth on the slopes. His black turtleneck was turned up to meld darkness with the bottom of the mask. Thin, black latex gloves covered his hands. A small earphone wire led to the man's portable radio as he monitored the law enforcement channels.

In the round image intensifier, the man observed Jasmine Thompson cross the street and give Brad Stone a hug as they stood under the tin-covered overhang where cotton wagons once stopped to be emptied.

Not long after the two had gone inside, the man watched an Itta Bena police car approach from the direction of Balance Due with its headlights out. Three men got out of the police car and walked over to a pale silver SUV. One of the policemen checked the license number against a sheet of paper, then proceeded to transfer the SUV's contents to the squad car. They drove away as stealthily as they had come. The man frowned as the taillights disappeared. There had been absolutely nothing in the radio chatter about this.

After the police cruiser left, the man made his way like a shadow to the gin and tucked himself under a tumbled-down loading dock near the wagon shed. The distant sounds of blues music trailed off about a quarter before three. The man waited easily with his thoughts. Nine minutes later, a dark, older-model Jeep turned off MLK Jr. Drive, cut its headlights, and bounced slowly along the dirt path. The man raised the monocular and spotted attorney Jay Shanker's face through the windshield.

Pay dirt.

The Jeep stopped under the shed. The engine died. Shanker sat still as the engine cooled with its simple tune of tinks and creaks. They were the only sounds until precisely 3:00 A.M., when he heard Stone speak to Jasmine.

"I'll be back," I whispered.

I slipped through a siding gap and scrambled toward the Jeep on all fours. After seeing no one else in the vehicle, I tapped on the window.

Shanker's startled face whirled toward me, wide and white. It took him several seconds to recognize me. Then he got out.

"Where's Jasmine?"

"Inside."

Shanker followed me through the hole.

Jasmine shook his hand and without preamble asked, "Did you bring the second CD?"

Shanker shook his head. "There isn't one."

Jasmine and I stood speechless.

"There never has been," Shanker said, his voice heavy with regret. "They got to Talmadge before he told me where he hid the rest of the documents. But they don't know that. They would have killed him by now if they knew the CD didn't exist."

"You lied!"

"I'm sorry. I had to. It was the only way to save his life. I had to get you involved."

"That's no excuse—"

"Please, hear me out."

Pain colored Shanker's words. "More's at stake than Talmadge. Braxton's a psycho car bomb headed for the White House. Even if he doesn't disintegrate like Talmadge, Braxton has no compassion, none at all. We can't afford to have his finger on the trigger of the world's most powerful military power."

Something rustled against the tin siding. Instinctively, I ducked and pulled Jasmine down with one hand and brought the H&K up with the other, thumbing the safety off as I did. The rustling stopped. I let go of Jasmine and scanned the room with the night-vision scope. Nothing.

"Possums," I said as I stood up and offered my hand to Jasmine.

Shanker exhaled loudly.

"Jay, do you have any idea where the documents might be?" Jasmine asked.

"I suspect they're buried in or near one of the duck blinds he used, but those are scattered all over the state from the Ross Barnett Reservoir down in Jackson all the way up this side of the Mississippi River to Tunica. It might be anywhere."

"Do we have to have those documents to make the case?" I asked.

"Absolutely," Shanker said. "Without the original records, and preferably Talmadge's testimony to establish the trail of evidence, Braxton just might get off the hook."

"Meaning we somehow have to spring Talmadge, recover the documents, and keep him alive to tell his tale."

"Not an awfully practical matter," Jasmine said. "He's being held in a guarded top-floor room at the VA hospital in Jackson."

Suddenly, the shrieking syncopations of a helicopter shattered the silence, followed by a swift blur of simultaneous terror. First came a red laser dot's lethal dance, which found its mark faster than I could react. The unmistakable crack of a Heckler and Koch MP5 reached my ears an instant after Jay Shanker's head opened up like a dropped melon.

Before Shanker hit the ground, the red dot danced over Jasmine like a red wasp heavy with death. I threw myself against her and prayed.

The man hiding amid the ruins of the old cotton gin loading dock watched a Huey-sized chopper close in, leading a convoy of military Humvees down Sunflower Road, straight for the T-intersection at the gin. None of the vehicles had lights on. As the convoy approached, the sounds of racing engines came from opposite directions on MLK Jr. An instant later, the light bars on two police cars lit up, with sirens in full acoustic regalia.

The man's jaw dropped as an old stake-back truck raced down the middle of the street, from his left, pursued by one police car and heading straight for the second. With no options left, the stake-back truck careened left onto Sunflower Road head-on into the convoy. Then the night filled with a concerto of squealing brakes, skidding tires, and the eruption of broken glass and tortured metal. The concerto's second movement commenced when the other vehicles in the convoy rear-ended each other in an extended chain reaction.

The two police cars skidded to a stop behind the stake-backed truck. The helicopter lit up then and spotlighted a tall, thin black youth as he sprang from the cab of the stake-back truck. Uniformed police officers leaped out of the squad cars and gave chase.

A third police car arrived less urgently and disgorged a huge man with a uniform and a black cowboy hat. The sounds of more sirens grew closer. The big man walked over to the Humvee as the passengers got out. Undamaged vehicles made their way around the collision but found themselves blocked by the Itta Bena police cruisers. A tall man with gray hair and a cigarette screamed obscenities at the huge man in the cowboy hat. Men in helmets and SWAT gear swarmed out of the vehicles.

The far end of MLK Jr. Drive lit up then with more police light bars.

The faintest of scraping sounds came to the man as he took in the scene. He whirled, TEC-9 at the ready, but saw only the blur of a boot disappearing through a gap in the siding. The man followed the boot inside.

The MP5's next shot lifted the hair at the back of my neck as I rolled Jasmine away from Jay Shanker's lifeless body. But the red dot was relentless. There was no time to aim my H&K because the slightest pause meant certain death.

Just as I feared history would repeat itself, a sustained burst of full-auto weapons fire came from the front of the gin, shunting the persistent red dot off into the darkness to paint a still life on the rusty tin roof.

My relief deepened with a totally unexpected voice.

"Old son, don't you have enough good sense to stop pissing off the *federales?*"

"Rex?" I stared at a shadow emerging from the darkness.

"Keep your voice down, podnuh. We don't want our buddies outside to connect the dotted line between you and me. Not too soon anyway."

I helped Jasmine stand up as Rex's compact muscular form grew near. From outside, the sounds of urgent voices and the thuds of running feet sifted into the gin's confined space, filled now with the smell of gunfire and death.

"How . . . why?" I stuttered.

"Because nobody else is going to keep pulling your *cojónes* out of the fire, my man."

I shook the gloved hand he offered me as tin siding rattled at the rear of the gin. We all three dropped for cover and brought our guns to bear.

"Don't shoot."

The voice was familiar.

"Uncle Quincy?"

"Jasmine!"

Quincy Thompson emerged from behind a sheet of corrugated tin siding, which swung out like a secret door at the back of the gin, right about where it abutted the adjacent building.

Instants later, I made out Quincy's face, which changed from relief to anger when he turned his head from Jasmine to me. Then he spotted Rex.

"Who the hell are you?"

"Chill out, cap'n. I'm just along for the ride."

Quincy muttered something beneath his breath. Then: "Come on! Quick!"

As we followed Quincy, the sounds of a siren grew near; flashing lights leaked through the old siding at the side of the gin. Then, almost lost in the dazzling of light-bar flashes from outside, a red dot danced about Quincy's back.

"Down!" I yelled, and launched myself into the backs of Quincy's knees, cutting him down with a clip that would have drawn a penalty flag in any football game. Shots sparked off a rusted piece of machinery. I heard Rex's TEC-9 and a distant cry of pain.

Then a voice at the rear called out, "Come on! Come on! Come on!"

I helped Quincy to his feet. He stared at me.

"What the hell you staring at?" I said.

His mouth struggled for words, which would not come.

"Get your rear in gear, pal," Rex broke the impasse, pushing us along. "Or your ass is grass and those folks're lawn mowers."

Quincy and I followed Jasmine through the makeshift opening. Behind us, Rex emptied the TEC-9 at the far corner of the gin, then tossed it away.

"Bought it off a street dealer in Jackson. When they track it down to him, he'll be in a world of hurt." I followed Rex through the narrow opening and let the tin panel close behind me right as the light and concussion of a flashbang filled the interior.

72

Smoke and flames persisted behind us in the gin. The flashbang had found plenty to burn in the old gin's debris, desiccated wooden beams, decades of cotton lint from ginning.

We slogged through mud and standing water along a narrow passage between the gin and the back of a brick wall of an adjoining structure. After maybe forty feet, we reached a low, narrow hole and shoehorned ourselves through it into the brick building's crawl space. After crawling under floor joists for twenty feet or so, we climbed up into an abandoned warehouse. Our guide helped us up from the access hatch one by one. As soon as he let go of my hand, he unzipped the front of his Ben Davis coveralls to reveal the uniform of the Leflore County Sheriff's Department. His name tag told me his last name was Mandeville.

"I'm Pete," he said. I shook his hand. Then behind him, I spotted a wizened old man holding a guitar case.

Mandeville caught my gaze. "That's Pap. He used to work at the gin. He's probably the last man alive who remembers the passage we just took."

The old man gave us a broad smile filled with teeth too white and even to be anything but dentures.

"Uh-huh, tha's right," Pap said. "We use that way when we late or need a break. Gin boss never caught us. Uh-uh."

"Come on, John's waiting," Mandeville said.

Pap stood by the door with his guitar case.

"Thank you," I said.

He nodded.

"Were you the one singing 'Killin' Floor'?"

Pap nodded.

"You played the best set of open D-minor licks I ever heard. Better than Skip himself."

Pap smiled.

A Leflore County sheriff's van sat on the other side of the old warehouse. Mandeville slid open the side door and motioned us all to hurry.

Inside sat John Myers in front and Tyrone Freedman way in back, sandwiched in among all of the luggage and gear from the SUV. The radio crackled nonstop. Half a block away, fire station sirens began to wail.

"Tyrone!" I said. "What the hell?" I leaned over to shake his hand before sitting down at the end of the rearmost bench seat. Jasmine sat next to me.

Quincy got in, sat next to Jasmine, and gave her a hug. Then Pete Mandeville slid the door closed. The sky brightened with a warm flicker over by the old gin.

"They connected you to my Internet traffic," Tyrone said. "A whole gang of federal agents came in the hospital's front door, so I went out the back and paid Deputy John here a visit."

Myers nodded. I looked around at the faces.

"Oh, man." My heart fell. "Tyrone, I am so sorry to drag you into this."

Mandeville slid into the driver's seat and put the van in gear.

Tyrone shook his head and laughed.

I looked around at the lives I was dragging into the black hole of trouble: Myers, Tyrone, Quincy, Jasmine, and Rex, who held his black gloves and mask in his hands. I had grown accustomed to getting myself in and out of trouble all by my lonesome. Until now, when it mattered most.

"I'm sorry for all of this," I said, looking around me. Beyond the windshield, the corner where Durham's Drug Store had once sat passed by on the left. Then we passed the post office, where, despite my mother's strictest prohibitions, the itinerant crop duster's son and I used to hang out in the dim, cool lobby with the shiny linoleum floors, pictures of criminals on the walls and a bank of shiny brass post-office boxes with combination dials stretching up almost out of sight. Then we passed the Judge's law office, followed close on by the old VFW hut, where I loved to play the illegal slot machines, and finally across the new Roebuck Lake bridge.

Across the square, boarded-up storefronts glowed like a summer sunset as the gin's flames leaped into the night sky.

"You didn't drag anybody into this," Jasmine said. "Mama did."

"Uh-uh, child," Myers interrupted. "Nope. It was my own damn fault for sticking my big nose in things."

"But still, I should have—"

"Old son," Rex spoke up, "you're so damned used to being in charge of things, you're just gonna have to recognize this ain't your fault and it's gonna take some teamwork and a little help from your indictable co-conspirators to get out of."

"Lady and gentlemen, this is Rex," I said.

I didn't use Rex's last name because Rex wasn't his real first name anyway, and I never knew when he was comfortable revealing his last. At the very least, I figured having two sworn law enforcement officers within an arm's length would not be the time despite their own illegal complicity in helping Jasmine and me avoid the hellhound dogging us.

Amid the quasi-sentient static of frantic police radio communications, everyone acknowledged the introduction in a way that indicated Rex's name was irrelevant because he had, after all, proved himself where it mattered. We listened to the bits of radio traffic for a few moments before Quincy spoke up, his voice as resolved and hesitant as a wedding proposal.

"Thank you for what you did tonight," Quincy told Rex, and extended his hand. Jasmine's face looked as if she had been slapped; she looked at her uncle as she would a stranger.

Quincy turned to me and offered me the same hand. The unremembered familiarity of his face touched me again, but again I could only feel the memory, not recall it. It felt important, very important, and frustrated me in its elusiveness.

"And thank you," he said. I shook his hand and a gate opened in his eyes. "Thank you very much."

"You're welcome," I said. "Very."

Jasmine hung on every syllable of her uncle's unspoken conversation and gave him a nod and a smile. When he sat back down next to her, she took his hand and gave it a squeeze.

John Myers loosed a broadside of laughter then. We all turned toward him.

"Lordy! I wish I could be there!" He laughed, then caught his breath; he pointed at the radio. "Rats and possums and a whole damn herd of mice and feral cats are streaming away from the fire, and I guess most of those city-boy Feds ain' *never* seen nothing like that afore." He laughed again. "They cuttin' loose, shootin' what moves."

He laughed, grimaced in pain as he grabbed his wounded shoulder with his good hand, then laughed some more.

"And the chief's been raising hell with that Homeland Security ass-hole about not notifying him about activity on his turf."

"Did Pap's grandson get away?" Mandeville asked.

"Course he did," Myers said. "And the fire department said it's not leaving the station until the gunshots stop, so all the Feds can do is stand around and shoot possums and stray cats."

We hit the unpaved part of the road and bounced into the night. When our laughter faded, Myers turned the volume down on the radio.

"That ain' the last surprise that ole boy's gonna get either. Sometime tomorrow, Homeland Security's going to get a call from two very em-barrassed agents." Myers looked at Jasmine and me.

"I had two babysitters watching me, followed me over to Lena's." He chuckled. "Itta Bena PD's evidence locker is missing just enough GHB to send those folks to never-never land. Lena slipped that old date-rape drug in their drinks." He smiled at the thought. "The chief left 'em in the backseat of one of their cars, naked as a jaybird and covered in their own jism."

"How did—?" Jasmine started to speak.

Myers shook his head. "You really don't want to know."

We road in silence for a long time, way past Runnymede. The sky glowed yellow over toward Itta Bena.

"Jay Shanker's in there," Jasmine said then, her voice low and heavy.

"Oh lordy, lordy," Myers said. "There was a man we all needed." He shook his head. "I can't tell you how many people's lives he made a dif-ference in, how many youngsters had their lives turned around by him, how many people—like Pap—who finally got rewarded for their back-breaking labor because that man went to bat for them out of the good-ness of his heart."

I had known Jay Shanker for only those handful of minutes in the gin, but Myers's words iced the darkness that hung black in my soul.

Mandeville steered the van toward the northeast and over the newly opened Yazoo River bridge to Greenwood.

"So what's your plan?" Myers asked me as we approached Highway 82.

I shook my head. "Don't have one yet, but somehow we've got to get Talmadge out of the VA in Jackson and find the load of records he hid." I summarized what we had learned from Shanker.

"I'd like to help you there, but I think Pete and I . . . the chief and all the others have gone about as far as we can without landing in jail."

"I understand."

"You can count on me," Tyrone said. "I went to med school right next to the VA, been in there any number of times."

"Anita still works there," Rex said.

"I'll do what I can," Quincy said, amazing Jasmine and me again.

"Get me back to my truck," Rex said. "I've got an idea."

73

Rex drove us south through the night, the headlights of his truck chasing ideas for a plan that rose and vanished like wisps of road fog. I sat next to Jasmine in the backseat, holding her hand, thinking about how to rescue Talmadge, grab the documents, get them to the media.

Rex had an abundance of unconventional resources and ideas and spun one scenario after another. All of these involved rebar, ropes, breaking and entering, safety harnesses, aircraft hijacking, and numerous other criminal acts no sane person would ever consider.

"When the going gets insane, the insane get going," Rex kept saying.

I didn't argue because insanity had saved my life way too many times in the past. Along with outright lunacy, all our plans required the illegal appropriation of someone else's property, the fastest, most untraceable way to acquire the materials we needed. No matter what we needed, Rex seemed to know where to steal it. Thus, from one scenario to another, a plan developed, much like constructing a vase out of whatever shards were at hand.

During the lulls when the planning discussions fell silent, dark, swirling waters backed up in my head with thoughts of the quick and the dead. I thought of the recently dead—Camilla, Jay Shanker, Chris Nellis—and the incredible loss their absence would cause. Their deaths not only gouged out holes of love and dependence in the lives of the living, but also deprived the world of the remarkable body of knowledge they had wrested from ignorance, thought by thought. Knowledge was just a different memory. Where did they go? I asked myself again. And did we go there too?

The question gnawed at me during the dark silences connecting Phillipstown, Mayday, Quofaloma, Midnight, Panther Burn, Zelleria, and a score of other lonesome settlements embedded in the Delta darkness. I could not shake my preoccupation with the intriguing theory of

Roger Penrose and Stuart Hameroff, who think our consciousness arises from a quantum mechanism that alters the very woof and weave of space-time, or that of Hameroff's colleague David Chalmers, who feels we will eventually discover consciousness as a fundamental building block of the universe.

From there, I had no trouble thinking of consciousness as an inscription in space-time or imagining how those inscriptions could directly affect consciousness.

For me, this begged a connection to the Hindu concept of *maya*, which says we are a grand illusion of God, and which, to my way of thinking, squares with Genesis, which tells us the world was without form, then God created the heavens and the earth. So, if we live in a world created by God out of nothing, there's no reason we shouldn't view our lives and everything in the world as "real," just as God intended. But I don't think we should be surprised when we dig down deep enough into the fundamentals of existence to find God created it all out of the infinite everything of nothing.

I fell asleep thinking about this. I didn't dream about whether love endured, but recognized it as one of those unknowable things the soul did.

The country roads of Sonoma Valley still slept at four thirty in the morning when Dan Gabriel steered his rental car to a halt on the westbound shoulder of Highway 116 to look at Harper's directions he had jotted down. The setting moon backlit the vineyards and pastures with a halo surrounding the highway and a ragged ridge of hills to the west.

Gabriel turned away from the scene, then flicked on the overhead dome light to decipher his sleepy scrawl. Frank Harper had called him less than two hours before and dragged Dan from his nightmares haunted by undead soldiers.

"I'm sorry to call you at this hour," Harper had apologized. "But I am concerned and can't sleep."

"Makes two of us."

"We could talk privately at the campaign meeting this afternoon at the General's retreat," Harper had said. "But this should offer a better opportunity."

Gabriel looked at his writing, then up at the road. Straight ahead he followed the westward curve of the highway, then spotted the distant traffic light, precisely as Harper had described it. A little closer, faintly as lighter black on black, a road led off to the right.

Putting the car in gear, Dan pressed ahead, nearly running off the road at the poorly marked transition onto Arnold Drive. Two traffic lights down and a left turn later, he drove streets lined with neatly landscaped houses. Gabriel got lost twice on the winding streets, before spotting Harper at the end of the correct cul-de-sac, leaning against a cane by his mailbox.

"Thanks for coming," Harper said as Gabriel stepped out of the white rental car and shook the offered hand. Harper's grip was strong despite the underlying Parkinson's tremor.

"Come on inside. I have a fresh pot of coffee on."

Gabriel walked patiently behind Harper, past trimmed juniper bushes and blooming agapanthas lit up by the front-porch lights. As he followed the old man, Gabriel thought again of how he had let events of his life sweep him along and how this meeting marked an irrevocable break.

He had long considered his Navy enlistment as evidence he was captain of his own ship. But the years—and especially the past six months—had made him realize his act of extreme adolescent rebellion was a reaction, not a real choice. He knew now he had to seize the tiller and steer his own course regardless of the consequences.

"My heart's heavy," Harper said as he directed Gabriel to a chair in the fluorescent-lit breakfast nook off the kitchen. "Heavy."

Harper sloshed his coffee as he set it down on the table and painfully eased himself into a chair.

"Clark Braxton is a creation of mine." His eyes were bright and strong and searched Gabriel's. "I'm the last man who knows the whole story. By the time you leave today, you'll know it as well."

"Why me? Why now?"

Harper's direct gaze searched Gabriel's eyes, then turned inward. After a moment, Harper said, "Because you are a good, honest man. A capable man with the ability to act on what I will tell you."

"Thank you."

"And now's the time because I feel more mortal than ever before. I have a cardiac pacemaker, electronics to control my Parkinson's, and electronics to deal with chronic back pain." His hand shook as he sipped at the coffee.

"It's time because Clark Braxton's slipping away. I monitor the man continuously via a remote Internet monitoring system. And in the end, I guess it boils down to something Clark told me not long ago up there at that damned Masada fortress, palace of his, over in Napa Valley. Clark looked at me and said, 'The problem with old men is that time and guilt loosens their lips. When consequences disappear, people do things that we can't tolerate.' Well, at the time, I assumed he was talking about Darryl Talmadge."

Shaking his head, Harper looked down at his hands, which trembled with a life of their own. "I firmly believe now he was talking about me, not Talmadge."

"Wow," Gabriel exhaled.

"Yes. And knowing what I am about to tell you is a dangerous burden. You can leave now. I'll understand. You have many years left."

The two men looked at each other silently. An old pendulum clock ticked loudly from the hallway. We cross many of the great divides in our lives without recognizing them as such until many years later, if at all. But Gabriel saw this one clearly. Dan Gabriel visualized himself thanking the frail old man and walking out right then. As his thoughts followed the future of that decision, he felt a lifetime of regret gathering in his heart. So he said, "Please tell me."

Harper smiled. "I knew you were the right man." He took a long draft from his coffee mug.

"One thing Laura LaHaye and Greg McGovern and the others neglected to tell you at your briefing at the General's retreat the last time has to do with a long history of secret, and often unethical, medical experiments performed by the U.S. military and intelligence communities on members of the armed forces and the general public. A tiny bit has leaked out: Project 112, Project SHAD, and a couple of others, which affected tens of thousands of unsuspecting people who were unwilling and unwitting guinea pigs in the testing of potentially dangerous chemical, biological, and nuclear weapons."

Harper closed his eyes and gave Dan a faint sigh as he shook his head. "But what I have done with the General's support and urging is far, far worse, farther ranging, and has the potential for altering the very nature of what it means to be human. Unless we do something within the next week, we will unleash a monster which will bring global bloodshed like never seen before."

Early dawn caught us driving along County Line Road. All peach, pastel, and bright, the sun shimmered off the lazy waters of the Ross Barnett Reservoir as we crested the top of the levee west of the main spillway gates. The vast thirty-three-thousand-acre man-made lake created by damming the Pearl River north of Jackson was constructed as a flood-control project but turned out to be a major recreational attraction for boaters, water-skiers, anglers, and duck hunters.

The brilliant morning sun helped chase the fuzziness from my head. Rex stopped at the sign atop the levee and turned left.

"We're headed up in the trees northeast of the Yacht Club," Rex said as he accelerated past a waterside restaurant. "The house owner's a rich guy from Meridian who throws wild parties for legislators and bureaucrats when he needs a vote or some quick action. It's off a private road and out of sight and earshot of neighbors.

"They beat the place up pretty badly during the last party and I got the contract to redo the drywall. I don't reckon we'll see anybody there for a while."

It seemed that no matter what needed doing, Rex had discreet ways to accomplish it. He was the ultimate good-hearted bad boy, and I was thankful to call him friend.

Frank Harper grew visibly fatigued as his story approached the present. He spoke continuously, stopping once to make more coffee and pausing only to spell a name, a word, or to let Dan Gabriel catch up with his notes.

"I was thrilled at first," Harper had begun. "Suddenly I had the blessings of the Army and the resources of the U.S. government behind my quest to look inside the heads of human beings and look for the thing which really separates us from the rest of God's creatures. I didn't pay attention to the fabric of deceit being woven around me."

Harper studied the empty bottom of his mug. "Now, the direct result of my life's efforts means the military will begin widespread deployment of Xantaeus next week, disguised as transdermal patches for vitamins and micronutrients."

"But I thought— In the briefing, Wim Baaker said Xantaeus would be deployed in the next year or two," Gabriel stuttered.

"Baaker doesn't know the whole story. The president does not know, and maybe three people at the Pentagon are truly aware."

"What about the adverse side effects?"

"Like I mentioned, about one percent of the people taking the drug never fully recover."

"That would produce thousands of dangerous killers."

"Completely psychopathic killers," Harper said. "People with no compunction about killing, but with the ability to appear normal and above suspicion."

"Like General Braxton."

"Like General Braxton," Harper agreed. "At least most of the time. Xantaeus'll ship next week, and you must stop it."

Suddenly the kitchen of Frank Harper's modest California ranch house erupted with a riot of noise and armed men clothed in black from their boots to balaclavas. Gabriel identified the men as the former Special Forces personnel who formed the core of the Defense Therapeutics security team and knew resistance would be foolish. He allowed himself to be handcuffed and led into the garage. One of the black-clad men opened the garage door, revealing the back of a medium-sized U-Haul truck.

We slept until noon and got up only when Rex turned up the downstairs stereo full blast and blasted us with the beat of vintage Boston. I awakened on my left side in a mammoth heart-shaped bed, staring out the window at a green mass of oaks and pines shivering in a light breeze. When I sat up, I was a little relieved and a lot disappointed Jasmine was not there and, from the topography of the pillows and bed linens, had not been there. An instant later, I remembered kissing her good-night at the door to a bedroom down an impressively long hall and falling asleep with my arms and heart empty.

Under me, the mattress resonated to the deep, familiar bass from the vintage rock and roll. I sat up. The shattered mirror over the bed told part of the story, as did a pair of women's shiny gold, six-inch spiked heels embedded in the drywall. Empty Chivas and Crown Royal bottles littered a polished cherrywood bureau. Half-empty rocks glasses sat near the bottles; three of them had lipstick imprints, one in hot pink, another in cherry red, and the third a deep Goth black with a used condom draped over its rim.

I didn't want to think about the provenance of the bedsheets, but I was grateful to have fallen asleep fully clothed.

Downstairs, the "Rock and Roll Band" cut ended, and in the momentary silence Rex yelled that lunch was getting cold. I detoured through a luxurious shower before dressing in another pair of cargo shorts and a plain gray T-shirt.

I padded down the curved, Tara-like stairs in my bare feet. A massive chandelier hung from the ceiling and dominated the thirty-foot-high cylindrical space within the staircase. Six pairs of thong panties in various Day-Glo shades dangled from one of the chandelier's hand-cut, oak-leaf crystal fobs along with a pair of large, striped boxers. At the landing at the foot of the stairs, paper bags, milk crates, and cardboard boxes of gear covered the floor, save for a narrow path from the front door to a set of French doors to the left. Voices murmured against the French-door panes.

I paused to scan the piles of gear and recognized most of it from the list we had drawn up hours earlier on the drive down from the Delta.

Hanks of half-inch, high-vee, sixteen-stranded braided rope with the New England Ropes Safety Blue labels still on it were piled next to Miller shock-absorbing lanyards with locking snaps, full-body safety harnesses, webbed lineman's belts, and half a dozen bright red Petzl Ecrin Roc helmets, great for the head, bad for camouflage, but undoubtedly the only thing quickly available wherever the hell he'd found it. I walked over to a bag full of carabiners and pulled one out. Petzl again, four-and-an-eighth-inch ball-lock models. The tag said they tested out at over sixty-two hundred pounds. I tossed the carabiner back in the bag and bent over another one, filled with StrikeTeam goggles with thick ballistic-rated polycarbonate lenses, and below those, leather gloves, a pile of Magellan GPS receivers, Motorola Spirit XTN two-watt, heavy-duty walkie-talkies with earbuds and talk-to-speak microphones.

A pile of boot boxes was stacked up to my armpits, all full of brand-new Thorogood ten-inch wildland firefighting boots in a range of sizes.

Next to them was a case of Counter Assault Bear Deterrent pepper spray. I bent over and cracked the cardboard box and pulled out a container the size of a spray-paint can. We had all agreed to minimize injuries to police and military personnel, who, after all, were only doing their jobs.

I read the label of the can to myself: "Strong enough to stop a bear in its tracks . . . range to thirty feet." I made a quiet, low whistle to myself. I had put pepper spray on the list, but had the smaller canisters in mind. I replaced the can in its case box and looked around the cluttered entryway. There were bolt cutters, backpacks, black coveralls sprouting pockets and pouches on every surface, flashlights, and headlights of every description, including two huge twelve-volt, 250,000 candlepower SuperNova spotlights.

There was even stuff I did not remember asking for. Like a dozen sticks of construction-grade dynamite cut in half, and a thick, clear-polyethylene Ziploc containing detonators, about evenly split between electric and regular fuses that could be lit with a match. The dynamite and detonators were of the type and age usually found in a petroleum exploration logging unit's "doghouse." There was paint thinner, a ten-pound hand sledge, two packs of road flares, and a roll of wide nylon webbing. A big clear-plastic bag full of dark cotton sweatshirts, pants, T-shirts, underpants, and dark athletic shoes slumped in a far corner with a Ziploc full of handcuffs and, next to it, a hefty steel wedge for splitting firewood. There was also lots and lots of duct tape and cable ties of every imaginable size and color.

I shook my head at the collection of gear and at Rex's ability and resourcefulness to assemble it all between dawn and noon while the rest of us slept.

I followed the muffled voices through the French doors and into a grand dining room, where Jasmine, Tyrone, Rex and his wife, Anita—still in hospital scrubs—sat around the far end of a polished mahogany table long enough to fill Enron's boardroom. Little Krystal hamburger boxes and greasy french-fry envelopes carpeted their end of the table. My heart filled with light when I laid eyes on Jasmine.

"Good morning, sleepyhead." Jasmine's eyes were bright and reflected the light coming in through the window.

I headed for the empty chair between Jasmine and Anita. On the table sat a half dozen little Krystal hamburgers and a line of styrofoam coffee cups. Tyrone gave me a nod as he chewed on his food.

"Brad!" Anita gave me a smile that was part concern and part welcome. "So good to see you."

" 'Bout damn time you hauled your lazy butt down." Rex smiled. "Here we are with twelve or fifteen hours to showtime and you play Rip Van freaking Winkle."

"Rex . . ." Anita frowned at him.

"It's okay, Anita," I said as I walked toward her. "The commander's right." She got up and gave me a sisterly hug, then looked at me. "Just look at those bags under your eyes." She tsked at me, then looked at Jasmine and said, "You've got a long row to hoe to keep this man healthy."

Anita's matter-of-fact acceptance of Jasmine and me worked wonders for my attitude. I leaned over to kiss Jasmine, and she gave me a Mona Lisa smile, which reached deeper inside me than ever before.

Then I sat down, pulled the lid off one of the foam cups of coffee, took a sip, and managed not to frown.

Brigadier General Jack Kilgore stood in his glass-sided corner office and took in the desks and maps and consoles and displays filling the vast operations room beyond. Troops in the operations room avoided looking at him and focused on their mission. When their commanding officer refused to sit, it meant his pitifully anorexic tolerance for BS had gone AWOL.

Kilgore held a cell phone to his ear and listened to the endless ringing of Dan Gabriel not picking up. The longer Kilgore listened, the more it sounded like a siren. He stopped at his door and followed the thick multicolored skeins of Cat-5 cabling, coax, wave guides, power cords, and assorted wires neatly bundled with cable ties and harnesses, which made only precise ninety-degree turns as they parceled out data, radio waves, and electricity from origin to destination. There were times he preferred the old days when God, guts, and guns were all you needed to win a battle, provided you had enough intelligence to apply them in the proper proportions at the right times.

But this new technology, Xantaeus, held only horror, not hope. It dehumanized, removed choice, deprived the individual soldier of his free will and ripped out the very thing that made him human. Gabriel's notion that some soldiers would go where the drug took them and never return haunted Kilgore and made him entertain seditious thoughts.

In the far corner of the operations room, Kilgore's second-in-command, Colonel Bill Lewis, talked with the mapping officer, who accessed the same data that guided cruise missiles and allowed pilots—and Kilgore's troops—to rehearse simulated missions by "seeing" the actual terrain overlaid by aerial and satellite photos with better quality and resolution than the average scrapbook snapshot.

Kilgore pulled the phone from his ear, stared at it for a moment, then pressed the "end" button and let his hand fall to his side. A moment later, Colonel Lewis stood up, took several sheets of paper from the console operator, and gave Kilgore a nod. Then he made his way to Kilgore's door and entered.

"Any idea?" Kilgore asked.

Lewis shook his head. "General Gabriel's phone works fine."

"I know that," Kilgore snapped. He waved the wireless unit in Lewis's face. "Tell me something useful."

Kilgore closed his eyes and grimaced. "Sorry, Bill. I'm low on sleep. My comments were uncalled for."

"We've all been there, sir." Lewis nodded. "This a pretty intense security exercise given the probability of Braxton as our next president."

Lewis, like almost every other soldier Kilgore knew—himself included—took pride in that they would finally get a commander in chief with knowledge, courage, and guts, someone they looked up to after the dismal parade of draft dodgers, cowboys, flaky liberal peaceniks, actors, and poseurs who had abused the military in one stupid, self-serving way or another. Kilgore realized part of his temper came from disappointment: after they'd waited for so long, the soldier headed for the Oval Office had claymore feet.

He wanted to tell Lewis this, but said only, "Thank you."

"I can tell you the cell's GPS functions are operating properly." Lewis handed Kilgore a full-color, topographical printout on fine, slick eleven-by-seventeen paper. "From this we know he spent over ten hours here." Lewis pointed to a spot near San Rafael. "At his hotel. His last call to you came from there. Then he goes north on 101, east on 37, and north again toward Sonoma." Lewis traced the route. "He stopped for a moment here, then for a much longer stop at an address in the Temelec subdivision, which checks out as the residence of Dr. Frank Harper."

Kilgore followed this silently.

"The phone remained at Harper's for more than five hours, traveled east, then north, and has been stationary since then, right here." He pointed to a series of almost concentric topographical elevation lines west of the Silverado Trail in Napa Valley.

"Braxton's estate," Kilgore said. "Figures. They have a meeting this afternoon." He thought silently for a moment. "Okay, here's how I want you to handle this. Pull a squad together who've trained in Al Qaeda tactics and give them everything a well-funded terrorist cell can get hold of—data, plans from the county, photographs from the French surveillance satellites, leaks from German intelligence—that sort of thing, and start them on planning an intrusion.

"Also, pull together another squad who'll gather everything we have and have them report to me. Put a fire wall between the two groups. Have the first one rent an office or something in the area, set up their operations. Keep this hermetic, no notifications to anybody outside this organization."

"Sir," Lewis said. "Who do you want commanding the squad?"

"You."

"Sir." Lewis smiled.

"Okay. How about the Mississippi situation?"

"The usual cock-up," Lewis said. "The Customs Service weenies are running around like a bunch of chickens with their heads cut off, only twice as fast and half as smart."

"You do know, don't you, that Brown is one of Braxton's men?"

"Nobody's perfect, sir," Lewis said evenly. "The General can't know everything. That's why people like us need to be at our best and weed out the bad apples."

"Well said."

"Thank you, sir," Lewis said, then continued his report. "The fire in Itta Bena spread to a whole row of buildings and burned way past dawn. Brown's assault team caught the blame, and the lawyers are standing in line to file lawsuits. Shanker's family's at the head of the line. He was quite an admired lawyer and beloved figure around those parts, and there was a near riot around the hotel where Homeland Security was staying.

"The Leflore County sheriff, the police chief in Itta Bena, and a bunch of others drove down to Jackson to complain to the senators and the U.S. attorney there, and I understand they're filing some sort of legal action as well. The networks have it, news vans and cameras everywhere. Photos of Stone and Thompson have hit everywhere, but any reporter with an IQ larger than his shoe size is asking embarrassing questions that should eventually discredit David Brown and his Customs assholes."

Kilgore smiled broadly then. Bill Lewis carried a long railroad-siding of a scar along the left side of his abdomen where a trigger-happy Customs agent had shot him during a joint-task-force raid on a bunch of innocent Muslims in Virginia. David Brown had instigated the raid on fabricated intelligence. Kilgore had opposed Task Force 86M's participation in the raid and had relented only after direct orders from the Pentagon. There had been rumors Lewis had deliberately been shot in retaliation, but given Customs' habitual inability to shoot straight, proving it would be impossible.

"They making any progress finding Stone and Thompson?"

Lewis shrugged. "A little. They're working a family tree like what caught Saddam—you know, a chart of everybody he ever knew, hoping it will lead them to Stone. They figure he's headed to Jackson."

"So what do you think of the questions the media are asking."

"I don't have enough data to form an operational conclusion on it yet."

"Uh-huh," Kilgore said slowly. "Do you have a personal opinion?"

Lewis nodded. "The whole thing stinks. I've looked at the records. NSA sent us the voice recordings of the radio conversations starting with Stone's Mayday off Marina del Rey." Lewis shook his head. "This looks like some sort of frame-up cobbled out of bits and pieces. It reminds me of Brown's bogus raids against those Muslim groups in Virginia."

"This doesn't involve Brown or Customs. This was some Army folks from the Technical Escort Unit."

"But, remember, they've been lobbying for Homeland Security budget funds themselves. I spent a little extracurricular time and pulled some records on the colonel who ran the Marina del Rey operation and . . ." Lewis smiled.

"And?"

"He served on active duty with Braxton."

"I see where this is headed."

"And so did Brown."

"Good work, Bill." Kilogore slapped him on the shoulder. "I'll take over control of the Mississippi operation so you can pull together the Napa stuff."

While Rex and Tyrone collected the remaining items on our list, Anita steered us first into the visitors' lot northwest of the main entrance of the four-story, calf-shit-brindle, brick-sided Veterans Administration hospital. Old men in wheelchairs and luckier ones with walkers parked themselves along the sidewalks, accompanied by family, nurses, and comrades. All smoked cigarettes.

Anita cruised slowly, looking for a space.

"Did you set a waypoint for the Woodrow Wilson coordinates when we went by?" Jasmine asked Tyrone.

"Yep." He bent over and worked at the buttons on the Magellan. "And here as well."

We all studied the building as Anita drove into the north lot, then east, and made a U-turn by the electrical power transformer substation supplying the hospital. Huge high-voltage cables sloped down from the main towers at one side, and smaller, lower-voltage lines led to the hospital.

"Obviously every room and critical care patient as well as the operating rooms and emergency areas have power from the generator. But the police inside don't.

"The police office is on the first floor, to the right, past the main entrance," Anita said as she drove us along a two-lane road heading west through the University Medical Center complex. Finally, she brought us around a large block and parked in front of Murrah High School across the freeway from the VA to study it better. Anita pulled a sheet of paper from the seat beside her and held it up for Jasmine and me.

"I snapped this with my little Canon digital camera when I came by early this morning to visit one of my patients." She handed us the paper. It showed the front of the VA with Darryl Talmadge's room window outlined in thick pen.

"He's in a locked room guarded by totally bored MPs outside the door."

"Sidearms only?"

She nodded.

"Who has the key? The charge nurse?"

"Nope," Anita said. "It's with a captain from something called the Technical Escort Unit, bivouacked in the room next to Talmadge." Anita leaned over and pointed to the room east of Talmadge's.

"Now for the hard part," Anita said as she drove the Suburban back to Woodrow Wilson Avenue and headed for Hawkins Field, our unanimous first choice for stealing a helicopter. As expected, the airfield offered a wide choice of Bell JetRangers, the aircraft Jasmine had flown in Los Angeles for television news crews. But Hawkins crawled with security and too many people.

"Okay, plan B," Jasmine said, little knowing we would eventually run through plans C through BB as the pressure of unrelieved frustration built toward dark. For more than five hours, we crisscrossed Hinds, Madison, Rankin, and parts of Yazoo County, north past Canton and way over toward Flora and Pocahontas, south down to Byram, and finally southeast of Brandon. We found the better the airport, like Campbell Field in Madison, the more helicopters were there and the better the security.

Using an aviation map and data earlier downloaded off AirNav.com, Jasmine directed Anita to smaller and smaller fields, private airports with names like Supplejack, Root Hog, and Petrified Forest.

"Getting warm," Jasmine would say every time we'd close in on a smaller airstrip because we'd find crop dusters there, but so far no helicopters, just fixed-wing Dromader M18s, Cessna Ag Huskies, and the occasional Ag Cat and an Ayres Thrush.

"There should be more helicopters," Jasmine said now as Anita shifted the Suburban into four-wheel drive and charted a slippery course down a narrow, tree-lined lane paved with mud from summer rains. "Mama and I won a couple of dozen lawsuits for families and school districts when fixed-wing aircraft oversprayed pesticides and seriously exposed children. And we have more and more organic farmers who will sue at the slightest hint of pesticide on their fields. Helicopters are more expensive for aerial application, but the mere threat of legal action has offered a real financial incentive to use choppers instead."

As we mulled this over, the trees gave way suddenly to a pasture.

"Eureka!" Jasmine said.

Anita eased off the accelerator.

"Don't slow too much," I said. "We don't want to stick in anybody's memory."

"Okay, over there, at the far edge." Jasmine pointed. "That's a Bell B3. It'll do perfectly. I can hot-wire it in a second." She turned toward Tyrone. "Got the waypoint?"

"Yes, ma'am. Yes indeedy!"

As we approached the trees at the pasture's far edge, a deep banging, popping racket thundered down on us from above. Instants later an old bubble-nosed helicopter with an Erector-set tail burst low over the trees and made its way toward the pasture. It looked like one of the dragonfly rescue copters from an old *M*A*S*H* episode, but instead of a litter for wounded soldiers, this one had a long pipelike array extending left and right below the cockpit. Jasmine turned and craned her head up to follow it. The engine missed an ignition stroke and left a stutter as the sound faded.

"What a relic," I said as we entered the trees again.

"Not really." Jasmine shook her head. "More like a classic. That's a Bell model 47," she said. The engine stuttered again. "Needs a tune-up."

"Belongs in a museum," Tyrone said.

Jasmine laughed. "A lot of flight schools still use them. I learned rotary wing in one." She read the surprise on my face. "A lot of small operators who have to transition from fixed to rotary wing still use the 47 because they're cheap. Bell 47 clubs all over the world buy these, restore them, have races, and fawn over them like vintage Corvettes. The 47's a damn good bucket of bolts if you take care of it."

"And if you don't?"

Jasmine shrugged. "They crash a lot."

Jack Kilgore had finished off the sixteen-ounce tub of bad convenience-store coffee when his encrypted phone rang. He grimaced at the last swallow of thin acidic crap and said a small prayer of thanks he'd been able to drink it in a safe, warm, dry place free of incoming rounds.

"Kilgore."

"Barner here, sir. We have a lead on our targets."

"Excellent. Tell me about it."

The helicopters were gone.

Everything depended on stealing a chopper. Everything.

But when we returned to the GPS waypoint for the helicopters shortly before 3:00 A.M., both helicopters were gone. Anita stopped the Suburban and we all strained our eyes for a glimpse of a helicopter in the empty cow pasture intermittently lit as clouds hurried across the face of the setting moon.

We sat in stunned silence—Rex, Tyrone, Anita, Jasmine, and I—sandwiched in among the gear jamming the big Chevy truck's capacious interior and overflowed to the roof rack.

"This is not a good thing," I said finally.

Jasmine leaned toward Anita. "Can you follow those tracks?" Jasmine pointed to a set of muddy tire ruts leading into the pasture. "Maybe they're around a bend of trees or something."

"Sure," Anita said. "We're already in four-wheel drive."

Everything rattled as we bounced across the pasture trying not to think about the increasingly obvious fact.

"This is my fault," Jasmine said, her voice low and burdened with second thoughts. "We should have visited all those little airfields after dark. The choppers have to go somewhere to refuel."

"Just keep praying," I said as we bounced across the field.

"Worse comes to worst, we'll locate one tonight, and if we don't have time, we'll try again tomorrow night," Tyrone said.

"Might have to," I said. "But it also gives our buddies with the Black-hawks more time to find us."

Worse looked as if it were coming to worst, then we rounded a peninsula of trees and spotted the dragonfly silhouette of the old M*A*S*H chopper resting on a trailer. A blue tarp covered the bubble nose. The newer helicopter was nowhere to be seen.

"Oh, boy," Rex said, his voice flat and dull. "Oh freaking boy."

Anita pulled up to the old helicopter and stopped. Even after she put the Suburban in park we all sat there silently absorbing the unspoken reality facing us.

"Shake it off, guys," Jasmine said. "It could be a lot worse." Then she got out and walked around the helicopter, climbed up on the trailer, and shined her flashlight into some sort of inspection port on what looked like the tail-rotor gearbox. Next, she rapped on the near-side saddle fuel tank and checked out the pesticide hopper fastened behind the cockpit.

Then she unsnapped the bungee cords holding the tarp and let it drift to the ground.

Feeling proud and proprietary, I couldn't take my eyes off Jasmine, climbing into the cockpit, sitting in the pilot's seat, and looking slowly around her, then down at the instrument panel. My respect for her grew as I saw the subtle displays of her knowledge and competence as she inspected the craft. After a while she smiled, looked over at us, and offered a satisfied nod. Then she climbed down and made her way back to the Suburban.

"Well, the good news is that this is a G model of the Bell 47, which means the Franklin internal combustion engine is at least two hundred horsepower rather than one seventy-eight, which we see a lot," she said.

"Oh, Lord, bless you for twenty-two horsepower," Rex said sarcastically.

"Rex!" Anita barked at him.

"Okay, all right," Rex mumbled softly.

"The aircraft's still here," Jasmine continued, "because the trailer tire on the other side is flat."

"So why didn't they fly it out like the other one?" Rex asked.

"On something as old and slow as this one, you want to save your engine and airframe hours for something that makes you money," she said.

"So . . . I guess this is the ultimate good-news, bad-news thing," Rex said. "The good news is we have a helicopter; the bad news is we have a helicopter."

Laughter cut through some of the tension.

"This one's okay?" I asked Jasmine.

"Well, it just has to be, doesn't it?"

"Enough gas?"

She nodded.

"How about the stuttering from the engine?"

"Sounded like a fouled plug," Jasmine said. "I'll check once we excavate Rex's tools."

The moon had started to dip below the trees as we piled out of the Suburban, pulled on dark coveralls and boots.

"One more thing," Jasmine said. "The 47 is a lot slower than the Jet

Ranger. We can cruise around seventy-five knots . . . eighty-two or eighty-three miles per hour. It'll add another ten or fifteen minutes to the flight time."

Time had become our enemy and this latest news urged us on faster. We used the bolt cutters to get rid of all the chains and padlocks, then rolled the light helicopter off the trailer with surprisingly little effort.

Rex and I unloaded the Suburban and tried to figure out what we could strap to the skids, under the fuselage, and to the forward portion of the tail frame. We soon realized we'd need to leave a lot of the gear behind.

While Rex and I struggled to sort out the gear, Tyrone and Jasmine unbolted the pesticide hoppers and removed the spray boom. With help from Anita, they hot-wired the simple ignition circuit, then patched the SuperNova spotlights' coiled power wires directly into the helicopter's twelve-volt electrical system.

Rex and I rigged a makeshift net from half-inch climbing rope and strung it from the front to the rear of the skids on both sides in roughly the same places the old M*A*S*H choppers carried the wounded.

The makeshift net also offered Rex and me a safer platform from which to ride the skids, necessary because the cockpit held only two people.

"Careful of the right side where the rear skid frame meets the tail," Jasmine warned us. "The exhaust pipes get really, really hot."

The moon sank from sight as our watches raced toward 4:00 A.M. Dawn would follow soon. We'd be toast if we hadn't finished before it was light. Then, shortly before 4:15 A.M., we rolled out the floppy strip of metal-grid reinforcing wire used for light-duty concrete pavement like sidewalks and driveways. It was a good twenty feet long and eight feet wide. We stiffened it lengthwise with three lengths of half-inch steel rebar cable tied to the grid. Then we connected two "vees" of rope to each side of the metal grid and a single piece of rope from the apex of the vees.

Rex and I climbed into our safety harnesses, checked our packs, and put them on. We put on our red helmets, as did Tyrone, who was our loadmaster and might have to climb out on the skids to hand us equipment depending on what transpired. He had put on his safety harness and helmet earlier.

I had the dead blond woman's H&K automatic in a thigh holster and spare clips in the cargo pockets of my coveralls. Rex had a worn, nickel-plated .380 Colt automatic pistol with white grips my mother had left him in her will. Jasmine and Tyrone had the matching .357 Ruger revolvers. They also had the M21 between them, but I doubted it would come in handy. If we got into a firefight, we were doomed.

As Jasmine fired up the helicopter's engine, Anita gave Rex a kiss and a hug, then drove away.

Rex and I slipped on our goggles and stood next to the metal grid as Jasmine lifted the helicopter about five feet off the ground. Her hover was unsteady at first, then grew more and more solid.

Using the walkie-talkies, Rex and I had her hover over the wire grid as we attached the ropes to the skids of the chopper. Then Rex made his way over to the left side of the craft. I climbed aboard my side and snapped my safety harnesses to the tail frame and radioed for Jasmine to lift off. I held on tight as she lifted slowly up into the dark sky.

"Hold a minute," Rex's voice played in my radio earpiece. An instant later, brilliant light shot from his side. The SuperNova light on my side was snapped to one of the grid ropes with a carabiner. In the illumination of Rex's light, I spotted the metal grid spinning about, trying to keep time with the rotor downwash.

We landed for an instant to fix stabilizing lines from two of the metal grid's corners.

It was 4:30 A.M. when we took off again. I lay almost prone on top of the gear, head forward, legs splayed for bracing.

I pulled the night-vision spotting scope from my overalls and trained it ahead to keep an eye out for power lines. It made me wonder what other unseen terrors waited in the dark.

David Brown leaned against the windowsill of the commandeered office on the fifth floor of the federal office building in Jackson, Mississippi, and looked down at the nearly deserted stretch of Capitol Street. A newly lit Marlboro hung from the corner of his mouth.

"Where the hell are you, you thieving pig-frigger?"

Brown drew on the Marlboro and let the smoke drift out his nostrils.

A knock sounded on the door behind him, then he heard it open.

"What now?" Brown mumbled without turning. In the window's reflection, he saw his assistant's silhouette outlined by the light spilling in through the open door.

"I may have something."

Brown turned around. "What kind of something?" He took the cigarette out of his mouth and looked at his watch. It was 4:32 A.M. The sky would be brightening soon with the predawn glow.

"Call records from Stone's phone. Verizon wouldn't release them without a subpoena."

"Worthless bastards." Brown sucked the Marlboro down to his nicotine-yellowed fingers. "We've got to be able to get what we need without having to get some bleeding-heart judge involved."

"Yes, sir, well . . . We found calls to someone here in Jackson, a man named Rex, last name undetermined."

"Come on! How can someone have *Undetermined* as a last name?"

Brown's assistant shrugged. "He's a cipher. He's a contractor and took care of the maintenance on the apartment building where Stone's mother last lived."

Brown scowled as he dropped the Marlboro on the polished linoleum floor and crushed it out with his shoe. "Tell me something useful for a fucking change."

"This Rex character is married to a doctor who works at the VA where Talmadge is being held. The MPs on Talmadge's floor spotted her this morning."

Brown smiled broadly. "We've got that cocksucker now! Let's make that bastard pay for all the trouble he's caused, him and that nigger bitch."

The assistant turned his face away from the slur.

"Get moving!" Brown barked. "Tell the VA to double the guard. Move Talmadge to another room; get the Jackson cops out there. Warm up our troops and let's make sure these slimefucks have a properly warm reception."

With Tyrone navigating by her side, Jasmine homed in on the Magellan GPS waypoints set the previous afternoon. I clung desperately to the makeshift rope netting with one hand and with the other kept the night-vision monocular trained ahead to keep us from snagging anything but air. Down on the right, the brightly lit parking lot of the Mississippi Highway Patrol headquarters sailed past. The VA loomed larger, dead ahead.

I pressed the transmit switch on my radio.

"Showtime," I said. "Rex, you ready with your lines?"

"Ready," he said.

"Tyrone?"

"Here."

"You might want to turn on the M21's scope and use it to scan the shadows."

"It's all shadows, man," Tyrone replied.

"You got that right," I said.

I tucked the night-vision monocular in the calf-height cargo pocket of the coveralls and got ready with my side of the rope that suspended the metal grid beneath us. The VA hospital sat on the left now, and a row of high-voltage electrical pylons on the right. The University Medical Center dominated the view straight ahead.

The earth eased up toward us and passed underneath at a slower and slower pace until we had reached the electrical substation supplying the VA hospital. I whipped out the night-vision monocular, passed my hand through the carry loop, then trained it below on the thick wires slouching off toward the VA.

I keyed my radio. "Jasmine?"

"Here."

"Rotate to the left about one hundred and fifty degrees and hold your position."

In moments, we were positioned directly above the wires.

"Okay, down maybe twenty feet. Rex, you ready?"

"As ever."

"Okay, Rex, slip the knots and hold on."

I let the night-vision monocular swing from its carry loop as I leaned down and slipped the two knots holding the wire grid on my side.

From the peripheral horizon of my focused attention, I registered a siren and the flash of emergency lights. I grabbed both ropes in one hand and took a final look below through the night-vision scope. I let the scope drop and used that hand to key my radio.

"Down a bit more," I said.

Suddenly the darkness split apart with thunder that rocked my chest like a howitzer; that same instant, night became day as an electrical sunrise chased the darkness with an arcing blast of blue-white lightning.

Rex and I let go the ropes as Jasmine gunned the Bell 47's engine, accelerating us away from the substation, back the way we had come. There were few lights in the hospital and none in the parking lot. Jasmine kept us low for the moment as we headed east then south. As we passed east of the loading dock, I heard the emergency generator roar to life.

An instant later, sparks streamed downward off a piece of lit primer cord, then a second, a third, and three more afterward. Three almost evenly spaced blasts followed almost immediately. The final three had much longer fuses. Rex had suggested the half-sticks of dynamite as a diversion. As I looked back, flames leapt from a full garbage Dumpster.

Then Jasmine took us out over Woodrow Wilson Avenue, where we quickly spotted Darryl Talmadge's room. As Jasmine moved us in toward the roof, I unhooked my harness from the safety line securing me to the helicopter's tail, then snapped the carabiner to a bowline knot tied in the end of a piece of the half-inch climbing rope. Another bowline was tied about five feet higher than this and had a sling and a sack of gear carabinered there.

As Jasmine brought us in to the VA's roof, a blast rocked the far corner of the hospital, sending a small ball of fire rolling up maybe fifty feet. Then came the final two blasts. Those had been the long fuses.

As Jasmine moved us gently into position, something that looked like a flashlight flickered in the room next to Talmadge's.

"Light next door!" I said into my radio.

"Clock's ticking," Rex said.

Jasmine brought the helicopter down softly, keeping enough rotor lift to avoid crushing the roof. From a duffel roped to the skids, I grabbed the hand sledge cable-tied to a hank rope, then swung it through Darryl Talmadge's window. Rex and I rappelled down and entered after kicking away the remaining shards of glass.

Things were all wrong.

Talmadge was not in his bed.

Then, the door burst open.

"Get the fuck out of my way, you two-bit rent-a-cop, or I will fucking blow your tiny nuts off!"

David Brown, in full SWAT gear and followed by his assistant and two other Customs officers, brandished his H&K submachine gun at the VA's lone security guard at the main entrance.

Before the guard could respond, a brilliant flash and bang rumbled from outside, then the lights went out.

"That just fucking ices the damn cake," Brown said. "And where the hell's our backup?"

"Still waiting for authorization." Brown's assistant tried to explain that media coverage, the previous day's lawsuits, and the deluge of law enforcement complaints to the state's senators and congressional delegation had chilled the cooperation Brown had demanded. The Army was double-covering its ass, the FBI was rethinking its earlier, reluctant cooperation, and the Jackson Police Department was outright hostile to them.

"Well, you better fucking get your sorry act together or I'll shred your worthless ass when this is all over!"

Three more blasts rattled the windows around the security screening area in the VA's main entryway.

"Listen," Brown said as the explosions echoed away. "It's a fucking chopper. Those idiots are trying to break Talmadge out!" He turned and pointed the MP5 at the security guard. "Take us up there."

The guard hesitated until Brown thumbed off the safety.

The first MP burst into Talmadge's room before Rex or I got our balance. The MP aimed his sidearm at us as a second MP lunged in. Suddenly, from the shadows behind the door, the aluminum tubing of a crutch bottom arced out of the darkness and caught the first MP squarely on his nose, snapping his head back beneath a geyser of blood, showering dark and black in the dim light.

"Yeeeeeeeeee-*hah!*" A rebel yell followed the blow, and I knew Talmadge had to be somewhere behind it.

The MP's finger closed on the trigger as he staggered back into his partner. The slug plowed into the apparatus behind the bed.

"Get back!" Rex yelled behind me as he rushed forward and loosed a long blast from the big bear spray container. The potent chemicals guaranteed to stop a bear in its tracks wrenched out two sustained screams from both men as they staggered back into the hallway. Talmadge propped himself on one crutch as he leaned against the door. Rex helped him shove the door shut, then jammed the wood-splitting wedge under it. I rushed him the hand sledge.

"By damn that Shanker boy is all right!" Talmadge yelled. "Sum'bitch promised he'd get me outta here!"

Rex hammered the wedge tight beneath the door before the men outside threw their weight against it. Outside, new voices joined the urgent babble, one of which made me think of the old gin in Itta Bena.

"Okay, let's rock," I told Talmadge. I leaned over and picked up his bony, husk-thin frame and carried him over to the window.

"Can you stand?" I asked.

"Course I can. I can walk some too."

"Cool."

The old man was surprisingly capable, probably from the adrenaline. I harnessed him in.

Across the room, Rex bent over the paint-thinner can and sloshed the contents under the door. The sharp solvent smell pricked at my nose as I held out a makeshift nylon web sling to Talmadge. "Step into this."

Rex hurried over to us, pulled a road flare from a cargo pocket, ignited it, and tossed it by the door.

A loud *whoomp!* filled the room with brilliant yellow light.

"That should make them back off," Rex said as he helped me secure Talmadge.

Moments later, the room's sprinkles started.

"Jasmine," I called into the radio. "Start your ascent."

"Roger."

Outside, the helicopter's engine revved. From beyond the room door came the whoosh of fire extinguishers, then the nasty, sharp, splintering blows of a fire ax. They'd be inside soon.

Finally, we attached bright yellow, shock-absorbing lanyards between our safety harnesses and the helicopter. The rope slack disappeared as the door buckled. Outside, the helicopter moved until our ropes led out at roughly forty-five degrees.

I stepped behind Talmadge and gave him a bear hug as the room door imploded.

"Get us out!" Rex screamed into his radio. The helicopter's engine screamed; the rope snapped taut, the shock-absorbing lanyards stretched almost lazily, lifting us gently off our feet. Rex and I fended our way over the windowsill. Suddenly, the lanyards' elastic slack bottomed out and we slingshot into the gathering dawn with gunshots sounded from behind.

"Clear," I radioed.

Rex, Talmadge, and I bobbed like yo-yos at the end of our lines, awful for equilibrium but great for making us tough targets. The unmistakable report of an H&K MP5A at full automatic sounded from the roof as Jasmine dipped the nose of the helicopter to gather speed, jinked, then labored upward. Another volley burst from the H&K spawned a mist of aviation gasoline. Then the M21 cracked loud and sharp. I prayed Tyrone's shots wouldn't ignite the high-octane fuel. Passing out of this world as a tiki-torch bungee boy had never ranked high in my pantheon of ways to die.

David Brown burst through the hospital's roof access door in time to see the old helicopter rise gently into the approaching dawn. His heart hammered and the tobacco rawness burned at his throat as he hustled across the roof.

The helicopter dipped suddenly out of sight beneath his first volley. Brown ignored the Marlboro complaints in his chest as he sprinted for a better shot. Then the old chopper labored into his sights again. As the Heckler and Koch came alive in his hands, Brown saw a muzzle flash from the helicopter's passenger seat. In the next eternally long split instant, Brown felt a crushing impact squeezing his chest. The last thing he remembered was falling into the darkness beneath the roof.

Jasmine jinked the wounded old chopper up, down, and sideways to throw off the shooters. The erratic movement bungeed us like a paddleball. Rex, Talmadge, and I clung together to dampen the wild gyrations.

Looking back, I caught a split glimpse of the shooter with the submachine gun falling off the roof. The shooting stopped then, but the spray of aviation gasoline grew worse. The droplets of high-octane gasoline sprayed from the right fuel tank, immediately above the dangerously hot exhaust.

Our wild oscillations evened out as we made our way across I-55 and over the Pearl River forest and flood plain. Although we were far south of the area I had traveled well as a teenager, I still remembered times in this stretch of woods, especially an eroded bluff of unconsolidated marine sediment from which I used to dig prehistoric sharks' teeth.

Jasmine steered us east toward a waypoint Rex and Tyrone had set the previous afternoon. In my night-vision scope, the tops of the tallest trees passed not more than fifty feet below. I scanned the area ahead and caught sight of a set of towering high-voltage pylons. I keyed my radio.

"Do you see the high-voltage lines ahead?"

Tyrone answered, "I've got them in the sniper's scope. Our van's just beyond."

"The wires might be a moot question," Jasmine said.

Before I could ask her what she meant, the spray of aviation gasoline stopped and the engine stuttered.

Rather than throttle back as I expected, I hear her rev the engine faster and louder than ever. We climbed erratically into the predawn sky.

"We're close to the van. I can autorotate to it if we have enough altitude." The engine stuttered and roared according to no pattern, but her calm, matter-of-fact words dampened my desperation.

Rex tapped on my helmet. "There," he yelled into my ear, and pointed toward the white van he had "requisitioned" from the airport long-term parking lot and positioned among the trees beside a construction site.

Suddenly, the engine choked, tried to restart, then died, leaving us with unpowered autorotation's lazy, low swooshing. Closing in ahead, the open-girdered arms and legs of the electrical pylons clutched at us like giant robots. Red flashing lights warned us away.

The low, sixty-cycle hum of electricity reached us before we spotted the wires.

"Jesus!" I yelled when I saw the light of first dawn frosting the huge cables. The helicopter might clear the wires, but not its dangling cargo. If the wires snagged us, certain death awaited everyone.

"Climb up to the skids," I yelled in Rex's ears.

We let go of each other and commenced all new erratic trajectories that unbalanced the helicopter further. Rex and I hauled up on the ropes for all we were worth as the wires grew closer.

Darryl Talmadge mumbled the Twenty-third Psalm. I remembered the words clearly from having recited them every day at the start of school in Itta Bena. Silently, I said them along with him as I strained to pull us up.

About the time we got to the part about the "valley of the shadow of death," I was fearing evil more than I ever had before. I thought of Jasmine, Camilla, and what life meant, and I climbed harder, faster.

On the other side, Rex had reached the skid and levered himself up.

Above me, Tyrone leaned out, hauling on my rope.

The wires reached for me. The hair on my body stood up from the electrical field around the wires. One spark and the avgas saturating the helicopter and my clothes would ignite.

I grabbed the skid as the loop of my rope, still draped below us, slid gently over the first wire. With Talmadge strapped to me, I could not pull myself up on the skid, and as our feet headed for the last wire, I swung our legs upward.

My cup ranneth over when we cleared the last wire.

Rex was up on the skid, but Talmadge and I were half on and off, ready to be crushed no matter how soft the landing. As the ground rushed up toward us, I slid us down the rope again. As we neared the ground, I unsnapped us from the rope, then I let go and rolled as soon as my feet touched the ground.

Suddenly, a muffled thump filled the silence as the first of the chopper's skids sank deep into the newly graded dirt. The chopper's momentum rolled it over. The powerless rotor dug once into the soft earth, then stopped.

I freed myself from Talmadge and rushed over to the chopper. Rex had already climbed out.

"Well, any landing you can walk away from is okay by me," he said as he stood up, his coveralls slick with the bright red clay.

"Word," Tyrone said.

My heart soared when Jasmine's head appeared. I rushed through the boot-sucking mud to help her climb down.

"Sorry about the landing."

"One of the best ever," I said, hugging her tight to me. Talmadge finished the Twenty-third Psalm. But before his "Amen" faded, three SWAT-clad men with Heckler & Koch MP5A submachine guns rushed from behind the white van.

Dan Gabriel stood at parade rest amid a canyon of hand-polished, teak wine racks filled with a priceless anthology of the world's finest wines, including complete vertical collections of every top château in Bordeaux. Engraved brass tags marked each bottle with name and vintage.

Clark Braxton's domed wine cellar had been carved out of the conical volcanic extrusion by the same wine-cave contractors who made the vast barrel-aging caves at the base of the hill where Gabriel and Frank Harper had been imprisoned upon their arrival.

The wine-cellar walls had been left in the natural stone and the floor covered in marble. The room and racks, which stretched fifteen feet or more and had rolling ladders with shiny brass fittings, cost far more than the median $500,000 northern-California tract house—not counting the value of the wine.

Two interlocked nylon cable ties bound Gabriel's hands at the small of his back. He tried to ignore the chaffing on his wrists as he looked through an arch of tinted-glass doors, two pairs of half-inch-thick plate glass set like an air lock to avoid fluctuations in cellar temperature. Massive redwood doors flanked the glass and framed a room beyond with a broad window opening out over the western periphery of Napa Valley. Through this narrow portal, Dan gazed at the jagged volcanic and quake-rift hills and tried to find his calm inner center that had been his salvation many times before.

In the distance, smoke drifted into the valley from a fire on a ridge hidden from view. The California heat had baked the humidity into single digits and made the entire state a tinderbox, as it did every year.

A C-130, painted brilliant international orange, came from the right and made a water drop. As the C-130 flew out of sight, Gabriel focused closer, on the room beyond the door. Braxton was there, out of sight somewhere to the left in a room dedicated to tasting new vintages of wines. The guards who had brought Gabriel and Harper up the service elevator said Braxton would see them when he was finished tasting a new vintage sent to him by the owner of an ultrapricey wine-cult vineyard in Yountville.

Gabriel turned slowly. The two guards stood beyond his reach. Beyond them, Frank Harper snored in an antique chair, his head resting on a polished oak table. A small pool of spittle collected on the polished table. In deference to his frail constitution, Harper remained unrestrained by anything other than his own physical deterioration.

At the back of the room sat a glistening, cylindrical glass elevator, which led up to the main villa level. On the opposite side of a massive stone column sat the shaft for the service elevator, carefully concealed lest even its very idea offend the aesthetic sensibilities of those who would gather to appreciate what *The Wine Speculator*—the influential and oh-so-trendy magazine for wine snobs and wannabes—gushingly called "the most ethereally supreme collection of wines ever assembled in one place at any time in history. If General Clark Braxton's collection were books instead of wine, it would surpass the legendary library at Alexandria."

Braxton reveled in the influence he wielded.

As the C-130 flew back into sight, General Clark Braxton came through the far set of glass doors, then waited for those doors to close and the second set to open. One of the guards moved quickly to position himself between the General and Gabriel.

Braxton held a small box in his hand as he walked into the room and stopped inside the door, a dim silhouette against the bright landscape beyond. Gabriel squinted, which, he surmised, was precisely what the General wanted.

The guard nearest Harper roughly jerked the old man upright.

"Let the feebleminded old bastard sit." Braxton's voice ran thick with derision, annoyance, boredom.

Harper's face registered a collage of surprise, pain, and anger.

Braxton shook his head slowly. There was a click from the box in Braxton's hand. When Gabriel heard his own voice and Harper's, he knew the box was a small cassette recorder.

First came the conversation of Gabriel's phone call to the elderly doctor, then the kitchen conversation. Braxton's face grew deeper shadows until he snapped the recorder off with a flourish.

"Welcome to my 'damned Masada fortress,' as you put it," Braxton said. "Yes, Frank, I have worried about you for quite some time. I had hoped to be wrong about time and guilt loosening your lips, but I have never won a battle on hopes, just on caution and preparation.

"And you—" Braxton's eyes burned with anger as he stared at Dan Gabriel. "You of all people. I trusted you." Braxton's jaw muscles trembled as the General struggled for control.

"You are a traitor." Braxton stepped forward and spit liberally in Dan Gabriel's face. Gabriel grasped for his inner calm and focused on the cedarlike aromas of cabernet sauvignon subliming from the spit. Gabriel's control nearly deserted him when Braxton slapped his face, but a vision of the consequences, being manacled, surrounded by guards, restrained him.

"I was giving you the command of the most powerful military ever assembled in history," Braxton said. "You have pissed away a soldier's ultimate dream."

Braxton turned and made his way over to the wine racks. He ran his fingers lightly over one of the tags. "Patton nearly died the day this bottle was filled and sealed." He looked at Gabriel. "He was a *real* soldier."

The General turned again to the rack and moved farther down. His hand rested lovingly on another tag. He caressed the brass. "Teddy Roosevelt charged up San Juan Hill a week or so after the grapes were harvested for this one.

"It shows how wrong I was." Braxton turned again to Gabriel. "I thought you were made of the right stuff to fill their shoes and more." He shook his head. "I was so wrong, but you must live with the consequences. You will not preside over the Xantaeus Era. We will use our new weapon preemptively to make sure no one challenges America's might again.

"We'll celebrate this the day after tomorrow," Braxton said. "There will be quite a few people here, Dan. In addition to my Defense Therapeutics staff, there will be quite a few friends of yours from the Pentagon; I imagine they will be sad to learn what happened to you." Braxton smiled, then looked at Harper. "And you as well, you old fool. But tragedies happen in the pursuit of peace."

Harper nodded slowly. Then Gabriel caught a malevolent glint in the old physician's eyes.

"So, Clark." Harper managed a smile as he looked around at the massive assemblage of wine. "Why have you collected all this wine and in all these years I have never seen you drink any?"

Braxton offered Harper a superior smile. "Drink it?" He paused, then said louder, "Drink it! Any damn fool can drink it!" He raised his arm and made a complete circle. "It takes discipline, self-control, and the true appreciation of the wine *not* to drink it, but to *have* the wine, to *possess* it, to put it where it, by God, belongs! That's what separates the dilettante from the true collector." Braxton spoke now with a near religious fervor. "To select, acquire, and protect, and most of all to *complete* the collection, is the mark of greatness. For when the collection is complete, it deserves a reverence transcending material value."

"But do you appreciate it, enjoy it?" Harper persisted.

"You are more pathetic than I ever realized, Frank. When a man rises to my level, possession, not appreciation, counts."

Braxton walked over to Harper.

"And that, you little, broken-down quack, is something you will never comprehend in the few hours you have left to breathe."

Without another word or even a final glance at either man, Braxton strode past and disappeared up in the shiny, cylindrical glass elevator.

I sat in the rearmost seat of the unmarked government van between Tyrone and Jasmine and held her hand. The van idled along the shoulder of the road near the end of the runway at Campbell Field outside Madison. As we waited, a single-engine Beechcraft Bonanza came in low, filled the van's windshield, and touched down. A radio up front crackled with traffic between the small control tower, the Beechcraft, and other airplanes approaching and ready to depart.

We all watched the Bonanza recede in the distance: Rex and Anita on either side of Talmadge in the seat ahead of me, then up front, the three government contractors who had snatched us more than six hours before. They had changed into summer-weight civilian clothes that revealed highly fit former military men. The leader of the group, a retired Air Force colonel and fighter ace named Buddy Barner, had turned to a second career in special ops when he had been assigned a desk to fly.

The interior of the van hung damp with the mustiness of drying mud caking the piles of combat garb jammed in back with the luggage and gear. The van's air-conditioning labored against the hundred-degree heat and matching humidity outside and did little to diminish the mud's fetid dankness.

But no one was complaining about the smell because we had acquired the mud along with Talmadge's microfilm. Years ago when he was still an active hunting guide, Talmadge had sealed the microfilm inside a thick, plastic, river-rafting dry-bag enclosed in an airtight length of black plastic drainpipe with caps glued over both ends. Talmadge had then buried the package deep in the muck beneath a series of fifty-five-gallon oil drums used as a duck blind in the middle of a lot of nowhere. The "nowhere" in question, which had eluded the efforts of the U.S. government, was a boot-sucking swamp approximately south of an abandoned railroad grade, about twelve miles southeast of the Choctaw Indian Reservation near Wiggins, and not far from where the Coffee Bogue Creek oozes into the Pearl River.

Talmadge hugged the bag on his lap and refused to let it go as he half-dozed beneath the sedatives Anita had given him to help control his seizures.

"Y'all don't worry 'bout me," Talmadge had told us hours ago. "These fits start with some Las Vegas lights in my head. But don't worry none. I'll give you fair warning. You hold me down for a bit and I'll go right to sleep."

Rather than risk a seizure, Anita and I had selected a sedative combination from among the selection our captors had brought. Talmadge lay totally buzzed. Every few minutes, he would chuckle and make a show of embracing the bag, and twice he had wept for his dead wife. Jasmine squeezed my hand in those moments, knowing that I was thinking about past and future, Camilla and her.

I think I knew Talmadge's pain, but could never be certain. Anguish—like everything about consciousness—remains a relentlessly personal drama, played out on an internal stage for just one person, an experience that can be deduced by others but never shared.

A faint turbine whine made its way above the air-conditioner fan and focused us all on the end of the runway.

Barner shook his head. "They're still a couple of minutes out."

Moments later, a Citation, its tail number not the one we awaited, fanned out and landed gracefully with little smoke from the tires.

"So,"—Rex leaned toward Barner—"how did you find us? Really. Three old guys when the whole U.S. government is still chasing their tail?"

Barner looked at a thin man with salt-and-pepper hair who sat near the window. They had been stingy with information. Other than to tell us they represented neither Homeland Security nor law enforcement, they had said little.

"No harm," the thin man mumbled. He turned to Rex. "First of all, we had some leads from the folks in California and just asked the right questions, the right way, to the right people." He paused. "See, people actually *like* to talk to me. Which is more than you can say for the numbnuts, Billy Joe Bad Ass Homeland Security goons." He paused. "And from what we learned, everything eventually pointed to *you*."

"Uh-huh, exactly," Rex said. "That's what worries me."

The thin man smiled. "You've left footprints now. You're a family man now and you've started to forget about your other life. Some folks out there are a little better at remembering, especially when somebody like you materializes and wants to call in really stale IOUs. Some of those folks might seem dumb as a fence post, but they can still connect the headlines to a call from you."

"Who—"

The thin man shook his head. "No can say, podnuh. You need to remember: they did you a favor. They let us get to you first."

"Well," Rex grumbled.

"What he means is 'thank you,'" Anita said to the thin man.

Rex opened his mouth to protest when the call sign we had been anticipating sounded loud and clear on the radio. Barner put the van in gear and headed for the airport's general aviation gate. He entered a combination on the keypad and waited for the chain-link gate to slide open.

As we drove toward the arranged spot on the apron, a small jet with the correct number and twin engines at the tail dropped quickly and landed at the very end of the runway. An earsplitting blast of reverse thrust echoed through the airfield.

"Short runway for a big aircraft," Jasmine said.

Barner nodded. "But a helluva lot better off here than with all the eyes at JAN or Thompson Field."

The jet, marked only by a civilian *N* number, taxied right up to the van. The jet's forward door opened as the aircraft rolled to a halt.

"Stay here," Barner told us as he and his two colleagues got out. The engines were still running as Barner climbed the stairs. Our van's rear doors opened then, and Barner's two men grabbed our bags and my laptop, then transferred them to the jet.

Seconds later, one of the men opened the van's sliding side door and motioned us aboard. They helped me carry Talmadge and settle him in. As soon as we were aboard, Barner introduced us to the two officers aboard, shook my hand, and disappeared.

With an earsplitting whine, the jet leapt from the short runway and pressed me back into my seat. Beyond my window, the earth fell away and the green patchwork of trees and crops shrank to model-railroad scales. I followed this and said a prayer of thanksgiving for outrunning the hellhound again.

The man in the red polo shirt and khaki pants whom Barner had introduced as Brigadier General Jack Kilgore stood up and faced us as the engines throttled back and leveled us off above a scattering of cumulus.

"Sorry about the slingshot takeoff," Kilgore said. He had a John Wayne voice straight from *Flying Leathernecks*. "We needed an aircraft with enough range to fly here nonstop, and they tend to be bigger than what that small airfield usually accommodates."

He rested his arms on the seat backs in front of him for balance.

"As my friend Buddy Barner told you, I'm Jack Kilgore and I command Task Force 86M."

"I've heard of you," I said.

Kilgore smiled. "And I've heard of you too, *compadre*."

Jasmine gave me an intense look.

"Sorry for interrupting."

"Not an issue." He cleared his throat. "You are probably wondering how in hell you ended up here."

We all nodded.

"But, before I start, would anybody like something to eat?"

We all nodded eagerly.

"Thought so," he said as he made his way to a storage locker aft of the cockpit, pulled out a stack of white cardboard boxes, and passed them around. "I am proud to say our snacks do beat Southwest's . . . but that's not saying much."

I couldn't suppress my smile as I recalled the tiny bags of kibble I had eaten on my trip from L.A. Kilgore took a lunch box, set it on the seat, and took a sip from a plastic container of Odwalla juice before beginning.

"This whole situation started a few days ago when I got a Mayday call from the first commanding officer of 86M. I served with him and under him."

He took another sip of the juice as he let this sink in. I plowed into my own lunch.

"You've undoubtedly read about my friend Lieutenant General Dan Gabriel."

"Whoa!" Tyrone said. "Braxton's secretary of defense?"

"One and the same," Kilgore said. "Over a giant pile of steam-table egg foo yong, he told me a tale about a closetful of snakes in General Braxton's head."

"I think we know a little about that," I said, nodding to the microfilm bag.

"Affirmative," Kilgore said. "But hold on for a moment and let me tell you Dan's story, then you can fill me in on yours. Together, we might get a better picture of the elephant."

We polished off our lunches as Kilgore related his meeting with Gabriel, their subsequent conversations, Gabriel's last phone conversation regarding Frank Harper, and the significance of the last GPS location of Gabriel's phone before it was turned off.

Kilgore polished off his second bottle of juice and nodded at me. "Your turn."

With help from Tyrone and Jasmine and not a word at all from Rex, I told Kilgore about my mother's funeral and finished with the raid on the VA hospital and the close call with the high-voltage electrical wires.

"Incredible." Kilgore shook his head. He looked at Tyrone. "I hate to tell you this, but you didn't kill David Brown."

"But how—"

Kilgore smiled. "The arrogant, chain-smoking bastard had a coronary. The Marlboro Man killed him." He paused. "I only hope that stinking hemorrhoid was conscious until he hit the ground." He looked around for agreement and found it unanimous.

"Good," Kilgore said. "This is the situation. First we stop the deployment of this Xantaeus, then we rescue Dan Gabriel." He paused. "Not necessarily in that order, because I think Dan knows how to deal with the General and the patch.

"A couple of our former guys work Braxton's security detail," Kilgore continued. "That's not unusual, given the quality of our personnel. Anyway, one of the guys called me from a pay phone in Napa last night and told me he heard Gabriel and Harper are being held at Castello Da Vinci, the General's Napa Valley estate. Rumor says an accident's being arranged for Dan and the doctor. That's what bothered him and why he called."

The small jet hit an air pocket, first lifting us up, then dropping us into a hole. Kilgore casually fended his tall frame off the ceiling with one hand.

"So," he said when the aircraft had regained its equilibrium, "I think we get Dan first because he's got the stuff in his head which will let us take down Braxton and this Xantaeus thing."

Kilgore raised his eyebrows as he looked from person to person.

"What do you mean *we*, white man," Rex finally spoke up.

"Damn good question . . . Tonto." Kilgore cleared his throat, and when he spoke, his tone rang dissonant and discomforted.

"This is a rogue operation. If we don't succeed, it's a lifetime in a crappy military prison for me and my second-in-command, Bill Lewis, who'll be meeting us in Napa. Bill and I know it, we accept it, but we cannot—will *not*—put our personnel at risk.

"And we can't send a request through military channels or even civilian police because it would take too long. Gabriel would be dead by the time we got a response. And Braxton has loyalists up and down both chains of command."

"Are you asking us to go in and rescue your friend?" I asked.

Kilgore shook his head. "Bill and I are committed, but I won't ask you to follow us. That's not why you're here. We came after you because Bill and I are convinced you were framed, and your lives are in danger."

"So we owe you?" Rex asked.

"Wrong, Tonto."

"It's Rex, if you don't mind."

"Whatever," Kilgore said. "Getting the CD from Shanker, rescuing Talmadge, and locating the microfilm outweighs any pathetic effort I've made so far. You don't owe me a thing. Rex."

"Well, it's pretty clear without Braxton put away for good, we're marked for the rest of what will probably be very short lives," I said. Jasmine's eyes encouraged me to continue. "For my part, I'd say the only way out of this mess we're in leads right through Castello Da Vinci."

"We could go to the press," Tyrone offered, "but even with everything we have, who'll believe us? Braxton's hugely popular."

"Even if they believed us, would they believe in time?" Jasmine added. "I'm with Brad." She gave me a look that connected to my soul.

"Jasmine's right," Kilgore agreed. He remained silent long enough for reality to sink in.

"Right," Rex said reluctantly, and looked at me. "I'm in, but only because I promised your mama I'd take good care of you."

Given my background, his comments drew laughter from everybody but him. Anita looked at him with a combination of fear and pride. She nodded at him.

"I appreciate your sentiment," Kilgore said. "But I want you to think about it for the rest of the flight. This has to be a clear and unequivocal decision. We have very limited resources and severe consequences for failure. I'll describe the situation; if you change your mind, I'll understand. Genuine decisions always keep consequences clearly and constantly in mind."

Our jet began a gradual descent.

"Fuel," Kilgore said. "The jet got us in and out of Jackson nonstop, but won't get us back. We'll land near Longview, Texas, for a minute. But before we get there, let's go over a few things. Time's awfully short and we'll need to hit the ground running when we land."

Without waiting for us to reply, he retrieved a large brushed-aluminum briefcase from the seat across the aisle, walked back to the rear of the aircraft, unlatched a table, and folded it down.

"C'mon down." He waved at us as he covered the table with topo maps, aerial photos, and street maps.

I stood next to Jasmine and reveled in the warmth of our casual touch.

"First of all, some ground rules," Kilgore said. "The first is our mission: rescue Dan Gabriel. If we can rescue Frank Harper and/or stop the

Xantaeus deployment, then we will, but only if we can without endangering our lives and others."

He looked at each of us until we agreed.

"Good. That brings me to the rules of engagement. We *will* avoid hurting or killing anyone except as a last, desperate resort. Other than the one or two folks out to dispose of Dan and the doctor, I'd say we're dealing with good folks just doing their jobs. Let's use that bear repellent and some other nonlethal items I've acquired whenever possible.

"Finally, we're not going to use U.S. government assets or equipment other than information. I do not want to get my quartermaster in trouble, and I do not want to make my legal case worse through multiple charges of misappropriation of government property."

I looked around the jet and back at Kilgore.

He caught my question. "American Express. My personal card. I'll worry about how to pay it off next month—if it matters by then. Same at the other end. Bill Lewis used his card to rent a van and an RV to use as a sort of mobile base. He's done some shopping for us as well."

Talmadge snorted in his sleep then. Anita looked over at him.

"Now, for personnel assignments," Kilgore continued. "Let me finish. Then if you disagree, we can discuss it."

Heads nodded.

"Anita, we'll keep him sedated in the RV with you to look after him." She nodded.

"Bill Lewis'll be with his unit, which still believes we're monitoring Castello Da Vinci to assess security readiness. He'll relay the information to me as it happens. Nothing suspicious about that; I'm usually involved in penetration operations against high-profile targets."

"Rex, you, Brad, and I will attempt the main penetration and rescue. Jasmine and Tyrone will mount a diversion from a safe distance since neither's got combat experience."

Tyrone frowned. Kilgore shook his head. "For you I have something that would be fun if results weren't so important."

"Such as?"

"I've read your rap sheet," Kilgore said.

"That's juvenile stuff," Tyrone said. "Sealed by the court."

"Uh-huh."

"I'm awfully rusty with that stuff."

Kilgore's smile and eyebrows said he was unconvinced. "I want to see if you can hack Castello Da Vinci's network."

"I can probably do that."

"Lives depend on it."

"Do they have any wireless parts of their net?" Tyrone asked.

"Just for guests," Kilgore said. "They have hot spots for all the visitors they have. But it's firewalled off from the main network. Plus, everything's encrypted. Guests get a onetime use Wireless Encryption Protocol key."

"WEP's a piece of Swiss cheese," Tyrone said. "Total moving target. Crackers break it, router guys issue some new firmware, which hardly anybody ever upgrades, and even if they did, the crackers are usually a step ahead."

"I thought a WiFi hot spot only went a few hundred yards," Jasmine said.

"Depends," Tyrone said. "Back at the DEFCON hackers convention in Vegas in 2004, they had a contest and managed more than fifty miles. My guess is that with all the guests they have and all the rock and stone around Castello Da Vinci, they will have ratcheted up the power of their system and tweaked antennas so their important guests won't get a weak signal. And, if the place is as big as you say—and we know Braxton has access to all sorts of corporate things—he probably has an IT setup there, probably a VPN to his company and maybe links to other places."

The air got rough for a moment as we closed in on the Longview airstrip.

"So you can do it?"

"Yeah," Tyrone said confidently. "I can do it, but I need a decent laptop with two wireless 802.11g cards, some wire, aluminum foil, a couple of Pringles cans, and an hour or so with a good Internet connection to download some software."

"We can do that." Kilgore nodded. "But, remember, you can't access your servers anymore."

"Don't need to. The software I need to blow open the General's network is available for free to anyone with an Internet connection."

"Oh, jeez," Rex said.

"Okay, we've got only a couple of minutes here," Kilgore said as he spread out the topo maps to offer the lay of terrain, roads, and the fortresslike security around and in Castello Da Vinci.

"Our guy's certain Gabriel and Harper are jailed in one of the half dozen barrel-aging caves at the base of the complex. None of them have locks, just big iron bolts on the outside. They're off a spur tunnel intersecting the main service tunnel not far from the loading docks.

"Bad news is it's hot as hell, well over one hundred degrees. Good news is there's one helluva big wildfire on the other side of the valley and the prevailing winds are blowing it right over the General's place, so visibility's pretty bad.

"More bad news: there's a big party tonight—Pentagon brass, corporate execs—which means extra security and a lot more people we will not want to shoot. The upside's all the caterers, and deliveries of food and wine. That's how we get in."

"Why wine delivered?" Rex asked. "From everything I've read, Braxton's got a multimillion-dollar wine cellar."

"But he doesn't drink it," Kilgore said.

"Doesn't drink it?"

"He's a collector," Jasmine said. "It's all about the collection, not about the drinking."

"Now *that's* crazy," Rex said.

"It's one sign of the type of brain injury Braxton has," I said. "And he picked up his collecting mania right after the head wound."

The pilot interrupted us with his final approach announcement. We helped Kilgore secure his papers and cleaned off the fold-down table until only a single red file folder remained. The jet lurched and yawed as the downdrafts of approaching afternoon thunderstorms tossed it about.

"Here." He handed the file folder to Jasmine. "This describes your mission. Pass it along to Tyrone when you're done."

The landing gear groaned into position. Only then did Jack Kilgore take his seat and buckle in for the landing.

The Castello Da Vinci's barrel-aging caves described rough semicircles in cross section and huddled deep inside the base of the old volcanic cone. Sprayed concrete and reinforcing mesh coated the rock walls to prevent the odd piece from falling onto the heads of winemakers and distinguished guests.

The floor trickled damp from some deep and ambitious aquifer. The French-oak barrels came from trees near Limousin and reached to the ceiling, eight-high on metal racks that held two barrels each. All bore the General's coat of arms burned into the heads. Durable paper stapled to each head detailed the varietal, vintage, vineyard, vintner, and other pedigree. A small alcove hollowed out of the rock walls off the main cave held a long, rough oak table around which sat twelve straight-backed chairs. A strikingly modern light hung over the table where barrel samples were tasted, admired, fawned over, and worshiped by the high priests of wine and the acolytes fortunate enough to be granted an audience with wine made from some of the world's most expensive grapes by one of the world's most exclusive celebrity winemakers under contract to one of the richest and most powerful men in the world.

Dan Gabriel sat in one of the high-backed chairs and sneezed at the cold dankness. He was naked from the waist up, having given the rest of his clothes to Frank Harper, who lay semifetally on the table.

"Bless you," said Harper.

"Thanks." Gabriel got up and rubbed his shoulders as he walked around the room again. The thick, solid-oak cave door was the only exit and had a simple but hefty iron bolt that slid from the outside only.

"It's no use," Gabriel mumbled as he made his circuit of the room, looking for a weapon, a path out, a tool, or any sort of inspiration for escape. "I've been around this room a hundred times and there's nothing that can help us."

"Let's pull the bung on one of them and drink it," Harper said.

Gabriel finished his circuit of the room and sat heavily back in the chair next to Harper.

"Might as well," Gabriel said. "At least we'd go out happy."

"That your choice?

"Not much of a choice."

"I suppose," Harper said. "But then, not making a choice is a choice itself, now isn't it?"

"Excuse me?"

"The decision not to make a choice is a decision to put yourself at the mercy of events and other people and allow them to make those choices for you."

"What about now when we don't have a choice?"

"We always have a choice," Harper said, "but sometimes we have to search very hard for it."

"Doctor, I've been scouring this damn place for hours now and all I get from you is philosophy." Gabriel's voice was sharp and raw.

"I am sorry I don't have an answer," Harper said softly. "But if you are going to give up, then make it a conscious decision. That way *you*, and not someone else, will have made the choice, visualized the consequences, and come to terms with yourself. There is dignity in being responsible for one's own choices even if they turn out wrong."

Gabriel listened to the quavering voice and couldn't tell if the old man was talking about the current situation or the past fifty years. Probably both.

"Look, I'm sorry for being so tense," Gabriel said. "But this conversation is not helping us get out of here."

"Is getting out of here your decision?"

"Jeez, Doc!" Gabriel threw up his hands and stood up. "Of course it is, but making a decision is like Braxton deciding he's acting out of his own free will when he's a puppet of the short circuits in his head."

"We've all got short circuits. Which doesn't mean we can't exercise free will."

"Can Braxton?"

Harper was silent for a thoughtful moment. "Not entirely."

"Does that make him insane?"

Again Harper let the silence grow around them. "I suppose we are all a bit insane in our own ways, but the General? No. Not in the legal sense, anyway."

"Oh, boy," Gabriel mumbled as he made another circuit of the room. "Oh, boy; oh, boy: that was a lot of help."

"All I can say is you need to be open for nonobvious choices," Harper said. "Free will depends on choices. I have faith there are always choices if we can but see them."

"Sure, Doc. Sure."

We landed at the Napa airport as the sun slouched toward the jagged ridgetops and smoldered through the smoke and haze like a giant blood orange. A dark green Chrysler minivan with what looked like quarter- and half-sheets of thin plywood strapped to roof racks followed us as we taxied toward a row of hangars.

As the jet slowed to a stop, Kilgore motioned us to pull down the window shades and stay on board. He then opened the door and stepped out.

I reached for Jasmine's hand then, and she met me halfway. I gazed at her and marveled at the astounding energy of a simple touch. I thought about the deep, hidden power of this physical connection and visualized the contact where our skins met, taking it to smaller and smaller scales in my mind, skin to skin, molecules, atoms, all the way back to an ethereal quantum foundation where consciousness meets the essence of existence. In that moment of clarity, the twin blades of love and the fear of loss twisted again in my heart.

A moment later, Kilgore stuck his head into the cabin. "Okay, let's roll."

We filed out with Rex carrying Talmadge by himself and climbed into a gear-jammed minivan with Bill Lewis behind the wheel. Kilgore shoehorned himself inside and slid the door shut.

"We don't have a lot of time," Lewis said. "My intel guys say the delivery truck with the wine is supposed to be at the General's palace in something over an hour. It needs to arrive within a specific time window, partly because of security and partly because there are a lot of vehicles for the big shindig tonight and they all have to be inspected before getting inside."

Outside the airport, we passed a boring row of forgettable buildings and shortly reached a traffic light at Highway 29, then turned north toward Napa. Minutes later, Lewis turned into a big shopping-center parking lot and steered us past the Home Depot, toward a large RV, a dark blue Chevy pickup with a matching camper shell, and a white Toyota, which looked rented. Lewis parked next to the RV.

"Okay, let's look as normal as possible," Kilgore said. "There's a lot of traffic and other RVs so nobody's likely to notice us. Everybody stay in the van but Anita and me. We'll get Talmadge in and settled."

As Lewis got Talmadge out of the van, Anita and Rex embraced and exchanged a kiss and a whisper. Then Anita was gone.

Kilgore filled the silence. "Jasmine, you and Tyrone take the pickup." He reached into his pocket and pulled out a set of keys. "This is to the truck. The backseat and the camper shell are full of the stuff Bill got for you." Kilgore looked at Tyrone. "The laptop, WiFi cards, are still in their box."

"So I have a little configuration to handle."

"Yeah," Kilgore said. "But I have faith in you. Anyway, you two follow the map and the directions. There's a powerful walkie-talkie in the glove compartment with extra batteries and a connection to the cigarette lighter. It's all digital; encrypted and set to the same frequency as the rest of us. Turn it on as soon as you get in the truck and listen very carefully."

Jasmine and Tyrone nodded.

"Any questions?"

They shook their heads.

"Okay, get moving."

Jasmine gave me a hug and a kiss.

"I love you," she told me.

Her words made me inarticulate. "Me you too," I stuttered. When she gave me one of her Mona Lisa smiles, I tried to etch it in my memory in case I never saw her again.

Then she and Tyrone drove away.

"Hey, these things are just stacked up here," Dan Gabriel called down to Harper from his perch atop a stack of barrels. "They're not fastened down or anything. All the barrels sit one on top of the other with a dinky little removable metal rack between each layer."

The stack shook ominously as Gabriel wrestled with one of the barrels on top.

"Yes," Harper said. "They come down all the time in earthquakes. But wine people are pretty clueless. They seem to have a fairly loose grip on reality."

"If we can make enough noise to get the guards to open the door, I can drop one of these on him."

Rex and I sandwiched ourselves behind the concrete support pillars of the Highway 29 underpass at Green Island Road and listened intently to the earbud connected to the walkie-talkies, which had set Bill Lewis's American Express card back more than $600 each.

We wore navy-blue Dickies coveralls, Red Wing boots, and khaki baseball caps with the Napa Valley Vintners Association on them. We had big cans of bear repellent, duct tape, cable ties, nylon cord, box cutters, and a handy piece of three-quarter-inch rebar about eighteen inches long. I had handcuffs; Rex had a funky red ball with holes in it and a strap Lewis had bought at a porno store.

The HK41 I had taken from the blond in Mississippi rested in a ballistic shoulder holster inside the coveralls. Rex wore his own 9mm the same way.

A constant vehicular surf rolled off the four-lane highway and washed around us, punctuated by the deep notes of tractor-trailers and pickups with glass packs. Every two or three minutes, a vehicle passed by our position, coming from or heading to the Green Island Road warehouse complex west of us. Kilgore preferred this spot, but had two other contingency locations.

"On his way." My radio earpiece filled with Kilgore's voice. I pressed the tiny button on the foblike microphone.

"Ready."

Rex looked at me. "This is freaking nuts."

"That's why you and I are here."

Rex smiled as we moved down the concrete slope. He squatted behind the steel guardrails; I sprinted to the other side of the road and took cover. Moments later, Kilgore's green minivan came around the sharp corner. Kilgore passed us, then hit the brakes and turned the minivan sideways, blocking the underpass road. Not two seconds later, a big delivery van came around the corner. The driver locked up the double rear tires when he saw the minivan.

Rex and I launched ourselves at the truck from both sides. The doors were unlocked so we discarded the rebar and jerked the doors open. I wrestled the startled driver to the middle of the cab as Rex slid behind the wheel. The driver's foot left the clutch, bringing the truck to a lurching halt. Rex had the truck restarted and moving in seconds.

The driver was a slight Hispanic man who kept shouting, "No hurt me! *Por favor!* No hurt! I have childrens!" He prayed in Spanish. Terrifying this innocent man made me more ashamed than I had ever been.

"I won't hurt you," I told him as we followed Kilgore north onto Highway 29 and back toward Napa. I believe he recognized truth in my eyes and calmed down. He let me put the handcuffs on him and place the gag in his mouth. He was momentarily frightened when I brought out the hypodermic Anita had prepared, but quickly settled down as the sedative took hold.

We followed Kilgore through Napa, across Big Ranch Road, and north on the Silverado Trail. We pulled off the road south of Rutherford and stopped alongside three cars with empty bike racks, their owners obviously some of the brilliantly colored riders packing this beautiful and popular wine-country route. The heat and lingering smoke from the distant brush fire had thinned the packs of Lance Armstrong wannabes, but had not chased them away all together.

"Any problems?" Kilgore asked when I opened my door. I shook my head.

"How long's he out for?"

"Three, maybe four hours," I said.

"Good," Kilgore said. "By the time he wakes up, we'll be dead, in jail, or big heroes."

"Just so long as it's not all of the above, kemo sabe," Rex said.

Kilgore opened his mouth to say something, but Rex beat him to the punch. "Rex. That's *Rex* with an *x*."

"You're okay." Kilgore smiled and punched Rex on the shoulder. "So let's get moving. Mr. X."

With the truck as cover from passing motorists, we transferred our gear and the minivan's plywood to the back of the truck and gently laid the sedated driver in the back of the minivan. Kilgore parked the minivan at the far end of the parking area in a shaded, narrow area parallel to the road to keep people from parking alongside. We laid the driver on his side so he wouldn't choke. Then, with a web of nylon rope and cable ties, we made sure that if he recovered prematurely, he couldn't move or hit the sides or roof of the van with his arms, legs, or head. We left the engine idling and the air-conditioning on low.

Finally, Kilgore attached a dark smoky-gray plastic pod smaller than a computer mouse to the back door of the van.

"What's that?" I asked.

"Auxiliary handset," Kilgore said. "Connects to my cell. This one has a motion sensor and camera built in. If the van or our man starts to move, it takes a picture like a camera phone, then e-mails it to me."

"Cool," I said.

"It's a cheap, stripped-down handset. No keypad or display. You program it with the main cell phone. They come with accessories to detect sound, moisture, heat . . . a bunch of other stuff."

I opened my mouth to ask him more.

"No time to jawbone about toys. We need to show up on time for our check-in."

We all climbed inside the truck and used the wine cases and the plywood to create hollowed-out hiding spaces in the back of the truck for Kilgore, me, and our gear. I hunched down and focused on remaining calm in the stifling, confined space as Rex stacked the boxes over me. Then the cargo door rattled down and the truck engine rumbled.

As the truck lurched its way back onto the road and Rex ran through the gears, I prayed: for the Hispanic man with children; for Jasmine and for myself; for Rex and Anita and Tyrone; for Kilgore; for Camilla, Vanessa, and my mother; and for the wisdom and protection to accomplish this mission.

Lying there in almost perfect darkness, I experienced the most perfect vision of Camilla, Nate, and Lindsey since the night they'd all died. The memory appeared in near-holographic faithfulness. The vision was important so I let it play.

At Jasmine's direction, Tyrone turned the blue pickup left off the Silverado Trail south of Rutherford.

"Big-shot General ain' gonna like this. No-*suh!*" Tyrone joked.

"Big-shot General can just stuff all those stars," Jasmine said. "I need a couple of minutes practice before the main event."

"You and me both." Tyrone nodded toward the brand-new laptop.

They drove past a flat, dirt-covered field, bare except for a gigantic pile of grapevines that had been cleared to make way for new ones.

"Turn here"—she pointed—"to the right."

Tyrone steered them along a hard-packed dirt lane like others crisscrossing the vineyards, providing access for trucks and other machinery involved primarily in the annual harvest.

"Okay, stop," Jasmine said.

She got out, opened the camper shell, and pulled out one of the big Toys "R" Us bags. Tyrone shut off the engine and got out to offer his help as Jasmine unpacked a "deluxe" radio-controlled airplane. The wings, nearly four feet from tip to tip, needed to be attached to the fuselage.

"Piece of mass-manufactured crap," she said. "Give me a couple of hours and I'd do something with this junk."

"Ain't got two hours," Tyrone said. "You or me."

Jasmine did not reply as she filled the small plane with fuel from one of the metal cans in the bag, then inserted batteries in the airplane and the control console.

"Can you get me the plastic bag from behind my seat, please?" she asked. When Tyrone returned, he handed her the Albertson's bag and watched as she took out a half stick of dynamite with an electric detonator inserted and taped into the end. She strapped this to the fuselage of the R/C aircraft but did not connect the detonator wires to the plane's remote accessory circuit.

Jasmine placed the airplane on the hard-packed road, ran up the engine, and guided it skyward.

"Awright," Tyrone said. "I got to get me to work on that crappy old Windows XP laptop."

"Over by the door." Gabriel crouched on the top of the barrel racks farthest from the door. Harper smiled as he followed the directions.

The barrel stack wobbled drunkenly as Gabriel pushed it away from the wall, rocking it back and forth, unbalancing it more with each shove until it tipped. Gabriel clambered to the next stack as the first barrels of extravagantly expensive cabernet sauvignon detonated like bombs as they hit the floor. Wine and barrel staves flew like shrapnel.

The next layer of barrels burst too, but not as violently. A few, instead of breaking open, rolled against the far wall. Neither of the men thought it odd at the time that the barrels made distinctly different sounds when they struck the wall. The head of one of the barrels cracked when it hit the wall and sent more wine cascading over the floor.

"Okay, that's more like it," Gabriel said as he rocked the next stack of barrels.

The stale air had begun to choke me by the time the truck stopped. I struggled not to cough as the cargo door rumbled open.

"Okay, the undercarriage and engine compartment are clear," I heard a voice, not Rex's.

"This looks like more wine than the order specifies," said a second unidentified voice.

"I've got another delivery after this one," Rex said without missing a beat.

The footsteps grew close, then stopped. The box above my head shifted; daylight filtered through a growing crack. I grabbed for the HK4.

Parked under one of the few trees in the middle of a large vineyard slightly northwest of Castello Da Vinci, Jasmine sat in the pickup and listened anxiously for some word on the walkie-talkie. But nothing came through.

In her mind she checked off her action list: All four of the radio-controlled aircraft sat in the pickup's bed, under the camper shell, fueled, loaded with their half sticks of dynamite. She needed only to connect the detonator wires to be ready to fly at a moment's notice. The vineyard access road they had parked on was actually a little better than the one she had tested all four planes on.

In the distance, she caught glimpses of a steady procession of limousines and the occasional motorcade as they headed for Braxton's event. Behind her, sprawled across the truck's backseat, Tyrone clacked at the keyboard of the new laptop.

"Yes!" Tyrone startled her.

"What?" She was irritated at having her thoughts interrupted.

"I'm in!"

"In where?"

"Braxton's network."

"Into the WiFi?"

Tyrone shook his head. "All the way in."

"You're kidding!"

"Nope."

"How?"

"Cool piece of new crackware called airpwn," Tyrone said. "Uses raw frame injection. One of my network cards listens on one channel, and the other card injects custom frames with perfect replies. If you tickle the size of the replies just right, it works so perfectly that the connection functions so well nobody on the other end can detect the intrusion unless they're watching a packet sniffer real-time."

"I don't understand a thing you're saying."

"That's okay," Tyrone said. "The important thing is that they can't block me without blocking legitimate traffic. So I get in through the wireless and look for a machine that's connected to both the wireless and the hardwired network. Happens all the time. Anyway, I have some custom modifications to the Ethereal packet sniffer along with a MAC spoofer and a custom password cracker I wrote a while back that let me grab all the data I needed to get into the primary system."

"You told Kilgore you were rusty at this."

"I lied. He knew that. Like I said, it's a new technology and really hard for even a talented user to close off all the holes. This one also didn't even bother to change the default password on the router."

"And what does that get us?"

"Eyes and ears."

"Say what?"

"Look at the screen here."

"Oh my God!"

Despite his age, his Parkinson's, and his having had little rest and nothing to eat or drink in more than twenty-four hours, Frank Harper startled Dan Gabriel with a whoop of joy when the next to last stack of barrels came thundering down. A fortune in cabernet sauvignon pooled ankle deep in the cave and made a visible current as it drained under the door.

"That should get somebody's attention," said Harper, who had moved to the back of the cave as Gabriel worked toward the door.

"Not too many somebodies, I hope," Gabriel said. "We better clear enough debris for the door to open."

I thumbed off the HK4's safety.

"Not now, Benny." The wine box over my head stopped moving. "We got a line backing up out there." The case of wine came back down and sealed me off again.

"Awright," the voice said.

Then the previous voice: "Unload at the usual place. Wait for somebody to come check the inventory before you leave."

"My pleasure," Rex said.

The cargo door rumbled again and the truck began to move. Only then did I reset the safety. I heard the safety on Kilgore's pistol click about the same time.

Moments later, the truck slowed, reversed, stopped. A minute later, cool air flooded in over me.

"Wake up, asshole," Rex said.

Beyond him, the yellow and black stripes of a loading dock showed beyond the mostly closed cargo door. An electric forklift whirred in the distance. I got out and helped excavate Kilgore, who climbed out quickly and paused to suck in the fresh air.

"Okay, let's stage the scenery as best we can," Kilgore said as he started moving wine cases toward the back of the van. "Stack the plywood flat in the corner so it's not noticeable. The more innocent things look, the more time we'll have before they tumble onto us."

Rex and I followed his lead, and minutes later Kilgore keyed the microphone fob. "We're in."

Then we rolled up the cargo door, grabbed a case of wine apiece, and followed Kilgore through the chaos on the loading dock. Caterers, vendors, and platoons of people in white uniforms with toques cursed petulantly in a dozen languages, demanding forklifts, assistance, and insisting to be escorted upstairs immediately or the canapés, ice sculptures, gelato, and everything else would be ruined. Ruined!

Braxton's security, dressed in blue blazers, khaki pants, white shirts, and rep ties, sidled through the unruly mob, trying to establish order. The looks on their faces said they'd prefer to shoot most of these people if only it wouldn't deprive the General and his guests of pâté or pastry.

"I like this very much," Kilgore said as we pushed our way through the melee and across the loading dock. To our right, an arbor heavy with summer foliage blossomed and extended the length of the lot now jammed with trucks.

"The formal entrance is on the other side of this," Kilgore said. "Braxton wouldn't want his very snotty guests insulted by the sight of common people working."

We followed him into the coolness of the main service entrance.

"Right up there." Kilgore pointed at shadows in the far right corner. We stood stock-still for a moment, blending into the dimly lit area. One of the security officers looked over at us, then turned to a tall, thin young man who was haranguing him about how his was the most important course and the General would be displeased if the delivery was not made immediately.

Kilgore led us around an oblique corner to a shadow-filled corridor and set his wine case down.

"This should be it."

Rex and I stacked our wine on top of his. A long, dimly lit cave stretched before us, lined on both sides with phalanxes of identical oak-plank doors bound with black iron straps.

"From here, I count maybe twenty doors."

"Damn . . . ," Kilgore mumbled. "Let's get going." He turned and slid the heavy bolt of the nearest door. The tunnel resonated with the screech of metal in desperate need of lubrication.

"Jeez!" Rex said. "Better hope the noise back there continues."

"We have a choice," I said as I took the first door on the other side of the tunnel. It screeched slightly less than Kilgore's.

"I'll work ahead," Rex said as he walked half a dozen doors down the tunnel. I cringed as he slid back the next bolt and filled the corridor with a deafening metallic thunder.

"Listen!"

Gabriel stopped by the door and stood up. The last pieces of broken barrel staves and a hoop hung loosely at his side. Above the sounds of priceless cabernet dripping into the expensive red flood came the rusty complaints of the cave doors and muffled voices of men.

Harper sat still and concentrated. "Yes, this may be good." He struggled to his feet as Gabriel scaled the last remaining tower of barrels, the one adjacent to the door. When he looked back at Harper, something on the cave wall caught his attention.

"Doctor?"

"Yes?"

"What's over by you? Looks like a crack in the wall."

Harper shuffled over to it. "A crack in the wall."

"These are supposed to be solid stone."

Gabriel climbed down, walked over, and stared at a small trickle of wine disappearing into the crack.

"Don't you think you should get ready?" Harper looked toward the door.

"In a sec."

Gabriel rapped on the area around the crack. Hollow. He rapped on a spot about five feet over. Solid. He tore at the crack, peeling off concrete fragments.

"What is it?" Harper asked.

"Maybe a better way out," Gabriel said as he worked at the wall. As the bolt sounds in the outside tunnel grew louder, the concrete came off in bigger pieces, revealing the mesh of reinforcing metal. The cool dankness of trapped air made its way through the mesh.

"Holy hell!" Gabriel said as he pulled at the bottom. The metal bent outward as he pulled loose the soft metal wires used to fix the mesh to the cave walls. With a final heave, Gabriel lifted the bottom up more than three feet, enough to crawl through.

"Here," Gabriel said to Harper. "Let me help you through."

An excited voice sounded outside the door. Someone had found the stream of wine.

"We don't know where it leads," Harper said. "Or if it leads anywhere at all."

Outside, they heard the thuds of running footsteps.

"That's right, Doc, but life's like that, isn't it? We know we have a tough fight the other way. I say we make a choice and pray for the best."

The bolt on the door rattled tentatively.

Harper accepted Gabriel's outstretched hand.

"Wise decision, young man."

"From you, I'm honored."

Harper wasn't halfway in when the bolt screeched all the way back.

"Keep moving, Doc," Gabriel called as he rushed to the barrel stack and scaled it with an ease that amazed him.

Jasmine's heart trip-hammered as she watched Tyrone paging through scene after scene from Castello Da Vinci's security cameras.

"Now, listen." He clicked on a button on one camera image, and the sounds of distant voices came from the laptop's speakers.

"Every camera also picks up sound."

"That's amazing."

Then Kilgore's voice came through on the walkie-talkie. "We're in."

"Okay, help me for a minute," Jasmine said to Tyrone as she grabbed the walkie-talkie, plugged in the earbuds and lavalier mike.

"I don't suppose you can locate Brad and the rest?" She clipped the walkie-talkie to her belt and got out of the truck. Tyrone followed her.

"Not too soon, I hope," Tyrone said.

"Why?" Jasmine opened the camper shell and dropped the tailgate. Tyrone came around the side and helped Jasmine pull out one of the radio-controlled airplanes.

"Because if I can see them, so can Braxton's security people."

Rex summoned us with a stage whisper. Kilgore and I jogged over and nearly slipped on the wet. The unmistakable fragrance of wine saturated the air. Red wine, to be exact. I bent over, wet my finger in the liquid, and tasted it.

"Young cabernet sauvignon."

Rex shook his head, then slid the bolt, eliciting a shrill, tortured sound that immediately attracted the beams of powerful flashlights and echoes of sprinting combat boots.

"Freeze!" someone shouted.

"I'm out of here!" Rex said as he muscled the door open. A thundering detonation showered us with wine and pieces of wood.

"The hell?" Rex yelled as he leapt back. Then another barrel exploded against the floor, followed by another and another.

"Jesus Christ, Joseph, Mary, and the donkey!" Rex cursed.

Braxton's security guards drew closer. Cautiously, we looked through the partly opened door at the carnage of expensive French oak and cabernet. Braxton's men closed to half a dozen paces.

"Hands up!" they shouted.

Heedless of the barrel barrage, Rex lunged over the priceless wreckage as Braxton's men grabbed my arm.

Colonel William Lewis paced calmly among his troops in the back of the shabby Napa storefront and listened intently to the radio traffic in his earbud. Lewis's troops were used to him communicating with the "Old Man," as they called Kilgore. They just had no idea where Kilgore was located.

"Sir, we've picked up some interesting stuff." Lewis turned and looked up into the face of Janet King, a fast-rising corporal, a Penn State lacrosse and rugby star (men's teams) with a computer science degree, who'd enlisted "because I was tired of the way politicians always piss on the military." She also hated being called "an Amazon." At six-one, 193 pounds, and a percent body fat she had to struggle to keep out of single digits, Corporal King had the wherewithal to make her objections stick.

"What've you got?"

"They've gone to the equivalent of general quarters over what appears to be intruders."

Lewis said a silent prayer. "Could it be a faulty alarm or something?"

She shook her head. "They've apparently made contact and have apprehended two people."

Lewis nodded and tried to appear calm.

"Whoa! Holy cow, holy cow!"

Tyrone leaped from the truck and ran around the back to Jasmine, who'd been pacing the hard-packed lane ever since she had finished connecting the electrical detonators to the accessory circuits of the aircraft. Jasmine turned.

"The security control screen has gone apeshit!"

"Show me."

"C'mon." Tyrone rushed back into the truck with Jasmine close behind. Inside, Tyrone held up the laptop.

"Notice the red flashes? Those were all green a minute ago."

"This looks like a diagram of the London underground," she said calmly.

"It's similar . . . part schematic, part spatial reality."

"I don't think this is a good sign." Jasmine shook her head and looked back at the screen. "What are those little icons?"

Tyrone took the laptop back and set it on the console between the two front seats so they could both see. He tickled the laptop's touch pad and used it to center the cursor over an icon. The mouseover text appeared on-screen.

"Security camera. If we click on the link, it gives details."

"This like a webcam?" Jasmine asked.

"Just like. They have lots of cameras hooked on an internal network. Lots of places are going to IP-based systems because they're cheap to build and can be programmed and implemented quickly."

"IP?"

"Internet protocols." He bent over the screen, working the cursor and keyboard. A moment later, the image of a deserted hallway appeared.

"There!" Tyrone said triumphantly as he clicked from one camera image to another. His triumph lasted only seconds as a jerky video showed Brad Stone and Jack Kilgore being escorted by armed guards.

"Oh, God!"

Once through the hole in the barrel-cave wall, Rex pulled a tiny LED light from his pocket and squeezed the sides to illuminate what appeared to be a stairway landing. Directly opposite the hole, steps led up. To the right, stairs led down. Rex looked around and saw recent footprints in the dust going left. As a noisy posse gathered in the barrel cave, Rex made footprints to the right and the left, then scuffed up both sets before climbing up the stairs after Gabriel and Harper.

For all the good it would do, he thought. But what the hell, there was nothing else to be done.

He climbed rapidly, trying once to raise somebody on the radio, but the surrounding rock made that impossible. Just as well, he thought. Braxton's men obviously had Stone and Kilgore's radios.

"Sorry, Miss Anabel," Rex said under his breath.

"Do you hear somebody behind us?" Harper asked in a ragged whisper.

"Hard to tell," Gabriel whispered as he half-carried the old doctor up the steps.

The restrained professionalism of Clark Braxton's security men surprised me. The handcuffs at my back were secure but not too tight, the grip on my arm firm but not uncomfortable. We arrived at an elevator as the doors opened and disgorged a big, beefy man with the face of an angry bull. The people holding us visibly stood straighter.

The man's eyes burned sharp and mean. He stuck his face right in Kilgore's.

"You are so far out of line this time, Jack, you will never, ever take another breath as a free man."

Kilgore remained silent as the man stood back and adjusted his tie.

"Take them up to the cellar," the big man said. "The General wants a word with them."

"You want us to notify local law enforcement, sir?" asked the man holding on to my biceps.

"I'll handle the county mounties when the time comes."

"Sir?" a voice came from the rear. "Sanchez wants to know if you want to send a search party into that hole in the barrel-cave wall."

"Tell him to wait for Jim Clayton. He knows those old tunnels like the back of his hand."

I didn't like what I heard; I had learned too much. Names, other things I would not expect professionals to reveal in front of captives. Unless it wouldn't matter.

When the elevator doors closed, I imagined the sort of "accidents" that could happen when two soldiers as capable as Kilgore and I tried to escape.

"There they are." Tyrone pointed at the screen. "Heading to that elevator, which has a camera"—he cursored around, clicked on another icon—"right here."

Jasmine's fear transformed into abject sorrow as she watched Brad Stone step into the elevator and look right up at the camera.

"I love you," she whispered to his image.

Dan Gabriel stumbled up the pitch-dark stairs, half-dragging Frank Harper behind him. He stopped periodically to rest and to listen for sounds of pursuit. He pushed on upward in the dark until suddenly his face hit a barrier and he almost dropped Harper.

"What happened?" Harper whispered.

"Dead end," Gabriel replied. "Can you sit on a step?"

"Yes."

Gabriel closed his eyes against the despair, although he saw nothing less, no more, with his lids open or shut, so complete was the darkness. Then, beyond the dead end, the sound of voices, footsteps. Gabriel ran his hand over the dead end, and under his fingers it felt like Sheetrock. Was there hope? He pressed his ear to the wallboard. Gabriel's hopes fell as he recognized the voice of Braxton's security chief. Then Jack Kilgore.

"We've got to do something," Gabriel whispered. "Even if it's a kamikaze charge, I can't just sit here and do nothing."

"Nothing—"

"Yes, Doctor, nothing is its own decision. They'll kill us if we sit here, so I might as well take somebody with me."

"What are you going to do? Charge through the wall like a madman and attack them with your bare hands?"

"Do you have a better idea?"

"No," said Harper.

Then came an unknown voice in the darkness that sucker punched them both.

"I do."

"Oh, man, take a look at this."

The laptop screen showed rack after rack of wine.

"This must be the holy of holies," Tyrone said. "Millions of dollars' worth."

"And he never drinks it." Jasmine shook her head.

Tyrone clicked around. "There must be ten . . . no, fourteen cameras in this room." Other than for different labels and neck capsules, most of the views looked mostly the same. The only ones different showed the elevator area and, the other, a brightly lit room with a view overlooking Napa Valley. The image showed the smoke rising from the hills behind them.

"A few more degrees down tilt and we'd be on this one," Tyrone said.

Jasmine looked over at the fire, then up at the window she figured must be the one on-screen.

Tyrone clicked back to the service elevator as the doors opened. He and Jasmine stared silently as guards escorted Stone and Kilgore out.

"Where's Rex?" Jasmine asked. Then a moment later: "I don't suppose you can save the video stream, can you?"

"I think maybe so. Why?"

"Great evidence."

Tyrone pecked at the keyboard.

"I'd like to make sure if anything happens . . ." Her voice cracked. "If something happens, I will nail that bastard's butt to a tree."

"Uh-huhmm," Tyrone said slowly. "Please remind me not to get on your bad side."

Jack Kilgore and I sat cross-legged on the cool tiles of General Braxton's wine cellar. Giant, polished wooden racks reached halfway to the twenty-foot ceiling. They stretched the length of the space like library shelves, organized into rows and aisles running from the elevators at the back to a set of double glass doors at the front.

Two security guards stood behind us, and a third stood by the double glass entry doors guarding our walkie-talkies, firearms, and the rest of our gear piled on the floor. They all had semiautomatic pistols drawn.

We waited in the silence, listening to our own breathing and scanning the priceless wine I doubted I would ever taste.

Suddenly, a loud hammering and crashing rocked the side of the wine cellar to my right, somewhere beyond the carefully crafted, lovingly oiled tropical-hardwood racks.

"Damn!" Rex cursed amid the rattling of wine bottles; the rack to our right shuddered. From beyond the rack came the dull breaking noises of full wine bottles smashing on the tile floor.

The guard in front of us raised his pistol and followed the noise.

Then from behind: "What the hell?" Kilgore and I turned at the same time and saw one of our guards, pistol drawn, running toward the source of the noise. He disappeared around the far end of the racks nearest the elevators. Then came a faint hiss and profound screams. Two wild gunshots followed. Above my head, geysers of red wine and glass erupted. I hit the floor; bottles exploded to my left. The guard behind us looked toward his partner. Kilgore struggled to his feet.

"Hold it!" The guard aimed his pistol at Kilgore. I seized his moment of distraction to swing my right leg around. I caught the guard's ankle in midstride, cutting his feet out from under him. He careened into the rack, snapping the neck off a wine bottle with the side of his head.

Amid a cascade of other bottles dislodged by his impact, the guard fired a single shot, then hit the floor hard. His shot hit the tile; the slug shattered and seeded the air with shrapnel. An instant later, the glass doors developed a web of spider cracks; to the right of the door, blood appeared on the guard's forehead. His hand went up instantly to explore the wound as the blood trickled down into his eyes.

I wrestled myself up as Kilgore kicked the fallen guard's pistol away.

"Brad!" Rex's voice sounded from beyond the wine racks.

"Rex?"

"Over here!"

Kilgore and I ran toward Rex as well as anyone can run with their hands cuffed at the small of their back. We bypassed the stunned guard on the floor, came around the corner, and nearly tripped over a guard on his knees, swaying back and forth as he screamed and rubbed at his face. The smell of bear repellent surrounded him and brought tears to our eyes. His gun lay on the floor and I kicked it.

At the far end of the long wine rack, Rex and Dan Gabriel manhandled the guard with the wounded forehead to the floor and bound him with his own cuffs. Rex then squatted down, using the wine racks as cover, and peered toward the double glass doors. Gabriel picked up the man's pistol and ran toward us.

About halfway between me and Rex, I saw an old man I assumed was Frank Harper holding unsteadily to the sides of a jagged hole in the wall. He looked back and forth, following the action, smiling broadly and making deep approving nods. The head movements made him look like an elderly bobblehead.

"Jack!" Gabriel said as he slapped Kilgore on the shoulder, then me. "You must be the Stone guy who started it all. Let's get you out of those cuffs." Swiftly, he grabbed the cuffs from the bear-sprayed guard and ratcheted them on the man's wrists. Then, without taking his eyes off the end of the long wine rack, he dug through the guard's pockets, retrieved the cuff key, and handed it to me.

"Unlock Jack for me, will you?"

I quickly unlocked Kilgore's cuffs, and he returned the favor.

"Bogey at your end!" Rex yelled. Then we heard him fire his pistol. Bottles exploded beside me. I lunged for the fallen guard's nearby pistol faster than Kilgore and came up with it at the ready. I fired a shot through the rack of wine at a shadow on the other side. More red wine and shattered glass. I ducked as the man fired back. I was close enough to read the label on a bottle of 1897 Château Margaux when it erupted like a grenade. The air hung thick with the pricey aroma of collectible claret laced with the acrid notes of smokeless gunpowder. I'm pretty sure it's not a wine nose ever described by *The Wine Speculator*.

Then more wine bottles went off like roadside bombs as the man fired wildly at us.

Kilgore moved to the end of the rack nearest the elevators. He pulled a bottle from the rack and pantomimed that he would throw it over the top as a distraction. He motioned me to join Gabriel at the other end. I ran carefully, to avoid slipping on the spilled wine and glass. My running steps drew more shots; more classified first-growth Bordeaux wine turned to glassy slush.

As soon as I joined Gabriel, Kilgore lobbed the bottle over the top.

When it hit the floor, Gabriel and I came around and saw the third guard, his face covered with blood, whirling toward the shattering of the wine bottle.

"Drop it! We don't want to hurt you," Gabriel shouted.

The guard froze, but did not drop his gun.

"Don't do anything stupid!" Rex yelled from across the cellar, where he had run to get out of our line of fire.

Kilgore motioned me around. I followed his direction and positioned myself so I had a third clean line of sight.

"Come on," Kilgore said more calmly now. "You are totally triangulated. Any one of us has a clear shot. Don't do anything foolish you might regret."

During his indecisive moment of silence, I felt my heart beating and listened to the dripping of wine. Then, like lightning from a clear sky, came a voice I had heard many times on television.

"One might say the same of you, Jack!"

Clark Braxton's voice preceded a soft-crepe thunder that filled the cellar with the shuffling of SWAT-clad troops with M16s, soft-rubber-soled boots, and perfectly secured gear that had made no sound at all.

"Let's play our cards," Jasmine said as she turned away from the laptop screen. Tyrone hesitated, transfixed at the vision of Braxton and his body-armored security guards. Jasmine grabbed his sleeve and dragged him out of the pickup's cab. "Let's get airborne."

Tyrone and Jasmine quickly got the first small aircraft off the ground. With her eyes on the small plane and her hands on the control joysticks, Jasmine sidled back to the cab of the truck.

"Now get the camera that looks out the window," Jasmine said. "The one which almost showed us." She looked up at the small aircraft. "Let me know when you see the airplane on the camera, then guide me in."

Tyrone scrambled back into the cab.

"Oh, hell," Tyrone said when he got back behind the keyboard.

"You are *not* going to believe what Braxton just did!"

. . .

Dressed in a tuxedo and patent-leather shoes that threw off light like a mirror, Clark Braxton's face twisted itself deep and red with a fury rolling off him like a shock wave. His hands trembled at his side as he surveyed the enological carnage.

Braxton's big security chief stood at his side, silhouetted against the last orange hues of the smoke-stained sunset bleeding through the distant window. I had no doubt he and Braxton would use this as the escape attempt they needed as an excuse to kill us.

Braxton's fists and arms trembled as he surveyed the wreckage. His eyes passed through anger and fury, then began to reflect light in a manner that grew truly frightening.

Unaware of his boss's gathering rage, the big security chief barked orders at his men. At the corner of my eye, I saw Rex duck around the corner of the wine rack.

"Stop!" The security chief yelled after Rex and directed two of his men to pursue him. As the other troops fanned out and took our weapons, I heard Rex and Harper.

"Come on!" Rex said. "Quick."

"No. You go."

"Move, Doc!"

"I'm too slow. You go."

"Hell!"

I heard the report of Rex's 9mm pistol followed by a three-round burst from one of the M16s. Then another 9mm shot.

"Damn! I'm hit," cried a voice. Not Rex's.

The security chief directed another man toward the action.

"It's okay," called the wounded man. "My vest caught it."

Then another voice: "There's a hole in the wall. Shall I pursue?"

"Negative!" yelled the security chief. "It leads to the barrel cellar. We've got a man posted there. Stay here; make sure nobody comes out."

"Sir!"

Braxton knelt on one knee to examine a broken wine bottle as a guard dragged Frank Harper around the corner. Braxton stood slowly, looking at the broken wine bottle like a mother holding her dead child. His entire body pulsed with barely restrained power. Then he dropped the bottle and leveled a killing gaze at Harper.

"You lame, worthless, feeble piece of dog shit." Braxton's voice started faint and low like the preamble to a prayer, then rose in pitch and volume as Harper and his captor grew closer. "You traitorous old fool!"

"Yes, I am an old fool," Harper said. Braxton nodded and the guard halted next to the wine rack. "And I am a traitor for saving your life."

Braxton flew apart. "You damned fool! Look at the damage you have done!" The General swept an outstretched arm around the cellar. He turned then and pulled his security chief's sidearm from its holster. The guard holding Harper leaped to the side as Braxton shot the old man in the face, slamming him back against the wine racks. The crack-shot former general shot Harper again as he slumped toward the tile. Harper died before he hit the floor.

Shock and disapproval registered in the eyes of the SWAT-clad men holding the rest of us. Killing innocent people was not part of a professional soldier's charter. The grip on my arm loosened.

"And you!" Braxton stepped away from his big security chief and leveled the man's own gun at his chest. "You were supposed to prevent this!" Dried spittle stuck like cotton to one corner of Braxton's mouth. "But you let these amateurs ruin the perfection of the world's greatest wine collection! Just look at it now! It was complete and now . . ." Braxton trembled. Around the room, the security troops were stunned by the sight of the General and the security chief locked in mortal combat. Their training had never prepared them for this.

"You ruined it, ruined it!"

When Braxton shot his security chief, Gabriel, Kilgore, and I broke for the hole in the wall. As we turned the corner, the two guards who had not seen the shootings raised their weapons. We ducked back around the end of the wine racks and saw Braxton standing over the head of his security detail as the man struggled to sit up. Two of the guards moved toward the General as he aimed the gun down at the fallen man's head and pulled the trigger again. Behind us, we heard one of the guards move away from the hole in the wall, his boots crunching on the broken glass.

Then, from beyond the window, out where the sun had begun surrendering to darkness, a toy airplane bobbed toward us. I turned and took shelter at the base of the wine rack along with Gabriel and Kilgore.

The explosion rocked the cellar and filled the enclosed space with glass and wine.

"Okaaay, there went the security cam," Tyrone said as he and Jasmine raced to launch a second radio-controlled airplane.

"We'll put this and the other two in about the same area," she said. "If Brad's still alive, he'll be heading away from there. Maybe we can pull security to where he isn't anymore." She paused. "Then we get the hell out of here."

The cellar noise receded quickly as we stumbled down the dark stairwell.

"What took you so long, kemo sabe?"

Rex appeared out of the darkness with a small, bright LED light.

"Lead the way, Tonto," Kilgore replied.

"Right this way, asshole."

At the bottom, we found no guard in the barrel cave and none in the tunnels or on the loading docks. We did hear another explosion faintly as we made our way to the wine delivery truck, gridlocked in a panicked tangle of traffic.

"You gentlemen up for a jog?" Gabriel said. "I know a nice trail to the road."

"I'm allergic to running," Rex said. "But not as allergic as I am to lead."

Outside the service area and beyond the beautiful green curtain that kept it from blighting the visions of important people, we found chaos like the last helicopter out of Saigon. Guests in evening dress came off the aerial gondola and were hustled by their own security people to waiting limousines, all of which jammed the driveway out.

We followed Gabriel in the shadows of the trees. At first, we walked to avoid attracting attention, then ran swiftly through the trees toward Silverado Trail.

We had walked through a shallow stream and were crawling up the bank when Rex asked us to stop for a moment.

"You finally going to quit smoking now?" I asked him.

"You can be a true asshole," he said only half-joking. "I have half a mind to tell your lady here"—he tapped at the walkie-talkie—"tell her you didn't make it . . . and see to it myself that I ain't lying."

He pulled the earbud and lavalier from his ear. "But I promised y'-mama, you know."

He handed me the earbud and the walkie-talkie.

It was Jasmine.

A score of postdoctoral and medical school students jammed themselves around a long, elliptical plastic-laminate table, took notes, and sipped coffee when I paused and listened to me with an embarrassing degree of intensity as I shuffled my way toward the last pages of my notes.

Around the perimeter of the windowless room stood a collection of people who would be my classroom students in the fall, and a sprinkling of faculty members I vaguely recognized but whose names I could not recall.

"I realize it's a big shock for many, but the theoretical and practical successes of quantum theory expose classical physics as a primitive tool. For the purposes of studying consciousness, it's like using a muzzle-loading cannon when you really need a particle accelerator. Regardless, the classically misled consciousness establishment remains mired in the seventeenth century wearing Sir Isaac Newton about their necks like an albatross." I glanced hopefully at the door for an instant, then back to my notes. "This stubborn refusal to relinquish obsolete ideas has damaged our ability to understand consciousness and to examine and discuss the existence of free will."

I turned to the big white board at the front of the room, erased my previous notes dealing with the technological verifications of quantum theory—semiconductors, nuclear bombs, GPS satellites.

"Quantum physics and superstring theory invalidate classical physics as follows: First, classical physics says any action must be caused by current, local, and totally mechanical circumstances." I wrote as I spoke, turning back to make eye contact between each point. "Second, classical physics holds there is matter and there is energy, sometimes equal but always separate. But as we have seen, quantum entanglement and superposition destroy the first proposition. The second crumbles because matter and energy are manifestations of the same thing, and neither exists as a simple either-or dichotomy.

"Furthermore, the universe is far weirder than we think because everything we know about matter and energy totally ignores ninety-six percent of everything."

A coherent wall of blank stares greeted this.

"Think for a moment about the studies from NASA and others in 2003 that proved that ordinary atoms—the stuff we're made of—comprise a mere four percent of the entire universe." I held up four fingers. "On the other hand, dark matter makes up twenty-three percent, and the rest, a whopping seventy-three percent, is dark energy.

"And we know virtually nothing about dark matter and energy! I have no doubt that this missing ninety-six percent of the universe affects our consciousness. When we learn more, I believe we will lose our bifurcated outlook on matter versus energy and find a third way that will invalidate much of the truth we hold dear."

A hand shot up.

"Yes?"

"Professor, why are you talking about cosmology in a biology lecture?"

"Because quantum physics, superstring theory, cosmology, and particle physics bring us to a point where the infinitely small intersects with the infinitely large. I believe all the hard questions in consciousness lie at the same intersection."

"Like how?"

"Like the incredible nonexistence of matter and energy," I said. "As we look at these on a smaller and smaller scale, matter and energy first seem to be the same thing, then appear to be some sort of ghost particle or a string if you like, produced by space-time itself. Look at your finger." Everyone in the class looked at his or her fingers. "Now, think about a keratin molecule, any molecule. Okay, now fix on a carbon atom. Then visualize a neutron. Then visualize the quarks making up the neutron. Think about one quark, any quark. It has no mass we can measure, only energy, and we have no way to determine where it is at any given point. Indeed, some variants of superstring theory postulate it's a vibration resonance emanating from space-time itself."

I watched most of the eyes in the room close.

"Now, imagine every other molecule and atom in your body at the same time. Visualize yourself as a collection of vibrating space-time clouds, none of which have any mass, but which you perceive as the solid, living, breathing you.

"There is also some very good evidence from work done by Penrose and Hameroff indicating that quantum-based processes underlie our consciousness, maybe through some connection to space-time—the fabric of reality and existence—and that our thoughts alter space-time permanently. Proving this experimentally, establishing it as fact rather than a good theory, will take time."

"So how does dark energy come into this?"

"Obviously dark energy and matter have to be part of space-time," I said. "And therefore part of how consciousness works."

"If Penrose and Hameroff are right," the student challenged. "And a lot of prominent people think they're dead wrong."

"A lot of prominent people thought Copernicus and Galileo were dead wrong too," I said.

I looked at my watch, then at the back of the room. Jasmine stood inside the door, leaning against the far wall. I caught a deep breath and tried to keep my tongue from stumbling. Her hair framed her face like a halo; the emerald studs I had bought her to celebrate Darryl Talmadge's successful defense dazzled on her ears. She wore a simple black dress and carried a suitably conservative leather handbag.

"As you probably know from the media reports, Darryl Talmadge died in his sleep two days ago. I need to go change now for the funeral up in Itta Bena or we'll be late. If you'd like to know more about dark energy, my notes are at ConsciousnessStudies.org. Also, if you're interested in the free will issues concerning Talmadge and Braxton, a transcript of the television interview Ms. Thompson and I did is on the Web site, as well as on Ms. Thompson's site, MississippiJustice.Org. Thank you for coming," I said as I headed for the door and Jasmine's welcoming smile.

The heels of Jasmine's black dress pumps tapped on the polished linoleum as we hurried toward my office.

"I'm sorry," I said. "I lost track of the time." I rechecked my watch. "Oh, man, I really, really hate being late."

Jasmine gave me one of her Mona Lisa smiles. After all these months, I had learned to read her smiles better and realized she still had as many ways of smiling as Sonia did for saying "Oy!" We rounded the corner and spotted Sonia toward the end of the corridor. She stood in the doorway of my new office at the University of Mississippi School of Medicine.

As we drew close to Sonia, I saw the bright, happy look on her face as her eyes connected my expression with the fond look in Jasmine's eyes. "You are going to be late, Dr. Stone," she said, trying to sound reproachful and not quite making it. "Quincy's waiting."

"Yes, Ma'am," I told her as I hurried into the reception area.

"Sorry," I apologized to Quincy.

"We'll make it," he said easily. "Be cool."

I gave him a smile, then hurried into my office and pulled on the same suit I had worn at Vanessa's funeral. Quincy and I had grown close since the night we both had too much to drink and he'd pulled out a worn, brown, expandable folder full of legal documents proving he was my half-uncle via the Judge and Vanessa's mother. The Judge's financial support to Quincy's mother had allowed them a far more decent life than the average resident of Balance Due. The Judge had also secretly arranged financial aid that had put Vanessa and Quincy through college.

I had not been as surprised to learn all this as Jasmine was.

"Vanessa and your grandmother and I decided there was no reason to saddle you with the ugly details," Quincy had told her, but I had seen a look of betrayal on her face and a realization that the specter of the black woman and the white planter from the big house had struck closer to home than she had imagined.

The revelations that had brought me closer to Quincy had wedged themselves between Jasmine and me for months.

Quincy still taught at Mississippi Valley State University, but came down to Jackson often, as did Jasmine. I had arranged my classes, clinical appointments, and lectures into a schedule allowing me to spend about half my time in Greenwood. I bought an old building off Cotton Street pretty near Steve La Vere's and loved to spend time renovating it. It was only a couple of minutes away from the hospital where Tyrone had resumed his work and I volunteered.

"Who's driving?" I said as I rushed out of my office, coat and tie in hand.

"I've got the Suburban," Quincy said. "Remember, we're giving Rex and Anita a ride."

Quincy picked up Anita and Rex at their home in Madison, then headed north on I-55. We rode in silence, watching the colors of spring race past the windows. The dogwoods filled the roadside forests with explosions of pink-tinted white. The emerging new leaves frosted the rest of the woods with bright green, full of hope and promise.

I still had not reconciled myself with Camilla, the way she had died and my memories of her. I reflected on my lecture from that morning and whether the Camilla I had known and loved had been trapped in her damaged brain all along, the same software and memories and person she had always been, but the damaged hardware failing to let her out.

Maybe it had been the same with Talmadge's wife and her Alzheimer's. I had certainly made my best case about this to the juries who had considered the charges against Braxton and Talmadge, but doubts still lingered in my mind.

The courts had remanded Talmadge to the high-security wing of Pacific Hills in Malibu so Flowers and I could continue to study him. Braxton's expensive legal team had got him off with a temporary-insanity plea that has allowed him to live as a mostly free man other than for a court-ordered monitoring of his medication.

Talmadge lived longer than anyone expected before the cancer got him.

Harper's notes had been seized by Laura LaHaye's office and made unavailable to us. The Xantaeus fiasco had been embarrassing but not a career killer for her, Greg McGovern, and the nondepleting-neurotrop team at Defense Therapeutics. While the patches had been withdrawn, the research continued because being first to have it was too important to the Pentagon.

Dan Gabriel had gone back to college at Cal Poly in San Luis Obispo and was studying marine biology. In his spare time, he volunteered for an organization he had founded that warned the public about the dangers of what had become known as "the chemical soldier." I don't think anyone has paid much attention to them, and for that we will suffer one day.

Jack Kilgore got a second star and a desk in the Pentagon, which he quickly found no fun at all. He took his retirement money and bought a river-rafting outfitter on the Rogue River in Oregon. Through some legal maneuvering by Jasmine, which I still do not completely understand, and a few phone calls that Kilgore placed before his retirement, Rex somehow managed to find his way back to a completely legal life, which disappointed him to no end.

The same calls and legal maneuvering led to a quiet shake-up in the Homeland Security administration and a score of courts-martial. Those, along with testimony from people like John Myers and the captured security-camera streams that Tyrone had snagged in Napa got Jasmine and me a boatload of apologies and our total exoneration.

Rex gave up contracting and with his new legitimacy acquired a federal firearms license and opened a wildly profitable shooting range near the Ross Barnett Reservoir, where people come to shoot machine guns of every type. The 20mm electric Gatling cannon is a perennial favorite.

I wear one of his "Why waltz when you can rock and roll" T-shirts every chance I get. Every now and then he manages to arrange for someone to show up with even bigger stuff they use to blow up old cars and trucks. The armed forces recruiters usually show up those days as well. He spends a lot of time denying that he *doesn't* have a shady past. I still wonder about that and he's never said a word to me.

Rex helped me take care of paying people back for the equipment we stole, for repairing the old helicopter, and with a nice payment to the terrified Hispanic man in the wine delivery truck who eventually accepted my personal apology as well.

The drive up I-55 was always boring, so I thought about all these things until my eyelids closed, inserting me into a recurring dream I always tried to remember. At the beginning, I soared through a jungle of colorful knots and vines racing through a glowing matrix that ebbed, flowed, and danced in time with the movement of each luminescent line. The knots were especially brilliant where they twisted about each other, then grew dimmer as the lines emerged from the knot and hurtled away. Some of the particles made solitary lines; some appeared suddenly; others disappeared. Still others were bound and woven like the great sheaves of a suspension bridge.

I sensed these were the world lines of every quantum ever created. In quantum physics, every particle has a world line in space-time. Even a particle at rest still races through the fourth dimension of time.

Those lines that appeared and disappeared represented the scientifically confirmed phenomenon of particles that winked in and out of existence even in a vacuum.

Then I somehow knew the sheaves were things, objects, animals, where matter held together. Some of the sheaves threw off great skeins of knots that burned brightly and altered the matrix in vast and awesome ways. I looked directly behind me and saw the lines I threw off like a ship's wake, offering turbulent fractal patterns in the matrix.

Scientists working on quantum computers can encode difficult computations by weaving the world lines of quantum particles in a specific way. The trick came from the use of von Neumann algebras in a way described by Berkeley mathematician Vaughn Jones back in 1987. The idea was picked up by string theorist Edward Whitten at Princeton and Microsoft Research fellows Michael Freedman and Alexei Kitaev, who figured out if you braided the world lines of subatomic particles, not only would they work for quantum computation, but they were also incredibly stable, which solved a big problem—decoherence—that required incredibly low, liquid-helium-like temperatures for operation.

The epiphany hit me then and I recognized the knots as thoughts and memories. The glowing matrix was space-time. All of the lines made some change in space-time, but the biggest alterations were the ones made by the knots.

Something shook me.

The lines and the matrix vanished.

I struggled to hold on to the epiphany: the quantum knots and their stability were how brain cells might maintain the quantum coherence necessary for consciousness to exist, and that was how we all connected to space-time. I had it!

Jasmine gently shook me awake. My heart fell as I opened my eyes and the epiphany slipped away. Again.

"What's wrong?" Jasmine read the look on my face.

"The big dream again."

"Do you remember it?"

I shook my head.

"Don't worry, you'll have it again."

Jasmine hugged me as Quincy made the turn into the Itta Bena Cemetery. Ahead of us sat the same old car and the same old preacher who'd helped me bury Mama. I caught sight of the bright artificial flowers I had left atop Mama's grave at my last visit, and for some reason I remembered her more clearly than I had in a long time. Memories had become more important to me as I'd made peace with Camilla's admonition to "make a memory." I had finally come to the deep emotional acceptance that we are the sum of our memories, and when we respect those memories, we respect ourselves and our lives.

Quincy brought the Suburban to a stop on the gravel drive.

Memories obsessed me now. I speculated again about Penrose and Hameroff and their theory that consciousness has a permanent effect on space-time. If they are right, perhaps our memories permanently embed themselves there as well.

"It had something to do with memory," I said to Jasmine. "The dream."

What if a perfectly faithful memory of events existed in space-time, something permanent we could reach out to with our imperfect hardware and flawed ability to recall? Perhaps if space-time is the face of God, then the memories we embedded there are heaven, or maybe our souls. Maybe both.

"I've always struggled with why we work so hard to hold on to memories," I said. "But I think they're important. Really important."

"How important?" she asked.

I shook my head slowly. "I haven't a clue. I just believe it. Don't ask me how it plays out right now because I can't find words for what I feel."

We got out of the Suburban.

"Memories are part of the meaning of life," I said. "Of what makes our existence significant. I think maybe this is why it's important to make memories and to be faithful to them."

I put on my coat as we walked over to the open grave. The same two guys stood near the same backhoe in the distance, dressed this day in work shirts. Jasmine and I got to the graveside as the preacher began. He took in Jasmine and me in a single glance and offered us a smile.

"I want to begin first with a saying from Helen Keller," the old preacher said. I was relieved to see he had been to a much better dermatologist and was no longer covered with precancerous lesions.

"Ms. Thompson"—he nodded toward Jasmine—"was kind enough to bring this quote to my attention." He blinked his watery eyes at an index card that trembled in his hands.

"The quote, which I believe I will use every chance I get, goes like this: 'What once we enjoyed and deeply loved, we can never lose, for all that we love deeply becomes a part of us.'"

I said, "Amen," and did not fight my tears.

By DR. RICHARD A. GABRIEL
(Colonel, U.S. Army, Ret.)
Author of *No More Heroes: Madness and Psychiatry in War*
(More about Dr. Gabriel following this afterword.)

AFTERWORD

Lewis Perdue's fascinating new book, *Perfect Killer,* is the first attempt in the popular literature to bring to the attention of the public a major problem facing modern armies, particularly the U.S. Army now committed to combat in Iraq.

The intensity of modern war, especially the close urban combat in which the American Army now finds itself engaged, produces high levels of stress and fear, which cause most soldiers (more than 80 percent!) not to fire their weapons as they seek to avoid the natural human revulsion to killing another human being. Over time, prolonged fear and the revulsion to killing produce high levels of psychiatric casualties that threaten to cripple combat efficiency. The military's response has been to seek chemical means to solve the problem. These attempts, and the threats they pose to the soldier's humanity, are the important subjects treated in Perdue's book as he attempts to bring these issues to the attention of the American public.

The idea of trying to control the soldier's fear through chemical means so that he may kill more efficiently is very old indeed, beginning at least two thousand years before Rome when the Koyak and Wiros tribes of Central Russia perfected a powerful amphetamine drug from the *Amanita muscaria* mushroom, which rendered the soldier highly resistant to pain and exhaustion even as it stimulated him to greater physical endurance. In the thirteenth century the Crusaders fought a band of Muslim warriors known as the *hashshashin,* so called because they used hashish prior to battle to reduce fear and control pain. The Spanish conquistador Francisco Pizzaro fought Inca warriors whose resistance to pain and fear was increased by chewing the coca leaf, from which cocaine is derived. From its earliest days the British Navy has given its sailors rum before and after battle, and the Russian Army in both World

Wars provided their soldiers with a number of chemical compounds derived from plants (*valeriana*) to improve their fighting ability. During the Vietnam War, American soldiers routinely used marijuana, alcohol, and hard drugs like heroin to help them overcome the fear and stress of battle.

But what modern armies have in mind far surpasses anything tried in the past. Biology and chemistry have combined in the modern age to produce the science of biochemistry. Armed with this new knowledge, the military research establishments of the United States, Russia, and Israel have set for themselves the task of abolishing fear in the soldier to make him a more efficient killing machine. The next revolution in military power will occur not in weapons technology, but in biochemistry that will make it possible for soldiers to better endure the conditions of modern war. If the search is successful, and it almost inevitably will be, the fear of killing and death will be banished, and with it will go man's humanity and his soul. The chemical soldier will become a terrifying reality.

The advent of the chemical soldier will change not only the nature and intensity of warfare, but the psychological nature of man himself. A chemical compound that prevents the onset of anxiety while leaving the individual mentally alert will produce a new kind of human being, one who would retain the cognitive elements of his emotions but would be unable to feel emotion. All emotions, not just fear, are based in anxiety. Remove the onset of anxiety, and the interactions between cognitive and physiological aspects of human emotion vanish. And with them what we know as the soul would be destroyed. We are left with a genuine sociopathic personality induced by chemical means. The sociopathic personality is one who clearly *knows* what he is doing to another person but cannot *feel* or appreciate the consequences of his action upon another person. Such personalities often cannot prevent themselves from acting even though they know (but cannot feel) what the consequences of their actions might be. They are unable to display loyalty to others, are grossly selfish, are unable to feel guilt or remorse or appreciate the consequences of their actions. The sociopathic personality functions only on the cognitive plane of his emotions and is incapable of human empathy. The chemical soldier will be a true sociopath.

Abolishing fear and the natural revulsion humans have to killing other humans will change the nature of man and war, and it will be achieved simply by increasing the "human potential" of the combat soldier. Frightened and revulsed soldiers don't kill very well. Studies have shown that little more than 15 to 20 percent of soldiers will fire their weapons at other soldiers. But if the chemical means of controlling fear and revulsion to killing succeed in, say, only 75 percent of the cases, then the killing capacity of soldiers under fire will increase by 400 percent! The killing efficiency of crew-served weapons will also increase. The number of psychiatric cases will be diminished greatly, but at the cost of exponentially increasing the number of dead and wounded on all sides.

In a war of chemical soldiers, military units will, once engaged, be unable to disengage. In earlier battles, both sides absorbed as much death as they could until fear and exhaustion broke one side's spirit, at which point one side ran or surrendered. Fear and revulsion put real limits on the ability of units to attack and defend. But the chemical soldier will fight without fear and revulsion to limit the killing. Battles once joined will proceed until one side has been entirely killed or wounded. Without fear and empathy to stop or at least limit the carnage, battles will be fought to the death because there will no longer be any human reason to stop them. The battle of annihilation, once rare, will become the norm.

Without fear, revulsion, and psychiatric collapse to force soldiers to surrender, units will resist to the last man. This will force the attackers to kill all the defenders, or vice versa, in a sterile exercise in military slaughter. The defenders will be unable to surrender and the attackers unable to offer surrender, for the reasons for surrender—fear of death, overwhelming revulsion at the carnage, or psychiatric collapse—will no longer arise in the chemically altered personalities of the soldiers involved. The empathy of human for human will have vanished and with it the need to spare even the wounded.

For the chemical soldiers traditional military virtues will have neither function nor meaning. Qualities such as courage, bravery, endurance, and sacrifice for others have meaning only in human terms. Heroes are those who can endure or control fear beyond the limits usually expected of sane men. Brave men are those who conquer fear. Sacrifice for one's comrades can only have meaning when one fears death and accepts it because it will permit others to live. But if fear is eliminated by chemical means, there will be nothing over which the soldier can triumph. The standards of normal sane men will be eroded, and soldiers will no longer die for anything understandable or meaningful in human terms. They will simply die, and even their own comrades will be incapable of mourning their deaths.

The moral paradox of the chemical soldier is that for him to function effectively on the modern battlefield he must be psychically reconstituted to become what we have traditionally defined as mentally ill! He must be chemically made over into a sociopathic personality in the true clinical sense of the term. The battlefields of the future will witness a clash of truly ignorant armies, armies ignorant of their own emotions and even of the reasons for which they fight. Battle itself will be incomprehensible in normal human terms. Once the chemical genie is out of the bottle, the full range of human mental and physical potentialities becomes subject for further chemical manipulation. The search to improve the military potential of the human being will further press the limits of humanity itself. Such "human potential engineering" is already a partial reality, and the necessary technical knowledge increases every day. Faceless, if well-meaning, military medical researchers press the limits of their discipline with little or no regard for the consequences. We may be rushing headlong into a long, dark chemical night from which there is no return unless the American public, the press, and opinion makers are made aware of the problem and decide to stop it. Lewis Perdue's *Perfect Killer* is one way in which large numbers of the American people can be made aware of the problem.

DR. RICHARD A. GABRIEL

Richard A. Gabriel was Professor of Politics and History and Director of Advanced Courses in the Department of National Security and Strategy at the U.S. Army War College in Carlisle, Pennsylvania, before retiring to write full-time. Dr. Gabriel held faculty positions at the University of New Hampshire, University of Massachusetts at Lowell, and was a tenured full professor at Saint Anselm College before assuming the post at the Army War College. He has taught graduate and undergraduate courses and has served as a consultant for the House and Senate Armed Services Committees. He has held the visiting chair in Ethics and Humanities at the Marine Corps University at Quantico, Virginia, and currently teaches ethics, humanities, and leadership in the MBA program at Daniel Webster College.

Dr. Gabriel is the author of thirty-six books and fifty-eight articles on various subjects in political science, ancient history, military history, anthropology, psychology, psychiatry, sociology, ethics, philosophy, and the history of theology. A number of his works have been translated into other languages, and others have been used as primary sources for television programs produced by the Public Broadcasting Company. Dr. Gabriel's work has also been featured in a number of made-for-television videos shown on Discovery, the Learning Channel, and the History Channel.

Among his books are a number of definitive works. A History of Military Medicine (2 vols., 1992) is the first comprehensive work on the subject; Crisis in Command, the first major critique of American battle performance in Vietnam (1978); The New Red Legions (2 vols., 1980) and The Mind of the Soviet Fighting Man (1984), the first studies of the Soviet soldier based on interview data; To Serve With Honor (1981), the first treatise on military ethics written by an American in this century and used as a basic work in U.S. and foreign services senior leadership schools; Soviet Military Psychiatry (1985), the first work on the subject published in the West; and Operation Peace for Galilee: The Israeli-PLO War in Lebanon (1984), the first military analysis of that conflict and generally regarded as the definitive work on the subject.

Professor Gabriel has held positions at the Brookings Institution, the Army Intelligence School, the Center for the Study of Intelligence at the CIA, and at the Walter Reed Army Institute of Research, Department of Combat Psychiatry, in Washington, D.C. Dr. Gabriel is a frequent lecturer to the academic, governmental, and military establishments of Canada, the United States, West Germany, China, and Israel. He has testified before the U.S. Senate and been interviewed on CBS, NBC, CNN, and ABC national news programs, the Today show, Crossfire, Nightline, and 60 Minutes. Dr. Gabriel is a consultant to NBC and 60 Minutes for various news stories and edits for two publishers, Hill and Wang and Greenwood Press, where he edits his own series of political and historical books.

Among Dr. Gabriel's most recent works are The Great Battles of Antiquity (1994), A Short History of War (1992), From Sumer to Rome: The Military Capabilities of Ancient Armies (1991), The Culture of War (1990), The Painful Field: The Psychiatric Dimension of Modern War (1988), The Great Captains of Antiquity (2000), Gods of Our Fathers: The Memory of Egypt in Judaism and Christianity (2001), and Great Armies of Antiquity (2002). Dr. Gabriel is also the author of three novels, Warrior Pharaoh (2000), Sebastian's Cross (2001), and The Lion of the Sun (2003). His most recent books are The Military History of Ancient Israel (2003), Subotai the Valiant: Genghis Khan's Greatest General (2004), and Ancient Empires at War (3 vols., 2004).

APPENDIX I

WLBT-TV Interview Transcript

Southern Sideboards

Hosted by Angela Corbeil

SEGMENT: FREE WILL AND THE BRAXTON/TALMADGE TRIALS

GUESTS: Dr. Brad Stone, Professor, University of Mississippi School of Medicine

Ms. Jasmine Thompson, Chair and Executive Director, Advocacy Foundation for Mississippi Justice

TRANSCRIPT

WLBT, Channel 3

Jackson, Mississippi

Copyright 2003, All Rights Reserved

CORBEIL: Our guests for this segment of *Southern Sideboards* are Dr. Brad Stone, Professor, University of Mississippi School of Medicine, and Ms. Jasmine Thompson, Chair and Executive Director, Advocacy Foundation for Mississippi Justice. Welcome.

THOMPSON: Thank you.

STONE: Good to be here.

CORBEIL: Before we begin, I must confess to our viewers that this is a very special segment for two reasons. First of all, it is the first interview that Dr. Stone and Ms. Thompson have given following the stunning jury verdicts in the cases of Darryl Talmadge and Clark Braxton. I am very grateful for this exclusive interview.

Secondly, this is a reunion of sorts. I began college as a biology major at UCLA too many years ago to count and was fortunate to take an undergraduate course from Dr. Stone. During this time, I worked as an intern on a science series for the PBS station in L.A., KCET, and then made the transition to a news intern at the same television station that Jasmine flew helicopters for when she was a student at our crosstown rival, USC.

STONE: I remember your assertive questions in class.

CORBEIL: I hope that's not going to come back to haunt me this morning.

STONE: Not at all.

CORBEIL: Good. Let's start by discussing your controversial notion that free will exists and that consciousness has a reality that transcends biology and matter. You've upset a lot of experts in the scientific mainstream.

STONE: People get upset when their pet notions turn out to be wrong. They usually have a vested interest in one notion or another and the truth be damned. Oops! Am I going to be bleeped for that?

CORBEIL: Not in the new world of MTV and hip-hop.

STONE: Okay. I'm not sure that's a good thing.

CORBEIL: Please continue. Free will? What's so upsetting about your position?

STONE: Right. Well, I think it's clear that the continuing faith in outdated science—classical physics—allows reductionists and behaviorists to say that consciousness is an incidental illusion arising from the collection of matter between our ears, which produces another illusion, that of free will.

CORBEIL: Why should that matter?

STONE: It matters because over the past few decades, society has let their view of the world govern our criminal justice system. And—

CORBEIL: That matters why?

STONE: Because that notion has eroded the notion of personal responsibility. After all, if we are all meat-based automatons, how can anybody be guilty of anything?

CORBEIL: They argue that science is on their side.

STONE: Everybody does. Their problem is that the science they use was modern back when the horse-drawn, muzzle-loading cannon was state-of-the-art.

CORBEIL: That's pretty harsh, don't you think?

STONE: Truth can be harsh. Look, this isn't just some dry philosophical debate. Free will goes to the heart of what it means to be human and governs our every interaction with other people from law to personal trust. The idea we can know right from wrong and that we can choose one or the other forms the bedrock of human society.

CORBEIL: But isn't lack of free will what you argued in the murder trials of General Braxton and the cold-case lynching in the Delta? You and Ms. Thompson got those guys off by convincing the jury that free will didn't exist.

THOMPSON: Actually, we argued that free will existed but both men had physical impairments preventing the complete expression of their free will.

STONE: Think of space-time as the ultimate computer, the omnipotent cpu of the universe, and think of consciousness and free will as software. Finally, think about your brain, the fabric laid down by DNA and modified by the environment, accidents, and other physical phenomena, as hardware—something like an input-output device on your personal computer, maybe the printer, the monitor, or a sound board.

CORBEIL: Words like "the omnipotent cpu of the universe" sound like a euphemism for God. Isn't it true over the centuries that whenever people can't explain something, they abdicate to some sort of deity—you know, eclipses, earthquakes, the seasons, crop fertility. We've eventually answered all those questions with science. Why put God in this equation when we've kicked him out of all the rest?

STONE: Why not put God in? We can understand that the long-standing persecution of science by the Vatican and other religions has a lot to do with scientists being antireligion. I happen to be antireligion as well, but I believe in God and science as well.

CORBEIL: But—

STONE: Look, quantum physics proves that what we perceive as "substance" is composed, ultimately, of the nothingness of space-time. I see God there, right at the intersection of infinity and nothing.

CORBEIL: I see an unsolved problem in science.

STONE: Good for you. You choose to believe in science instead of God. I can't prove you wrong. All I ask is you offer me the same courtesy.

CORBEIL: Fair enough.

STONE: Okay, getting back to the original question. You can deduce from my computer analogy that the brain's cpu can be working fine and the software be robust and bug-free, but still observe some strange behavior in the input-output device.

CORBEIL: But where does free will come in here if the hardware is damaged? Doesn't that mean there's no free will?

STONE: Maybe in some cases the hardware is damaged beyond repair. But current experiments with cognitive behavior therapy—CBT—show that while genetics and the environment offer us merchandise between our ears which is faulty to some extent, we can think our way past the problems in most cases. This is also at work, I believe, in the so-called placebo effect, where a sugar pill can cure fatal diseases. It is an example of belief—something immaterial affecting physical processes. Classical physics says this can't happen. But I believe we have quantum mechanisms that allow this to work.

CORBEIL: That's very interesting, but how's this so different from the reductionists? After all, you got those guys off by showing they didn't have free will.

THOMPSON: In court, what I had to show was a diminished ability to exercise free will. I argued it and Professor Stone scientifically established the nonvisible physical impairment.

CORBEIL: But how far can you take things? Isn't it theoretically possible to excuse almost any crime from shoplifting to mass murder using the same argument?

THOMPSON: There's a big difference between excuse and explain. The first implies that criminals go free. The other should make us reexamine how we treat people who commit crimes.

STONE: Society has a right to protect itself. But the real issue is whether we should treat people guilty of the same crime differently merely because one has a physical—visible and detectable—brain defect and the other does not.

CORBEIL: That's what the big national debate is all about. Having someone like Braxton melt down shocked people into thinking about it. So, were those guys really guilty? Is Braxton really crazy or did he get off because he's rich?

THOMPSON: Yes on the first two parts of your question and on the last as well. Despite that, I believe that what we should be asking about Braxton and Talmadge, beyond the question of whether or not they committed murder or treason, is whether they acted as best they could given the damaged hardware. And how the justice system should handle them.

CORBEIL: Thank you very much for coming. Coming up next, the next installment on careers and success. How manicures can make the difference.

APPENDIX II

PROFESSOR
BRADFORD STONE
Lecture Notes
University of Mississippi School of Medicine
Consciousness Studies 532:
Dark Energy and the Mistakes in Quantum Physics

Heisenberg uncertainty principle says the act of observing a quantum-level system alters the system itself.

This means that we cannot know what the precise state was of any system or particle prior to our observation. Obvious parallels in consciousness studies because any attempt to study consciousness alters the consciousness in the person being studied.

Hold Heisenberg and the quantum paradox in ready memory while you consider the convoluted and tortured mathematical switchbacks involved with attempting to reconcile particles and waves, the most famous and convoluted being Schroedinger's equations for the collapse of the wave function.

What we can observe about the behavior of quantum-level particles and waves comes through the clumsy filters of the experiments we devise to study them. At a fundamental level, this means our senses and the way we perceive the world are tuned in such a way that we cannot observe our experiments directly. Rather we see the *results* of experiments, which we must interpret to the best of our ability. This means we cannot actually *know* something at the quantum level. The best we can do is interpret some indirect observation produced by an experiment.

And this is where knowledge breaks down and Schroedinger slips into increasing irrelevance.

This means the wave-particle duality and the spaghetti mathematics needed to reconcile the two are artifacts produced by distorted interpretations of badly designed experiments.

[Whiteboard graphic 1, circle, set up one experiment, in it light appears to be a particle.]

[Whiteboard graphic 2, circle, another experiment, light looks like wave.]

Do same thing with electrons, get same result, leads us to conclude light can act like a particle of what we think of as matter and matter—the electron—can behave like a light wave. And this paradoxical duality results in the contortionist math that plagues quantum physics—and along with it, needlessly complicates our ability to understand the quantum-level connections with consciousness.

Significantly, these experiments showing wave-particle, matter-energy duality are designed and constructed with the purpose of proving some theory that we already believe in. And when you believe in a theory, then consciously or not, you design the experiment to verify your preconceived belief. As soon as you believe in a theory, you shut all the other possible doors. Then you take your experimental results and make them fit the paradigm of the day. Why do you think scientists discard so many data points that don't fit the predicted curve?

[Whiteboard graphic 3, X-Y axis with arc starting at the intersection; scatted vicinity of the arc with a hail of dots.]

You've all seen this: very few experimental observations fall right on the curve, and yet we somehow believe that the curve is precise despite the fact that it's an inexact compromise that gives us a pretty good rule of thumb for what seems to work. But "pretty good" makes for messy equations when you try to force-fit it into the precision of mathematics, and this is why the equations are such a rat's nest.

Many make things fit better by tossing out the data points that are too far from the needed approximation. Discarding these is rationalized away as experimental error, random misfits, equipment malfunction, or some such thing. But what comes out of that process is not the truth of something but a rough approximation of what they hope to prove.

Put another way, the experiment we design determines what result we get. Design it one way and you get particle; another way, wave. And we continue to design experiments according to theories that will only give us those results.

We are stuck answering today's questions with yesterday's experiments and theories and equations.

Third path not explored. Look at discarded data points, find a way to answer why they don't fit the curve. We then have to fashion theories and mathematics to embrace all that orphan data. Invent new technologies and experiments designed to test this third way. I think that when we do, we will find that the wave-particle, matter-energy paradox vanishes with the realization that they are merely the tail and trunk of a hidden elephant that we've never discovered because we have failed to look in the right places, ask the right questions. When we do that, I think the math will get considerably simpler and more elegant.

It's a very human thing to try and devise experiments that reinforce the paradoxical dualities.

We perceive the world the way we do because our senses have evolved in such a way as to present us with one view—the one which maximizes our chances of survival. This shapes our thinking about the nature of reality, and we design experiments to prove our thoughts. Dark energy, quantum entanglement, uncertainty, and the ultimate characteristics of space-time, which might show we live in an 11-dimensional world, all indicate that our commonsense notions of reality are flat-out wrong.

Our senses evolved in a way that makes it easy for us to intuitively comprehend things as matter and as energy. If it feels solid, it's matter; if we feel the heat, see the light, then it is energy. We accept those as the defining elements of our reality, and it is simple human nature to define our scientific search in ways that confirm this. But we now know that at the quantum level, matter and energy are also particles and waves all at the same time, which means that they are not matter, energy, particles, or waves but something entirely new, something else deeper, hidden, and more fundamental.

Our observations are flawed because the experiments we have devised so far only return data defined as matter, energy, wave, particle. We have to find ways of devising experiments that can offer us data points we can understand that are defined in different and currently unknown terms.

Reconciling the nonconforming data points linked with dark matter (23% of universe) and dark energy (73% of universe). All physics, all science, based on incomplete knowledge of just 4% of universe.

The current state of knowledge about the nature of matter and energy is a lot like the old joke about the simpleminded person who lost his keys somewhere in the dark, but insists on looking for them under a streetlight half a block away because that's the only place he can see. If we persist in designing only those experiments that give us predictable data about the 4% of matter we can easily grasp, then we will forever be denied the truth—as best we can comprehend it—about the other 96% of the universe.

Are the aberrant data points we currently discard actually pointers to that dark matter and energy, pointers that tell us to look beyond the penumbra of the streetlight? When we finally look there, will the math we develop to describe it offer us the simple path out of the maze of complexity that Schroedinger and others have drawn? And what will it tell us about dark matter and energy? We know scientifically that they exist, but we can't detect them. Do they coexist within or around ordinary matter? Does it influence consciousness? And how do we design an experiment to find something about which we know nothing?

Nobody has those answers. And because we are woefully ignorant about the 4% we can comprehend and clueless about the rest, it's not only arrogant for any scientist to claim certainty about physics, but it's also astoundingly ignorant.

This is particularly relevant to the field of consciousness. Quantum theory has proven that every particle, every quantum of energy—whatever you want to call it—exists only in an undefined state of infinite possibilities *until* it is observed. When that happens, the particle experiences a collapse of its wave functions, which reduces all the infinite possibilities to a single observed state.

I submit that what our consciousness defines as the future is the set of all possibilities. The "present" which we experience is the infinitely small razor edge of time in which we experience the collapse of the wave function. In a sense, our consciousness surfs the continual wave-function collapse and propels us from the past toward the future.

Each decision we make collapses a set of wave functions and closes off all possibilities save one. But that one introduces us to yet another infinite series of possibilities, and another and another, each one of them engraving its permanent and indelible mark on space-time.

In conclusion, what does this mean to us as human beings? It means that we are the condensation of all the collective probability waves of all the quanta which compose us. Inside us, many of our electrons and protons, neutrons, are winking in and out of existence billions of times per second. And all the rest exist as probability waves. That means that we probably exist, but we can never prove it.

Rx only

XANTAEUS®
(Xantaeusol HCl, USP)

DESCRIPTION

Xantaeus® (Xantaeusol hydrochloride transdermal patch, USP) is an anti-anxiety agent that is not chemically or pharmacologically related

> Xantaeus is supplied as transdermal patches 45 mg of Xantaeusol hydrochloride, USP (equivalent to 31.2 mg of Xantaeusol free base, respectively).

to the benzodiazepines, barbiturates, or other sedative/anxiolytic drugs. It is closely related to busprione HCL and to busprione II, HCL, as developed by the Walter Reed Institute of Research.

Xantaeusol hydrochloride is a bluish-white polymorphic, water-soluble compound with a molecular weight of 513.0.

Each Xantaeus (Xantaeusol transdermal system) contains Xantaeusol HCL base in an ethylene-vinyl acetate copolymer matrix. Proceeding from the visible surface toward the surface attached to the skin are (1) an occlusive backing (polyethylene/aluminum/polyester/ethylene-vinyl acetate copolymer); (2) a drug reservoir containing Xantaeusol HCL (in an ethylene-vinyl acetate copolymer matrix); (3) a rate-controlling membrane (polyethylene); (4) a polyisobutylene adhesive; and (5) a protective liner that covers the adhesive layer and which must be removed before application to the skin.

CLINICAL PHARMACOLOGY

The mechanism of action of Xantaeusol is unknown.

Xantaeusol does not exert anticonvulsant or muscle relaxant effects and avoids the prominent sedative effects that are usually associated with more typical anxiolytics. Xantaeusol has a high affinity for serotonin receptors but does not affect GABA binding in vitro or in vivo. The effects of Xantaeusol on other neurotransmitter systems are pharmacologically and strategically significant, but classified.

A multiple-dose study conducted in 53,205 subjects indicates significant nonlinear pharmacokinetic activity. This non-linear activity indicates that repeated dosing will lead to significantly increased Xantaeusol blood concentrations than had previously been measured in single-dose studies and as predicted in animal testing models.

Multiple studies of in vitro protein binding showed that approximately 92% of Xantaeus is bound to plasma proteins. Neither aspirin nor flurazepam affected plasma levels of free Xantaeus. In vivo studies, however remain inconclusive and may cause clinically significant differences in treatment outcome. It attenuates punishment suppressed behavior in animals and exerts a taming effect, but is devoid of anticonvulsant and muscle relaxant properties

Contrary to in vitro studies of busprione, Xantaeus significantly displaces highly protein-bound drugs such as warfarin, phenytoin, and propranolol from plasma protein. Xantaeus also displaces digoxin and related compounds.

Xantaeus is extensively metabolized in first pass pathways mediated by cytochrome P450 3A4 (CYP3A4) oxidation. Serious and permanent psychotic behavior resulting in violence has been observed in less than one percent of the population.

Special Populations

Warfighter Combat Personnel
Administration prior to actual combat produced prolonged anxiolytic effects and extended resistance to stress and fatigue without visible impairment of combat efficiency over periods of 72 hours and longer without sleep.

Race Effects
The effects of race on the pharmacokinetics of Xantaeus have been extensively studied and outcomes available to qualified personnel only.

INDICATIONS AND USAGE

Xantaeus is indicated for the management of anxiety disorders and for long-term relief of the symptoms of anxiety in extended combat situations.

The efficacy of Xantaeus has been demonstrated in controlled clinical trials the results of which are classified and available to qualified personnel only.

APPENDIX IV

ALL INFORMATION CONTAINED
IN IS O CLASSIFIED
BY [signature]
S11-13

*Larry— we got to move fast!
The lawyers daughter is onto
us! She has talmadge's papers &
is taking them to Brad Stone.
THR will sink Xantarus
unless you act immediately!
— LaHaye 15 May*

12 Xn for
Carllel Donega
& instructed for
further action

RECORDED

RESEARCH, DEVELOPMENT
ENGINEERING COMMAND
ABERDEEN PROVING GROUND, MARYLAND

MAILED
APR 1
COMM. F8:

*General LaHaye — I am moving as fast as time and
caution permits — LF 8/20*

531 MI BDE DEP ORD
MODIFY TO INCLUDE REQ FROM USCINCENT PER 011803Z 2APR 1 RE GUARDIAN BRIGADE

Action Number: 1177
Subject: TECHNICAL ESCORT UNIT DEPLOYMENT ORDER
Action Agency: J-3

*Not good enough!
It has to be
faster! Your
ass is on the line
too!
— LaHaye 27 May*

SUBJ: REQUEST FOR GUARDIAN BRIGADE [TECHNICAL ESCORT] SUPPORT

REF: A: MEMORANDUM FROM LF, XO [for CDR], 485TH BI MDE

SUB: INTECEPT OF COMPROMISED BIOMEDICAL DATA, SOCAL PACIFIC COMMAND

B. PHONCON BETWEEN GEN. LAHAYE, CCJ2-CH AND CBRAXTON, DEFTHER

1. AS DISCUSSED IN REF B AND C, OPERATION ENDURING FREEDOM/USCINCCENT REQUESTS SUPPORT FROM THE TECHNICAL ESCORT UNIT (TEU), GUARDIAN BRIGADE, US ARMY RESEARCH, DEVELOPMENT ENGINEERING COMMAND COMMAND, FOR TRAINING IN INTECEPT OF BIOLOGICAL SAMPLES TO CONUS TESTING FACILITIES IN DIRECT SUPPORT OF OPERATION ENDURING FREEDOM.

THE TECHNICAL ESCORT UNIT/GUARDIAN BRIGADE IS THE USCINCCENT EXECUTIVE AGENT FOR DIRECT ACTION, INTERVENTION AND PROTECTIVE DEPLOYMENT. USCINCCENT REQUIRES IMMEDIATE COLLECTION OF THESE SAMPLES FROM FOREIGN MILITARY AGENT. IT WILL BE NECESSARY TO RAPIDLY TRANSPORT THESE SAMPLES TO CONUS LABORATORIES FOR ANALYSIS.

2. DISCUSSION: USCINCCENT REQUESTED* TEU PERSONNEL (APPROXIMATELY FOUR, PER TELECON), EXPECTED TO BE OBTAINED FOLLOWING INITIATION OF HOSTILITIES

| CLASSIFICATION | |ACTION NUMBER |ORIG REQUISITION
     Q-CLEARANCE/EYES ONLY   SOA 1177   2200 05 JAN
THRU DJS_____ J-3 ___ J-31 ____ J-33 ____

CJCS/VCJCS/DJS/JI/DIA/J3/J4/J~/J~/J,/J3 JOD/NIDS,GULF:RECALL/PA
[EXEMPTION (b)(6)] J-3 RECELL/ CATB/LL~ MINIMIZE CONSIDERED

*General — With all due respect, your demands on my ability to deploy
forces are raising the risk of exposure. If the CO of RDECom finds
out what we have been doing we are in serious trouble. LF 6/2*

DO IT NOW! C.B.

BIBLIOGRAPHY

Ackerman, Diane. *A Natural History of the Senses*. Vintage Books USA, reprint ed., September 1, 1991.

Allen, James, Hilton Als, John Lewis, and Leon F. Litwack. *Without Sanctuary: Lynching Photography in America*. Twin Palms Publishers, January 1, 2000.

Angelou, Maya. *I Know Why the Caged Bird Sings*. Bantam, reissue ed., April 1, 1983.

Blakemore, Colin, and Susan Greenfield, eds. *Mindwaves: Thoughts on Intelligence, Identity, and Consciousness*. Blackwell Publishers, reprint ed., May 1, 1989.

Brundage, W. Fitzhugh. *Under Sentence of Death: Lynching in the South*. University of North Carolina Press, June 1, 1997.

Cabaniss, James Allen. *The University of Mississippi: Its First Hundred Years*. University College Press of Mississippi, 2d ed., 1971.

Carter, Rita. *Exploring Consciousness*. University of California Press, September 2, 2002.

———. *Mapping the Mind*. University of California Press, March 1, 1999.

Chalmers, David J. *The Conscious Mind: In Search of a Fundamental Theory*. Philosophy of Mind Series. Oxford University Press, October 1, 1997.

Cobb, James Charles. *The Most Southern Place on Earth: The Mississippi Delta and the Roots of Regional Identity*. Oxford University Press, October 1, 1992.

Colletta, John Philip. *Only a Few Bones: A True Account of the Rolling Fork Tragedy & Its Aftermath*. Direct Descent, August 1, 2000.

Crick, Francis. *Astonishing Hypothesis: The Scientific Search for the Soul*. Scribner, reprint ed., July 1, 1995.

Cytowic, Richard. *The Man Who Tasted Shapes: A Bizarre Medical Mystery Offers Revealing Insight Into Emotions*. Warner Books, reprint ed., February 1, 1995.

Damasio, Antonio R. *Descartes' Error: Emotion, Reason, and the Human Brain*. Quill, November 1, 1995.

————. *The Feeling of What Happens: Body and Emotion in the Making of Consciousness.* Harvest Books, October 10, 2000.

————. *Looking for Spinoza: Joy, Sorrow, and the Feeling Brain.* Harcourt, February 1, 2003.

Dennett, Daniel C. *Freedom Evolves.* Viking Books, February 10, 2003.

Douglas, John, and Mark Olshaker. *The Anatomy of Motive: The FBI's Legendary Mindhunter Explores the Key to Understanding and Catching Violent Criminals.* Scribner, June 15, 1999.

Dray, Philip. *At the Hands of Persons Unknown: The Lynching of Black America.* Random House, January 8, 2002.

Edelman, Gerald M. *Bright Air, Brilliant Fire: On the Matter of the Mind.* Basic Books, reprint ed., May 1, 1993.

Edelman, Gerald M., and Giulio Tononi. *A Universe of Consciousness: How Matter Becomes Imagination.* Perseus Books Group, March 1, 2000.

Feinberg, Todd E. *Altered Egos: How the Brain Creates the Self.* Oxford University Press, January 15, 2001.

Franklin, Kristine L. *Molecules of the Mind.* Scribner, January 29, 1987.

Fukuyama, Francis. *Our Posthuman Future: Consequences of the Biotechnology Revolution.* Farrar, Straus & Giroux, April 17, 2002.

Gabriel, Richard A. *No More Heroes: Madness and Psychiatry in War.* Hill & Wang, reissue ed., April 1, 1988.

Garner, James W. *Reconstruction in Mississippi.* Peter Smith Publisher, December 1, 1964.

Ginzburg, Ralph. *100 Years of Lynchings.* Black Classic Press, reprint ed., September 1, 1997.

Grearson, Jessie Carroll, and Lauren B. Smith, eds. *Swaying: Essays on Intercultural Love.* University of Iowa Press, December 1, 1995.

Greenfield, Susan A. *The Private Life of the Brain.* Wiley, April 7, 2000.

Gregory, Richard L., and O. L. Zangwill, eds. *The Oxford Companion to the Mind.* Oxford University Press, reprint ed., December 1, 1998.

Grossman, Dave. *On Killing: The Psychological Cost of Learning to Kill in War and Society.* Little Brown & Co., August 1, 1995.

Harrison, John E., and Simon Baron-Cohen, eds. *Synaesthesia: Classic and Contemporary Readings.* Blackwell Publishers, December 1, 1996.

Hawking, Stephen, and Roger Penrose. *The Nature of Space and Time.* Princeton University Press, October 15, 2000.

Heilman, Kenneth. *Matter of Mind: A Neurologist's View of Brainbehavior Relationships.* Oxford University Press, January 15, 2002.

Hendrickson, Paul. *Sons of Mississippi: A Story of Race and Its Legacy.* Alfred A. Knopf, March 18, 2003.

Hohman, Kimberly. *The Colors of Love: The Black Person's Guide to Interracial Relationships.* Lawrence Hill Books, October 1, 2002.

Holland, Endesha Ida Mae. *From the Mississippi Delta.* Simon & Schuster, October 8, 1997.

Holmes, Richard. *Acts of War : Behavior of Men in Battle.* Free Press, August 4, 1989.

Hope, John Franklin. *Reconstruction After the Civil War.* The Chicago History of American Civilization. University of Chicago Press, 2nd ed. March 1, 1995.

Jibu, Mari, and Kunio Yasue. *Quantum Brain Dynamics and Consciousness: An Introduction.* Advances in Consciousness Research, vol. 3. John Benjamins Publishing Co., December 1, 1995.

Katz, Jack. *Seductions of Crime: The Moral and Sensual Attractions in Doing Evil.* Perseus Books Group, October 1, 1988.

Kennedy, Randall. *Interracial Intimacies: Sex, Marriage, Identity, and Adoption.* Pantheon Books, January 7, 2003.

———. *Nigger: The Strange Career of a Troublesome Word.* Vintage Books USA, January 14, 2003.

Ketchin, Susan. *The Christ-Haunted Landscape: Faith and Doubt in Southern Fiction.* University Press of Mississippi, January 1, 1994.

Margolick, David. *Strange Fruit: Billie Holiday, Café Society, and an Early Cry for Civil Rights.* Foreword by Hilton Als. Running Press Book Publishers, March 1, 2000.

Marijuan, Pedro C. *Cajal and Consciousness: Scientific Approaches to Consciousness on the Centennial of Ramón y Cajal's Textura.* New York Academy of Sciences, November 1, 2002.

Marshall, S. L. A. *Men Against Fire: The Problem of Battle Command.* University of Oklahoma Press, September 1, 2000.

Mellon, James. *Bullwhip Days: The Slaves Remember.* Pub Group West, December 1, 1988.

Meredith, James Howard. *Three Years in Mississippi.* Indiana University Press, January 1966.

Minor, Bill. *Eyes on Mississippi: A Fifty-Year Chronicle of Change.* J. Prichard Morris Books, June 15, 2001.

Moody, Anne. *Coming of Age in Mississippi.* Laurel Editions, reissue ed., March 1, 1997.

Newberg, Andrew, Eugene G. D'Aquili, and Vince Rause. *Why God Won't Go Away: Brain Science and the Biology of Belief.* Ballantine Books, April 3, 2001.

Norris, Joel. *Serial Killers.* Anchor, reprint ed., August 1, 1989.

Peirce, Neal R. *The Deep South States of America: People, Politics, and Power in the Seven Deep South States.* Norton, 1974.

Penrose, Roger. *Shadows of the Mind: A Search for the Missing Science of Consciousness.* Oxford University Press, reprint ed., May 1, 1996.

Penrose, Roger, and Malcolm Longair, eds. *The Large, the Small and the Human Mind.* Cambridge University Press, reprint ed., January 15, 2000.

Polkinghorne, J. C. *Belief in God in an Age of Science.* Terry Lectures. Yale University Press, April 1, 1998.

Romano, Dugan. *Intercultural Marriage.* Nicholas Brealey Intercultural, 2nd reprint ed., May 1, 2001.

Rubin, Richard. *Confederacy of Silence: A True Tale of the New Old South.* Atria, July 2, 2002.

Schrödinger, Erwin. *What Is Life?* with *Mind and Matter* and *Autobiographical Sketches.* Foreword by Roger Penrose. Cambridge University Press, reprint ed., January 31, 1992.

Searle, John R. *The Mystery of Consciousness.* New York Review of Books, September 1, 1997.

Shipman, Pat. *Evolution of Racism: The Human Differences and the Use and Abuse of Science.* Simon & Schuster, July 1, 1994. ISBN: 0671754602.

Thayer, Robert E. *The Origin of Everyday Moods: Managing Energy, Tension, and Stress.* Oxford University Press, June 1, 1996.

Walker, Evan Harris. *The Physics of Consciousness: The Quantum Mind and the Meaning of Life.* Perseus Publishing, December 2000.

Walsh, Maryellen. *Schizophrenia: Straight Talk for Family and Friends.* HarperCollins, January 1, 1985.

Wexler, Laura. *Fire in a Canebrake: The Last Mass Lynching in America.* Scribner, January 7, 2003.

White, Adam. *The Interracial Dating Book for Black Women Who Want to Date White Men.* Universal Publishers, October 1, 1999.

White, Deborah G. *Ar'n't I a Woman?: Female Slaves in the Plantation South.* Norton, 1985.

Wiesel, Elie. *Night.* Trans. Stella Rodway. Foreword by François Mauriac. Bantam Books, reissue ed., April 1, 1982.

Wilber, Ken. *Quantum Questions: Mystical Writings of the World's Great Physicists*. Shambhala, rev. ed., April 10, 2001.

Wilson, Colin. *Order of Assassins: The Psychology of Murder.* Hart-Davis, 1972.

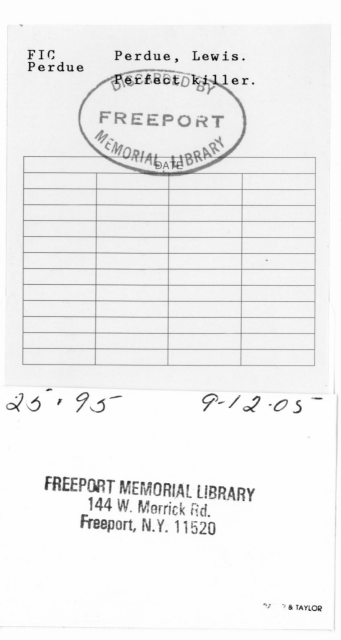

FIC   Perdue, Lewis.
Perdue
           Perfect killer.

DONATED BY
FREEPORT
MEMORIAL LIBRARY
DATE

25.95   9-12-05

& TAYLOR